ANGELS
OF ISLINGTON

First Published in Great Britain 2017 by Mirador Publishing

Copyright © 2017 by Sam Davey

All rights reserved. No part of this publication may be reproduced or transmitted, in any form or by any means, without permission of the publishers or author. Excepting brief quotes used in reviews.

First edition: 2017

Any reference to real names and places are purely fictional and are constructs of the author. Any offence the references produce is unintentional and in no way reflects the reality of any locations or people involved.

A copy of this work is available through the British Library.

ISBN: 978-1-912192-38-0

Mirador Publishing
10 Greenbrook Terrace
Taunton
Somerset
TA1 1UT
UK

Angels of Islington

Sam Davey

~ ~

"The hottest places in hell are reserved for those who, in times of great moral crisis, maintain their neutrality."

— Dante Alighieri

~ *Acknowledgements* ~

Thanks to my lovely "beta readers" Janet Davis and Liz Pursglove; to Elly and William Burrows for their input, suggestions and real-world critique, and finally to the ever supportive and practically encouraging Colin Davey for nurturing me through the creative process.

This book is dedicated to my father.

~ *In The Beginning* ~

The knife was sharp and some would have called it beautiful, if an object so clearly created for killing could ever be described that way. Its subtle blade, thrice forged and adamantine strong, tapered to a point as deadly as a stiletto. It was designed to enter flesh with the precision of a scalpel but with a shaft that widened out by several inches to give the bearer the power to cleave through bone and sinew.

The girl was quiet now and had ceased to struggle, although involuntary shudders rippled through her as she stared in hopeless terror at the hooded figure and the monstrous creature lurking at its side.

They had stripped her naked before binding her in chains that caught the light each time she quivered, sending tiny refractions chasing across the tiled floor. The beast pawed at them as they flashed before him, weaving his head and opening his jaws in a vain attempt to catch the motes of light.

"Enough." The voice was low, accentless and as dark and empty as a ravaged tomb. He placed his hand upon the beast's head and immediately it quietened. Leaning forward, he reached for the chains that bound the girl and pulled her upwards until she hung, feet first, before him.

He took the blade and slowly traced a pattern on her skin, tiny drops of blood flowering on the path the knife marked upon the living canvas. The hand moved deftly with a gentle but implacable precision and at first, it didn't hurt. He leant forward and hooked the chains to the wall, leaving both his hands free to slowly twist and turn the shuddering body, etching an elegant latticework of cuts across her thighs, stomach, back and breasts.

In her terror, she felt the drips of blood upon her face and saw them slowly pooling on the tiles beneath her before she felt the sharpness for the first time. And then it was quick.

With one perfect and unforgiving movement, he sliced upwards, from her sternum to the base of her abdomen, slicing clean through skin and muscle, creating one single narrow line through which the blood began to flow.

Finally, as the girl's involuntary tremors started to slow and the dancing motes of lights ceased their enticing oscillations, with a practiced and sinister elegance he made the final cut, a small incision just above her collar bone.

He stepped back, pulling a piece of cloth from his robes to wipe the bloodstained blade and as he did so, the now drooling beast moved forwards, its head lowered and began to lap from the warm and still un-clotted pool.

As the beast drank, the air began to thicken; a mist forming around the creature and the dying woman suspended above it. The silver specks still refracting from the bloodied chain brightened and became more intense and as the creature drank, the lights grew stronger, burning brighter and growing in number until they joined together in a single, burning line of concentrated platinum fire.

Then, the man stretched out his arm and touched the light with the tip of the now unsullied blade, pushing it into the brightness, like a key into a lock. When the blade was fully inserted, he turned the knife gently to the right until it could turn no further.

There was a click, so quiet that he almost failed to hear it above the noisy lapping of the creature as it rolled its tongue across the tiles, seeking every drop, licking every smear. But he didn't miss it. His task was done.

Pushing back his hood, he spoke quietly, but with undoubted triumph: "The door is open."

~ *Chapter One* ~

After the boss had hung up on me, I slammed the phone down and indulged myself in a cathartic but ultimately futile operetta of obscenities. Then I farted, loudly and dramatically, a crescendo of resentful derision.

It wasn't nice; goat curry the night before was more than a little unforgiving, if that's not too much information, and the residual odours only added to my recognition that the pressing needs of a full bladder ought to be attended to. Throwing back the duvet, I urged my aching and still unwilling body to assume a standing position and shuffled resentfully to the bathroom. Checking the clock on the landing as I grumbled through the doorway, I saw it was even earlier than I'd thought. Five thirty-five. What sort of hellish time was that? Five thirty-five on a dark, damp and utterly un-lovely November morning. Not even daybreak... and for what?

Manny knows missing persons aren't really my thing. I tend to favour the classic hit job - find the target, do the business and back to Charlie's Bar no questions asked. But there is always the exception. And this, apparently, was one hell of an exception. Before he had hung up on me in exasperation at my rather less than enthusiastic response to his request for assistance, Manny had told me that one of the Guardians had gone AWOL on the Saturday late-shift and in less than twenty-four hours the whatsit had hit the proverbial. Big time.

He had been assigned protection duties for this cute Italian girl – and not just any Italian girl, but a girl with 'Family' – if you know what I mean? Her normal Guardian hadn't travelled with her – there'd apparently been difficulties with visas because of some rather dodgy dealings in Egypt a while ago - and we had been called in to provide emergency cover.

Up until last night, all had been rolling smoothly, no noise, no problem...

~ 9 ~

But at least three hours before the shift was due to end and without a word to Control, our man buggers off early and young Sophia disappears.

I am not saying that the two events were related – Manny vets our Guardians pretty closely and the chap in question had been with the Agency since Methuselah was a boy. In fact I had worked with him a couple of times myself over the years and would have sworn that Isra was kosher; a little too fond of the good times when he wasn't working, but not the type to sell out to the opposition – and definitely not someone I would have thought could ever leave a client unprotected.

So when Manny's call had come through before sparrows-fart, I didn't exactly leap at the chance of being dragged into what sounded like a piece of real grunt work. I'd been looking forward to a leisurely and carb-filled breakfast followed by a session with the Sunday papers over a pint down by the river, but instead I was out of my rather run-down flat just behind Dalston Junction within fifteen minutes.

I might have been pissed off with him for disturbing my slumbers, but both Manny and I knew that I would never refuse an assignment. That wasn't how the Agency worked and the old bastard knew he could rely on me. It's my job, and I signed up to it a long, long time ago. Too late now to re-negotiate terms; and to be honest, the consequences of breaking my contract were not ones that I ever wanted to dwell on.

As the streets were clear, I could fly through them and I made it to the office in Canonbury well before six thirty. Manny, a tall, spare-framed guy who's aged well, keeping both his hair and his waistline, was dressed rather formally; his normal uniform of old cords and a check shirt replaced today with a sharp grey suit, and, quite surprisingly, a fedora. He was sitting at his desk, engrossed in reading the contents of the manila file in front of him. He didn't look up, so I walked over and flicked the brim of his hat.

"So, Manny, what gives – what happened to Isra?"

Manny looked up. His face seemed strained and there were dark shadows beneath his eyes: "Zach." He acknowledged me and nodded to the seat by the window.

I sat.

"You know the one about how many angels can dance on the head of pin?" he said.

"Well, it turns out the answer has nothing to do with how many, but more about the sort of dance they're doing. It seems that our friend Isra got carried away last night after watching bloody *Strictly*. He had about 8 Jagerbombs and then decided to experiment with a fiendishly difficult Paso-doble. He's damaged his pollex and his primary remiges will take at least a month to grow back."

"Ouch," I said, instinctively giving a reassuring stroke to my own wings.

Manny, or the Angel Emmanuel[1] as he is more formally known, gave me a rueful glance.

"Ouch indeed – and what's more worrying is that when he fell, he must have lost his phone – there was no sign of it when he arrived at St. Basil's – so he'd no way to let us know what had happened. The ward sister called me around two this morning – and it was only when I went over there and spoke to him that it finally came out that he had signed off early."

"That's the bit I don't understand," I said. "Surely Isra[2] knew the protocol – you don't go off shift until the next guy's turned up – what made him skedaddle if there was no-one to take over?"

'Angels of Islington' is one of the oldest justice and protection agencies in Europe – we've had the same offices in Canonbury Tower[3] since 1509. Manny knows the business – and we just don't make mistakes like this - or rather - we shouldn't...

Manny shrugged and gestured to the folder on his desk. "Well, according to Isra, he didn't leave her alone. He says the next chap turned up early, they did the normal handover – including the Abracadabra before you ask – and Isra was at Charlie's by half past six."

This got me thinking. The Abracadabra is the most ancient of all the Angelic talismans, created way over seven thousand years ago to channel celestial protection, and pretty much foolproof. Only a fully qualified Guardian could use it and it took many decades of study to perfect.

---

[1]"Emmanuel is an angel from the first celestial sphere, a seraph. He has the ability to open multidimensional windows through which magic and miracles can travel and has headed up Angels of Islington since his retirement from fieldwork in 1209. Emmanuel loves the colour orange, fresh flowers and scuba diving." *The Angels' Yearbook*, 2014

[2]"The Angel Israfil is a Guardian Angel from the third sphere. He is also known as the Angel of Music and features as such in a poem by Edgar Allan Poe. To him is also accorded the privilege of blowing the last trump when the day of judgement dawns." *The Angels' Yearbook*, 2008

[3] "The manor house of Canonbury was constructed by William Bolton of St. Bartholomew's Priory between 1509 and 1532. In addition to the Angelic Agency, the tower has been occupied by many historical figures, including Francis Bacon and Oliver Goldsmith. The Tower Theatre Company was based here from 1953 to 2003. It is currently used as a Masonic research centre." Preface to *The Angels' Yearbook*, 1973

"Who was next on the rota?"

"Well that's the strange thing," Manny replied.

"Isra said that the original guy – the one from Italy who'd been Sophia's Guardian all along – turned up out of the blue. Said the visas were sorted, he was back in the driving seat, and that he would be resuming full-time duties from now on. Isra checked the ID – all seemed fine – did the handover and left. He said the Italian bloke seemed pretty anxious for him to be on his way, so he leapt at the chance of an early night, and just thought nothing of it."

"What's odd though, is this." Manny tapped the folder he had been reading when I came in. "According to the file, Ely – that's the regular Guardian – is highly unlikely to be granted a visa – which is why the Vatican branch came to us. They're much more relaxed about past peccadillos over there, but when the powers that be at Border Control found out that we were proposing to send the angel responsible for the Plague of Hail over to the UK, just when the Egyptian situation is so sensitive, they put their foot down big time – and as far as I know, that hasn't changed."

At that moment, the desk phone rang. Manny picked it up and listened carefully. Whilst he made some notes on his pad, I began to think things over. I had met Ely (aka the Angel Elyon) some time ago. I'd been drafted in to help manage the fall-out from the Carbonari scandal and Ely was my local contact. He was a good guy - if a tad obsessed with climatic conditions - and he cooked a mean Bolognese. He was more the type who would welcome a chin-wag over a Peroni and a plate of pasta "like mama used to make" than someone who would hustle you out the door- which was just one more thing that didn't add up about Isra's story.

As I finished musing, Manny put down the phone. To say he looked worried would be an understatement.

"That was the Vatican. Ely's back in Rome; when the visa stuff didn't look like getting sorted anytime soon, he just decided to head on home. Whoever it was last night at Sophia's – it wasn't him. What's worse, his nexus has gone down – Sophia is not just missing – he can't sense her at all."

The relationship between a human and their Guardian is intensely personal and complex. The connection - or nexus - is there from birth, but can only be activated by the human. We angels can't influence or interfere – we only get involved if we are invited in (a bit like vampires – but playing for the other side).

Most humans never recognise or connect with their Guardians at all during their lifetime, so if you hear a Guardian moaning about their caseload, you should just take it with a pinch of salt – it's likely that only one in ten thousand nexuses are ever actually activated.

However, once they are connected, the nexus provides a constant and irreplaceable link between the Guardian and their charge. That is why we couldn't provide a fulltime replacement for Ely. Once it's been activated, you can't transfer a nexus, so all we could do in this case was work shifts to provide a temporary minder, but as Sophia was only supposed to be staying in London for two weeks, that had seemed, at the time, to be a reasonable solution.

I looked at the file on Manny's desk. On top of the standard documentation was a picture of Sophia, a slight and uncertain half-smile upon her lips. Her dark hair was pulled back from her face. She had brown eyes – and was definitely worth at least a second glance.

She was sitting at a table, cup of coffee in front of her and a book turned face down by its side. She looked as if someone had just said her name, and she'd turned instantly towards them. I sensed fear. Her eyes had the haunted look of one who has seen things she is unable to forget. I looked again – the book in front of her was quite worn, but I could make out the title; it was a copy of Dante's *Inferno*.

I flicked quickly through the file – the picture had been taken a couple of days ago, outside a coffee shop just off Old Street, and she had not been alone.

Sophia was in London to meet someone; someone who had been on the run for years. A man her father had tried to have killed – and the one person who stood any chance of bringing him – and potentially the whole damn bunch of evil bastards she called 'Family' - to justice.

The man she was here to meet was her brother.

I looked up from the file. "Manny, what about the brother?" I looked again at the notes, "Says here his name's Alessandro – but now known as Alex… Doesn't he have a Guardian? He's been in London for nearly five years – so he must be one of ours."

Manny sighed and shook his head. "Oh yes, he has a Guardian alright - and one of the best… Alessandro left Italy nearly ten years ago and if it hadn't been for Jaoel[4], he would have been a goner many times over."

---

[4] "The Angel Jaoel is a Guardian from the third sphere with a pretty impressive CV, which includes guiding Abraham on his journey to Paradise. He is also a good friend of the Archangel Michael and their blessings are intertwined. Jaoel is soft voiced and has a true understanding of the Human condition." The Angels' Year Book, 2006"

At the sound of the name, I looked up. I had heard rumours about Jaoel.

I should also tell you that my full name is Zachriel[5] – otherwise known as the Angel of Memory – and the mention of Jaoel had got my synapses buzzing.

Manny continued: "He must have been about twenty-five when it happened – Sophia was not quite ten and they were both living in one of the family homes just outside Palermo. The trouble started when their father decided it was time to bring the boy into the business. Until then, neither he nor Sophia had any idea about the family's operations – they lived quietly at home, went to good local schools, and didn't see very much of Dad - story was, he travelled a lot on 'business'.

"However, unlike his father, Alessandro had a conscience. He and Jaoel had been connected since his early teens and when he began to understand exactly what the 'business' entailed, he was disgusted... horrified. He wanted out. But the family couldn't risk letting him go. Things came to a head one weekend following a particularly unpleasant piece of turf-warfare in Mexico. To cut a long story short, there was an argument, things got out of hand, his father pulled a gun... but it was Alessandro's mother who took the bullet – and the boy himself got away."

Manny got up and walked towards the window. I stood as he approached and moved aside so we could both look down upon the still, quiet street. It was not yet full light, but in the tower garden I could just make out that the leaves were starting to fall from the old mulberry tree planted by Francis Bacon when he was an associate of the Agency back in the 1600's. Everything looked drab, messy, and unkempt.

Maybe it was just my state of mind, but I was more than a little uneasy – and I could tell that Manny felt the same. As we stood together, the tips of our wings touched and I started as I felt the sharp current of his tension and anxiety. Angels are intensely attuned to each other and as a result very rarely engage in any form of physical contact – we find it quite literally shocking.

I shifted my position, walking away from the window, and he continued:

"Jaoel kept him safe over the next five years until finally, Alessandro came to London, and built his new identity. On their return from Mexico, her father and his brothers convinced Sophia that her brother was responsible for her mother's death and she was sent away to school, grieving and confused. She

---

[5] "The Angel Zachriel is a seraph from the first sphere. He is the Angel of Memory and Remembrance. His team has won the International Choir of Angels annual pub quiz for the last millennium." *The Angels' Year Book*, 2000

heard nothing from Alessandro until last month – just around her twentieth birthday – and that was Jaoel's doing.

"Over the years, he and Ely had kept in close contact; the one thing they were both worried about was Sophia finding out the hard way about the family business - and they had permission to intervene."

This was serious – Guardians are only given permission to intervene in situations of life and death.

Manny continued: "They decided to use the dream nexus to communicate, and so night after night, Alessandro appeared to his sister in her dreams, talking to her, telling her the truth about their father, and finally, showing her exactly what happened on the night their mother died."

"And so young Sophia just ups and runs to England because of some nightmares…?" I sounded sceptical – the dream nexus used to work really well a few hundred years ago, but humans just don't get spooked like they used to.

"Well, this is where things got a bit out of hand," confessed Manny. "The dream nexus unsettled her, sure enough, but it didn't seem to be getting us where we needed to be. I approved a full manifestation."

"God's blood, Emmanuel, you did what…?" I was so shocked I reverted to a medievalism I haven't used for decades. "We haven't approved a manifestation since the Tunguska event in 1908."[6]

He nodded, and moved towards me - spreading his hands forward, palms flat – as though to calm me down. "You don't know how important this is, Zach. We need to keep Sophia and Alessandro – or Alex as he calls himself now, alive, safe – and most importantly, together. The Agency – both here and in Italy – must make sure they testify."

"Ely and Jaoel produced a full manifestation – they had worked together in the past, in fact that little business with Dante and Beatrice was one of their concoctions – and they used the same technique again this time."

Now I remembered what I had heard about Jaoel and also I understood exactly why Sophia had looked so haunted – and why she had a well-thumbed copy of the *Inferno*.

I was not happy; in fact I was verging on full-on fury – and this must have shown on my face.

"You gave her a full manifestation of Hell… that's what that old bastard

---

[6] "A large explosion over the sparsely populated Eastern Siberian Taiga flattened 770 square miles of forest but caused no known casualties. There are more than 700 eyewitness testimonies to angelic manifestation at Tunguska." *Annual report of the Heavenly Host*, 1908

Jaoel specialises in – he may well have taken Abraham to Paradise, but he really gets his jollies by conjuring up visions of eternal torment. Don't you know how vulnerable the human brain is to that type of thing? You say you wanted to keep Sophia safe – but surely you didn't want to drive her insane?"

"Now, Zach, you know that we always operate for the greater good – and sometimes hard decisions have to be made. Look at Job.

"Sometimes we need to make tough choices – for a higher purpose, for the greater good." He was staring into the middle distance and using his bureaucrat's voice, quoting from the little known apocryphal Book of St. Richard (otherwise known as the Book of Cop-outs and Bullshit). I was having none of it.

"Basically, you have driven a young girl from her home and sent her, terrified and isolated, to a city where the only person she knows is her brother – who she hasn't seen for ten years – and who she has always believed is a murderer and responsible for her mother's death.

"And now she has disappeared and you want me to find her."

"Not quite," said Manny, who now turned his head slightly, looking me directly in the eye. "Yesterday afternoon the nexus connection between Jaoel and Alex also broke down. It is not just Sophia who has gone missing.

"I also haven't been quite up-front about what happened with Isra. The Vatican also told me that the angel claiming to be Ely was actually Eligor – one of the most powerful of the Fallen."

He closed the file and pushed it towards me. "My theory is that they have been taken into the Inferno. And I need you to go get them."

~ *Chapter Two* ~

I stared at Manny in disbelief. The day had not started well and was showing no signs of improving.

"Now hold on," I said, "you called me in to pick up on a simple MISPER, and now you expect me to go tooling off into the nine circles of Hades... I do not need this. I so do not need this – and you know it."

Before you think that I was acting like a pampered princess preparing for her sweet sixteen, I should tell you that I had only just got back to London from a particularly filthy mission, working with the Al Malaikah[7] in Syria. To say it had been like Hell on earth would not be an exaggeration – I did not want to dwell on the things I had witnessed working with the Kirama Katibeen[8]. And Manny knew exactly what I'd been through – he was the one who'd sent me.

I leant forward and picked up the manila folder and was just about to throw it across the desk and storm out of the office when the picture of Sophia fell on to the desk in front of me.

Manny had not yet responded to my outburst and he now leant forward and deftly picked up the photograph.

"She is very young; very young and very brave," he said in an annoyingly unctuous and 'holier than thou' tone. "She came to London to find her brother and to urge him to testify, to bring to justice those who have done great wrong

---

[7]"The Islamic angels, or the Al Malaikah, do not take on individual guardianship of human beings and, in the main, work more closely with the dead than the living." *The Angels' Year Book,* 1994

[8] "The *Kirama Katibeen,* otherwise known as the "honourable scribes" are appointed to watch over humanity and to record both their good and evil acts and intentions. This is one of the most stressful roles in the heavenly hierarchy, and the Katibeen suffer burn-out more quickly than almost any other of the angelic hosts." *The Angels' Year Book,* 1994

and who have gone unpunished for many years. And now we believe she has been taken into the darkest place imaginable…"

Once again he didn't look at me, preferring to fix his eyes on the picture in his hand. "But I understand, you're tired, you don't feel well. Go home, Zach." He raised his head, looking me full in the face. "I am sure you have better things to do."

There was silence between us.

"You utter bastard," I replied eventually. "You know I can't do that."

I took the picture and once again sat down. "But if I'm going to do this, then you are going to have to give me more background. And you have to come clean about exactly what the Vatican knows – and why this has suddenly become so important."

"That's fair enough," said Manny, "and you'll need to be fully briefed before we let you go."

I looked at him quizzically. Manny could be annoying, and more than a tad bureaucratic, but he was not pompous – and not one to usually adopt the third person.

"We?" I questioned.

"Yes. We. Head Office is all over this one like a rash, and we will need to… co-operate. I informed them of the situation before I called you in and they were with the Vatican earlier. They have already spoken to Ely and I've been informed that London is their next port of call." He looked at his watch. "In fact, I think they will be with us any moment."

I realised that it was now nearly eight o'clock, although from the light I would have thought that it was still much earlier. I looked out of the window. By this time, I would have expected the sky to have brightened; even on a dull day in November the sun was usually up by this time. But it was still dark, grey and overcast, as if night was clinging to the Heavens and did not want to let go. In fact, I thought, it was darker now than when I left Dalston Junction.

"Who's coming?" I asked uneasily, thinking that I was finally about to find out why Manny was so uncharacteristically suited and booted. I had my suspicions – and Manny didn't take long to confirm them.

"Well, this is a big one. K is managing it personally – and I think he is bringing Sara along for the ride."

That explained what was happening outside; Sara (aka Sarandiel) is the angel responsible for the twelfth hour of the night – and she[9] was clearly working overtime, providing top cover so she and the big guy could travel safely without being seen.

I had only met K[10] once – and it hadn't gone well.

He had spent so much time at the top of the tree that he took the deference of others for granted and really didn't like it when it wasn't automatically forthcoming. I was an operative who knew how to follow orders when I had to, but in my book, respect is something you have to earn; just having a set of fancy titles wasn't enough.

If he didn't like my attitude, he liked my appearance even less. He expected his agents to look the part, and always dressed impeccably himself. I could make a shirt look rumpled within thirty seconds of putting it on and had never truly mastered the art of making a tie sit like it naturally belonged around my neck.

Looking across at Manny, I saw he was just brushing what must have been an imaginary crumb from the sleeve of his jacket. There was no doubt about it; he looked sharp. I was wearing old jeans, battered trainers and a sweatshirt that had seen better days. As I had been dragged from my pit so unceremoniously that morning, I hadn't shaved and since getting back from Syria – where I had let my hair grow longer - I hadn't had chance to visit my favourite Turkish barbers in Stoke Newington. I looked like a tramp.

"Great," I said, without any visible enthusiasm.

Manny gave me a quick glance. He could sense my rising hostility. "Come on, Zach, it'll be okay – you have a strong reputation, and you are the best guy for the job. Just listen, nod and say yes – and then we can get on with what we need to do to get Sophia and Alex back home."

"It's just that I am fed up with the way that Head Office talks about 'nurturing talent, focusing on delivery and exercising our execution muscle' and other meaningless platitudes and then just sets up another bloody

---

[9] "Angels are gender neutral as they have no biological requirement to reproduce. Individual angels often have a preference for particular gender characteristics and will choose the pronoun they prefer to use in reference to themselves. This choice then influences their physical materialisation, so that angels who chose the male pronoun will grow facial hair, those who chose the female will develop breasts and will usually be of a smaller and slighter stature than their 'male' counterparts." *The Anatomy of Angels*, 1935

[10] "Known as 'K', the archangel Lord Kemuel is Chief Executive of the seraphim, Permanent Secretary to the Heavenly Host and commanding officer of the Angelic Powers. Prior to his appointment he was part of the 'seven day team' responsible for the creation of oil and gas." *Annual report of the Heavenly Host*, 6003 BC

committee to do bugger all. We were at least 50% short of cover in Syria – and all this talk of austerity doesn't wash with me. I bet Sara is still driving the latest model, four wheel drive chariot; I can't even afford a car with the rent I have to pay."

Even as I spoke, I heard a sound outside. The skies darkened further and the clouds lowered, becoming thick and almost tangible. The chariot descended and pulled up neatly and undramatically in the space just to the rear of the tower.

Just to avoid confusion, I should point out that the chariots we use nowadays are rather different from the one famously spotted by Ezekiel[11]. We no longer favour flaming wheels and the full accompaniment of the combined vocal powers of the choirs of the Heavenly Host. Angelic transport has become rather more discreet over the years and Sara was, in fact, driving a brand new *Mercedes GLE.*

Once the Merc was securely parked in the Tower's only business parking bay, the sky began to lighten and I could clearly see our visitors getting out of the car. Sara was quite small for an angel, probably about 5'6, with a cloud of unruly hair framing a strong yet sympathetic face. She wore a tailored grey suit and carried an attaché case. She opened the rear passenger door and a long, thin figure unfolded himself. In direct contrast to Sara, K was remarkably tall, his chosen materialisation not dissimilar to his true angelic form. His face was saurian and he looked extremely intelligent, but not kind. Like Sara, he wore a grey suit; his had the addition of a subtle green pinstripe, and a green silk tie. Neither Sara nor K had chosen to materialise their wings[12], possibly to avoid drawing attention to themselves in the short time they would be outside, but more likely because having wings makes it damn uncomfortable when you are travelling by chariot nowadays.

Manny and I stood up and moved towards the door, which opened as K, followed by Sara, came into the room.

"Emmanuel, good to see you; this is a bad business, a bad business indeed." K spoke quickly, clipping his words, a hint of a trans-Atlantic undertone in his

---

[11] "Early angelic chariots, such as that seen by Ezekiel, were composed of four angels, each with four wings. Two of these wings spread across the length of the chariot and connected with the wings of the angel on the other side. This created a sort of 'box' of wings that formed the perimeter of the chariot. Chariot design has improved significantly in the past a hundred and fifty years." *What Chariot?* April 2004

[12] "As angels are not, in their true form, corporeal, they are able to suppress or alter certain aspects of their appearance when they choose to materialise." *The Anatomy of Angels,* 1935

voice. He did not smile at Manny; he didn't see fit to so much as nod in my direction, and walking behind the desk, he sat down in Manny's chair and picked up the manila folder.

Sara followed him into the room, smiling warmly at Manny and, whilst K was giving his attention to the folder, shooting me a quick wink.

She was alright was Sara. A bit too career orientated for my liking, but I knew she had a sense of humour. I'm a little older than her, but back in the day, we both had summer jobs as security guards on Jacob's Ladder. It was boring, but we got on, and some days we actually had a bit of a laugh. Sara would cover for me if I turned up late (or fell asleep…) and I ended up being a shoulder to cry on when things didn't work out the way she wanted. At the time, she'd had a bit of a crush on Samael, the angel responsible for guiding dead souls to the place of judgement. Not surprisingly – given that he then held the rank of Archangel, whilst she was just a college leaver marking time until her first assignment, he did not reciprocate. And besides; he was married – which was most unusual for an angel - and turned out to be a thoroughly bad lot. But that's another story.

I returned the wink – and wouldn't you know it, K spotted me. He looked disapprovingly in my direction and then nodded meaningfully to Manny, who cleared his throat. "Zach, come and sit down. We need to get on. K does not have all day, and the situation will only get worse the longer we leave it."

I picked up a chair from the corner of the room and joined the other three at the desk. Both Manny and I had already got rid of our wings as it is considered very bad form in angelic circles for a more junior angel to be fully alated[13] when someone higher up the pecking order is not fully materialised.

K looked at Sara, who picked up her attaché case and took out a file. She placed it on the desk, opened it, and began to speak. "This is Alessandro Maniscalo, now known as Alex Mason."

She took a picture from the file and placed it in front of us. Like his sister, Alex had an elegant head, dark hair, and dark eyes. In the picture he was smiling. I had a sense it was taken quite a while ago.

Sara took out another picture. "This is Sophia Maniscalo, Alex's sister." Again, the photo looked like an old one – Sophia's face was plumper, more childlike than she had looked in the shot I had seen earlier that morning. "They

---

[13] "**Alate**: adjective: having wings or wing-like extensions. Word origin from Latin *ālātus*, from *āla* meaning wing." *The Shorter Angels' Dictionary*, 2001

met for the first time in nearly ten years last week, at a café in London." A third photo was placed on the desk. It showed Alex and Sophia sitting together at a pavement café – they're talking animatedly and seem close. Sophia's hand resting on the table, Alex's lying close to it. Their shoulders are nearly touching and the proximity doesn't seem to bother either of them. "This was taken two days ago. Within twenty-four hours, the nexus between Alex and his Guardian, Jaoel had been terminated. Six hours later, the nexus between Sophia and her Guardian, Ely went down. We have no terrestrial record of any activity for either human since that point."

She reached for a fourth photo, but before she could pull it from the file, I intervened. "You just said the nexus between Alex and Jaoel and been terminated." I looked accusingly at Manny. "You didn't tell me that earlier, you just said it had broken down."

This was more than serious. The nexus connection can break down for a number of reasons; for example, if the human loses their faith, if they are suffering from extreme emotion, such as overwhelming grief, or if there is deep loss of consciousness. In such cases, the connection can quite easily be restored. But for a nexus to be terminated, it means the connection has been destroyed – and that can only happen if the Guardian Angel severs it. If this had happened then I could only think of two scenarios which could have caused it. Either Jaoel had ceased to exist[14] – or he had fallen.

"There was no need for you to know." K spoke sharply. "Manny did as he was instructed. We still have not established exactly what happened to Jaoel and greater minds than yours are already working on it. Continue." He gestured to Sara, who placed the fourth photograph in front of us.

"This is Eligor, otherwise known as Duke Eligos." The picture was of a classically handsome man, dressed in a uniform which looked to me like the ceremonial uniform of the Blues and Royals, one of the regiments which form the Queen's Household Cavalry. He was fair, with aristocratic features and what I couldn't help but think of as a 'noble brow'.

"Eligor is one of the big boys," Sara continued. "He commands sixty legions of the Fallen, and is a deadly deceiver." She pointed at the photo. "His human materialisation is always like this, so it will be fairly easy to recognise him in this dimension." She consulted her notes. "This is what they said about

---

[14] "As angels are not corporeal beings, they cannot die in the true sense. However, they can cease to exist in the celestial spheres, a process known as *evanescence*, if they no longer have faith in their true angelic purpose." *The Anatomy of Angels*, 1935

him in 1563 – which is the last time we have any record of him operating openly in England: '*Eligor is a great duke and appeareth as a goodlie handsome knyght... He answerest fullie of thyngs hidden... he knoweth of things to come and procureth the favour of lords and knyghts'.*"

"But I know who wrote that." I was both surprised and excited to recognise the words of one of my old companions. "Manny, do you remember Johan, Johan Weher, Dutch guy, 16th century – did some work for us as an associate on a contract job in Germany?"

Manny shook his head. "It rings a bell," he said, "but I am not sure... you're the one with the memory, not me."

Sara looked interested and moved towards me as if she was about to speak, to question me further about Johan and the work we had done together. K, however, dismissed what I was saying with a sharp cutting gesture of his right hand. "Distractions are not helpful," he said. "Carry on."

Sara then took out the final photograph. It showed Alex, Sophia and the person we now knew to be Eligor. Sophia was in the centre of the picture, with Alex and Eligor on either side of her. They seemed to be at some sort of party – or maybe a nightclub. Sophia wore a red dress, cut tight and clinging to her body. She looked amazing. The guys both wore open neck shirts with jeans and all three of them were drinking what looked like champagne – and there was a bottle of Krug standing in an ice bucket just to Alex's left.

"This was taken on Friday night at a party in Hoxton," Sara said. "Jaoel sent it to Ely, and we retrieved it from his phone earlier today. There are a few more pictures and quite a lot of texts, sent Friday night and then a couple on Saturday morning. Nothing after half past twelve on Saturday, and the nexus between Jaoel and Alex terminated at precisely one forty-five. It looks like Jaoel was keeping Ely informed of what was going on over here, but it is odd that he doesn't seem to have sussed straight away that Eligor was one of the Fallen."

That was strange, because although very few humans have the psychical and spiritual sensitivity to actually tell if someone they meet is a materialised angel, we angels can always sense the presence of a celestial companion - or one of the Fallen.

Getting another document from the file, she handed out transcripts of the texts Jaoel and Ely had exchanged on Friday night. "Have a look – nothing to indicate any concern – he just seems a bit worried that his charge was going to have a hangover the next morning – he wasn't bothered that Ely was still waiting for his visa and that Sophia didn't have a permanent angelic presence to guard her."

I had a quick look. Just as Sara said, the texts were straightforward, even light-hearted.

Jaoel had been in the same room as one of the Fallen and he had said nothing about it to Ely.

His last text on Friday read: 'Finally… going home. Big day tomorrow. YOLO'.

I considered those words, and it dawned on me that they could mean something very different from the reassuring message they had first seemed to be. Alarm bells had been ringing ever since I remembered what Jaoel had done to Dante Alighieri back in the 14th century. I didn't trust him then; I certainly saw no reason to trust him now. I put the transcript on the desk and pointed to the final text Jaoel had sent Ely on Friday night.

"Much as I hate to say it," I said, "this suggests to me that what has happened to Jaoel is not evanescence. I think we have a rogue Guardian on our hands."

~ *Chapter Three* ~

All three of them turned to look at me, but no-one spoke. The index and forefingers of K's right hand began to tap the desk in a gesture of ill-concealed irritation.

He turned to Manny, and to say he did not look best pleased was an understatement. "As you know, I had wished to avoid this. Our aim this morning was to brief the Angel Zachriel and get the rescue operation underway immediately. There are certain…" he paused, clearly seeking the appropriate words, "aspects of this case… which we did not wish to release at this point. However, it seems that our friend here," he nodded his head curtly in my direction, "is more than usually…" he paused again, "perspicacious."

By which, I thought, he means 'bloody annoying and a shade too good at putting two and two together'.

"Zach has full security clearance," said Manny. "He has just returned from a mission with the Katibeen and won't have heard any of the recent rumours. I can personally vouch for his integrity and…" he paused and looked a little embarrassed as if he was about to refer to something rather personal, "his purity of spirit."

I started back in my chair and then half rose to my feet. To question an angel's purity of spirit is to question their fundamental being; you couldn't get more personal. Sara could see that I was dis-comforted and gestured reassuringly towards me, placing her hand just an inch from my sleeve. I could feel the warmth from her emanation, and I relaxed a little, sitting back down.

K's reaction was somewhat different. He looked at me appraisingly, seeming to actually relish my discomfort. A rather grim smile played quickly across his thin lips. "Well in that case, Emmanuel, on your head be it; perhaps you had better tell the tale. But do it quickly." He checked his watch. "Time is pressing and I would have thought that Eligor and our Italian friends are likely to have progressed into at least the second circle by now."

Manny cleared his throat and began. "Zach, whilst you were in Syria, we finally confirmed what we have suspected for the past year or so. We have obtained absolute and irrefutable proof that a serious number of angels have recently joined the Fallen. Twelve or possibly thirteen Guardians, three messengers and one of the cherubim. We suspect that at least two others are involved, but have yet to break cover. We don't have sufficient information to confirm their identity."

This was shocking news indeed. The Heavenly Host had been fairly stable for at least sixty years; the last serious defection I'd heard of had taken place in America in the 1940's, and there had been a couple of big names who went over in Europe a few years before, in the late twenties. Since then we had seen just the occasional rebel, most of whom had been dealt with before they caused too much trouble.

Perhaps I should explain a little here. Angels are incorporeal beings, and despite my comment about chariots, we don't covet material goods or wealth. We are genderless and don't feel the pull of sexual desire – although we do appreciate beauty and can even fall in love (this is not particularly encouraged and often ends in tears...). No, for angels, it is not about sex or money... Our weakness is power.

Getting back to basics, angels are not necessarily nice creatures. Being nice and being good are really two very different things, and sometimes following the rules to the letter brings with it some rather tough calls. Saying that, it is actually a lot easier nowadays, as there is rather less smiting involved on a daily basis; divine justice being more likely to be meted out by a preponderance of identity scams and emails from friendly Nigerian princes than a plague of locusts.

Nonetheless, the most important thing, in the words of the pledge we all take when we gain our wings is that we: '*at all times act as the instruments of the higher power, acting to further celestial good, retaining our spiritual purity and acting in obedience; we will seek out and punish that which is evil*' [15]

---

[15] "The articulation of the pledge acts as a catalyst within the angel, empowering and conferring the full range of the individual angel's celestial powers. It is also the symbolic statement of full spiritual maturity, the physical manifestation of which is the angel's wings." *The Anatomy of Angels,* 1935

We must remain spiritually pure if we are to fulfil our purpose within the Heavenly Host. Those of us who work outside the celestial realms have just three functions: to guide and protect mankind, to act as messengers between Heaven and earth (like the Katibeen) and - the big one - to execute divine judgements.

This can mean doing some pretty unpleasant things; just look at Sodom and Gomorrah, which was a tough gig if ever I saw one – and not one that we are particularly proud of now. It's actually been wiped from most of the text books and I remember Isra really pissing off the PR department by sending them a huge consignment of salt one Christmas. Some angels have no sense of humour.

Just in case you are wondering about other angelic careers, having a desk job in the celestial realms may be more of a soft option, but it doesn't attract me. From what I can see, it mainly consists of 24/7 praising of the holy name – with quite a lot of choral work thrown in. Not my scene really – I prefer a more active life and to be honest, too much singing really does my brains in.

Joking apart, the bottom line for all angels is that when the chips are down, we do what we are told. As the Book of St. Richard phrases it, 'our role is to implement the power of celestial policy, not to create it'. But for some of us, the temptation to take that power for ourselves becomes irresistible – and once we give in, we fall.

And according to Manny, that had been happening.

A lot.

"As you know," Manny continued, "significant surges in global negative activity are an indicator that there has been a shift in the balance of power. What we have experienced recently has been heading off the scale. You've seen for yourself what it's like in Syria – add to that Paris, Egypt, the Ukraine, Bosnia, Sudan – and it's not just war and terrorism. International crime, human trafficking, fraud, exploitation - you name it, they're getting worse."

"But there has always been war," I said, "destruction, conflict, rivalry, murder. It may not be pretty, but it's surely just part of the human condition? Go right back to the beginning, Cain and Abel – a classic tale of jealousy, anger and blood-lust – you know how it goes – it's just the way of the world, surely?"

Manny shook his head. "There is much more to it than that. Ever since the fall of man, we have had responsibility for the maintenance of cosmic harmony. Putting it crudely, there has always been a balance between good and evil – and it has always been on a knife edge. Human beings have free will – they can always choose which side they want to be on – and in the main, most of them stick somewhere in the middle. Generally honest, but happy to break the speed limit or get by without paying their TV licence, they won't actually cause someone harm, but will probably walk by on the other side if a situation gets dodgy. Of course, there are exceptions – and they are usually the people we work with."

I nodded. This all made absolute sense. I had never been particularly bothered about understanding the thinking behind organisational policy – I just liked being out in the field, doing my job - but it was clear that I needed to brush up on a few things if I was going to get my head around what was going on.

Manny continued, "Our role is to guide, to guard – and sometimes to exact punishment. As you know, once a nexus is in place, we can usually help to keep someone safe – and protect them from spiritual attack, even if we can't always prevent actual physical harm. We work through those with the moral courage to stand up and speak out for what is right; people like Mandela, Malala, Martin Luther King. Going back through history, the list is a long one. We don't expect to eradicate evil; it needs to remain in any case if humanity is to retain its free will, but we must ensure that the balance remains in our favour. That there continues to be more good than evil, more kindness than hatred, more joy than suffering."

"And if we don't?" I asked.

It was K who answered. "Then the power shifts. We become the opposition."

I considered this. There was not one perspective from which this could ever be seen as a nice thought. "So," I said, "just how bad is it? And why are Sophia and Alex so important?"

"We have dealt with rebellion before – and in the big scheme of things, this is actually quite small beer. As K has already indicated, the Potestas[16] are involved, and there is genuinely no need for you to concern yourself with the Fallen. Leave it to the experts."

---

[16]"The *Potestas*, otherwise known as the Angelic Powers or Authorities are warrior angels whose primary function is to ensure that the cosmos remains in order. They fight the forces of evil and are responsible for casting the vanquished back into Hell, often chaining them to their places of punishment and detention. Their battlegrounds are usually cosmological, so there is little evidence of their activity within the material realms." *The Angels' Year Book,* 1952

Here Manny looked straight at me – and I could see that he was serious.

"However," he continued, "we do suspect that Jaoel may have defected – and we don't know just how close he is to Eligor and his plans. Alex and Sophia are part of the Maniscalo family. Our charges apart, crime doesn't get more organised, or dirtier than the Maniscalos." He turned slightly, looking across the desk at our visitors. "Sara, I think you're best placed to brief Zach on this one."

Sara had been politely listening to the previous discussion – but in a way that made it obvious that none of it was news to her. She had developed a more serious side since our time together back at Jacob's Ladder. Reaching once more into her attaché case, she pulled out some papers and passed them across to me.

"We are old souls," she said, "but that doesn't mean we can always second guess what is going to happen out there – or even grasp that it is actually happening. Particularly nowadays; crime is a very different beast with the darkweb behind it and whilst we angels may take some time to understand how it works now, you can bet the human brain is working nineteen to the dozen to exploit it."

She had a point – one of the primary differences between angels and humanity is that humans are generally far more creative and inventive. They have to be – they need to change, evolve, adapt to their environment – and at times adapt the environment to them. We, on the other hand, are immortal, celestial beings, divinely constituted, with a pre-ordained purpose. Any changes to the angelic nature or abilities tend to be slight, often cosmetic – and always take a long time to perfect.

She leant forward and picked up a cutting – I could see it was an extract from the *New York Times*. "This was written a few months ago," she said, "the author has lived under police protection since 2006 because of threats to his life from organised crime."

Pointing to a section of the article, she began to read:

"'Mafia organizations are more of a threat than terrorist groups because they modify democracies from within by introducing their illicit earnings into the legal economy... As difficult as it is to track the routes of drugs, it is even harder to follow a money trail in the era of online banking and cyber-finance... The strength of criminal organizations is the lack of attention they receive from governments and their ability to garner social consensus – in cases where the state is absent, the mafia 'offers services' to citizens. Their winning formula is simple: an extreme tendency toward economic evolution combined with a minimal tendency toward cultural evolution'.[17]

"In other words, these groups are invidious, they get under the skin of society, making use of new technology, moving money wherever they want it to go – and yet they still remain based within the old communities – using the old-fashioned tactics of fear and corruption just as much as they manipulate and exploit via social media and the darkweb. We have been watching the Maniscalos for years. They sit at the centre of the operation in Italy – and if we can destabilise them, we will be going a long way towards destroying the whole, damned lot of them."

She paused. I took a look at the papers she had pushed towards me. It was not a pretty sight. Photos showing the victims of shoot-outs and torture, news articles highlighting corruption – and the lack of any action to prevent it. I scanned through bank statements, revealing multi-billion dollar transactions – and remembered something I had heard a few years ago.

In 2009 the United Nations Office on Drugs and Crime had revealed that money from organised crime was one of the only sources of liquid investment capital available. Between 2007 and 2009, banks in the United States and Europe had lost more than one trillion dollars on bad loans and toxic assets. Liquidity had become the main problem of the banking system. As a result, banks loosened their protections against money laundering and opened up their safes to the Mafia's dirty money, which was primarily from drug trafficking. These funds were then laundered and absorbed into the legal economic system. This was serious shit.

Sara continued, "When Alex came of age, it became clear that he'd made his choice; with his own free will he was going to disassociate himself from evil. We thought at that point that we had the chance of a way in. But then came the confrontation and his father's murderous attack – leaving his mother dead and turning Alex into a fugitive.

"We could do nothing but make sure that Jaoel stayed as close to Alex as possible. We approved a semi-permanent materialisation[18], gave them new

---

[17] Extract from *The New York Times*, April 2014, by Roberto Saviano

[18] "Permanent or semi-permanent materialisations, in which the angel adopts a material form (usually human, although there have been rare examples of animal materialisations) either forever or for a long period, require significant amounts of celestial energy to maintain and need the approval of the permanent secretary. In such a state, the angel can access and make limited use of all of their angelic powers with the exception of the ability to alate." *The Anatomy of Angels*, 1935

identities, and the two of them travelled together, finally setting up home here in London about five years ago. We also made it our business to ensure that both Guardians – Jaoel and Ely - worked together to forge the bonds we needed between Sophia and her brother.

"When Sophia made the same choice, this improved our chances of finding a way to unite her with her brother and to use their testimony to bring down the Maniscalos. Over the years, Sophia had become suspicious of her father's stories. Then we invoked the dream nexus connection, which planted yet more seeds – and she made it her business to do a little gentle digging into her father's affairs.

"When she left Italy, she brought with her evidence which links the family to crimes committed not just in Europe, but in the US and Mexico and this, combined with Alex's testimony regarding his mother's murder and the attack upon himself, will be enough to indict their father and at least three of his brothers."

Sara looked directly at me. "We need to reach Alex and Sophia before it is too late. If they remain for too long within the Inferno, the chances are that the balance of their minds will be disrupted – and they will not be fit to testify. You heard what Manny said about the balance of power; the increase in numbers of the Fallen has tipped it dangerously away from us.

"We need to destabilise the Maniscalos; we need to break up the Italian cartels." She paused and pulled out from the folder a picture of a man, tied to a chair, his head lolling to one side and blood seeping from the deadly pattern of knife wounds etched across his naked torso. He had no hands or feet, just bloody stumps.

She thrust the picture in front of me. "We need to prevent things like this from happening."

Sara sat down and began to gather up the documents from the desk, returning them to their folders and putting them back into her case. Despite the dramatic nature of her last few words, she appeared calm, unflustered and surprisingly business-like.

She zipped up the case and stood up. "Right," she said, "are you ready, Zach? I think we have work to do."

I started, "I'm sorry, but what exactly do you mean by 'we'?" This was news to me. Although I had had a couple of partners over the years, I tended to prefer working solo, and despite my fondness for Sara, I really wasn't sure that I wanted an untried bureaucrat coming into the field with me. She was clearly a shit-hot analyst, and her cosmological force-control was impressive – she had done a great job darkening the skies that morning, but surely this didn't qualify her for a rescue mission into the Inferno?

I turned towards Manny and K, who had moved towards the window, looking out at the garden beyond the ancient mulberry tree. Their heads were close together and they appeared to be deep in conversation.

"Um, Manny… Is that it then?" I said somewhat lamely.

He looked up and gestured towards the door. "Yes, take what you need from resources – stay in touch using the normal channels and get back as quick as you can. We really don't have any more time to lose on this one."

I nodded questioningly towards Sara. Manny shot me a quick grin and nodded back.

Sara seemed to think that we were now partners on the Maniscalo case – and it looked like she had got that one right as well.

"Is it okay if I take the car, sir?" Sara addressed K. "I have a feeling we may need to make a couple of calls en-route, and that is probably the quickest way to travel."

"Yes, I have further business to discuss with Emmanuel. I'll summon transport when I need it." K paused and looked at both of us. "I am sure you understand the critical nature of this mission. We cannot tolerate failure. Good luck and Godspeed, Angel Sarandiel, Angel Zachriel."

K turned back to the window and he and Manny resumed their conversation. We were dismissed.

Sara and I walked silently from the room and down the stairs, making our way to the rear of the tower where the Merc was parked. "Come on then, Sara," I said, "if I am going to be saddled with you, at least give me the keys – I've been wanting to have a go in one of these babies for ages."

She looked at me, opened the rear door and placed the attaché case neatly in the pocket behind the driver's seat. Then she straightened her jacket, opened the driver's door and got in.

"No way," she said, "I haven't forgotten how you always used to go up the down lane on Jacob's Ladder. You caused utter chaos. And besides," she smiled at me sweetly, "you're not insured."

~ *Chapter Four* ~

I conceded with a good grace. She had a point about the insurance and anyway, if she was trusted to drive the permanent secretary around, who was I to complain? I looked at the clock on the dashboard – just a little after nine o'clock. Only three and a half hours since Manny's phone call. I couldn't help thinking that it seemed a hell of a lot longer.

"Right," I said, "before we go anywhere else, I need to shave and change into something rather more appropriate, and there are a few bits and pieces we are going to need to pick up."

I looked across at her, once again taking in the impeccable cut of her suit and the undeniable elegance of her shapely legs, encased in sheer nylon. I looked down at her shoes as she moved her left leg slightly in order to depress the clutch. Black, probably designer – and utterly unsuited to the work in hand. "I think you could probably do with a change of image as well."

Sara grinned and nodded towards a green canvas bag on the back seat. "I've got my field clothes and kitbag ready. Let's head round to yours – and then I think a visit to St. Basil's is in order."

I had to hand it to her, she wasn't missing a trick. I was extremely keen to find out exactly what had happened last night and Isra, safely nestled away at St. Basil's, was probably our best lead. I also thought it was highly likely that Isra would have been in contact with Jaoel. Given the sensitivities around the Maniscalo siblings, it seemed inconceivable that Sophia's stand-in wouldn't have got in touch with Alex's permanent Guardian. And if Jaoel had been involved in their disappearance, if he was in cahoots with Eligor – in short, if he had joined the ranks of the Fallen, I needed to find out as much as I could about the events of the last forty-eight hours.

Sara swung the car right onto the Balls Pond Road, past Dalston Junction and then took a swift left into Ashwin Street. Not the most salubrious part of town, but it had been home for a while now – and to be honest, I've never really been that fussed about my surroundings – just a place to lay my hat – if you know what I mean? The road comes to a dead end just outside my front door; Sara parked the car, undid her seat belt and took a swift appraising look out of the window.

"Lived here long?" she asked, conversationally.

"No, not really, just over a hundred and forty years, I moved in around 1870. Before that I had a place near the Holloway Road.

"I like it here," I said – perhaps a tad defensively, as I could see she was looking a little uneasily at the graffiti on the walls. The dead cat in the gutter didn't help either.

We both got out of the car. "How about you – where do you live nowadays?"

When we first met, Sara and I had both lived in the city, in the part of the Heavens known as Ma'on[19]. I had taken the first chance I could to move out; with my job it made sense to have a permanent bolt-hole on earth, and to be honest, I sometimes found the atmosphere of the celestial realms more than a little stifling. But she was an Angel of the Hours and I assumed she would have been expected to remain pretty close to the centre. I was not wrong.

"Oh," she gave a little, half embarrassed cough, "I have a place in Araboth, nothing much." I might have known it. Araboth, otherwise known as 'Seventh Heaven' is the most prime piece of real estate in the celestial realms. This only served to make my neighbourhood seem even less appealing.

I said nothing; Sara grabbed her bags from the back seat. Looking round once again at the old takeaway boxes discarded on the pavement and the broken windows of the building across the way she asked, "Do you think the car will be okay here? We could always dematerialise it – just to be on the safe side."

"Whatever," I grunted noncommittally, recognising the sense in her suggestion, but not taking kindly to the implication that my street was not a safe place to leave K's car for a few minutes.

"Let's do it," she said. "You take out the CCTV, I'll do the car."

---

[19] "Ma'on, otherwise known as the Fourth Heaven, is one of the celestial planes most sought after locations, home of the vibrant and multi-cultural city of New Jerusalem. Ma'on is well served by the angelic highway and with close links to both the Garden of Eden and the gates of paradise, an early viewing is recommended." *Heavenly Homes and Gardens*, 1994

All angels are chronoprohiberists – in other words, we have the ability to freeze time – not forever, but for long enough to cover our tracks. How else do you think we manage just to appear and disappear with no-one actually seeing where we came from? It also comes in pretty handy if you need to make something happen that you don't want caught on camera. Once I had dealt with the CCTV cameras which overlooked my end of Ashwin Street, Sara touched the car firmly with the forefinger of her right hand. She nodded once, and the car vanished.

It didn't take us long to get changed; within ten minutes we were both dressed in fatigues; my trainers and Sara's Jimmy Choos swapped for combat boots. Whilst she took the opportunity to force her mass of curls into a rather severe bun, I shaved and grabbed my kitbag from the place I always stored it – the laundry basket at the foot of my bed. I didn't really fear sneak thieves – but just to be on the safe side, I always thought that the last place anyone would choose to look for my valuables would be underneath my unsavoury and, to be honest, rather crusty cast-offs.

I went into the kitchen, filled two water bottles and went to the cupboards for some Red Bull, a dozen protein bars and a slab of Kendall mint cake; all of which I stowed safely away in the depths of my kitbag. As celestial beings, food and drink isn't necessary for us, but our physical bodies still need to be fed and watered, and I wasn't quite sure how long this trip was going to take.

"There are a couple of things we are going to need if we are to have any chance of getting Sophia and Alex out of there safely," I said. "I am not sure what sort of arrangement Eligor has made for managing their corporeal status in the realms of the dead, but I think we had better assume that it won't hold good once we get hold of them."

Sara nodded. "I did a bit of research into this whilst K was in conference with the Vatican. There have been instances of other mortals safely navigating the Inferno, but they have always had some sort of celestial protection. The best bet seems to be the Golden Bough – which is how Aenaes managed it when he went through the underworld."

"Who's this Anus when he's at home," I asked, "and how long ago was this?"

Sara sent me a withering glance. "Not Anus, you idiot." She pronounced the word carefully. "A-nay-us; he was only one of the most important humans in early classical civilisation," she replied. "One of the few survivors of the Trojan Wars, he escaped after Troy fell to Agamemnon and the Greek army

~ 35 ~

and travelled to Italy where he founded the city of Rome. On the way he wanted a bit of advice from his dear old dad - like you do - and was advised by this wise woman that he would need to visit the underworld. He used the Golden Bough as a sort of entry ticket – and left it hanging on the doorway when he came out."

"Well, that is really helpful," I said. "Let's just place all our faith in a gilded twig that some human left hanging on a door frame over two thousand years ago."

Sara looked at me triumphantly. "It's still there – with a sort of blue plaque thing next to it, on the gateway in the Elysian Fields. I saw it only a few weeks ago when I was out there for a run. It would be quite easy to pick it up on our way in – there's still an entry to the Inferno on the northern side of the fields you know."

"Okay, well, be that as it may, we don't have it to hand now and as people keep telling me, time is pressing. I suggest we take a few other precautions. I'm going to make sure they have the protection of the right talismans, and I'm also going to ask at St. Basil's about medication for reviving humans who have experienced excessive exposure to celestial radiation." I opened my wall safe and took out a couple of small bottles, plus two golden amulets embossed with one of the strongest of our protective talismans.

Sara looked a little crestfallen. She had been spending so much time thinking about this Anus bloke that she clearly hadn't spent any time considering the more practical measures we would need to take. To me this was clearly just another example of her inexperience – and her lack of suitability for the mission we had just been sent on.

"Listen, Sara," I said. "It's been great to see you again, and we must have a proper catch up sometime, but this job is not really your cup of tea.

"You've been a desk bunny for years. I know you understand the theory better than me – and you could probably quote policy and regulations until you go blue in the face and I evanesce out of sheer boredom. But do you really think you've got what it takes to go into the Inferno and rescue Sophia and Alex?"

I picked up my bag and walked towards the door. "What say we just drop you home and I take it from here…?"

The force hit me like nothing I had experienced before. My face was rammed up against the door with my ear pressed agonisingly into the Yale lock. There was an excruciating pain coursing through the back of my neck and

~ 36 ~

my kidneys. Sara had rushed me, pushed me up against the door and was now using her full force to hold me in place, with one hand clamped firmly on the nape of my neck, the other in the small of my back. Given the reciprocal nature of angelic connectivity, she must have been in severe pain as well, but she did not flinch.

After what seemed like eternity but must only have been about forty-five seconds, she let go.

"Let's pretend you never said that."

Picking up both our kitbags, she walked down the stairs.

By the time I got out on to the street, the car had rematerialised and Sara was sitting at the driving wheel looking poised and efficient. "Get in," she said. "Next stop, St. Basil's."

~ *Chapter Five* ~

"Did you remember to unfreeze the CCTV cameras?" I asked as we drove through Shoreditch and onto Bishops Gate.

"Oh, I did better than that," she smiled in a rather superior way, "I arranged a small temporal realignment for the whole of Ashwin Street. In fact, we left before we even had chance to arrive."

I looked at the clock in the car.

It said five past nine.

"How on earth did you do that?" I asked, astonished.

"Don't forget, I am one of the Angels of the Hours. We're in charge of time." She looked at me again and said a little smugly, "In other words, time does what we tell it."

"Well in that case, smart-arse, why can't we just go back to Friday night and stop all this from happening?"

"For three good reasons," she answered, as she steered the car expertly past Charing Cross station, turning left at Trafalgar Square. "Firstly, the practical reason: if we just went back in time and took Alex and Sophia away from that party in Hoxton, Eligor would guess his plan had been rumbled. He would inform his contacts on our side and they would retreat, leaving us with no way of uncovering the remaining rebels. You know that thought and deed are not the same thing – and we can't truly know if an angel has fallen until they actually give into temptation and perform an act of treachery. If our guess is right and Jaoel is the one responsible for this, he must actually betray his charge before we can bring an accusation against him and get him cast out."

I thought about this. "That seems a little unfair on Sophia and Alex," I said, "making them go through all this just so we can improve our crime management figures. Surely they should come first? They are the victims here after all."

"That brings me to the second reason. If we go back in time and change things, we create a different future. That means different outcomes and different risks. Just say we went back to Friday night, took Alex and Sophia away and then on Saturday morning, Sophia goes out to buy a paper and gets run over by a car. The evidence is lost, she can't testify, and we can't indict the Maniscalos. Going back in time might actually make the future worse for Alex and Sophia, not better.

"It is one thing to create a small temporal realignment in a very limited space, but quite another to actively go back in time and change things. And that brings me to the third reason. It's forbidden. If I was tempted to do it and gave into that temptation, then you would have to arraign me. I'd have become one of the Fallen."

I considered this in silence as Sara drove on down Whitehall, making her way around Parliament Square onto Victoria Street. We were heading for Chelsea.

We had reached the Embankment and now Sara began to slow down, finally stopping outside some tall, wrought iron gates on our left. As we approached, the gates began to open; we drove through, in to the southernmost part of the Chelsea Physic Garden. We parked under the trees, behind the most ancient of the hothouses and taking our kitbags, got out of the car. The gates, which had been there ever since the 17th century, when the Heavenly Host agreed to join forces with London's Worshipful Society of Apothecaries, gently swung back into place. We had arrived at St. Basil's.[20]

Although angels can't die in the same way that humans can, their physical bodies can be injured or even destroyed. Those of us who work away from the celestial realms actually become quite attached to our corporeal forms. We spend a lot of our time inhabiting them and from my experience; most of us would always rather pay a visit to hospital for a fixer-upper than go through the hassle of generating a new body.

The gardens face south and have an undeniable atmosphere of peace and well-being, aided in no small degree by the presence of St. Basil's. Although

---

[20]"St. Basil's Hospital for angelic care and rehabilitation has been situated within the Chelsea Physic Garden since 1673 and provides treatment for any physical illnesses or injury sustained by angels during corporeal manifestations. Common ailments include breakage or damage to bones or plumage and avian influenza. In recent years, the hospital has expanded its services to provide a range of cosmetic treatments and holistic therapies." *The Anatomy of Angels*, 1995

the hospital can't be seen by the humans who also occupy this space, its powerful curative emanations are one of the reasons why healing flowers and plants have flourished here for over three hundred and forty years.

There was no-one around. The gardens weren't open to the public on Sundays in November anyway, and the volunteer gardeners were all working on preparing the beds at the other end of the garden for winter.

Having dematerialised the car (it made sense not to take any unnecessary risks) we brushed past the richly scented winter jasmine and eucalyptus and headed straight for the ancient glasshouses. Passing through the small, narrow and oppressively heated rooms, we had to walk in single file. The glasshouses hadn't been designed to accommodate many visitors; we'd never wanted to encourage interest in this part of the gardens.

We reached the final door, which always remains stubbornly shut if one of the gardeners or an inquisitive visitor tries to open it. I put out my hand; it opened smoothly to my touch and we walked into the main reception hall of St. Basil's. I checked my phone – no messages or missed calls. The time was nine forty-five.

Everything about the hospital was white: glaring, intense, almost hallucinatory white. Think of the whitest thing you could possibly imagine – say a snow drop in the beak of a white dove, sitting on a Swiss alp, covered in snow, with the UV glare to the max; and then imagine it a hundred times whiter. My eyes hurt as I reached into my bag for my sunnies and crammed them on.

That was better; but only slightly.

I hadn't been here for over five years and I had forgotten just how weak the human body was in the face of celestial radiance. I would be about as much use as a bacon sandwich at a vegan's banquet if I didn't do something soon. "Sorry," I said to Sara, "but this is too much for me. I am going to have to dematerialise. Grab my bag will you?"

Without waiting for an answer, I tossed her my kitbag and raised my arms up, into the light. I emptied my mind of human concerns and focused every atom of my being on thoughts of the eternal. As I did so, I felt my corporeal shell begin to fall away, dropping to the floor at my feet like a large and unwanted rag.

I had resumed the true form of the Angel Zachriel.

Now that I had eyes which were properly adjusted to the light, I turned back to Sara, who was prodding my corpus with her left foot. "You can't go dropping litter in here you know. We had better tidy this up or one of the nurses will take it away." She bent down, picked up my body[21] as if it weighed no more than a discarded crisp packet and carried it towards the side wall, where she plonked it none too gently on a bench. Sara had decided to remain in her corporeal form but I could now see that she was wearing a pair of UDs[22] which she had probably put on just before we came into the reception area. I bet she had brought them with her from the celestial realms this morning; it was just the sort of annoyingly well organised thing that I was beginning to expect from her.

"Are you going to stay like that?" I asked her, indicating her physical form. She was still corporeal, but she had fully alated and her wings, which were glossy and the colour of copper beech leaves, were folded neatly behind her. She was carrying her kitbag over her shoulder. I picked mine up from the floor where she had dropped it.

"Yes, this is still a bit of a novelty for me, I haven't had a material body for about three hundred years – and these UDs work really well. K gave me a pair this morning. He said we might need to pop in to St. Basil's."

"Nice of him to give you a pair for me too," I said pointedly.

She shrugged and bent over to adjust the shoulders of my limp and disused corpus. On the wall behind the bench was a poster which read:

'November special – book your body in for a full service and get three cosmetic treatments for the price of two*. Terms and conditions apply.

(*rhinoplasty and penile enhancement not included.)'

I dumped my kitbag on to the bench next to the body and was about to hold it more securely in place by putting one of my corporeal hands on top of it, when someone came flying straight towards us.

---

[21]"Categories of Physical Manifestation: 1) Transient: Angels who work predominantly in the celestial realms or angels whose work requires them to work with humans without being seen (i.e. Guardian Angels and Recording Angels) have no need of a fully corporeal body. If a physical form is required, a transient body is created by the transfiguration of local atomic matter (usually dust) and the body returns to dust when it is no longer required. 2) Temporary: Angels whose work regularly requires them to be visible to humans and other creatures (e.g. Justice Angels, Divine Messengers) require a fully corporeal body. In such cases, the body is created using the appropriate alchemical ingredients and takes a little over nine months to perfect. Once created, it becomes the property of the angel, who is required to maintain it appropriately to ensure it remains fit for purpose." *The Anatomy of Angels*, 1935

[22] "Umbra Divinus shades are specially designed to protect the eyes of angels on earthbound missions who need to return temporarily to the celestial realms. Everything looks better with UDs – protection, style and comfort." *Umbra Divinus catalogue*, 1675

"Good morning, angels," said a gratuitously cheery voice, "is this one in for a service?" It was one of the receptionists, who had decided to come over and try a spot of triage. She pointed to my corpus. "It does look like it could do with a little TLC doesn't it? Now why don't you leave it with me and we will have it ready by three o'clock. You can always go and relax in our all-inclusive spa and health club whilst you are waiting. Let's have a little look shall we?"

Manoeuvring herself in front of my rather less than fragrant body, she grabbed a handful of hair and pulled my head upwards none to gently in order to take a look at the empty, vacant face. "Oooooh," she exclaimed in satisfaction, "hairline going, crow's-feet and bags under the eyes..." She turned to look up at me and wagged her finger. "Who hasn't been getting his beauty sleep then?"

The cheery voice was becoming more irritating by the second.

As I watched, impotently, she expertly put a finger in its mouth and took a quick look at the teeth. She tutted. "Could do with a bit of a clean-up in here as well." She pointed to the poster, "Teeth-whitening is included in the offer if you're interested?"

"Actually, no, stop it," I said. "It doesn't want a service. Please just get out of my face and leave my corpus alone. It may be a bit battered, but that's the way I like it."

I moved to stand in front of my poor, poked about body and pulled out my ID, which I shoved, rather roughly in front of her. "We are here on Agency business; I just want to leave that here for a bit whilst we go talk to one of your patients. The Angel Israfil."

The receptionist sniffed as if she was quite disappointed that she was going to miss out on giving my discarded body a bit of a wash and brush up. She considered my ID and then looked questioningly at Sara, who obligingly took hers from her pocket and handed it over. After some deliberation, both seemed to pass muster and we were asked to follow her to the front desk so she could take some details.

Within five minutes, we were on our way to the ward.

"Don't be too long," said the receptionist as we headed towards the swing doors. Her voice was remarkably less cheery. "It's really against regulations to leave an unanimated corpus lying around. If an Inspector turns up, I will have to move it." We assured her that we'd be as quick as we could be and rushed through the doors in search of the Aquinas ward and Isra.

~ *Chapter Six* ~

We found it pretty quickly; one thing I can say for the AHS (Angelic Health Service) is that it is well organised and efficient. Well, there has to be some advantage to being on the side of the angels.

Aquinas ward specialised in wing damage; we passed two bays containing angels looking bored and a bit sorry for themselves, their pinions bandaged or wings extended in traction. They were all wearing the ubiquitous UDs.

Isra was in the third bay, and as luck would have it, none of the other beds was occupied. He looked up as we approached; we weren't exactly friends, but we knew each other and had worked together on a handful of jobs for the Agency in the past. He was not bad looking, but his carefully styled hair, casual leather bracelets and trendy designer tattoos made me think that he cared rather more about his image than was good for him.

As we entered the room his face broke into a smile of recognition. "Hey, Zach, what brings you here? I didn't think hospitals were really your thing."

He was right, I don't like hospitals – or any other institution if truth be known, too many people, too many rules.

"Here on business I'm afraid, mate. Sorry to hear about your accident, Manny filled me in first thing this morning."

"Bit of an embarrassing thing to do really... I'll bet they'll be having a right laugh in Charlie's this lunchtime." He grinned a little ruefully. "Still, Sister says it's not that serious, the pollex is bruised but not broken, and I should be out by tomorrow – as soon as they have straightened out the damaged plumage."

As Isra gave his slightly battered feathers a gentle stroke, Sara moved round to the other side of the bed and put her kitbag down on the floor; they are a bit hard to manage with wings sprouting out of your shoulder blades and I could see she was getting fed up carting it around.

"Hello," she said, "I'm Sara." She smiled reassuringly at him, like someone from an advert for toothpaste or car insurance.

"I know we haven't met before, but do you mind if I call you Isra?"

He looked rather nonplussed; this was a little contrary to angel etiquette, which usually demands that one angel bestows on the other the permission to call them by their more informal name. It really isn't done to actually ask for the right to do so.

Still, Isra was basking in the warm glow of Sara's smile, and he wasn't the boy to turn down a pretty face, even if she was being unconventional. Isra blushed a little as he nodded feebly, and Sara continued introducing herself.

"I work in K's office and, as Zach says, this is business not pleasure, although I must say that I'm glad to hear that your injuries are not that serious." She glowed down at him again, and I could feel Isra starting to get all gooey in the process.

I gave a slight cough, which caught both their attentions, and dragged Isra back into the here and now. Unseen by him, Sara gave me a crafty wink. Little madam.

"What's this about then?" asked Isra and I realised that he probably didn't know about Alex and Sophia.

We explained.

Isra turned pale when he heard about Sophia's disappearance and it only got worse when we told him that Alex had also vanished. He sank down onto the bed with his head in his hands and when we let him know that the nexus between Alex and Jaoel had been terminated, he began to shake... He turned away from us and curled himself up, making himself as small as he could, raising his knees against his chest, his broken wings attempting unsuccessfully to shield him.

As we watched, he started to rock, back and forwards on the side of the bed. I heard him begin to murmur to himself but couldn't quite pick up the words; if he had been human I would probably have pulled him towards me and slapped him round the face, but the additional shock of the full force of physical contact between two celestial beings would probably have knocked him out – and that was the last thing we needed right now.

"Isra, calm down, this isn't helping. We need to know exactly what happened. You have to pull yourself together." I spoke urgently, but there was no response. Isra just kept on rocking.

Sara was taking in the situation and could see that we weren't getting very far. Opening her kitbag, she took out a pair of gloves and, pulling them on swiftly, sat down beside Isra. She placed one gloved hand gently on his shoulder, and with the other, began to softly stroke his damaged pinions. She said nothing. Almost immediately, the rocking slowed down; soon it had stopped altogether. Isra raised his face to look at Sara.

"I am so... so sorry." He was stuttering as he attempted to regain his composure. "I knew something was wrong on Friday – b...b...but I let that bastard Jaoel convince me that he had it under control. And on Saturday - when the regular guy - Ely - turned up and just wanted to get on with the job without even a thank you, I got a bit pissed off. I could see that I wasn't wanted, so I just thought 'to Hell with it'. I didn't need the grief on some second rate temp assignment – and I just walked out of there without a second's thought. And now they are gone. Oh God..."

He was starting to get distressed again; I could see Sara resuming the stroking so I moved round to face him and spoke to him rather more gently this time. "We need to know first-hand exactly what happened in the forty-eight hours leading up to the disappearance. Isra, you are the only one who can help."

This seemed to get through to him. He looked up at me, big eyes seeking my approval, but all the while leaning in towards Sara as if wanting to make sure she was still there for him. I gave him the nod, making it clear that I was there to listen, not to make judgements... and then he started talking.

"So," began Isra, "on Friday morning, Sophia moves out of her hotel and goes to stay with Kathryn, Alex's girlfriend. She had told him that she didn't feel safe in the hotel, she was sure that someone was watching her and they agreed it would be better for her to move somewhere else. Kathryn lives not far from Old Street – she's got a flat in Cranwood Street, nice place, but a bit poky."

This was news to me. There had been nothing in the file to say that Sophia had relocated, and nothing about the involvement of this Kathryn person. Assuming she was a person, and not another one of the Fallen, disguised, like Eligor, in human form. This was starting to get to me; if there is one thing I can't stand it's being treated like a mushroom. Being kept in the dark and fed nothing but shit did not make me happy.

Isra saw my face and began to splutter apologies... "I hadn't had chance to update the files, I was going to do it on Saturday after the regular guy showed up..."

"But instead you went off to Charlie's and got arse-holed... you bloody idiot." I was not pleased and felt like ripping nine strips off him, but Sara threw me a warning look. We needed to hear Isra's story – and fast. I knew she was right, an argument at this point would not be helpful. I reined in and sat back in my chair, letting Sara take over the questions.

"What time was this, Isra?" said Sara.

"About half ten. It didn't take long to get her settled, Sophia travelled light, she only had a couple of cases with her, and when everything was sorted, the girls decided to go out for a coffee. Naturally, I went with them, they had lunch, checked out some shops... nothing much happened until around four."

"One question," asked Sara. "Were you material? Did Sophia know you were there?"

"No, strictly by the book on this one," said Isra.

So, at least he'd done one thing right. It was rare for a Guardian to reveal themselves materially to their charge, particularly if it was a temporary arrangement like Isra and Sophia's.

"They went back to the flat to meet Alex and Jaoel and stayed there for around three hours. I had them under observation for a while, but the conversation was going nowhere. Kathryn didn't seem to be in the picture at all about the Maniscalo situation, it wasn't mentioned once, so I assumed that Alex and Sophia had decided to keep it to themselves."

This was good. At least the humans seemed to have some common sense.

"How about Jaoel?" Sara asked. "He's fully materialised, right? How did he fit in with all this?"

I had forgotten about that. Jaoel had been given a semi-permanent materialisation around ten years ago. Such a thing was almost unheard of and in this case had only been granted to provide cover for Alex whilst he was on the run. Usually angels who work outside of the celestial realms need to uncouple themselves from their corporeal forms at least once a month, for cleansing and general health purposes. I must admit that I feel a bit sullied if I go for more than a couple of weeks without a good dematerialisation; Jaoel must be really scuzzy by now.

"Oh, he was fine." Isra was relaxing now, even starting to get chatty as Sara continued to gently stroke his damaged pinions. "He and Alex were really close, like brothers, you know? And he seemed to be very, very fond of Sophia. I could feel him generating surges of energy in her direction. He knew I was there, but his powers are limited, so he just acknowledged me on arrival and ignored me from then on, no meta-conversations on the ether, if you know what I mean?"

Sara nodded, and carried on stroking.

"Anyway, they were talking about football, TV, stuff like that. It got a bit boring, so I zoned out.

"At around seven, they started thinking about going out. Alex said that he wanted to take in a party at some guy's house. I can't remember the name – it sounded American – Earl, Lord, something like that."

"Duke," I said quietly, leaning towards him. "The name was Duke Eligos." Sara and I exchanged glances. We were getting somewhere.

"If you say so," said Isra, not picking up at all on our heightened interest. "I hadn't heard of him before. The girls said they had to get ready, so the guys headed off and they all arranged to meet at the Dragon Bar on Shoreditch High Street at around nine. They stayed at the Dragon until around eleven and then decided to move on to this Duke guy's party."

"Had he turned up at the Dragon to meet them? Did you see him?" Sara asked.

"No, the four of them stayed together, didn't talk to anyone else – I took a few pictures on my phone, they seemed to be having a good time, although I think Alex was worried that Sophia was drinking rather more than was good for her. Anyway, this party was on Old Nichol Street, just a few blocks away from the Dragon and it wasn't a cold night, so they decided to walk." Isra was getting in to his stride now; this was his story and he clearly wanted to tell it his way.

"Everything seemed fine until we got to the front door. Straight away I sensed trouble. The place was… not normal. Not human. I didn't like it. Given the sensitivity of the situation, it didn't seem like a safe sort of place for Alex and Sophia. But Jaoel just walked inside."

Isra turned towards me, like everyone else, he was wearing UDs, but even behind his glasses I could sense his disquiet.

"I thought Jaoel must be able to sense it too; even with the deterioration in his powers, it was not exactly subtle, but he didn't seem bothered – he had an arm round Sophia's shoulder, sort of keeping her up, keeping her steady. And he was just walking in there. I messaged him, and he picked up. I know he did. But he didn't reply."

I thought about this - and it sort of made sense. Jaoel's angelic powers would have been gradually deteriorating over the years because of his inability to cleanse himself and realign his celestial energies - and would get more so the longer he remained within a human form.

"Are you sure he felt it?" I asked.

"Yes," Isra replied, "he texted me… I'd show you, but I lost my phone at Charlie's last night."

"What did it say?"

"Something like: *'Don't worry, all groovy… I know what I'm doing'* and a smiley face. This didn't fill me with confidence, so I thought I had better instigate a transient materialisation, just in case we were going to need some actual muscle in there. I found an alley about 100 yards away, but it was easily five minutes before I was ready to try to get in to the party.

"It wasn't hard to get inside; the place was busy, but not really crowded. I just walked in, looked like I knew where I was going and no-one bothered me. Downstairs, all seemed normal. Just humans, music, drink, drugs, dancing. Nothing I was concerned about. And no sign of Alex or Sophia." Isra was on a roll now. He wasn't looking at either of us; his eyes had glazed over, gazing into the middle distance as he told us his story.

And all the while, Sara continued her gentle stroking, running her fingers along the length of his plumage.

"I decided to head upstairs, I could sense there was something there, but there were so many different emanations that I really couldn't work out what. As I said, it was a warm night, but it began to get very cold. I remember looking at my arms and seeing the skin prickle into goose bumps. I was on the second landing now. I could still hear the party below, but I could also hear noises coming from the door at the end of the landing. Sort of grunting, moans and furniture creaking. I suppose I thought it was just someone taking advantage of an empty room for a quick shag and almost ignored it until I heard a scream."

Isra looked across at me. We were getting there, making progress… but he wasn't happy. His shoulders tensed and I could see fear beginning to gather in his eyes. I knew that he didn't really want to talk about what happened next. But that didn't matter. I had to know. I leant closer, gave him a brief nod and a curt smile, willing him to continue.

From the corner of my eye I could see Sara's hand continuing to move, slowly, hypnotically up and down.

Isra coughed, trying to clear his throat; I passed him a glass of water. "What happened next?" I asked him. "What did you do when you heard that scream?"

Again, he wouldn't meet my eyes. "The door at the top of the stairs opened and someone came out. I think it was a man – tall, and broad shouldered. He wore a cloak and I couldn't see his face. I pushed myself back against the wall and he didn't notice me. There was another scream and he hurried towards the door at the end of the corridor. He pushed it open and as he stood on the threshold, I caught a glimpse of what was inside."

Isra looked up at Sara. I could see he was shaking.

He was out of his depth here. But then, he was only a Guardian. Music was his thing, doing his job, keeping his head down and playing his horn. He had never had to get up close and personal with the big boys before, and I could see he was rattled to the very core of his being.

"What happened then?" I asked. "What did you see?"

"I only caught a glimpse, just a few seconds... before the door shut, but it looked like a human male, tied up, chained on a hook hanging down from the ceiling. He was upside down. The man was naked and he was cut – sliced all the way down one side." Isra was shaking his head... not wanting to remember.

"I saw... saw that his blood was draining into a huge bowl... and behind... behind the bowl was a... thing. It was monstrous. Oh God... It grunted and slavered and its vile tongue was licking the blood from the bowl." Isra was staring straight at Sara. He had stopped talking, unable to bring back the memory, unable to face what he had witnessed.

Sara had stopped stroking his wings and was now holding his chin in her right hand, whilst her left hovered against his chest, just above Isra's heart.

"Tell us what happened." Sara's voice was low, gentle. "It's okay, Isra... just tell us... I won't let anyone hurt you."

He relaxed slightly, took another sip of water, and continued.

"The man had clearly been gagged, but he had somehow managed to twist himself free of it. As I looked, his eyes caught mine and he opened his mouth, but before he could make a sound, a hand with a knife came from behind him and cut his throat.

"Then the door shut, the guy in the cloak was inside and I heard voices. There was a dull, heavy thud and all went quiet. I crept to the door. Nothing. I waited for about five minutes. When there were no more sounds, I decided to risk it. I banged on the door, and shouted a bit in a sort of drunken voice... I banged again and just walked in. The room was empty."

Isra looked up at me. "Completely empty, clean, no blood, no bowl, and no knife. No disgusting Hell-Beast. But I know what I saw. I know they were there."

He felt better now, he'd stopped shaking, and Sara had moved back from him. I could tell the worst was over, but we still didn't have the full picture. "Go on, Isra, what happened next?"

"The noise from downstairs was getting worse. There was nothing doing up on the second floor, so I thought I had better try and find Sophia and the others. As I got to the bottom of the stairs, the door next to the kitchen opened and Kathryn came out. She didn't look happy. The others were behind her and they were clearly all set to leave the party. Sophia was looking very much the worse for wear. She had her arms round Alex and some other bloke - a big, blond guy - was helping to steady her through the door. Jaoel was behind them. It was dark in the hallway and I couldn't see them that clearly, but I was close enough to hear what they were saying. Alex was apologising to the blond guy, said his sister was not really used to drinking, and that last glass of champagne was clearly one too many.

"The blond guy said not to worry or something like that and went back inside. Jaoel put out his hand, stopped a taxi and they all got inside. I went round the corner and dematerialised and was back at the flat just before they got there."

The story was over, and Isra relaxed, looking down at his feet and then stretching his wings, wincing a little at his bruised pinions. "That's it," he said, "that's what happened."

Sara pushed her chair away from the bed and stood up. "That's some story," she said slowly, clearly trying to take in the implications of what we'd been hearing. "And what happened when you got back to the flat? Did you speak to Jaoel?"

Isra shook his head. "It was about half twelve when they got back. Sophia had been sick in the cab and then there was a big row with Kathryn. She hadn't wanted to leave the party and she wasn't happy about having to look after Alex's sick little sister all night. Alex calmed her down and said he would stay with Sophia until she felt better and Kathryn went to bed in a right huff.

"Alex took Sophia to the bathroom and that's when I took the opportunity to speak to Jaoel. I told him what I'd seen and he said I must've been imagining it." Isra shook his head indignantly. "Okay, so there was some pretty strong weed at Eligor's place... but he implied I must have had a toke and hallucinated. Bastard. As if. I haven't touched that stuff since Haight Ashbury.

"Anyway, he did admit that he'd felt a little uncomfortable at the party; he and Alex had only met this Duke guy a couple of days ago, and from what he saw at the house on Old Nichol Street, Jaoel didn't like the crowd he was running with. He told me he stayed with Alex, Sophia and Kathryn the whole time they were in there and that this Duke guy seemed pretty keen on Sophia and kept trying to make her go off alone with him. At least Jaoel realised that this wasn't a good idea, and when it became clear what Duke's game plan was, he acted pretty fast and slipped her a mickey. She got all woozy, Duke had to back off, and they all went home."

"So it was Jaoel who drugged Sophia, not Eligor?" I wanted to find out as much as I could about Jaoel – and everything I heard about him served to confirm the warning bells that had been ringing since Manny first mentioned his name.

"Yes." Isra's voice was stronger now, clearly thinking that the spotlight was now no longer on him, but pointing straight at Jaoel. "I couldn't ask him anything else because we heard sounds from the bathroom; Alex and Sophia were coming back. Jaoel just winked at me and told me not to worry. Said he had it all under control. And God help me, I had no choice but to believe him." Isra looked up at us. "He had been Alex's Guardian for twenty years, Manny trusts him. He's one of us. It was unthinkable to doubt him."

Isra stood up. He walked across to the window and looked down into the gardens for a moment. When he turned back to us, he was calm and seemed fully in control. "Zach, I am telling you, his story doesn't ring true. The emanations in Eligor's place were incredibly strong and no angel could have missed them – even one who had been manifested for a hundred years – let alone ten. Thinking back, I could tell he was uncomfortable. He didn't meet my eyes at all when we were talking. I am pretty sure now that he was lying."

Sara and I exchanged glances. "Don't beat yourself up about it," I said (although I didn't really mean it. Isra's incompetence, speedy desire to pass the buck and overall lack of initiative were starting to really get on my wick). "There's many a better angel than you that's been taken in by the likes of Jaoel."

"We think he may have fallen," Sara explained. "And if he has, then he may well be the key to the whole situation, but we don't know for certain. We know nothing for certain – apart from the fact that Alex and Sophia are missing – and we need to find them."

Isra nodded. "And I want to help you.

"I need you to believe me when I tell you I wasn't hallucinating and that what I saw in that room was not just random torture; it was some sort of ritual.

A human sacrifice. That man was being drained of all his blood and we all know what that could mean. I'll tell you something else; I have been thinking about that Hell-Beast lapping blood from the bowl ever since they brought me in here; and I think it was Belphegor's familiar."

Sara and I gasped. This was not what we had expected to hear. Belphegor[23] certainly was one of the big boys. He's one of the seven Princes of Hell, also known as the 'Lord of Opening'. He can open the gates of Hell from any place in the mortal world; all that is needed is for the ritual to be performed by an adept.

I knew from bitter past experience that this requires little more than the living blood of an innocent to be drained into the profane chalice and the chanting of a few rather nasty incantations.

If his familiar was present, then Belphegor could not have been far behind.

If Isra was right, it could only mean that there had been an attempt to make an opening into the Inferno as early as Friday evening – and from then onwards, Sophia and Alex had just been living on borrowed time.

We carried on with our questioning and Isra told us that Saturday had started out pretty normally. Sophia slept off her hangover and was dead to the world until around 11.30 and in the meantime, Kathryn, Alex and Jaoel went out to Borough market, getting home just after noon laden down with poncey artisan hipster stuff which they all ate for lunch.

After the duck confit sandwiches and kale and beetroot smoothies had been consumed, Isra said there had been a bit of a barney between Kathryn and Alex. She was feeling a tad neglected and wanted some one on one attention, so they had agreed to head over to Alex's for the rest of the afternoon.

This left Jaoel and Sophia alone in the flat.

"Jaoel and Sophia... alone?" Sara asked. "But shouldn't Jaoel have stayed with Alex? He was his Guardian after all."

I agreed. Even if he didn't want to play gooseberry, Jaoel should have tailed them, staying out of sight and waiting nearby... it's not as if there aren't a million coffee shops in Shoreditch for him to hang out in. A Guardian should never desert their charge for any reason – no ifs, no buts. End of.

"What time was this?" I asked. "We know the nexus between Alex and

---

[23] "Belphegor was once one of the seraphim and is amongst the first and most mighty of the Fallen Angels, holding great seniority in the Hierarchy of Hell. He has the power to open the gates of Hell in any worldly location and he tempts men by encouraging sloth and laziness." *Register of the Fallen,* 1876

Jaoel was terminated just before two o'clock on Saturday - and after that there was no connection at all between them. This must have happened at around the time they left Kathryn's flat."

I turned to Isra, my anger building, but still just about managing to remain calm. "Didn't you sense the change? There was just you in there, with one human and another angel. You should have been constantly attuned to the celestial frequencies – that's one of a Guardian's most basic responsibilities. You must have felt the nexus breaking. You must have been aware of it..."

I stood up and began to pace the room, clenching my fists in an attempt to keep composed. It was no good, my control was slipping. "What the hell were you playing at, Isra?"

Isra began to bluster. "Well, as I said, the connection was weak anyway, Jaoel's emanations were not always clear – and I didn't... I couldn't." He looked up at us helplessly.

It was at this point that I lost it.

~ *Chapter Seven* ~

As you might have already gathered, I am an Angel of Justice[24]; that being the case, my job doesn't involve very much of the harp playing or fluffy cloud stuff. In fact, it is actually fair to say that in the past I have been no stranger to a reasonable amount of smiting. I will also admit that I have a bit of a short fuse – that's just the way I'm wired. I can't stand incompetence. And Isra had been a damn fool.

Not stopping to think, I grabbed Isra's shoulders and pulled him to his feet. The minute I touched him, I felt the celestial power flowing between us. What shocked and weakened Isra simply added to the strength of my righteous indignation. I felt myself growing larger, taller... my wings extending, and my radiance intensifying as the power of divine vengeance began to flow through me.

By now I was towering above the others. My wingspan filled the whole of the back wall, obscuring the doorway, my head nearly touching the ceiling. Looking down, I could see that Sara had moved close in towards Isra's limp and sorry body as if to try and shield him. She had one hand over her eyes; clearly those UDs were not designed to withstand the full force of a vengeance manifestation and my radiance was now filling the room with a light that was so refined and intense that I could have used it to break every pane of glass in the hospital if I had chosen to do so.

Isra was now a dead weight in my arms. Ignoring Sara, I gathered him up and walked towards the window. The gardens below lay still and silent, nothing moved and no birds sang. The fierce, flaming rage solidified into an intense,

---

[24]"The mission of the Angels of Justice, headed up by the Archangel Raquel, is to bring fairness, promote harmony and to wreak divine punishment on those who have transgressed the sacred law." *The Angels' Year Book*, 1984

white heat which proceeded to forge within me the steely certainty of judgement. As I had done so many times before, I began to consider both crime and punishment and to determine how divine justice would be delivered.

I thought about Isra, reflecting on what he had done, feeling once again how he'd angered me. He was weak, foolish and irresponsible. He had failed in his duty. He had failed as a Guardian. I judged him and I found him wanting. Raising my arms, I lifted the pathetic bundle and prepared to hurl him through the windows to the ground.

But as I did so, I felt rather than saw Sara move towards me. Looking down, I noticed that she had taken off her UDs and her eyes were closed. She approached me slowly, her arms outstretched to guide her as she walked. She had removed her gloves, and her pale, slender fingers slowly reached out and touched the feathers of my frenetically extended wings. She did not try to restrain me. She used no force and instead of the shock which I had expected, her touch was like a cool and gentle current, a clarifying flow of pure and brilliant reason which began to move within me, calming the white hot furnace of vengeance and retribution.

Neither of us spoke and in the silent pause, I looked down at Isra. *Yes*, I thought, *he's weak, but he's also scared and confused; a Guardian Angel suddenly facing the forces of the inner legions of the Fallen and not really sure he's up to it.*

We had all been there.

My mind reached out towards him, taking in the emanations his unconscious spirit was still emitting and I sensed his guilt, his sorrow and his repentance. And I recognised that it was my responsibility as an Angel of Justice to take this into consideration.

I had been on the verge of passing judgement, and I would have been wrong.

My eyes were drawn to some words written just above the doorway – a quotation from the divine doctor himself, Thomas Aquinas, after whom the ward itself had been named. They read: *'The work of divine justice always presupposes the work of mercy and is based on it'*[25]. I had learned that text by heart when I was at the Academy; it was one of the basic rules of field work. And I had been about to ignore it.

---

[25]"The *Summa Theologica* by St. Thomas Aquinas is the set book for all angels wishing to join the ranks of the Angels of Justice. Additional background reading should also include *A Theory of Justice* by John Rawls and *Horton Hears a Who* by Dr Seuss." *Prospectus of the Angelic Academy*, 1971

Without a word, I moved across the quiet room and laid Isra down on the bed. As my anger subsided, my radiance began to return to a manageable level and I resumed my normal size. I looked at Sara. She opened her eyes and held my gaze, waiting for me to break the silence.

"Thank you," I said finally. "I've become a bit too quick to anger. It's no excuse, but I am still wired about all the shit I saw in Syria. I took it out on Isra. He's an idiot, but he's not evil. He's just been a bloody fool."

She smiled. "You know you're quite terrifying when you do that 'righteous indignation' thing. I've never seen it before; there's not much call for it in Araboth."

I shrugged, "You think that was full-on righteous indignation? You should see Manny when he's riled – that was just a hissy fit in comparison. Even so, I should've had more control. We still haven't heard the full story and Isra's neither use nor ornament at the moment."

I looked down at him, lying crumpled and motionless upon the bed. Sara had turned away from me and was rummaging in her kitbag. She extracted her gloves; pulling them on, she reached over and stroked the hair back from Isra's forehead. She then touched his temples, gently. Her fingers didn't move and she said nothing. There was a look of intense concentration on her face. Gradually, I saw his muscles lose tension and relax. His body loosened and the rictus of fear upon his face began to ease and smooth away.

"What's with the hand thing?" I asked. I had first noticed it this morning, at the meeting with K and Manny, when her emanations had provided an almost physical reassurance to me. Since then, she had done the same thing to Isra, calming him down so he was able to tell us his story and she had over-powered me twice, once in the flat and just now, here on the ward.

I've already told you that angels usually avoid touching each other because of the unpleasant physical impact of getting too close to each other's emanations, but Sara seemed to have some special way of directing and controlling her celestial vibrations.

"Oh, it's nothing really," she said. "Anyone could do it if they wanted to. It is all about focus. I've been studying with Raphael[26] for about three hundred years now and I'm nearly ready to take my finals as a healer.

---

[26] "The Archangel Raphael is an angel from the first sphere, with celestial responsibility for the medicinal arts. Since his success at healing the injuries sustained by Jacob following his titanic eight hour wrestling match with the Angel Phanuel, he has specialised in sports therapy." *The Angels' Year Book*, 1993

"That's one of the reasons I wanted to come on this job with you. I think I'm fine on the theory and I've had some really good feedback from the volunteering I do at the Holistic Therapy centre in the Elysian Fields, but I really needed some time out in the field under my belt. It's a requirement and I can't qualify without it."

She looked up at me and grinned. "Being a desk bunny is not really my thing you know."

God, she made me feel like a fool. If I knew how to pronounce it, I would say that chagrined was not the word.

"I've been a bit of an arse-hole really, haven't I?" I said, expecting her to deny it.

"Yep," she said, continuing to focus her gaze upon Isra, whose eyelids had given the slightest flutter. He was beginning to stir. Hopefully he would wake up shortly and we could find out exactly what happened on Saturday night.

"I think the best thing now is for you to head off and get those supplies you wanted. I'll stay here and sort out Isra. I think he will feel a bit safer if it's just me in the room when he comes round."

She looked at her watch. "I don't think it'll take long," she continued, "so why don't we meet back in reception in thirty minutes?"

I was a bit taken aback by this. When did Sara get to be in charge? But I didn't want another row and to be honest, I was still feeling a bit sheepish about the whole righteous hissy-fit thing.

"Okay," I said, "I'll head to the pharmacy. I'm just going to grab some germanium; it works really well for celestial radiance sickness. Is there anything else you want me to pick up?"

She thought for a moment. "If they have some dried asphodel, it may be an idea to bring that along. We don't know what sort of state they'll be in, and that works wonders if we need to tranquilise them."

I nodded. Looking down at the bed, I saw Isra's eyelids flutter again and decided it might be best if I wasn't the first thing he saw when he woke up.

"See you downstairs in thirty."

I walked out of the room, just in time to hear Isra asking feebly (and rather predictably) "Where am I?"

~ *Chapter Eight* ~

It wasn't hard to find the pharmacy and once I showed the dispenser my ID, I got what we needed without any trouble. As he poured the germanium into two glass phials, one with a handy eye-dropper in the lid, and packed the dried asphodel neatly in a small brown parcel, the dispenser asked where I was heading.

I told him, expecting at the very least a sharp intake of breath and an admiring glance, but instead he nodded matter-of-factly, saying, "In that case, here's a couple of other bits and pieces you might find useful." He went back into the dispensary, returning with a brown bag containing what looked like three pigs ears. He sealed the bag and passed it to me, along with a small pouch containing a small phial of eucalyptus oil, a couple of dirty old coins and a leaflet advising on the health risks of underworld travel, which mainly comprised of advising travellers not to eat anything and to keep one's eyes fixed firmly on the road ahead when leaving.

Deciding it would be best just to humour him, I said thank you and headed back towards reception, determined to dump the offal and the other rubbish as soon as I was out of sight.

All seemed fine as I walked back into reception; my dear old battered corpus was just where I left it, sitting rather forlornly in the waiting area with my kitbag balanced on its knees. No-one appeared to have touched it and I smiled blithely at the receptionist, who gave me a rather grumpy look, pointing meaningfully at her watch. I looked around for a bin, but no joy, so I had no choice but to stow everything away in the side pocket of the kitbag.

I was just refastening the straps when Sara joined me.

"How did it go? Is Isra okay –did he fill you in on the rest of the story?"

She nodded.

"Yes, he's fine, feeling a bit sorry for himself – and you did a fair amount of damage to his primaries when you were heaving him about up there, but apart from that, he's ok."

She shot a quick glance at the receptionist and nodded meaningfully towards the farthest wall. She had something to say that she didn't want anyone to overhear, so we moved quickly out of earshot.

"Isra told me that the angel claiming to be Ely turned up at Kathryn's at around 17.30 last night, he was fully materialised and not alated, but the ID seemed kosher, so Isra gave him permission to enter.[27]"

"Did he know the guy?" I asked.

"He says not – when I pushed him a bit harder, he said it could have been the blond man from the party, but he hadn't seen his face, and he definitely didn't make the connection last night. By this time, Alex and Kathryn and come back and were having a drink in the kitchen with Sophia. Isra got the guy claiming to be Ely into the back room and summoned Jaoel, who for some reason had been communing with nature on the balcony. Isra says that as the other two had material forms, it seemed like good manners to do the same, so he assumed his corporeal form before doing the handover.

"Didn't Jaoel say anything?" I said. "He had spent time with Eligor on the Friday night; surely he would have recognised him?"

"According to Isra, Jaoel acted as if he had never seen the guy before. If you remember, he left Sicily ten years ago, before the nexus between Sophia and the real Ely developed – they had clearly communicated for years over the ether, but they had never actually met. Isra didn't sense trouble, but he was surprised at how quickly both Jaoel and the fake Ely wanted him out of the way. They performed the Abracadabra, and five minutes later, Isra was out of there and heading for Charlie's Bar."

The Abracadabra charm is one of the oldest of the protection talismans. In the dim and distant, the Guardian would write a description of the person to be protected on one side of a piece of parchment, inscribe the incantation on the other and once the talisman had been activated it would provide protection for around twenty-four hours. Talismans made of precious metal last longer, but

---

[27] "Permissions, Passes and Exeats: once a property is under guardianship, no celestial or spiritual being may enter until direct permission has been given by the aforesaid Guardian. Equally, no Guardian may leave a building which is within the remit of their protection, unguarded, requiring an official exeat to demonstrate the transfer of responsibility." *The Guardian Angel's Handbook*, 1895

are more difficult to activate quickly and nowadays we tend to use a photo rather than a written description.

"Who provided the picture?" I asked.

"Isra says that he offered to print one, but that the fake Ely already had one in his wallet, so they used that."

"Did he actually see the picture? Do we know if it was really an image of Sophia?"

Sara stared at me, a worried look beginning to appear on her face. "I don't know… I didn't ask… I just assumed that it must have been Sophia." She was blustering, but she got over it and admitted, "I didn't think to ask. He said that the angel he thought was Ely just gave the picture to Jaoel, who wrote out the incantation, they did the charm together and Ely replaced the talisman in his wallet."

I was pacing now. "But that must be it. I couldn't understand how Sophia could have been harmed if the Abracadabra was functioning. It was the bit of the story that just didn't make sense."

I hit the wall with my fist, causing the receptionist to look up from her paperwork and give me another angry look. "This proves that Jaoel is in cahoots with the Fallen. I can't believe that he wouldn't have turned over the photo to take a look – anyone would. And if he did and saw that it wasn't Sophia and just carried on with the charm without saying a word, there can be no other explanation."

Sara nodded. "Yep, things don't look good on the Jaoel front. It seems that K's suspicions are absolutely on the button as far as that is concerned, but like he said, that's not for us to worry about." She could see that I was about to object to this, so she quickly changed the subject: "Did you get the stuff from the pharmacy?"

I told her I had and she looked at the clock on the wall. It was nearly one o'clock. "We should get a move on."

"Hang on, what about Kathryn?" I said. "No-one has said a word about her. She was there last night when Eligor turned up. She may still be there. She might even be able to shed more light on what actually happened. I think we should go check it out."

"No," said Sara, "absolutely not. K didn't mention her to me, and I don't think Manny knew about her either. I think she is just a civilian, a bit of a hanger-on. It will just waste even more time going to see her. We've found out what we needed to know. We need to get into the Inferno."

~ 60 ~

As she was talking, she began walking swiftly towards the exit. "You had better get back into your corpus. I'll see you at the car."

I wasn't happy, but I wasn't sure what to do about it, so decided just to play ball.

I walked over to the seating area and placed my hands on the shoulders of my inanimate form. I focused on re-entering my body; sending waves of pure energy into every artery, vein and capillary, feeling the blood begin to flow, the heart begin to beat. I took a single, deep breath, and exhaled, opening my eyes, and closing them immediately – I had forgotten about the impact of the celestial radiance on human pupils.

Grabbing my kitbag, I stumbled rather clumsily in the direction of the front door, where I bumped into Sara. She had taken off her UDs, but she seemed to have had nowhere to put them and she was looking more than a little put out. She turned back towards the reception.

"Sorry, Zach, I've left my bag up on Aquinas ward. You stay here, and I'll see you in five minutes."

Without waiting for me to say anything, she was gone. *Ha!* I thought. *So much for Miss Perfect…*

This was my chance. I needed to find out exactly what had happened last night; there was still a lot that didn't make sense, and there was a real possibility that Kathryn could fill in the final pieces of the jigsaw. If Sara wasn't interested, that was her lookout, but I was heading back to the flat in Cranwood Street to see if Alex's girlfriend could give me the answers that I was looking for.

~ *Chapter Nine* ~

She couldn't.

In fact, Kathryn was never going to be answering anyone's questions ever again.

I took a taxi from the Chelsea embankment and was outside the flat in Cranwood Street within twenty minutes; the cabbie had played a blinder and I gave him an extra twenty for his trouble. I told him I might need his services again in another forty minutes or so and indicated that I would make it worth his while if he could hang around, so he agreed to park up and grab a sandwich whilst I went inside.

The front door to the buildings was locked, but I struck pay dirt quite quickly and was buzzed in by an elderly Irish chap who responded to my third attempt at random button pushing and opened the door when I told him I had a delivery for flat seven.

Inside the building's dingy foyer, I took my bearings and allowed myself a moment of contemplation, checking for spiritual energies, both angelic and demonic. There were some strong residual traces; I could clearly sense the presence of supernatural activity and these weren't just little lingering smidgeons - the latent demonic energy still present in this building was heading towards the top end of the scale. By now, I was fairly sure that something pretty big (and probably pretty unpleasant) had occurred here within the last twenty-four hours.

The building seemed unnaturally quiet. The neon strip lighting above the resident's pigeon holes was flickering feebly, and the stairwell was dark. I waited a moment, thinking my Irish friend might decide to come onto the landing to check on me, but nothing stirred and all the doors remained shut. As I climbed the stairs to the second floor, the lingering emanations became stronger, but I was pretty sure that I was the only non-human presence in the building.

The entrance to Kathryn's flat was on the third floor, right at the end of the dark landing. Wishing to play safe, I didn't press the light switch and walked on cautiously towards the door, which was pulled almost shut, but swung open noiselessly to my touch. I decided not to call out – I had no idea what I might find there. I was reasonably confident that Eligor would not be inside, I was very aware that most of the big boys had a seemingly inexhaustible supply of unpleasantly eager human initiates to manage the more mundane side of the business and it would be best to proceed with caution.

The hallway was dark, but I could see a light under the door at the end of the corridor, so I walked slowly towards it, checking out the rooms on either side of the hall as I went. The kitchen door has half-closed and in the gloom seemed to be completely empty; moving further along the hallway, the bathroom and bedroom doors were shut. There was a faint and irregular dripping noise coming from the bathroom and I could hear the muffled ticking of a clock through one of the bedroom doors. Apart from that, the flat was silent.

I had reached the end of the corridor. I turned the handle and very slowly opened the door. The room was large and full of light; my eyes had become so accustomed to the gloom that I blinked and took a while to focus. It was a big room, taking up the whole width of the flat and had long windows opening on to a balcony which even in November was alive with greenery. The light I had seen under the door frame was natural, pouring in from the un-curtained windows and it would once have been a pleasant, even beautiful place to unwind in. It wasn't anymore.

The long, pale blue curtains that had hung at the windows had been pulled down, slashed into shreds and now lay in a pathetic muddle in front of the up-turned sofa. Every picture had been pulled from the wall and shards of glass mingled with broken picture frames and shattered ornaments upon the wooden flooring. To the left of the room, an old refectory trestle table and trendily mis-matched chairs had been forced back against the wall; two of the chairs remained standing, the rest were in pieces, and the table had been broken in two. A bottle of wine had been knocked to the floor, its contents mingling with the soil spilling out from a large stone plant pot, which had been upended on the rug in front of the fireplace. The scent of the wine, however, did little to overpower the smell which hit my nostrils as I looked around the room. Under the window was a huge pile of evil-smelling shit and weaving to and fro across the floor was a pattern of muddy, bloody footprints which looked like they belonged to a gigantic animal.

The room was deserted and there was no sign of Kathryn. Scanning the room quickly, I spotted a mobile phone plugged into a charger on the right hand wall. I picked it up, and noted three missed calls from Saturday night, all from a caller who had withheld their number. I righted the sofa and found a handbag and a rucksack on the floor beneath it. Taking a quick look inside I found Kathryn's wallet and keys inside the handbag. The rucksack seemed empty, but when I shook it, a small photograph fluttered to the floor. It was a copy of the picture of Sophia that Sara had shown me earlier that morning – and there was no writing on the reverse - it couldn't have been the photo used last night as part of the Abracadabra ritual.

Already worried, I now I began to fear the worst – who leaves home without their phone, keys and money? If Kathryn had gone, then I thought it likely she had been made to leave against her will... and if she hadn't then where was she and what had happened to her?

Looking across the room, I noticed that the giant footprints came into the room from the hallway. It has been too dark for me to spot them before, but I could now see that they seemed to have come from the bathroom. I moved quickly down the hall, and knocked urgently on the bathroom door.

Strange how these vestiges of human etiquette take root within our celestial consciousness – I knew that chances were Kathryn would not be in there – or if she was, she would probably not be in a fit state to respond, but my human form had become so hard-wired to convention, that I couldn't just open a bathroom door without knocking first.

No answer. I turned the door handle, calling out Kathryn's name as I did so. The sudden noise unnerved me, I had not realised just how overpowering the almost complete silence had become. There was no reply, just that irregular dripping sound from the other side of the bathroom door. As the door opened, the light came on automatically. I had found Kathryn – and it wasn't a pretty sight.

She was naked and had been hung upside down in the bath tub; her feet were tied together, the metal chains which bound her, hooked around the shower stall. I could not see the expression on her face as her hair fell, tangled and bloody, across her face and shoulders, which were resting at an unnatural angle, with one of her arms splayed out along the bloodied porcelain surface, the other bent and ungainly against the back of her head.

She had been slit open cleanly down one side. The wound was narrow and had clearly been inflicted with an extremely sharp knife and by a person who knew exactly what they were doing. This was no random or frenzied hack-job – this was a professional hit. I could tell at once that she was completely exsanguinated, that the blood had been drained slowly from her body, and that this was likely to have been the gradual and painful cause of death.

I reached across and touched the side of her face, gently cupping her cheek in my hand. Her skin was still warm, her flesh pliable. She couldn't have been dead that long. By the side of her head, I saw a clear white circle, where the bath's surface had not been stained with her dripping life-blood. Remembering Isra's description of the ritual he had witnessed at Eligor's flat on Friday night, I reckoned that this was where they had placed the bowl they used to catch her blood as it fell, before feeding it to the vile Hell-Beast and performing the ritual which would open a door into the Inferno. I looked around me and sure enough, there on the bathroom floor on the other side of the sink pedestal, was a brownish-red circular stain, looking about the same size as the circle in the bath. Next to the circle were four footprints, and peering closely, I saw a number of coarse grey animal hairs caught in a knot on the skirting board.

As I continued to examine the skirting and the area around the wash basin, a single drop of water fell from the shower head into the bath. In the absolute silence, it seemed unnaturally loud and startled me. I turned round to look into the bath tub, and as I did so, I heard something move out in the corridor. Before I could do anything, the door was pushed violently open and something hard and heavy hit me. I crumpled onto the bathmat and knew no more.

~ *Chapter Ten* ~

There was a disgusting smell of burnt feathers and a bright light, and someone was slapping my face none too gently.

"Wake up you idiot." It was Sara, dressed in her combat gear but fully alated. She seemed slightly taller than before and she was simultaneously shining a pinpoint torch into my eyes and waving something under my nose; a small bunch of feathers, gently smouldering and giving off a highly potent and unpleasant aroma. She put down the torch and pulled back her arm as if she was preparing to slap me again. I grabbed her wrist just in time to prevent another ringing and quite unwarranted blow to my right cheek.

I looked at the feathers – they were copper coloured and fine barbed, with slightly reddish quills. "You used some of your own? I'm honoured."

Sara said nothing and as I let go of her arm, she extended her hand to help me up.

I got to my feet somewhat unsteadily and looked into the bathroom mirror. Apart from looking slightly dazed, I seemed little the worse for wear but I could sense the mother of all bruises beginning to make its presence felt under a bump on the back of my head that was at least the size of a golf ball.

"Needs must," she replied. "But don't get any ideas about it – there weren't any smelling salts to hand and you were completely out for the count. Don't think this means anything other than the triumph of necessity over convention."

"If you say so." I turned back to the mirror. It is very rare for an angel to pluck feathers from their wings. I was aware of a couple of occasions where one angel had given another a magnificent quill as a sign of respect or perfect friendship. In fact, some of these have found their way into the hands of humans and have been used to compose some of the most sublime oratorios[28]. I had also heard human legends about times where angels had used their feathers to tip the arrows of particularly favoured warriors, but such cases were few and far between – and I was not even sure there was any truth in the tales.

Put it this way – I had never given any of my plumage away – and no-one before has ever come close to plucking their wings for me.

"How come you're here?" I asked. "And I assume you have seen this?" I gestured towards the bath and what remained of Kathryn. "And what the hell happened? Last thing I remember, someone came charging in here and hit me, I didn't see them, but I have a pretty good idea who it was. What's going on?"

Sara did not look happy. Her wings were folded back, but I could see from the little shudders running through them that she was having difficulty keeping her mood under control.

"What's going on is that I have to keep getting you out of bloody stupid situations that wouldn't have happened if you had behaved like a professional. And we are still no closer to actually finding Alex and Sophia. When I got back to reception and found you had gone, it didn't need a genius to work out what you were up to, so I dematerialised and made my way over here. When I arrived, I materialised round the back and found a taxi waiting nice as pie outside the front steps. I described you to the cabbie and he confirmed that he'd dropped you off and you'd asked him to wait for you. I told him that there had been a change of plan and that you'd be heading back with me. He looked a bit disgruntled, but drove off after I insisted that you were not going to need his services any more today.

"I pressed a few bells and this grumpy old Irish guy let me in. I asked if anyone else had been by; he said someone had called with a package for flat seven, but he hadn't heard anyone since then. I checked out the building and could sense your presence. I also picked up on a lot of unsavoury emanations – spiritually speaking, this place has got a really bad smell."

"You're not wrong there." Now I was beginning to feel a bit more compos mentis I could see how pissed off she was. "But what I don't know is if it's the result of recent activity, or if dodgy stuff has been going on here for a while.

---

[28] "The human composers Bach, Haydn and Handel were all the possessors of Angelic quills, given to them by the Archangel Sandalphon. Sandalphon is one of only two angels to begin his existence as a mortal (he was previously known as the Prophet Elijah) and he keeps a close eye on humanity; taking particular responsibility for musical endeavour. He has worked closely with a number of musicians and his recent successes include the last three winners of the Eurovision Song Contest and Bjork." *The Angels' Year Book,* 2006

Isra didn't mention any underlying issues - but then he's got about as much sensitivity as a door knob."

I continued to rub the back of my head; Sara wordlessly rummaged around in her kitbag and threw me a tube of something.

"Arnica. Rub it in to the bruising. It'll help reduce the swelling."

She wasn't going to rise to the jibe about Isra, so I did what she suggested whilst she just carried on telling me what had happened whilst I was out for the count.

"When I got to the third floor, I saw light coming from the door at the end of the corridor and I heard noises. I ran inside, fired one round of tranq dust which should have knocked out any human in the vicinity and found you crashed out on the bathroom floor with Kathryn dead in the bath tub. There was no-one else here, but the kitchen windows were wide open and I reckon that whoever it was must have used the fire escape to get away before the tranq could get him."

"Why do you think that?" I asked. "They might have been gone ages before you arrived."

"No," Sara said, "I heard a noise like a window being flung open when I was out on the landing – and I also don't think you would be standing here all fine and dandy if whoever hit you had had time to finish the job. Come with me – I need to show you what I found in the kitchen."

I followed her out of the bathroom; she was standing by the kitchen window, holding a large leather-bound book.

"This was on the kitchen table. It was held open at page 285."

I reached over to take the book from her. As my fingers closed on it I felt a deep revulsion. My skin tingled unpleasantly as I touched the binding. I looked more closely.

"This binding is not normal leather. That's human skin," I said, swiftly putting it down and looking at it in distaste. "What is this thing?"

"It's called *The Necronomicon*," replied Sara, handing me some sterile hand cleanser from her kitbag. "Originally known as the *Al Azif*,[29] it is a human transcription of arcane demonic lore."

---

[29] "The Al Azif is a literal rendition of the howling of demons, their incantations, blasphemies, spells and rituals, first transcribed in 783 BC by the followers of Yog-Sothoth (the eater of souls) and the dread Cthulhu. It was translated into Greek in 950 BC and went to number one on the Catholic Church's list of banned books in 1232. Despite this, the Elizabethan magician John Dee obtained a copy and translated it into English in 1585, giving it the title it is more commonly known by – The Necronomicon." *Notes from the Angels' Year Book*, 1907

"Oh right," I said, giving my hands a more thorough cleanse than I'd bothered with back at St. Basil's. "I know all about the *Necronomicon* – just never actually come across one in the flesh so to speak…

"Now you don't find things like this hanging around your standard hipster apartment. In fact, no-one since Aleister Crowley has ever even claimed to have laid eyes on one. If we needed any further proof of demonic activity beyond the seismic destruction, the Hell-Beast turd and the cadaver, this is it. So go on, enlighten me… just what is on page 285? What do you reckon old matey-boy – who looks increasingly like being our pal Jaoel – was up to?"

Sara looked at me quizzically, and I realised she hadn't ventured into the front room yet.

"Page 285 describes the detailed ritual for casting a soul permanently into Limbo. If they had succeeded, I would have found two dead bodies when I got here, Kathryn's and yours. Once your soul had been ripped from your corpus, you could never come back to it – even if you managed to get out of Limbo."

She was right. Although killing an angel is well-nigh impossible, there are certain places it is hard for even a celestial being to escape from and Limbo is one of them. The gates won't open for the inhabitants until the last trump is sounded – and I don't think that Isra is going to be playing that funky little number any time soon.

I was silent for a moment as the full magnitude of what might have happened swept over me.

"We need to get rid of this," I said, gesturing towards the *Necronomicon*, "and we also need someone to come and do some serious troubleshooting here. It's not just a dead human; the front room looks like a bomb went off, and I would be really surprised if everything went down in total silence last night."

I realised that I hadn't used Kathryn's name; just called her a 'dead human'. By doing so, I had actually de-humanised her, made her into just another corpse, an anonymous victim, like so many I had seen in Syria. That was the only way to cope with stuff like this.

As I talked, Sara and I walked through into the front room. She was definitely taller, probably about 5'10 now and her hair was slightly darker. I guessed that she had taken the opportunity of her dematerialisation to slightly amend her physical body; something we often do when we're getting used to a new physical form.

As Sara was taking in the destruction, I continued theorising. "I think that once Isra was out of the way, Eligor summoned Belphegor and they used

Kathryn to perform the ritual and open the gateway. Eligor then took Sophia and Alex through into the Inferno, and he probably needed Belphegor to close the gateway on the other side.

"That would leave Jaoel here with the Hell-Beast; they have a taste for human flesh and I'm thinking that Eligor and his cronies need to keep Alex and Sophia in one piece, for the time being at least. If they simply wanted to kill them, they could have done it days ago.

"My guess is that they probably decided to leave old Fido here rather than risk a little accident in the Inferno. I reckon Jaoel got a bit jumpy and shut the disgusting monstrosity up in the front room, where it proceeded to run amok until one of Eligor's minions turned up to send the little darling home to daddy. I bet he was probably just about to go his merry way when I arrived."

Sara nodded, and as the stench in the room was becoming unbearable, we both decided to move elsewhere. The choices were limited, so we headed back towards the kitchen.

"He must have come up behind me whilst I was examining the body, coshed me and was about to give me a one-way ticket to Limbo-land when you put a spanner in the works – for which I am eternally grateful by the way. He must have decided that dealing with two celestial beings was more than he could manage and legged it, leaving his nasty little book behind."

"That seems plausible," said Sara, "and you're very welcome".

She looked straight at me. Her bun was tighter than tight, but there seemed to be the beginnings of a smile playing around the left corner of her upper lip. She gave a slight wiggle of her shoulders and her wings vanished, putting us back on equal footing.

Rubbing her left shoulder, she continued, "I am getting a little fed up of saving your sorry ass from certain doom, but I also have to admit that your hunch was right, we did need to come here."

She gestured at the book and looked out towards the hallway, clearly thinking of poor Kathryn and the horrific ritual which had taken place just few short hours ago.

"I can't think of a better explanation for what must have gone on here. Not sure about one thing though... you seem pretty certain that the guy who hit you was Jaoel. I'm not so certain – I only sensed one other non-human presence in the building when I arrived."

I opened my mouth to object, but she took no notice.

"Whoever, whatever, it doesn't really matter. K's guys, the Potestas, will be dealing with that side of things, and we don't know anything for definite. And now is not the time for an argument about hypotheticals. You're spot on about needing some troubleshooting though. I assume this is something the Agency can handle?"

"Yes, but…"

"But nothing. First thing is to call Manny to sort out the body, the book and the mess – and then we need to get on with the job we have been given." She checked her watch. "Do you realise what time it is?"

It was nearly two o'clock; roughly five hours since we had left the Agency. She was right, however much I hated to admit it and however much I disagreed with her about Jaoel. I took my phone from my kitbag and gave Manny a call. Reluctantly, I had to go back into the front room to get a signal; I gestured to Sara to stay where she was – there was no need for both of us to suffer.

To say he was unhappy would have been something of an understatement. Not only were we no further forward with rescuing Alex and Sophia, we had the suspicious death of a human to account for – and there was no way that Kathryn's poor exsanguinated body could be passed off as accident, suicide – or even death by misadventure.

We had built good links with the Home Office over the years, in fact we've had someone on the inside since the days of Francis Bacon; it never hurts to have the Attorney General on your side. Although we are not quite that well connected these days, Manny would be able to sort this out without too much trouble. Not that that stopped him from giving me one hell of a bollocking and threatening to pull me off the case and send me straight back to Syria.

"Now hang on, Manny, you yourself said I was the best guy for the job. And we know a lot more now we've spoken to Isra and actually seen the scene of the crime." I was grasping at straws here – and Manny knew it. But what he said about Syria made me think of something that might help.

"Listen, Manny, do me a favour, in fact do us all a favour. Speak to the guys out there and see if we can get hold of the Katibeen. Kathryn would have had a Recording Angel just like every other human, and they would know exactly what happened in her dying moments. They would also know if she intended any harm to either Alex or Sophia, and it might help fill in a few of the gaps. Sara and I can't hang around to hear what they say, but we'll follow the protocols once we're inside and you can give us an update when we check-in."

Without waiting for an answer, I pressed the button to end the call and dumped the phone back in my kitbag.

~ 71 ~

As I did so, I looked out of the window. An unmarked car had just pulled up outside the building and two impeccably dressed MI6 types were getting out.

If I was not mistaken, our troubleshooters had arrived. Sara had seen it too and we both thought that it wouldn't be a good idea to be found hanging around the scene when they got here.

Not that we were worried about the forensics; Manny would have sorted all that, but we just didn't have time for pleasantries and conversation. Chronoprohibery seemed the obvious solution; I did the honours once more and froze time for exactly two hundred seconds. Enough for us to get out of the building and to casually observe our two men in black pressing entry buttons at random until the by now even more irritated Irish chap agreed to let them in.

Isra's story had confirmed much of what we had already guessed; it had given us a lead on Eligor and the ritual he had used to open the gateway. I was also convinced that my intuition to come to the flat had been the right one. We now knew both how and where the gateway had been opened. Finding Kathryn's tortured and discarded body had been a deeply unsettling experience even by my jaded standards and I vowed on my oath as a Justice Angel that I would mete out some pretty solid retribution for her suffering before this case was ended.

But there were still a number of questions completely unanswered.

If the Abracadabra had been cast, how could Sophia have been taken into the Inferno on Saturday night when she should have been protected for at least twenty-four hours? How much had Kathryn known about Alex and Sophia? Was she just an innocent, or had she played a more sinister role in luring Sophia to Cranwood Street?

And the biggie – what was going on with Jaoel? If he hadn't joined the Fallen, how come he had just accepted Eligor when he turned up pretending to be Ely? Isra was sure Jaoel would have recognised him from Friday night, so what was he doing allowing Sophia to be left guardianless and alone in a hostile city? And if he had defected and it was Jaoel who attacked me whilst I was examining Kathryn's body, why had neither Sara nor I sensed any other non-humans in the building?

But we had no time to go looking for any more answers. Alex and Sophia had now been Eligor's captives since yesterday evening, and we had little doubt where he had taken them.

Sara and I were now finally about to set out on the highway to Hell.

~ 72 ~

~ *Chapter Eleven* ~

Unfortunately, the Satnav didn't recognise 'Highway to Hell' as a bona fide location and so Sara and I were now back in Chelsea, sitting in the front seat of K's chariot, poring over a map of the underworld and arguing the toss about the best route to take.

As there was no angelic equivalent of Belphegor's ritual for opening a gateway into the Inferno, we needed to decide which entrance would be our best bet. It may come as a surprise to you, but there are at least twelve ways into the realms of the dead and I was quite keen to take the quickest and most well sign-posted – via the grotto of Cumae at Lake Avernus, just west of Naples. Sara, on the other hand, favoured what seemed to me to be a more circuitous route via the Elysian Fields and the boundary lands just beyond them.

The reason I wanted to go in via the Avernus gateway was quite straightforward. We had no idea how far Eligor, Alex and Sophia would have travelled by now, or in what direction. The quickest way into the nine circles of the Inferno lay just beyond the main gates and was not particularly strongly guarded. If we wanted to find them fast, it seemed to me that we should get into the Inferno as quickly as possible and search through each circle in turn, although I already had a hunch as to where Eligor was headed. If his main aim was to shatter the balance of their minds and drive them into insanity, then I doubted he would be spending too much time in the regions devoted to lust and gluttony. No, for my money, he would have side-tracked the sins of the flesh and would be heading straight into deeper and darker regions: greed, anger, treachery and violence.

I also knew that there were beings in Hell's hinterlands that, although not exactly kosher, were not out-and-out villains, and if we went in through the

~ 73 ~

main portals, we stood a reasonable chance of meeting up with someone who might have seen Alex and Sophia and who, with a little bit of persuasion, might be prepared to help us out.

Sara was a bit dubious about this idea until I reminded her about Aeneas and his visit to the underworld. He'd wanted a quick word with his dear old dad, who had unfortunately snuffed it some time ago, and he had gone into the underworld to find him.

"You have to remember," I said, "not everything in the underworld is necessarily evil; some people live there because they like that frisson, that sense of living on the edge. Some of the real estate around the Hell-mouth is actually quite sought after." I knew what I was talking about. I had once taken a vacation on the shores of Lake Avernus and had met up with a couple of nymphs who lived in a beautiful art deco villa overlooking the Styx. I won't go into details, but suffice it to say that those girls REALLY knew how to party.

Sara still did not look convinced. I tried again.

"There are countless places where the boundaries between the realms of the Fallen and our celestial territories are very narrow indeed. In fact, the gateway through the Elysian Fields is a case in point."

I took the map from the dashboard to show her what I was talking about.

"Look - you walk too far along the eastern boundary and you run slap-bang into the perimeter fence surrounding the Tartarus prison - the deepest dungeon of Hell and home to the absolute class A, unrepentant degenerate villains – the sort you would never want to mess with. Whereas going in by the main gate, we steer clear of Tartarus and go straight into the Inferno."

Sara considered this. "I see your point, but I think you've forgotten one thing. By now, I bet they know we're on to them. Whoever it was we disturbed in Kathryn's flat will have reported back; they'll know that we've found the body and have figured out about the ritual and I guess they know that we will be planning to come after them into the Inferno. I would bet anything that they will be expecting us to go in via the Avernus entrance because it's the quickest route and if we try, by now it will be anything but plain sailing. At the very least, they would spot us the minute we went in and any chance of surprise will have vanished. At worst, they will have put defences in place and we'll be too small a team to get through."

I considered what she said. She had a point; our main chance of success lay in the fact that there were only two of us. We could move quickly, without drawing too much attention to ourselves. But if we were facing serious opposition, we would need reinforcements. And that would take time – time that we didn't have if we were to rescue Alex and Sophia before it was too late.

"But if we go in the back way," she continued, "via the Elysian Fields, we are entering the underworld from celestial territory and the chances are that we are less likely to get challenged or to appear on their radar." Now it was Sara's turn to grab the map, and she swiftly pointed out the route she had in mind. "We can skirt round to the west, alongside the River Lethe until we get to the Lake of Fire and then head through Malebolge, straight into the eighth circle."

"The eighth circle?" I questioned, wondering if Sara was thinking along the same lines as I was.

"Yes, the eighth. I reckon Eligor will be making straight to the centre. They'll probably skirt by Belphegor's place for a pit-stop." She pointed to the map as she spoke; Belphegor's domains were in the fourth circle, their boundaries guarded by Hell-Beasts, on the permanently darkened shores of the Stygian Lake. Not exactly the kind of place you would choose for a mini-break.

I nodded. "Yes, I think you're right. They'll probably cross the river here," I pointed, "and then head in via the Medusa Gate, down on to the Burning Sands and the ditches of Malebolge. Eligor isn't going to bother with the support acts, particularly not now, if he suspects we are on to him. He'll be going for maximum impact. And I'm not quite sure how long the human brain will be able to endure it."

I took the map back from Sara and folded it, placing it in the side pocket of my kitbag. "Come on," I said, "fire up the chariot. We need to get moving."

"The Elysian Fields?" She looked at me questioningly.

"The Elysian Fields."

With a small but remarkably satisfied smile, Sara closed her eyes, preparing to summon the darkness of the twelfth hour of the night to this secluded and still leafy corner of Chelsea. Even though the rear entrance to the Physic Garden is a fairly out of the way place, as we ascended we would be in full view of anyone sauntering along the Chelsea Embankment or out on a boat on the Thames so it seemed like a good idea to stay within the clouds on the way up.

In less than five seconds, the skies had darkened. Grey and black mists swirled around the car, becoming denser and darker and finally blotting out the trees and the Physic Garden walls completely. Visibility was down to zero as Sara turned on the engine, put the car in gear and accelerated in a straight, vertical climb. We were on our way.

Less than a minute later, the skies cleared as we crossed the border into the celestial domains. Sara fumbled in the glove box and pulled out a pair of UDs, which she tossed in my lap.

"You'd better put these on," she said. "Grab mine from my bag will you?" I leant over to the back seat and pulled her kitbag onto my knees. I began to undo the strap when Sara reached across and rapped my knuckles.

"They're in the side pocket, the left one... no need to open the bag," said Sara a tad sharply. I found the glasses and handed them over to her without saying anything. I must admit to being a little hurt – we had been through a lot over the last few hours, and I was a bit surprised at her reaction.

"Sorry, I just hate people going through my stuff." Sara put on her own UDs and smiled brightly across at me.

I didn't reply and she didn't seem to notice, probably because we had just arrived at our celestial destination. We had come to a halt outside golden gates, flanked with tall and imposing marble columns inlaid with pearl. Sara put the Merc into neutral and we waited for the car to be scanned. I felt a faint judder as the interrogation beam checked my spiritual purity and next to me, I felt Sara quiver and reach for my hand as the beam passed through her. I felt a slight shock at her touch, but it was over in a second, the red light above the marble gatepost turned green and the golden gates began to open.

This was a new thing. Last time I made a home visit, you still had to go through the whole question and answer rigmarole with Rocky the security guy, but K's Efficiency and Reform group had recently introduced digital services at all celestial border points and Rocky[30] had been pensioned off.

He had been a bit of a grumpy old git, but I sort of missed the personal touch now it had gone. Still, there was no doubt the new system was quicker. Sometimes it would take an absolute age for him to find your details in the filing system and once he mixed me up with the Angel Zazriel, who is the strongest of the seraphim and we wasted about ten minutes when he challenged me to an arm-wrestle and wouldn't let me through until I had won best out of three.

Within seconds, the gates had opened. Sara gently but firmly removed her hand from mine; without realising it, I had curled my fingers tightly through hers, and she had to give a little tug to pull herself free. She put the car in gear

---

[30] "Rocky, otherwise known as the sainted Simon Peter, first vicar of Rome, delivered many years of diligent and devoted service as gatekeeper to the Heavenly Host and will always be remembered for his rigorous attention to duty. On his retirement, he was presented with a gold watch by the Permanent Secretary himself and now spends his time fishing and messing about in boats." *Celestial Times*, April 2001

and we drove through the pearly gates, making our way along the pure white highway, lined on either side with flowering cherry trees, whose blossom, it being Heaven and perfect and all, remained permanently on the trees all year round.

Although the windows of the car were closed, I could just about hear the sweet harmonies of the angelic choirs, whose role it is to perpetually sing praises to laud and magnify the holy name. It gets in your face a bit for the first hour or so, but you sort of forget about it after a while – like living under a flight path or slap-bang up against the rail tracks at Dalston Junction.

"You okay?"

Sara gave me a quick glance and I nodded in return. I hadn't been back in some time and, as always, it was a bit of a culture shock. I didn't really want to talk about it, so I quickly found another subject for discussion.

"So, I reckon we'd be best to stick with our materialised bodies whilst we're here. It'll be easier to make contact with Alex and Sophia if we have a material form."

"Yes," agreed Sara, "and as Eligor is probably on to us anyway, any tracking they're using is likely to be sweeping for our Angelic entities as well as our physical bodies, so it would give us no advantage to change."

"Where are we heading?" I asked, as the avenue broadened out and we arrived at a crossroads.

"Straight to the Elysian Fields I think," she replied. "I can leave the Merc at the Healing centre and ask Raph to look after it. If K needs it in a hurry, he can just arrange for it to be collected, it'll be perfectly safe at the centre."

We were getting close to a junction, so we slowed down. So far, the road had been quiet; in fact we hadn't seen a soul since we'd passed through the gates. Ahead of us, there were fewer trees; instead banks of snow-white calla lilies grew in graceful clusters at the edge of the roadside. The gleaming highway broadened out and for the first time, we saw another vehicle, approaching us from the right.

It was a silver truck, with high cabin and an open back. The red and black symbol of the Potestas was marked clearly on the cabin door and sitting in the back of the truck were about a dozen angels, all fully alated, silent and cross-legged. These were some of the Warrior Angels, directly under K's command. Crack troops, programmed for loyalty, single-minded in their commitment to the Celestial Order and the utter destruction of the Fallen. It has been said that the Potestas are the only division within the Heavenly Host to have never contained a dissident or to have included in their ranks an angel who subsequently fell from grace.

Actually, I had heard a rumour which suggested otherwise, but I had no real evidence that there was any truth in the scurrilous story that the first commanding officer of the Potestas had been none other than Lucifer himself. It might surprise you to know that there's still a lot of confusion even now regarding exactly what happened in the First Rebellion. Everyone knows it took place – and of course everyone knows what the end result was, but there are quite a few versions still doing the rounds about what made it kick off in the first place. However, in addition to providing defensive forces, the Potestas are also the Keepers of Celestial history so I'm not surprised that they may want to keep some of the less savoury factoids to themselves.

The truck swept past us on the other side of the road, heading in the direction we had just travelled. At the junction, we took the left fork and continued on our way. Once again, the highway was deserted.

"Reckon they're the guys K's got searching for Jaoel?" I asked Sara as I watched the truck disappear around the corner, totally obscured by the flowering cherry trees.

"Could be," she replied. "I know he'd already mobilised Nat's[31] division before we left this morning – but if Manny's filled him in on the developments at Kathryn's flat, he might think they need reinforcements."

"Do you know him – Nat, I mean?"

I'd never met him, but his reputation was legendary – and not necessarily in a good way. As I've already told you, I've got a bit of a temper, but mine is nothing compared to Nathanael's. Like me, he's an instrument of divine justice, but unlike me, his role is simply to punish, not to judge. And from what I've heard, he is absolutely merciless. Back in the day, he was the angel assigned to work with the Prophets Elijah and Elisha, and some of the stories of what he got up to are right up there with Sodom and Gomorrah on the list of things the PR department would rather not talk about.

"I've met him." Sara sounded noncommittal. "He does a good job – and he's never failed yet." She glanced across at me. "Doesn't mean I have to like him."

---

[31] "The Warrior Angel Nathanael is an angel of the second sphere. Utterly dedicated to the cause of celestial justice, he has never failed to exact punishment or to wreak divine vengeance upon the Fallen. In his spare time, he enjoys gardening, Pilates and the music of Demis Roussos." *Notes from the Angels' Year Book,* 1974

As she spoke, she manoeuvred the car into the left hand lane and we began to slow down, preparing to turn into another tree-lined avenue – magnolias this time. On the grass verge at the side of the road was a large and elegantly lettered sign bidding us *'Welcome to the Elysian Fields'*.

"Anyway," she said as we drove on past the sign board, under the magnolia trees' waxy canopy of pearlescent blossom, "I told you that K had the situation under control – and to be honest, after seeing what those bastards did to Kathryn, I am actually quite glad Nat's in charge. He'll make sure they get what they deserve."

"He's not always very measured though is he? Remember that case on the West Bank? Those poor school kids? Mauled to death, just for having a bit of a laugh. Forty young boys ripped to pieces just because Elisha's nose was put out of joint.[32]"

"Well, you weren't exactly 'measured' back there at St. Basil's," she retorted, "you nearly threw poor Isra out of the window."

"Yeah, difference was, I didn't. Nat's a loose cannon and I'm not sure if that's what we really want on this case – particularly as Alex and Sophia are still out there – and Nat doesn't really give a flying one about who gets in the crossfire."

Sara turned right into the driveway of a strikingly modernist building, all steel, glass and right angles, not a softening curve or colour to be seen. There was a large metal plaque on the wall at the entrance. It read *'Elysian Fields Holistic Healing and Therapy Centre – abandon all hopelessness, all ye who enter here'*.

"I told you," she said without taking her eyes away from the road, "I don't have to like him. But, personally, I trust K's judgement and if he thinks Nat's the right guy for the job, that's good enough for me."

I said nothing as she negotiated the car into a fairly narrow space at the front of the building and turned off the engine. She had reminded me, none too subtly, of an angel's first duty – to act in obedience - and I couldn't disagree with her now without it looking as if I was calling into question the judgement of the Heavenly Host's most senior officer, an act which could easily be seen as a prelude to rebellion.

---

[32] "Reference to the unfortunate incident can be found at 2 Kings 2:23-24. The Office of the Permanent Secretary has offered its sincere condolences to the families involved and has commissioned a report which is awaiting the arrival of Sir John Chilcott within the celestial realms." *Annual Report of the Heavenly Host,* BC 2001

~ *Chapter Twelve* ~

The mood between us was none too cordial as we both got out of the Merc. We grabbed our kitbags from the boot and Sara locked the car.

We were standing outside one of the ugliest buildings I had ever seen. It was about the size of a standard soccer pitch, eight storeys high and constructed entirely from steel and concrete. The top two floors were longer than the floors below them, but not balanced centrally to create a 'T' shape, instead they stretched out at least 10 yards to the left of the building, making it look disconcertingly unstable. Narrow glass balconies ran the length of each storey, climbing upwards at a slight angle like an Escher puzzle; each room had a huge picture window, unadorned with curtains or blinds, giving a desolate and almost unfinished air.

Sara marched purposefully ahead of me, making straight for the front steps and then on into the reception area. I followed more slowly, mulling over our last conversation. When we had talked about the Potestas' involvement before, she had really just glossed over it – but it was clear now that she knew all about the operation, even down to who K had assigned as the patrol's commanding officer. So why hadn't she mentioned that Nat was involved until just now? And what else was she keeping from me?

As I slowly began to climb the steps, I asked myself how much I really knew about Sara. I hadn't seen her for years – and it suddenly struck me as more than a tad strange that out of all the desk bunnies they could have landed me with for this assignment, it just happened to be the angel I used to hang out with, someone I had actually liked and probably would be expected to trust, who had turned up this morning – and was now pretty much running the show. Was there a deeper game being played here? Or was I just feeling a bit sore about the dressing down she had just given me?

Whichever, I decided that I was going to have to step up on the vigilance front – and I resolved to check in with Manny at the first possible opportunity, thinking that he might be able to fill me in a bit more on what was actually going on here.

As I completed my musings, I reached the top of the stairs and walked through the glass doors into the open plan reception area, where Sara was standing, engaged in animated conversation with someone who could only be an Archangel[33].

Sara's mood had lifted and she turned happily towards me. "Zach, what took you so long? Come here and say hello to Raphael – I've told him all about the case we're on and he is dying to meet you."

As she spoke, Raphael turned towards me and I was surprised to see that there was an equally welcoming smile on his face. Like K earlier, he was dressed impeccably, but that was where the resemblance between the two Archangels ended. Raphael was tall and sturdily built, with white hair and a salt and pepper beard; his face was lined and weathered and he looked more than a little care-worn, but despite that, the smile seemed to sit quite naturally on his lips. To be honest, he reminded me quite a lot of Morgan Freeman.

"Zach, welcome to the HTC – hideous building isn't it? Bloody Michael decided to give Le Corbusier free rein when he got up here – and this is the result. Stood empty for years, and when I needed somewhere for the centre to expand into, it was the only place big enough that I could get at short notice."

"So what do you actually do here?" I asked, quite surprised to find that they needed so much space for what I would have thought would have been a bit of a niche enterprise.

Sara picked up a leaflet from the desk and handed it to me. The centre offered a whole range of activities which seemed to be aimed mainly at angels who worked in the terrestrial zones – things like spiritual consolation and resilience courses, basic and advanced talisman and amulet design and usage, nexus development and dream therapy.

---

[33]"The Archangels are first in rank and power within the celestial realm; amongst their number, Gabriel, Michael, Raphael, Uriel, Kemuel, Jophiel, Raquel, Sandalphon and Zadkiel are the leading members of the Heavenly Host, each taking specific responsibilities within the celestial cabinet. They are also concerned with non-celestial matters, and act as the Guardian Angels of specific nations and countries, concerning themselves with politics, military matters, commerce and trade. Their primary function is to ensure the balance of power in the eternal struggle between good and evil remains firmly stacked in favour of the existing administration." *Introduction to the Annual Report of the Heavenly Host*, 1876

"Okay – so you teach basic techniques for Guardians – the stuff they need to support and protect their charges. But I wouldn't have thought that there is more of a demand for that now than there was a thousand years ago."

"It's not just stuff for the Guardians, Raph also runs master classes here - for angels who want to become healers," said Sara, sounding a little defensive. She clearly didn't like me questioning her Guru. "Like I said, I have been studying with him for about three hundred years."

"Sara is actually one of my star pupils," said Raphael fondly. "But you're right, Zach, my classes are small – I take one student every hundred years, and the Guardian Angel support and refresher work doesn't need that much space either. No, we needed to move in order to meet the demand for Angel Therapy that has just grow'd like Topsy over the past twenty years."

I looked at him quizzically. I knew that Angel Therapy had become ridiculously popular back on earth, but I had no idea that the Heavenly Host was now seriously involved in it.

"Come with me," said Raphael, "let's take a very quick peep into the call centre." He led us through the double doors at the back of the reception and gestured towards an open elevator. Once inside, he pushed the button for the eighth floor.

"The call centre takes up the top three floors of the building; the fourth floor is devoted to re-charging the batteries of the operators once they come off shift."

The elevator doors opened and we walked out on to a circular landing which ran around the whole of the eighth floor. The walls of the offices were glass, and looking through, I could see bank after countless banks of desks, all equipped with display screens and keyboards. At each desk sat an angel. Most of them were wearing headphones. They all had a look of absolute concentration on their faces and none of them was talking. As I looked, I became aware that even through the glass, the volume of the ongoing and persistent celestial praising had definitely gone up a notch.

"This floor serves Europe, the Middle East and Africa," said Raphael. "The Americas are serviced downstairs, and everywhere else gets channelled to the agents working on floor six."

"So what are they doing?" I asked, still not really understanding what I was seeing.

"They're responding to requests for service," said Raphael. "We've recently introduced prayer recognition software, which filters the service request to the appropriate agent. You know, stuff like 'if you require consolation services pray 1, for prophecies, predictions and forecasts, pray two, spiritual guidance and advice, pray four' etc. etc. It's actually pulled our productivity stats up by around 15%. We've had some complaints from people who think it de-personalises the service, but you can't quibble with the stats now can you?"

As he spoke, Raphael gestured towards a display board up on the wall on which flashing LED lights pulsed out the current performance ratings:

Prayers waiting:	*15,087*
Average waiting time:	*10 seconds*
Prayer abandonment rate:	*28.6*
Average prayer handling time:	*32 minutes*
Fulfilment rate:	*75.06*
Current customer satisfaction rate:	*84.7*

"Everything is up by about 10 percent on last month, which is going down extremely well with K's Efficiency and Reform group. And of course, it's all cloud-based technology. You've got to move with the times you know, Zach." Raphael could clearly see that I was looking sceptical.

"I know we always used to offer a more individual service," he said, with a slight shrug, "but we just can't afford it anymore."

"Why not?" I asked. "I thought one of K's big things was that we become a... what was it... 'customer-centric organisation', with the needs of humanity at the heart of everything we do?"

"Yes, but, Zach, these are times of austerity; with the headcount down on earth getting bigger by the day, our resources can't possibly grow to accommodate the need if we just stick with our old business models. You and I both know that we don't have enough angels to go round. And it's not just that. Even if we could throw resources at the problem, it wouldn't be the solution. Things are different now. Even you Justice Angels must have noticed that the old fashioned reliance on the traditional establishments has fallen by the wayside over the last hundred years?"

I didn't take too kindly to his comments about Justice Angels. "I hope you're not suggesting that we're out of touch in the Agency?" I was beginning to bristle with indignation. What did some celestial desk jockey know about what was happening out there in the real world? "We see humanity at its worst down there – and all the traditional vices, sins and depravities are as bad as they ever used to be – with just as many people out there calling on us for vengeance and divine retribution. We've seen no let-up in demand in that department I can tell you!"

"Hey, calm down, Zach." Raphael's voice was conciliatory rather than aggressive.

"That may well be the case for you guys, but we know that at least fifty per cent of our Guardians don't have the caseload they need to work at maximum efficiency; most humans just don't have a strong enough faith in the old traditions to build and maintain the nexus any more. They're looking for new ways to find guidance – the internet, social media – and we just had to find a radically different way to service the market."

"It also keeps the Guardians properly occupied," added Sara. "Anyone whose case load is below 75% has to make up their time doing shifts at the centre. We channel service requests from all the registered Angel Therapists across the globe and we are now even looking at setting up direct services – Raph's got Steve Jobs on board on this one and the early designs for the iAngel app look really good."

She paused and gave me a bit of a rueful grin. "Head office is not so sure about the logo though; apples have still got a bit of a bad press up here."

As she was speaking, a green light started to flash just above the door leading into the call centre.

"Oh look, the shift will be finishing in thirty minutes," said Raphael, "and we don't want to be trampled in the change-over, so I suggest we head back downstairs."

We trooped back into the elevator and emerged a few seconds later back in reception.

"Well, thanks for the tour," I said to Raphael, "it's amazing how much has changed up here since my last visit," and, I added silently, how little I liked it.

"A pleasure to meet you," he responded; "I hope all goes well with your mission. Sara's told me the basics. Eligor's a tough customer – I had a few run-ins with him during the First Rebellion, but happily I lived to tell the tale."

He smiled briefly, before rearranging his features into a more serious expression. "Just don't underestimate him. Yes, he is indeed a mighty warrior, with at least sixty legions at his command, but his main weapons are more psychological. Eligor is one of the most practiced and talented deceivers within the ranks of the Fallen – who are all, by nature, masters of lies and deception. He will try to trick you, out-manoeuvre you and undermine your faith in each other."

~ 84 ~

There was nothing genial about Raphael now. He looked gravely from Sara to me, and back to Sara; his eyes lingered on her affectionately, finally coming to rest on her face, framed by her gleaming copper hair which was still pulled back tightly into a bun.

"I mean it. You need to trust each other implicitly and absolutely. If you don't have each other's backs on this mission, you might as well give up before you go any further. I don't know you, Zach, but Sara is very, very important to me, and I do not want to lose her just because of some screw up."

I started forwards at this, more than a little annoyed that Raphael seemed to be suggesting that I was the liability on this mission, but before I could speak, Raphael held up his hand and gestured for me to keep quiet. I let him continue.

"Whatever you may think, Zach, both your souls are important to me. I know Manny of old, and he wouldn't have given you this job if you weren't up to it. But neither of you has faced anything like Eligor before and if you can't depend on each other 100%, you will fail.

"You need to let me know right now if you have any doubts, any doubts at all about each other… Because if you do, I am pulling this mission."

At Raphael's words, Sara gasped. I turned to look at her. Did I trust her? Could I really rely on her 100%? I remembered that just before I entered this very building I'd resolved to be extra vigilant, uncertain as to why she had not told me earlier all she knew about the Potestas.

I thought about the way that all day, she'd always seemed one step ahead of me – did she know stuff that I didn't, stuff that she clearly was not going to share – or was she just damn good at her job?

Whilst I was thinking these rather uncharitable thoughts, Sara reached out and placed her hand in mine, gently lacing our fingers together and clasping me tightly. Unable to stop myself, I returned the pressure, feeling the warm, strong emanations flooding through me as her fingers encircled mine. There was no pain when we touched, no shock or jolting, just a warm, gentle radiance; something I had felt with no other angel.

Raphael looked at us, and gave a bit of a humph.

"Well, that answers my question. You couldn't do that if you didn't trust each other."

I could not quite make out if he was pleased or disappointed that we had passed the test.

"It only remains for me to wish you luck. Sara, give me the keys to K's chariot, I'm seeing him tomorrow, so I'll take it over to him myself."

Sara did as he requested. Raphael then touched her lightly upon the shoulder, raised his hand towards me in benediction and gave us both the formal and traditional farewell:

"Good luck and Godspeed, Angel Sarandiel; Angel Zachriel."

~ *Chapter Thirteen* ~

As we walked through the shaded reception area, out of the tall glass doors and down the ugly concrete steps into the unremittingly blazing sunshine, I turned to Sara and said,

"Didn't you think he looked a bit like Morgan Freeman?"

Sara adjusted her UDs and grinned at me – "Yup – last time Raph went earth-side, he saw a picture of him up on a hoarding and decided to adjust his look accordingly… It's kind of cute really." She paused thoughtfully. "Still, I must admit, I sort of preferred it when he was channelling Bob Marley. He looked really cool with dreads… Anyway, what did you think of him?"

"Well, he clearly rates you," I replied, not wanting to commit to an opinion at this point. In truth, I had quite liked the old guy, even if I didn't really approve of his call centres and his reliance on statistics. He'd seemed rather more approachable than K, although to be honest, that wasn't a particularly difficult thing to achieve.

"What did you think about all the doom and gloom stuff he came out with right at the end? You know the '*if you don't trust each other, you will fail*' line - all a bit heavy don't you think?"

I wanted to see how Sara would respond to this – to be honest; I was still a bit sore about what had happened back in the Merc. I wanted to push her a bit – just to see what she was really thinking about us working together.

"I think he's right, Zach. And maybe you still don't really understand just how important this is to me. You do dangerous stuff all the time, so I guess you might be a bit blasé – but this really is a big deal to me. But don't forget, I've been in training for three hundred years – and I am not about to let all that go to waste. I'm going to see this through, if it's the last thing I do. And I trust you absolutely. I always have."

As she said this, she stopped walking and began to fasten her kitbag securely round her waist.

"Come on," she said, "we've got a demon to find – and two souls to rescue – and I reckon it's time to get moving. Race you to the gates..."

And without another word, she stretched out her wings, sprang into the air, and was off.

"Oy... that's cheating," I shouted, fumbling with the straps as I fastened my kitbag in place.

Within seconds, I too was airborne, my heart rate increasing with every beat of my wings, adrenalin storming through my system as I scanned the skies, trying to spot Sara amongst all the other soaring, wheeling and gliding angels; there even appeared to be a small flock of cupids and cherubs playing kiss chase in the clouds.

This was why everything had seemed so dull and deserted down on the ground. With the exception of the Potestas and the poor desk-bound angels up in Raphael's call centre, we hadn't seen a soul since we had arrived. If we had just thought to look upwards...

The skies were full of angels.

To my right, stretching out towards the horizon, an entire Angelic choir was hovering just above the gold-tinged cloud tops, every angelic mouth wide open, every set of lungs working fit to burst as they moved into an a-Capella version of *The Long and Winding Road*.

A squadron of seraphs, held in tight V formation[34] circled above me, heading off towards Ma'on. They were probably due to report for duty in New Jerusalem. Ahead of me, and to the left, I saw a flash of copper. Sara, the sunlight glinting on her wings, was darting between the tree tops in the Elysian Glade. She saw me, and pulled up into a vertical hover – the posture most terrestrial artists use when portraying angels in flight. She pulled out her tongue and then turned her back on me, before launching herself forward into a glorious swan dive.

Keeping my arms tight against my sides, I increased my speed, climbing upwards as I forced myself forwards, always keeping an eye on that flash of

---

[34] "The wingtips of the leading angel in a squadron create a pair of opposite rotating line vortices. The vortices trailing an angel create an underwash which in turn, creates an induced drag for the angel creating it; at the same time these vortices create an upwash which can aid the flight of any angel following. A study by the Efficiency and Reform group has shown that each angel in a V formation of 25 members can achieve a reduction of induced drag by up to 65% and as a result increase their range by 71%. V formations have subsequently become the required formation pattern for all Angelic flight." *The Anatomy of Angels*, 1979

copper which darted unhesitatingly, far in front of me, just ahead of the horizon. I had not had the chance to fly like this for years. On earth, even in the most deserted of places, I'd never felt able to indulge this element of my Angelic nature as I could in the celestial realms. At this moment, there was almost no other thought on my mind; I was utterly and almost overpoweringly aware of the beating of my wings, the blood and oxygen pounding through my body and the joy, the absolute, indescribable, all-encompassing joy of being an angel, in flight. Unable to help myself, my mouth opened and as I flew, I began to sing.

It didn't last long. I have the voice of an unhappy bull-frog at the best of times, and even to my tolerant ears, my choral offering was adding nothing to the tone and tenor of the celestial harmony. Seeing the pained expression on the faces of a number of my colleagues as I flew past them, I quietly subsided into a gentle and relatively Pooh-like hum.

As I reached the pinnacle of my flight path, I took the opportunity to hover in silence for a second, once more scanning the skies ahead of me and spotting Sara about 200 feet below me, closing fast on the tall black gates that marked the boundary of the Elysian Fields.

Fixing my eyes on the gates, I dived, tucking my head close in to my chest and slightly folding my wings; concentrating on nothing but speed, I seared through the air. The wind whistled in my ears, finally blocking out the heavenly orisons; I was conscious of nothing but the exhilaration and power of controlled flight, the copper of Sara's wings below me and the tall, black gates that marked the entrance to the Inferno. I had stopped humming, by the way.

In less than five seconds, I was almost there. I stretched out my primaries, slowing down my speed considerably and carefully adjusted my head and neck to a position more suited to looking round me. As I knew to my cost, it was easy to injure yourself just by stretching your neck and head too far out of kilter when flying on the horizontal[35].

---

[35] "Unlike other creatures gifted with the power of flight, the primary purpose of an angel's wings is aesthetic; the power of flight is a heavenly blessing designed to create wonder and at times "mighty dread" in the sometimes troubled minds of humanity; rather than to facilitate hunting or for defence. In addition, the Angelic form has been celestially designed and is not subject to the terrestrial laws of evolution. This has meant that an angel's physiology is not necessarily suited to all possible forms of flight and injury to the upper back, shoulders and neck often occur if care is not taken to protect these areas when flying at speed. Treatment for such injuries and advice on how to avoid them is provided by the Angelic Osteopathy Clinic at St. Basil's Hospital." *The Anatomy of Angels,* 1765

I looked to my left and saw that Sara was now flying alongside me. As we slowed down to prepare for landing, we both moved into vertical flight mode and came to ground simultaneously and, even if I say it myself, rather gracefully.

"Beat you," said Sara, "and I even took time out to pick this up." She waved something shiny at me and then proceeded to stow it away down the side of her kitbag. It looked like an old piece of wood that someone had sprayed gold as a bit of a minimalist Christmas decoration.

"Yes, it's a fair cop… you fly well." I had decided to be gracious in defeat. I had enjoyed the exercise, but I also knew that I had used less than half my potential flight power in our chase through the skies. I don't know why, but something was telling me I would be wise to let Sara think that once again, she had the upper hand. "So what's that thing?" I gestured to the top of the shiny twig that was just sticking out of her bag.

"The Golden Bough. Remember? I told you about it this morning."

"Are you sure it's okay to just walk off with it?" I asked her.

"Yeah, no problem," said Sara, "I'm sure Raph'll be fine about it. Anything to help Alex and Sophia get home safely. And talking of which, have you heard anything from Manny? Do we know anything more about what's happened with Jaoel?"

I shook my head. "No, I want to check in with him as soon as we have got safely into the Inferno, there's no way I am getting in touch until I can at least tell him we're inside. He'll do his nut otherwise."

I looked at the sky; the sun was now large and rosy gold and clearly heading towards the horizon. "I reckon we have about three hours max until sunset and we may need to camp down for the night. I'll call Manny once I'm clear what our next moves are."

I looked at Sara to see if she was going to object to this strategy, but she simply nodded and together we walked towards the tall black gates which marked the edge of the boundary between the Elysian Fields and the lands of the Fallen.

Now what you have to remember here is that the boundaries between the two realms are actually a tad blurred. Permanent residence in some of the more exclusive areas – such as the Isles of the Blessed[36] and the Heroes Hall

---

[36] "The special magic of these truly spectacular islands is reserved as a permanent residence for those souls who chose to be reincarnated thrice and who are then judged as especially pure on all three incarnations. The islands are owned by the Estate of the Heavenly Host and may be visited

(otherwise known as Valhalla) is limited to those souls who meet the entry criteria. There are also the places of punishment, such as Tartarus and the hideous dungeons of the Flame Pits; souls consigned to damnation or those who are serving a sentence imposed by the Potestas or the Angels of Justice currently have little choice about their living quarters, it's Hell fire or the frozen lake – no question, no argument. I had heard a rumour that the Efficiency and Reform group were looking to introduce digital tags for grade B offenders, allowing them to be resettled in some of the less popular areas of celestial space, but so far, objections from a significant cadre of Archangels seems to have put the kibosh on that one.

Anyway, apart from these restrictions, there is actually quite a lot of freedom for those souls who are not earth-bonded[37] and who don't want to reincarnate to live pretty much wherever they want to once they have shuffled off the mortal coil.

This means that those who genuinely wish to spend eternity basking in the radiance of divine bliss will usually choose to settle somewhere like Ma'on, the celestial New Jerusalem, or if they are really fortunate, in Araboth, the Seventh Heaven (the place where Sara was currently hanging her hat).

But not everyone wishes to have quite such a full-on exposure to divine radiance, and the whole multi-faceted nature of terrestrial belief systems has created such a mares-nest of complexity that many a newly liberated soul spends his or her first few hours on the celestial plane having a bit of a hissy-fit because it just is not what they expected AT ALL.

Not surprisingly, the indomitable human spirit of invention and adaptation has been at work in the Heavens, and now, most people's visions can be accommodated fairly easily. We have heavenly gardens, conservatories, universities and museums. There are alpine villages, jungle retreats and lake-side pleasure spots. There are also at least two areas in the territory classically designated as 'Hell' devoted exclusively to the composition and performance of music, and another three for other aspects of the performing arts.

---

by less fortunate souls on the feasts of Pentecost and Ascension." *Heavenly Homes and Gardens,* 1997 ("Don't bother; they're all a load of smug bastards." – AG – *Trip Advisor* 2015)

[37] "Bonded-souls; otherwise referred to as "ghosts", "wraiths", "spooks" or "spectres", are those souls who refuse to give up their bond with their terrestrial habitat following the demise of their physical body. Experts are still uncertain as to the cause of this unwillingness to transition, but most theories suggest that either excessive fear of uncertainty or unusually high levels of retained connection with a terrestrial place or individual lie at the heart of this phenomenon." *A Guide to the Three Realms,* 1945

We have celestial dwelling places for dog lovers, cat lovers and equestrians, and even entomologists, campanologists and taxidermists have their own little dedicated homelands, located on the furthest reaches of the Heavens. Although it is true to say the last three domains seem to be relatively undersubscribed and it's widely rumoured that they're the areas most likely to be targeted for the community release of digitally tagged prisoners, if the Efficiency and Reform group get their way.

So, all this meant that there are certain zones within the celestial space whose inhabitants are quite likely to not be what you might have expected or believed them to be. I knew that many who had served out their sentences in Tartarus now lived cheek by jowl with the souls of young urbanites, who saw the lands on the boundary as somewhere a bit edgy and 'vibrant' and thus preferable to what they viewed as the bland, polished and conventional portals of New Jerusalem.

It was also fairly common knowledge that many of the lesser Fallen Angels had taken up residence on the outlying plains of the boundary lands, acting as spies and informers for the big boys, most of whom, like Belphegor, had huge mansions in the fourth and fifth circles.

So, as Sara and I prepared to pass through the gateway, out of the Elysian Fields onto the bleak isolation of the plains of Lethe, I actually was starting to have second thoughts about what we had got ourselves into, and some real concerns about what exactly might be about to happen next.

Once we passed though that gateway, we moved away from safety and the automatic protection of the Heavenly Host. We were entering hostile territory - on a mission that the Archdukes of Hell would do anything in their power to sabotage or terminate.

We could not make any assumptions about the people we met now and whether they were friend or foe, we would have no way of knowing.

~ *Chapter Fourteen* ~

There were no sentries on the celestial side of the gateway and just a single security cam which faced out, over the boundary, clearly focused on people trying to get in, rather than those aiming to leave. We approached slowly, on foot.

"Shall we ditch the wings?" I suggested. Sara nodded. Once into the boundary lands, we wanted to draw as little attention to ourselves as possible and without wings, we could be taken for boundary dwellers or tourists, we wouldn't be immediately identified as angels.

With a shake and a shudder, Sara's beautiful copper wings folded in upon themselves, grew smaller and smaller and then disappeared, leaving no trace, not even the tiniest feather. I focused my mind and concentrated intently on returning to the simplicity and frailty of the standard human form and felt my own wings do likewise. As always at such times, I felt both vulnerable and somewhat diminished. An angel without wings is an altogether more fragile entity.

Suddenly I thought of Jaoel, who had willingly spent almost ten years in a fixed materialisation. Unable to alate, he would have been cut off completely from the spiritual cleansing of the celestial realms, separated from his true self, forced to remain, day after day, year after year, within the confines of a weak and relatively unresponsive body. For the first time, I truly began to understand the burden that he had taken on; for the sake of Alex's soul he had agreed to a voluntary banishment from almost everything that defined and supported him as a celestial being. This would have meant exclusion from the rituals and activities which would make his physical manifestation bearable – and for the first time, I began to comprehend why he might have been prepared to betray everything to escape it. As Isra might have phrased it, "Heavy shit there, man."

~ 93 ~

So it was in a rather sombre and reflective mood that I approached the gates. Sara walked slowly beside me. She said nothing as I reached out and turned the large black handle. Like me, she seemed wrapped in thought; the exuberance and frivolity of our flight across the Elysian Fields replaced by something more serious as the reality of the task we had undertaken was now actually staring us full in the face.

The handle turned and I pushed the gate inwards, carefully and with some deliberation. It was heavy and did not respond easily at first. The wrought iron hinges made squeals of protest and the bottom edge of the gate ground with some resistance against the paving stones as I pushed it open. These were clearly not well-trodden ways.

Once the gate was open, there was no point in delay. I walked through. There seemed to be no security on the other side either. No-one appeared to challenge me or ask for identity or travel papers. In fact, the place seemed to be completely deserted. Sara followed close behind; I felt her hand rest lightly on my shoulder and I shut the gate behind us with a slight, but still resonant, clank. Once the gateway was closed, I was aware that the celestial radiance had vanished and everything had become darker and less brilliantly defined.

It was very strange. As I turned back to look through the gates into the fields we had left behind, I could still see blue skies and a sun which had a fair way to go before setting. But on this side of the gate, dusk was already on us, the sky was a deep and cloudless midnight blue; there were as yet no stars, but a crescent moon had risen, casting a sort of eldritch light on Sara's face, which now seemed as hard and pale as alabaster. We both took off our UDs and stowed them away in our kitbags. We weren't likely to need them on this side of the boundary.

"Have you been in this way before?" she asked, hanging slightly back, as if uncertain of her surroundings, and not quite sure what she should do next.

I looked around me at the encroaching woodland to our right and, ahead of us, about half a mile away, the shadowy pathway leading to an old stone bridge – one of the many crossings over the River Lethe. Beyond the bridge, possibly a mile or two further on, I thought I could make out a small collection of rather ramshackle cottages just visible on the skyline. Nothing much seemed to have changed since my last visit.

"Yes," I replied, "I've been here a few times, but not for years. I don't think I've been anywhere near the boundary lands on this side of the Inferno since sometime around the end of the 16th century. One of our old associates had settled here after he passed over and I needed to consult him on some outstanding business. Manny sent me up here on a day trip, but I've not been back since."

As I spoke, I was conscious that my voice sounded harsh; my throat felt dry and quite uncomfortable. I realised that I'd not had anything to drink since first thing this morning. The events of the day had thrown me from my normal Sunday routine, which would usually have involved a square meal and at least a couple of pints over at Charlie's.

Angels don't actually feel hunger or thirst, but we still enjoy food and drink and, perhaps more importantly, our physical bodies don't lose the need to be sustained. I was normally quite good at making sure that I kept it topped up with essential supplies, it had been good to me and I was fond of it. Opening my kitbag, I took out the water bottle and after a long and satisfying swig, found the slab of mint cake, had some for myself and then passed a few squares to Sara, along with the water.

"Come on, you had better get something inside you," I said. "The last thing we need is physical collapse – and the first rule of survival whilst we're in here is not to eat or drink anything that is offered to you by anyone we meet or to take anything which you find within the boundaries."

Sara nodded and drank, passed the water bottle back to me and bit off a piece of the mint cake. We began walking, following the path towards the bridge, heading in the direction of the settlement we could just see in the distance beyond the edge of the forest.

"So it's true then, all that stuff about not eating the food here? I thought it was just prejudice and old wives' tales."

"No, it's true alright," I answered. Rummaging in my kitbag, I pulled out the leaflet the pharmacist at St. Basil's had given me and handed it to her. "Like it says in here, once you consume something that belongs to the underworld, it remains with you forever. You see, it can't pass through your system like food and drink from the land of the living; instead, it'll remain within you; binding you permanently to this place. The only way out would be to ditch the body and resume your angelic form – which I suppose is not such a big deal in the long run, but would quite severely mess up our chances of connecting with Alex and Sophia."

"Yes, you're right. That would be problematic." Sara seemed more than a little cross with herself. She clearly didn't like being wrong-footed this way. "I wish I'd realised it was a real risk, I thought it was just small-minded tourist types being all snobby about the local cuisine. I didn't think that we literally couldn't eat or drink anything whilst we were in here."

She patted her kitbag dismissively. "I haven't got any supplies with me – and I suppose we can't fill your bottle from the river can we?"

"No," I said somewhat dryly. "Not unless you want to indulge in eternal forgetfulness. That's the Lethe – river of oblivion. Even if the first rule didn't count, you wouldn't want to drink that stuff. That's what they give to the souls who are about to be reincarnated. It makes them forget everything about their past, their identity and all the things they did when they were on earth before. That's part of the bargain – you only get to go back if you are prepared to start from scratch. Anyway, I've enough water for a couple of days if we're careful."

Sara looked at me and her nose wrinkled in distaste. "Urgh... that re-born-souls thing has always given me the creeps. I just think it's a bit... unhygienic. You know, putting used souls into a fresh, clean new body."

I shrugged. "I think it's quite a good idea... and it would be a hell of a lot busier up here if we didn't do it... Can you imagine what it would be like if every single soul that passed over had to be accommodated in a suitable dwelling place? Forever?"

I'd always thought that reincarnation was just a pragmatic solution to the problem of overcrowding in the afterlife.

"You may think it's a bit messy," I continued, "but don't you think the alternative would put rather unwanted pressure on the Heavenly Host's ability to deliver on its promise of everlasting bliss? The way I see it, they can offer the bliss-stuff as part of the morality bargain because they know full well most humans are going to get bored to tears sitting on their bums on a beach up here and will want to get back down to terra-firma within a hundred years or so."

We had arrived at the bridge, and we stood for a second, gazing down into the clear, dark waters. The Lethe ran slow, but was not sluggish. Few plants grew in its chill and forbidding depths and fish did not flourish.

I pointed down into the river. "Just a mouthful and the slate is wiped clean. Total oblivion; a new life with no baggage. Can't be bad really. And we can still create new souls[38] when we need to, there seems to be no decline in demand."

---

[38] "In recent times, human theologians have speculated intensely upon the nature of the soul. Indeed, many philosophers have suggested that they may be finite in number and that amongst that number, some souls may be pre-destined or 'elect'. In reality, the Heavenly Host has long adopted a sustainable approach to the generation of souls and will always seek to re-use and re-cycle when possible." *Annual Report of the Heavenly Host*, 954 AD

"Hmm… I've heard of a few slip-ups though," said Sara. "Humans born with memories of past lives, strange demonstrations of knowledge they couldn't possibly have acquired through their day to day lives. That sort of stuff. It all just seems a bit sloppy and slapdash."

We moved away from the parapet and carried on walking, our pace fairly slow. "Yeah, maybe," I said, "I think there probably are a few slip-ups now and again. And I know for a fact that the department concerned has a huge backlog, so maybe a few little souls slip through the net without proper processing, but what's the big deal?"

As far as I was concerned, the reincarnation of souls was the least of our worries. It was now really dark, and although we had seen or heard no-one since we'd walked through the gateway, that didn't mean that we'd not been observed. I had no idea if our plan to outwit Eligor by coming in via the Elysian Fields had been successful, or if he had anticipated us and we were already under surveillance. I had to admit that I was uneasy; we were way too exposed where we were; I wanted to get under cover and contact Manny for an update as soon as possible.

On the other side of the bridge, the ways divided; one path heading straight ahead along the edge of the forest, towards the small settlement we had spotted when we came through the gates, the other, which ran along the bank, seemed dark and uninviting and I had no idea what lay beyond the bend in the river a few hundred yards away.

Quickly and quietly, I let Sara know what I was thinking; we agreed that the best thing to do would be to head for the village and try to find a place to crash down until daybreak. It was pretty late already, and with any luck, we would only need to wait a few hours. It would also give us chance to contact Manny and get our bearings.

Once we got to the settlement, we might also be able to find someone who could give us some news; if Eligor had brought Alex and Sophia into the Inferno, that would be too juicy a piece of gossip to be kept quiet, and I was pretty sure that someone would be able to give us some info.

I also cherished a faint hope that my old mate Johan might still be around. He'd been living here alone last time I saw him, but had been hoping his wife, Lisl, would find a way to join him when she passed over. He was a Dutch guy, a demon expert and alchemist – and an absolute dab hand with talismans and protective sorcery; one of the best associates the Agency ever had. He'd been on my mind ever since Manny had told us that we were dealing with Eligor;

Johan had been involved last time that particular Archduke of Hell had been operating openly in England.

But it had been a long time since I'd ventured into the boundary lands on this side of the Inferno, and he might have moved on if it had turned out that boundary dwelling didn't exactly float Lisl's boat. And even if it had, by now they might well have decided to cash in their eternity chips, and gone back to earth for another go.

Having agreed our next steps, we walked off the bridge and took the path that led towards the village. At that moment, the still night air was broken by a single noise, which sounded like the stifled whinny of a horse. I took a swift look over my shoulder and what I saw set all my alarm bells ringing.

Deserted no longer, the clearing to the front of the gateway now thronged with activity. There were at least six horsemen, their mounts the darkest grey with wild black manes and eyes that gleamed red in the gathering darkness. They stood, silhouetted against the gateway; illuminated by the faint light which still remained in the celestial skies behind them. Each horseman was horned. Three had antlers like stags, reaching skywards, sharp, wild and forbidding, whilst two of the others had a single horn emerging from their foreheads. These appeared, from the way the light gleamed upon them, to be tipped with steel. The horns of the final rider, long, pointed and menacing, curved slightly as they stretched upwards. I took a second glance, almost disbelieving. This was no man; this wasn't even one of the Fallen. This was a Minotaur.

We had not heard them approaching and I had no idea how long they had been there. Sara followed my eyes and as we watched, we caught the faint jingle of a bridle and heard hooves stamping on the stone pathway. At the feet of the horses gathered a pack of creatures which may once have been dogs. They were horrible.

Despite their rather terrifying appearance, the small group seemed quite confused and disorganised. Whoever they were, they had either not yet picked up our trail, or were waiting for orders. Whatever the reason, their lack of organisation gave us one small advantage.

Without a word, I grabbed Sara's shoulder and thrust her round, pointing back the way we had come. She grasped the situation instantly, and together we ran to take cover beneath the arch of the bridge.

"Don't talk. Keep quiet. Can you do the dark thing?" I whispered as we huddled ourselves tight against the ancient and unpleasantly clammy stone

~ 98 ~

wall, being careful to keep a good distance between ourselves and the edge of the river.

"Already on it," she replied, and within seconds we were shrouded in impenetrable shadows as the darkness of the twelfth hour of the night surrounded us.

~ *Chapter Fifteen* ~

And so, we clung together, motionless and silent, wrapped in darkness beneath the ancient bridge that spanned the River Lethe and the dark waters which promised oblivion to any who drank them.

For some time nothing happened. We heard the stamping of the horses and the faint jingle of reins and harness. One of the dog-things began to bark, but almost instantly there was a harsh crack of a whip, followed by a whimper and then silence.

And then without warning, the silence broke. A horse was racing towards us, steel-shod hooves ringing hard against the stone paving. Whoever it was seemed to be approaching from the path that led through the forest; as they neared the river the headlong gallop began to slow to a canter and then a gentle trot, which became walking pace as they mounted the bridge. Then the noise stopped. We could see nothing, and I assumed that whoever it was had reached the top of the bridge and was now in full view of the horsemen assembled at the gateway.

Then, directly above us, we heard the sound of a horn; three long notes spilling out into the silent darkness, calling to the hunters at the gateway with imperious command. This was clearly the signal the horsemen had been waiting for. In a matter of seconds, we heard the horses approaching and with them came the dog-things; panting and occasionally baying despite the repeated sounds of the unforgiving whip and the whimpers which followed its application.

"Good evening, my huntsmen, and hopefully..." a pause, "well met." The voice that rang out from the bridge above us was confident, commanding, full-bodied – and female. "What news for Lord Eligor?"

At first, there came no answer from the horsemen who we guessed must

~ 100 ~

have gathered at the foot of the bridge. Then we heard one horse begin to walk forwards, its hooves ringing on the old stones of the bridge. A dark, guttural male voice began to speak.

"Greetings, Lady Enepsigos, as always it is a pleasure to serve you..." There was a jingle, a thump and a slight creaking sound, and then the speaker continued, his voice somewhat muffled, as if he was talking into his chest. He must have dismounted and was now probably bowing or abasing himself in some other way before this high ranking Hell-Queen.

"And may I say, Your Ladyship, you are looking particularly ravishing this evening, those are truly the most becoming helmets... " Whoever it was, he was beginning to bluster.

"Get up, you fool, I have no time for pleasantries, and neither have you. Lord Eligor is waiting. What news of the angels?"

The creaking over-head came again. The speaker had clearly got back on his feet. "Your suspicions were right, my Lady, someone has been here, we can tell you that for sure. The gate has been opened recently, and at least one angel has come through into the boundary lands. But the signs are confusing, and the trail isn't strong." His voice wavered. He knew he wasn't giving her the news that she wanted – and he clearly knew that she wasn't going to like it.

"When did you get here? And how long ago was the gate opened?" The woman's voice was sharp, peremptory. I made up my mind that I really didn't want to get on the wrong side of this one. Next to me, I felt Sara shiver.

"We only just got here, just afore you did, my Lady." The man sounded nervous, uncertain. "There was no-one to be seen, but I reckon the gates had not been closed long. They still felt warm-like, and an angel's touch don't linger long in these parts."

"Well, where are they then? I have ridden the straight road from Erebus and met no-one but boundary dwellers and tourist-scum. They cannot have gone that way or I would have found them. Have you searched the forest and the riverbank?"

"Not yet, my Lady."

"And do you think that is good enough?"

But there was no answer; instead we heard a strange whirring and a sickening thud as something sharp and hard hit something soft and unprotected. There was silence for a few seconds, then a whinny and another soft, sharp whirring, followed by a clattering shudder as the dead weight fell to the ground.

Then the dog-things began to bay and the remaining horses stamped and whinnied as the strong, ferrous smell of blood rose in the otherwise scentless air. The clear, powerful voice of the woman soared above the noise of the pack.

"The rest of you, look here; this is fresh meat. This is your reward, and there will be more of it, if you do your job well."

And now we heard other sounds, several long slashing noises, followed by the disgusting and distressing sound of flesh being ripped apart and thrown onto the pathway.

"But remember, this will also be your punishment if you fail me. You are the Wild Hunt and you will bring me the angels, or I will rip each and every one of you to shreds and feed you to my Hell- hounds."

At this, the noise became unbearable as the barking and howling of the dogs was joined by the bellowing of the Minotaur and the harsh, rough sounds of the other hunters.

"I have given you blood. I have given you flesh of the unworthy. Eat... and then we ride."

The sounds above us became unbearable: the crack of bones being pulled apart, sinews splitting, muscles tearing; the bestial sound of raw meat being devoured, and the slavering noises of wild creatures tearing to shreds the body of their former companion.

And when it was done, we heard her voice again, strong, commanding and determined.

"Now, ride, ride like the very Devil himself. Prove to me that you are truly the Wild Hunt. Find me my quarry and you shall feed upon the flesh of angels before this night is over."

The horses galloped across the bridge, the dog-things barking at their sides. We heard them ride into the distance, heading along the path by the bank of the river. And then there was silence.

For a long time we did not dare speak. Then, when all had been quiet and undisturbed above us for at least twenty minutes, I felt Sara pull away from me, the darkness moving with her as she crept towards the edge of the stone archway. Then she was gone.

Stumbling after her, I climbed back up the riverbank and, looking around me to check the coast was clear, hoisted myself up on to the pathway and slowly walked back on to the bridge. It was messy, really unpleasant and I picked my way carefully through the ghastly remnants of blood and bone, not wanting to get any of the grossness on my boots. I reached the middle of the bridge and positioned myself next to Sara, who was looking down at the bloody mess that was all that was left of the huntsman whose lack of diligence had so annoyed the Lady Enepsigos – and the horse whose only fault had been to have been carrying the wrong rider, in the wrong place at the wrong time.

"Close call," Sara said.

I nodded . "And we'd better not hang round here. Who knows what other scavengers might get drawn to the scent of all that blood. We need to be off - and pronto."

One good thing about being stuck under the bridge; we were both rested and antsy and so we found no difficulty in setting a good pace, running hard down the edge of the road, keeping close to the forest and heading towards the small village about two miles ahead of us. Faint lights shone from some of the cottages, but the path ahead was shrouded in almost total darkness.

"Why do you think they didn't spot us?" asked Sara, after we had run about half a mile or so and felt fairly certain we weren't being followed by outliers from the hunt.

"Not sure, and I don't really understand why they couldn't tell how many of us had come through the gateway," I replied, panting a bit. Sara's pace was unrelenting. "But I think when we were under the bridge, the Lethe waters confused the dog-things; we were so close to the waters of oblivion that they just couldn't find our scent."

"What were those creatures? And who was that woman?" Sara didn't seem bothered by the pace at all.

I was in no fit state for discussion. "Let's just get there, and then we can talk." We had reached the edge of the village. It was only a small settlement, perhaps twenty or thirty houses, clustered together around a village green, which was traditionally furnished with both a duck-pond and a thatch-roofed wishing well.

When I had been here last, Johan's house had been close up against the forest, surrounded by a white picket fence. I think he even had honeysuckle and roses round the door.

There was a light on at the cottage that had been Johan's.

I gestured to Sara, and we slowed down, coming to a halt by the side of a large oak tree which stood right at the edge of the village green.

"I used to know the guy who lived there, but that was quite a while ago. If he's still there, then we should be good for a place to crash, he used to work with the Agency and I can vouch for him."

~ 103 ~

"But if not?" Sara questioned.

"I know," I shrugged. It was a poser. Not everyone who lived in the boundary lands was a bad-guy, but we now knew for sure that the hunt was after us. There was a price on our heads, and it would be risky for anyone to help us.

"Look," I said, "I'm just going to go for it. We can't stay out in the open much longer. You stay here, I won't be long. I'll come get you if everything's okay." I prepared to step out of the shelter of the forest, into the road, in full view of the nearest houses. Instantly, Sara's hand shot out and she grabbed my sleeve. I felt a sharp shock run through me and gave an involuntary yelp.

"No way," answered Sara. "I've got another idea. You say that your guy's house is that cream one over there? The one that backs on to the forest?"

I nodded, rubbing my arm a little ostentatiously.

Sara looked across at me, suddenly aware of my discomfort. "Oops. Sorry, didn't mean to shock you... Anyway, my idea is this. Why don't we circle round the back, see if we can look in through the windows without being seen? If this guy's still there, you might even see him, but even if you don't you could still get a sense of whether it's his place or not by what it looks like inside."

I had to hand it to her. This was not a bad idea. In fact, Johan did have particularly pronounced personal tastes when it came to decor. As I told Sara, he was the only person I'd ever known who collected bird skulls. When I'd first met him, his entire house had been covered with them, from the tiniest wren, right up to his greatest treasure – the skull of some strange prehistoric creature, which I hadn't recognised at the time, but now knew to be the remains of a giant ostrich.

His obsession had been moderated slightly when he married. Lisl was a good woman; she admired her husband's learning and found his eccentricity amusing rather than annoying, but even she drew the line at skeletal remains inhabiting every nook and cranny of her home. She had limited Johan to five shelves in his study and a small cupboard under the stairs, but I knew that if I peeped through his windows and saw even one little bird skull, chances were we were on to a sure thing.

We worked our way through the trees and bushes that provided a natural boundary between the village and the forest, keeping under cover and taking care not to make a sound. We soon found ourselves standing by a white picket fence, looking in through the windows of the drawing room of a small, well-

~ 104 ~

appointed cottage. The curtains were not drawn and the lights were low, a fire was burning in the grate and we could just see two figures, sitting close together on what looked like a battered old leather chesterfield. They were facing the fire, with their backs to the window. I couldn't make out either of their faces. There were chocolate box pictures on the wall and a number of spindle-legged reproduction side tables, groaning with the sort of porcelain statuary you see advertised in the more down-market Sunday supplements. I wasn't getting a good vibe. Last time I was here, Johan's house had been more hovel than haven.

I was about to let Sara know that I didn't hold out much hope that Johan was still living here when she hissed, "Look... Over there." She was pointing out across the garden. It was laid out neatly, with raised beds, roses rambling against the side walls, a lawn punctuated with the little clusters of ornamental grasses and flowering cabbages that garden designers say are so essential and finally, to the far side of the house, a rockery. The rockery was decorated with small, white objects. I looked more closely; these weren't stones or sea shells. These were bird skulls. Hundreds of them. There could scarcely be any doubt about it, against all odds, and despite my previous misgivings, I was now almost certain this meant that Johan was still living here.

As I stared at the rockery, one of the figures got up from the sofa and slowly walked to the window, reached up for the curtains and began to pull them to. The light shone full on his face and if I had had any doubts before, they were now gone entirely.

"Come on." I grabbed at Sara's kitbag and pulled her along with me; we jumped over the fence and ran through the garden, reaching the window just as Johan was about to pull the second curtain in to place.

That was a mistake.

~ *Chapter Sixteen* ~

Half an hour later, when Lisl had picked up a dazed and disorientated Johan from the floor and Sara and I had apologised, explained and begged very nicely for admittance, we were all sitting together in the small, rather chintzy dining room. Lisl had prepared coffee and cake, tea and sandwiches and finally, wine and olives. Sara and I had played our parts to perfection, refusing each and every offer politely and ingeniously; all part of the complex code of etiquette[39] which needed to be followed pretty strictly if you were to visit the underworld unscathed.

Recognising that some sustenance was probably in order, Sara and I were now both eating protein bars washed down with Red Bull, whilst Johan and Lisl had ignored the tea and coffee and were by now quite determinedly stuck into the second bottle of ghostly Gewürztraminer.

"So, Zach, it must be, what, five hundred years?" Johan looked at me over his glass. "It was just before Lisl joined me I think... So that would make it around 1600."

"1601," I confirmed.

One of the perks of being the Angel of Memory is that I have a pretty good head for dates.

"Just after that little bit of bother we had with the Earl of Essex. You'd been here for about twelve years. The place was a little more..." I searched around

---

[39] "Dining out in the underworld is a tricky business for the visitor, as the consumption of food or drink, even if unwittingly, will instantly make it difficult or impossible for the visitor to leave the host's dwelling – an embarrassing situation all round! However, the rules governing behaviour are universal and a little charm goes a long way in dealing with what could otherwise be a tricky moment. Your host is honour bound to offer you sustenance, but if you decline, politely, but with grace and gentility, you should find this leads to minimal disturbance." *Debrett's Etiquette of the Underworld,* 1876

for an adjective which would describe the transformation which had taken place at Johan's without giving offence, "*basic* back then."

"That's my Lisl." Johan's rather gaunt face relaxed into a quick grin, taking in the floral cushions, mock candelabra table lamps and special little antimacassar things hanging off the armchairs for the TV remote controls. The only discordant note came from a pair of short-swords, mounted on a shield and hanging above the fireplace.

"I think her happiest moment in half a century came when the guy who started the *Betterware Catalogue* passed over and started up a little round in the boundary lands for old time's sake.

"Anyway, however good it is to see you, I'm pretty sure this isn't a social call." Johan sat back in his seat and slowly swirled the wine in its cut crystal glass. He looked up at me, with questions in his eyes. "We've heard some rumours, Belphegor's Hell-Beasts have been baying for blood on the other side of the Styx, and someone said that there are two humans, live ones, kidnapped and imprisoned in Eligor's stronghold."

I said nothing. I wanted to find out just how much Johan knew.

"And then," he continued, "only a few hours ago, the Wild Hunt was out, we heard them across the fields, riding hard along the banks of the Lethe." He put down his glass and looked straight at me. "They don't ride for sport; they ride to kill. They seek live prey, not the spectral flesh of border-landers."

As he spoke, he reached out towards me, touched my arm, and his hand passed right through me. "We have the appearance of solidity, but we're not flesh and blood. Not like you."

"We heard that two angels had been seen, entering at the Elysian Gate," Lisl spoke, looking first at her husband, and then at me and Sara.

"But there was no-one there," Sara said. "The place was deserted when we came through."

"Oh no," replied Lisl, "we always have a watcher, even though the border's not officially guarded. We take it in turns. But you wouldn't have seen us," and to demonstrate what she meant, she gradually melted away, every part of her slowly fading into nothingness. The last things to go were her startlingly blue eyes. She winked; then there was nothing.

"Just 'cos you can't see us, don't mean we aren't here." From out of nowhere came a sing-song, rather childish voice. Then there was a sort of extended wet fart sound which seemed to come from the edge of the room, nearest the door.

~ 107 ~

Then someone else spoke, from over by the window. "Angels think they know everything... but the ghasts and the spectres can still show them a thing or two." This voice sounded older and deeper.

There was a giggle and a sudden draft as the curtains began to billow out into the room; the window opening and banging closed several times in rapid succession. A pile of books flew one by one from the shelves, landing with a thud on the floor beside me. I looked up to see a vase of flowers was now appearing to float slowly and rather jerkily across the room, coming to rest on the table behind us. Lisl reappeared and went to stand behind Johan. She was not looking amused.

I was on my feet. "What the...? Johan, what's going on? Who else is here? This is no time for poltergeistery." I stood up and addressed the room. "Whoever you are, show yourselves like honest souls."

"Yeah, come on, guys. This isn't really the right time and place for a spook show. I told you to go to bed." As Johan spoke, the air seemed to wrinkle like a heat haze, and two figures slowly solidified. A young man and a girl. The girl had the same cornflower blue eyes as Lisl.

"Zach, Sara, meet our children. This is Heinrich," Johan gestured towards the youth standing at the window. He looked a bit sullen and was conspicuously examining his nails. "And Lottie." A little girl ran forward, head-butted Johan in the stomach and then hid herself behind her mother's skirts. She looked about six years old.

"I didn't know you had children?" I looked quizzically at Johan.

"They both died before I met you. Lottie caught pneumatic fever and passed just a few weeks before her sixth birthday. Heinrich died at sea. For a long time, Lisl and I did not speak of them." He looked down and a pained shadow of remembrance seemed to pass across his face.

"Talking about them, letting people know we had had children, and had lost them... It was just too hard. But, in the end, it was actually Lottie's death that was responsible for my profession. When she died, I was driven to seek the truth about the spirit world, to find out what I could about the hidden truths. I became an alchemist, an expert on the dark craft and the secrets of other worlds." Once again, he gave that wry smile. "In a way, you could say that she is responsible for making me what I am."

He reached for his daughter and pulled her towards him, ruffling her hair. The affection between them was tangible. "But even so, you two, it's bed time; we've a long day tomorrow. Particularly you, Heinrich." He nodded somewhat

~ 108 ~

curtly towards his son. "Now, say goodnight to our guests and do not come downstairs until breakfast," he said firmly.

The children murmured rather vaguely at us and trooped out.

"They weren't with you last time I came?"

"No, they both passed many years before I did and they were living with the other orphans on the far side of the boundary, in the Elysian Fields. It took a while for us to find them. When Lisl joined me, we dedicated our lives here to tracking them down, and for many years now we have been a family again."

He paused, and muttered, more to himself than to us, "Whatever that means…"

Johan looked out into the hallway, towards the stairs; we could all hear the muffled sounds of the children getting ready for bed. I could tell he was troubled about something, but he had always been a very private person and I hadn't seen him for a very long time. It didn't seem like a good idea to intrude.

"Still, I'm sorry they startled you. Now, where were we?"

"You were telling us about the rumours." Sara spoke softly, but there was an edge to her voice. I could tell she was getting a little frustrated. Like me, she was conscious of time passing. We needed to find out where Sophia and Alex were being held, and we had to establish just how much was known about our presence in the boundary lands.

"Ah yes. The rumours. It's been a long while since any of the living has been seen in these regions. Why don't you tell me exactly what is going on? And if we can, we'll help you." He turned to his wife, who nodded, giving us both a brief smile.

Between us, we brought Johan and Lisl up to speed. Whatever was bothering him, it clearly hadn't got in the way of his critical faculties, and within a few moments, they had the gist of why we were here and what we had to do.

"This all makes sense," said Lisl. "We don't really get much news about the realms of the living, but over the last few years, the atmosphere has been changing." She looked at her husband, who gave a nod in agreement. She continued, "Here on the boundary, we're supposed to be left in peace, this is a place for all souls, but we've noticed a lot more activity from the dark side." She paused and looked at Sara, as if weighing her up. "Do you know about the defections? The angels who have joined the Fallen?"

We both looked startled. Manny and K had implied that this was some big secret. They hadn't wanted to even let me in on it – and yet here were two ex-humans, who seemed to be completely in the know.

~ 109 ~

"Yeah, we know," I murmured, not wanting to make a big deal about it.

Sara added, in her most official sounding voice, "That's classified. We are not authorised to discuss it."

Johan shook his head and gave a wry smile. "Classified for you maybe, but out here they make a big song and dance about it. When an angel joins the Fallen, there's always a huge celebration over in the fifth circle – and the bells have been ringing overtime the last twelve months or so. What did we calculate, Lisl? Twelve Guardians and a couple of Messengers?"

"Yes," she replied, "and there was talk that one of the cherubim had fallen too, but I'm not sure if that was just gossip."

"It was actually thirteen Guardians," I told them, "and yes, we lost one of the cherubim as well." Before I could say more, Sara was out of her seat, and right in my face.

"What do you think you're doing?" she hissed at me. "I just told you that's classified. We do not discuss this," she lowered her voice so only I could hear her, "with these... ex-humans. This is celestial business. Have you forgotten who you are?"

I caught Johan's eye and glanced towards the window. He and Lisl moved away and I took a step back, leant against the door frame and folded my arms.

"Sara, these 'ex-humans' are my friends. Johan was one of the best associates the Agency ever had. And I bet you he knows more about Eligor than any other soul in the universe. They've invited us into their home, and have offered to help us, even though there is clearly something going on that's upsetting them." Sara looked away at this; she even had the grace to look a little shamefaced.

"When it comes to trust and confidence, I would rather have Johan on my side than your Potestas friend Nat. Any day. And if you don't like it, you know what you can do." I pushed away from the doorframe and walked past her towards the window, joining Johan and Lisl who were now seated back at the table, talking quietly.

When you're out in the field, you learn to trust your instincts and sometimes you just don't play it by the book.

I knew Sara was inexperienced, but her knee-jerk reaction had pissed me off. What was the point in dissembling, or coming over all official and superior, when they clearly knew more than we did? We needed to find out everything Johan and Lisl could tell us, and if that meant breaking a few protocols, well, so be it.

~ 110 ~

"So politically, the balance of power is wavering?" Johan had got to the heart of the matter immediately.

"Yeah," I replied, "and if we want to start pushing it back in the right direction, we need to find Alex and Sophia whilst they are still compos mentis and take them back to the land of the living."

"Please tell us what you know." Sara had walked over to join us. She had regained her composure and now spoke calmly again. She didn't actually apologise, but before taking her place at the table, she looked at first Lisl and then Johan, who both nodded. As she sat, she bent forward, taking the map from the side pocket of my kitbag.

"Where do you think they've been taken?"

Johan and Lisl pored over the map.

"Well, we heard that the humans had been taken to Eligor's stronghold. That's here." Lisl indicated an isthmus of land, bordered by the Stygian Lake at one end and the rivers Styx and Phlegathon to the left and right sides.

"It's not far from the Medusa Gate; on the outskirts of Dis." Dis was the largest city in the underworld, home of demons and monsters and a refuge for some of the more flamboyant of the Fallen Angels. I took a good look at the map. The place that Lisl was pointing to was on a curve in the River Styx; on the other side of the riverbank were the first two circles of the Inferno, Limbo and – most encouragingly - the road to the Avernus gateway.

If we could get Alex and Sophia out, we would only be a few hours from the border. I was far better acquainted with the lands on that side of the Inferno than the regions we would need to travel through to reach Eligor's stronghold. If we were going to get there quickly, we would need to move out of the boundary lands into the heart of the Inferno - and that was going to be no picnic.

"Do you know anything about how well they're being guarded? Is Eligor's place fortified, or is it more of a country mansion?" Sara's question was a good one; we needed to get an idea of what we were up against if we were to develop any kind of plan.

"The strongholds of the Archdukes of Hell are all well-guarded," answered Johan. "And if the stories about the baying of the Hell-Beasts are true, Belphegor has joined forces with the Arch-Duke. I heard that they've been let loose to roam freely along the banks of the Styx. They can't hurt the Fallen or the souls of the dead who are coming through from Avernus, but they are quite capable of ripping any living body to shreds within seconds."

"Well, I reckon we can find a way round the Hell-Beasts, they may be ugly and unpleasant, but they're not very bright." I refused to sound downhearted. "We just need to find a way into the strong-hold."

"Easier said than done," Johan continued. "Don't forget that Eligor commands sixty legions of the Fallen and my guess is that the palace will be under constant guard." He looked up at me. "You won't be able to fight your way in, and I doubt that you'd be able to get in through the normal entrances via trickery or guile either. Eligor's too smart for that."

I was reminded of Raphael's words as we were leaving the HTC. Why was everyone so keen to point out how impossible this was all going to be?

"Look," said Sara, "I don't think there is any point trying to make detailed plans now. We don't even know how we're going to get through the Inferno, let alone break into Eligor's dungeons." She was running her finger over the map. "We'd originally thought that we would go along by the side of the Lethe, here... then circle round the Lake of Fire.[40]" Her fingers traced out the route as we watched her. "Then, we cut straight through the ditches of Malebolge and in at the Medusa Gate." She stared up at Johan. "Can you think of a better plan?"

"Hmm..." Johan pondered. Her plan still seemed to me to be the best one, but I was keen to hear what my old comrade would say.

"Keeping hard by the bank of the Lethe is probably a good idea. You should get protection from the waters – it will be more difficult for Eligor and his minions to detect you if you keep close to the vapours of oblivion and the Lake of Fire should give you some protection as well. There's so much spiritual energy discharged around that place that you may not show up on the radar. What do you think, Lisl?" Johan looked questioningly at his wife.

"Well, the Lake of Fire's pretty grim. I wouldn't want to go back there. I wouldn't want anyone to have to go through that again." She looked at her husband, and we could both see tears starting to form in her eyes.

She blinked and wiped them away with the back of her hand. "But I think you're right," she continued. "Once they're away from the Lethe, they need to keep to the places where the spiritual energy is strongest. It won't be easy, but I think it's their best shot."

---

[40] "On entry into the underworld, all souls other than those who have priority purity passes must journey across the Lake of Fire, where they will present themselves for judgement. Souls requiring redemption will be transported to their place of punishment or penitence, where they will serve their allotted sentence. Those souls who have reached the required levels of benevolence will be couriered to their preferred location within the afterlife. Any soul which is judged to be beyond redemption will be devoured." *A Guide to the Three Realms*, 1945

I'd had enough. I wasn't going to ignore their distress any more.

"Lisl, what is it? It's bloody obvious that there's something bothering you." I went over to the old woman, and put my hand gently on her shoulder. "We've just turned up out of the blue this evening, and we're so grateful to you for taking us in." I looked at both of them and made sure Johan held my stare.

"If we'd stayed out there, who knows how long it would have been before the hunt picked up our scent. I don't want to pry, but what's going on – and is there anything we can do to help you?"

Johan looked at Lisl and she gave a faint, almost imperceptible nod.

"It's Heinrich," said Johan. "He's fed up of this." He waved his hand dismissively, taking in the cottage the garden and village beyond. "He wants to leave us. To put it bluntly, he wants another life." At Johan's words, Lisl gave a small shudder and her tears began to flow more strongly this time. I saw Sara reach over and take her hand. Lisl grasped it and did not let go.

I looked over at Sara, who was comforting Lisl, and then back at Johan, who continued, "He never was an easy child. Always full of questions, challenging everything, wanted to run before he could walk. He was bright. Could argue the toss with anyone. And always wanted his own way. I wanted him to join me in the business, but he would have none of it. Instead, he was apprenticed to a sea captain just after his fifteenth birthday." Johan looked at his wife.

"He wanted to see the world," said Lisl, "to travel. To have adventures."

Johan was having trouble keeping his voice strong. "The only adventure he had was to the bottom of the ocean. His ship ran aground on his first voyage; he was dead before he reached sixteen."

"But you found him." Sara looked up at Lisl. "You and Johan found him and Lottie, and you got your family back."

"Yes, and Lottie is so young, she's quite happy, playing with the other children, running wild in the woods. She doesn't care that she will never grow up. Never be anything but a little girl. But Heinrich is different." Lisl took her hand away from Sara's and went to stand beside her husband.

"Heinrich wants another chance. He wants to grow up, see the world, fall in love." She gently touched her husband's cheek, catching a tear, and wiping it smoothly away.

"He wants the chance to have a full life. The sort of life we had." She turned to me. "Zach, he goes with my blessing, however hard it is, but Johan... he

~ 113 ~

can't deal with it. If Heinrich goes, we lose him forever. He will drink the waters of Lethe and enter another body.

"And when he returns here, he won't know us. We lost him before, but this time it will be forever."

"Yes. And he wants to do it on bloody reality TV." Johan was angry now, shouting the last three words. He pulled away from Lisl and began to pace the room. "The whole of the after world will watch him. Will see us exposing our grief and looking like fools. I can't do it, Lisl. I just can't."

And with that, Johan walked from the room, slamming the door behind him. Lisl collapsed on the sofa.

"I'm sorry, but you have completely lost me... what is he talking about?" I was confused. "Reality TV?"

To my surprise, Sara didn't seem to be quite as confused as I was about this. "I think I may know what all this is about," she said, picking up a magazine from the table, and turning a couple of pages to reveal a picture of two grinning angels and a photo montage of football players, rock stars, wealthy businessmen and actors. At the bottom of the page was a little black and white picture showing a small, dirty and rather bedraggled child. Stamped across her face was the words 'fickle finger of fate'.

"What is this?" I asked – the pictures meant nothing to me, and I was more than a tad disturbed by the picture of the little girl.

"*This is your next life,*" replied Sara. "It's a reality TV programme that's got really big in the celestial realms. Basically, six contestants compete for the prize of a celebrity reincarnation. Each week, there's the chance to be born into a life of success or privilege. The winner gets the top prize, the next four contestants just get something random, but each week one poor soul gets the booby prize – the 'fickle finger of fate' sends them into their new life as one of the dispossessed and the disadvantaged."

"Is this for real?" I was gobsmacked. "Since when has reincarnation been material for entertainment?"

"Well, you know I think the whole reincarnation thing is a bit... well... creepy. And I think that quite a few people think that the idea of a show based on celebrity future lives is a bit tasteless, but K actually thinks it's a good thing." Sara had her official head back on. "The show's incredibly popular, and that helps keep people entertained, which in turn keeps them quiet, which we really need during these difficult times." She was on a roll.

"It's also helped drive a positive surge in overall reincarnation rates – which is a priority area for the Efficiency and Reform group. The increased demand on celestial services has been a worrying trend for some time, and the more souls we can find who are prepared to head back to the terrestrial realms, the better it is and the less drain there is on our resources."

Lisl nodded. "That's what Johan says. Still, you can't get away from the fact that it's incredibly popular. Heinrich has been a huge fan since it started."

"Johan and I don't really watch it. We prefer a good book to be honest, but when Heinrich told us that he'd been offered a slot on the show we've seen it a couple of times and I must admit that Araton and Dalquiel[41] are actually not bad, although I'm still not sure which one's which."

"Arat's the one with the spiky hair," said Sara.

"So when's this happening?" I asked.

"Tomorrow," replied Lisl. "We heard last week that Heinrich had been selected. They ask you for preferences when you apply. You know, do you want to be a film-star, or a model, a basket-ball star or a President... that sort of thing. He said he wanted to be an explorer, and of course, when he found out that the top prize for tomorrow is to be reincarnated as the first human to walk on Mars, Heinrich could hardly contain himself." She got up and went to the window, through which we could just make out her husband, still pacing furiously around the bottom of the garden.

"Johan's tried to forbid him, but Heinrich is actually five hundred and thirty-five years old, so legally he can make these decisions for himself. The TV Company is sending a chariot round here tomorrow at 09.00."

Sara and I looked aghast "So tonight..." I began.

"So tonight," Lisl completed, "is Heinrich's last night with us. Whatever happens, he won't be coming home with us. As of tomorrow night, his new life will have begun."

We didn't know what to say, then, in the silence, I heard a sound which chilled me to my core. Through the window came the faint sound of a hunting horn. It echoed around the room, faded out, and then it came again, louder this time. We could hear the distant baying of hounds and the jingle of bridles.

As Sara and I looked at each other in panic, Johan burst through the door, wild-eyed and terrified. "It's the hunt," he shouted, "the Wild Hunt is upon us."

---

[41] "The Angels Araton and Dalquiel, otherwise known as Arat and Dal are two of the most popular personalities in Celestial Broadcasting. They have won the award for most entertaining performance on a celestial channel for the last two hundred years." *The Angels' Year Book*, 2001

~ *Chapter Seventeen* ~

Lisl said nothing, but turned and ran into the hallway, her thoughts clearly with Heinrich and Lottie who were asleep in the rooms above us.

Sara swore under her breath and reached into her kitbag, searching for something.

I instantly moved over to Johan and tried to grab his shoulder, but my fingers went straight through him.

"Calm down, Johan, it'll be ok. We're leaving". I swiftly looked across at Sara, who to my astonishment had pulled out a military issue crossbow and was calmly and efficiently assembling it. That angel never ceased to astound me.

The horn sounded again, closer this time.

Her eyes met mine and she nodded almost imperceptibly towards the garden. Turning back towards Johan, she said gently: "We're sorry to have brought this upon you, particularly tonight of all nights. We'll go now and the hunt will follow us." She'd worked fast and had finished her task; carefully placing the crossbow down on the table whilst she checked her arrows, their golden tips bright and deadly in the lamplight.

"Come on, Zach, let's go." Sara began to move towards the back of the house. "We'll head out that way and with any luck they'll pick up our scent and ignore this place completely."

Lisl came into the room, her face grey and her eyes full of panic. She was muttering under her breath, her fingers clasping the cross she wore around her neck as if seeking reassurance. At first I couldn't make out what she was saying, but then I realised she was praying in her mother tongue. "*Lieve God, behouden en ons redden.* (Dear God, protect us and save us.) *Lieve God, behouden en ons redden. Lieve God behouden en ons redden.*"

Johan put his arm round her and held her tight. He seemed to take strength from her fear, and it was with his usual considered calm that he now spoke.

"There is another way." He looked at me. "The old wounded rabbit bluff. It worked the last time; I can't see that it won't work now."

"Yes." I'd been hoping that he'd say this, but it was going to be incredibly risky and I would never have asked it of him. I turned towards him. "Are you prepared to play your part?"

He nodded, and bending to kiss the top of his wife's head, he unfolded her from his arms and came towards me.

I called for Sara, and quickly outlined the strategy. Within seconds, we were in place. Operation Wounded Rabbit had begun. The idea was simple and it was a plan I relished.

Lisl had called out to the Heavens for protection. And her prayers would be heard.

Ignoring the call of the hunting horn, which was becoming increasingly intrusive as the hunt careered towards us, I focused my energies upon the need to protect this family and to see justice done. I felt myself leaving behind the coarse trappings of my corporeal body and experienced the growing sense of power and exultation as celestial fire burned through my veins and the power of divine justice, vested in me and mine to administer, possessed me.

Once again, I was the Angel Zachriel, albeit a pocket sized version. Given the size of the rooms in the cottage, I had deliberately not assumed my full height, but even so, my wing-tips brushed the ceiling and I dared not fully alate.

The instant my corpus was empty, Johan hastened towards it and placed his hands upon its cold and empty shoulders. This bit was always a bit creepy. Johan pushed himself against and into, my vacant body. With each push, a little bit of him was gone, and very soon, Johan had vanished, and my corpus was reanimated.

The me-Johan got up and stretched. It bent its knees, reached out its arms, put its fingers together and cracked its knuckles with relish. It turned to me and winked. "You're in good shape, Zach. I haven't felt this sprightly in a long while."

"Look after it, mate." I gave a short glance at the corpus which had been my companion now for so many years. "It's been mine for a long time, and I am actually quite fond of it."

"Don't worry; I'll look after it like it's my own."

"That's what I'm afraid of."

We grinned conspiratorially. In his day, Johan had been fearless, one might even have said reckless, and on more than one occasion had risked life and limb on behalf of the Agency. There was one time in Northumberland when he had been injured so badly... but that's another story.

"Right," said the me-Johan, walking to the wall and taking down one of the rather vicious looking short swords displayed artfully above the fireplace. "Lisl, you must stay here. Do not let anyone in. They can ride through the garden, they can trash it if they want to, but they can't enter this house without your permission. Do you understand?"

Lisl nodded. The me-Johan secured the sword in his belt and turned to Sara. "Are you ready?"

Sara's only answer was to grab her crossbow, check her arrows and dip her head towards the door. I could tell she was eager to be off.

"Just one more thing." I looked hard at both of them. "There can be no survivors. You know that don't you?" They both stared back at me without flinching. "When we are through with our business tonight, we must have destroyed them all; we can't risk any news getting back to Eligor. And that includes the lovely Lady Enepsigos."

At the doorway they turned. Sara looked straight at me, her beautiful face set hard and determined and the light of battle in her eyes. "Good luck and God speed, Angel Zachriel."

I blew her a kiss. "Good luck and God speed, Angel Sarandiel. We'll be back here safe and well in time for breakfast."

Next minute, they were on their way, running low across the garden, into the woods, heading towards the path that led out of the village.

They had gone not a moment too soon. As Sara disappeared beneath the trees, the horn sounded again, and within seconds the dog-things surged out of the woodland and onto the lawn.

Their heads were down seeking the scent of their quarry and their blood was up. With teeth bared for the attack and eyes reddened with blood-lust, the pack cast to left and right, following our tracks right up to the back door.

Lisl quivered with fear as one of the beasts hurled itself against the wood and their howling intensified as they smelled traces of the flesh they had been promised. Above the noise of the pack, came a cry from upstairs. Lottie had woken up.

"Go to her," I told the terrified Lisl. "And Johan's right, they can't actually come in if you don't invite them. Just go to the children. All will be fine. I promise."

I could see she didn't believe me, but she was glad to put what distance she could between herself and the Wild Hunt. She ran upstairs and I heard a door open and shut. She was with Lottie and I was now free to play my part in the proceedings.

Another howl from the garden told me that the pack had picked up the new trail and as the dogs streamed back into the woodlands, the riders emerged, with the demon Enepsigos[42] leading the way.

As she came out of the trees, she reined in her mount. The horse slowed to a walk as she crossed the lawn, stopping just outside the window of the room where, but a few hours ago, Lisl and Johan had been sitting together. It shook its head temperamentally and whinnied; instantly Enepsigos pulled out her crop and hit the beast sharply across its muzzle. Its head went down mutinously, but it made no more sounds.

Behind her, the rest of the hunt assembled. Five riders now, their horns and antlers silhouetted against the sky, flecks of foam visible around the mouths of their horses, which stamped and whinnied until, following the example of their mistress, the other hunters used their whips to bring silence.

"I know you are in there, ghast or spectre, ghost or phantom... I sense your presence still." Enepsigos urged her horse forward, her voice harsh and her anger barely controlled.

"Did you think you could conceal the angels from me? How dare you be so arrogant? And so stupid. You may be dead, but you can still feel pain... and I can promise you pain beyond anything you have imagined."

I just hoped that Lisl remembered what Johan had told her. Despite her threats, Enepsigos could do nothing unless Lisl actually asked her over the threshold.

"My Lady, the pack has moved on," said one of the hunters as he rode up to the demon. He bowed his head, his antlers nearly touching his horse's ears as he abased himself. "My Lady, the scent is fresh; it continues over here." He pointed in the direction that Sara and the me-Johan had taken. "Back into the woods, but heading towards Erebus."

---

[42] "The Demon Queen Enepsigos is a two-headed huntress who used to live on the moon until the great King Solomon bound her and cast her into Hell when she told him his temple would collapse. She has the powers of prophesy and shape-shifting and has absolutely no sense of humour." *Know your enemy – The Angels' Guide to the Legions of the Fallen,* 1987

She turned one of her heads in the direction he pointed, the other remained staring fixedly at the cottage. Could she sense me? Or was the presence of Lisl and the two children strong enough to confuse her.

"How fresh is the scent?" She turned both heads towards her huntsman.

"Just minutes, my Lady. We will have them. I know it."

"And when we do, you will be rewarded." She reached over towards the man, who tried not to flinch as her scaly hand cupped his face, one finger gently running down his cheek in the mockery of a lover's caress. "But if you fail... remember this," and instantly her hand ceased its stroking and the sharp talons ripped smoothly through his flesh.

She raised her fingers first to one mouth, then the other and licked them with surprising delicacy. Then she laughed and, turning her horse towards the forest, moved away from the house. As she neared the bottom of the garden, she stopped to call back over her shoulder.

"Don't think you have escaped that easily, spectre. I will not forget this place. You and I have unfinished business and don't you dare forget it." And with that she brought her whip down hard on her horse's flank and raised the hunting horn to her lips.

The hunt following behind her, and with the sound of the horn still echoing in the darkness, she put her horse to the fence at the bottom of the garden, was over it in one clear stride and soon she and the rest of them had gone, swallowed up into the black depths of the forest.

There was no sound from within the house. Good girl, I thought proudly. Lisl had kept her head. The game was afoot and it was my turn now.

~ *Chapter Eighteen* ~

As soon as the last horse had vanished into the forest, I left the house and alated. As my wings opened behind me, I leapt into the air, growing larger and stronger as I gained altitude. I felt no fear. There was no fear. I was an Angel of Justice, responding to a call for divine help and protection. I was an Angel of Justice and the vengeance of the Lord was mine.

I flew upwards, high, high above the woodland, but always keeping my eyes fixed upon the tree tops, looking out for the spot that Johan had described, the place where, with any luck, he and Sara were baiting the trap with the wounded rabbit.

As I flew, I thought of Sophia, of Alex, captured, imprisoned and subject to who knew what Infernal tortures at Eligor's hands. I thought of Kathryn and her terrible and lonely death and of the untold people whose lives would be destroyed if we did not succeed.

With every thought, my power increased, my strength burgeoned within me and I felt the burning certainty of divine justice consume me. There would be no question of mercy this time. Enepsigos was no Isra, she was no misguided fool, she was a double-headed bitch queen from Hell and she deserved every single thing that was coming her way.

And as for me, the Angel Zachriel, I was no longer one being, no longer a single angel setting out on a foolhardy mission to fight a demon and the Wild Hunt. I was the power and the principalities, the virtues and the dominions. They were now embodied within me and I was their instrument. This was what I lived for, and oh my Lord, how I had missed it.

I circled, looking out for a clearing about half a mile away from the cottage, and concealed from the road. I flew down, skimming the tree-tops and as I did so, the sounds of the hunt filtered up to me.

The baying of the dog-things was incessant now. The horn sounded, again, and then again, but this time a different note. I heard the sound of horses' hooves, pounding the forest floor. And there it was.

The clearing.

There was no sign of Sara, and on the floor, spread-eagled as though it had fallen, was my body. The me-Johan just lay there, motionless and un-protesting as the dogs poured into the clearing and the horses came to a standstill, forming a semi-circle around it.

Three of the dogs were on the body, ripping at the jacket and trousers, trying to get to the sweetness of the flesh below, but when Enepsigos saw this, she uttered just one word of command and the beasts fell back, their hackles up and teeth bared, growling at the rest of the pack. They had been forbidden the feast, but they would not give up their prey lightly to any of the others.

"Only one angel?" Enepsigos sounded surprised, and looked round her, casting to left and right, trying to see into the shadows beneath the trees. She gestured to the Minotaur and one of the antlered huntsmen, who dismounted and moved into the bushes, beginning to search for traces of Sara.

The huntsman with the disfigured face moved hesitantly towards her. "My Lady, please remember, we couldn't tell if it was one or two angels who had entered through the gateway… the tracks weren't clear, so maybe this," and he nodded towards the still, silent body lying in the centre of the clearing, "is the only one."

Enepsigos shook her heads at this. "Our intelligence said otherwise… we were certain there were two of them."

She paused, saying almost to herself, "It was a foolhardy mission by anyone's standards, but to send just one…" One head gave a faint smile, whilst the other gave a slight, disbelieving shake.

"Just one angel against the might of the Fallen." She laughed. "Lord Kemuel's arrogance grows surpassing strong. One would think he was ready to join us, his pride is so great."

By this time, the Minotaur had finished his searching and had now returned to the clearing. He went up to his mistress and bowed low saying gruffly, "Nothing, my Lady; no sign of anything but this one."

"Well you clearly have not looked hard enough. Look deeper, search further. There must be another one and we need to find where it is hiding."

He gave a slight bow, and went back in to the forest.

Of the antlered huntsman, there was no sign.

"Let's take a look at this angel." The demon queen gestured to the huntsman with a single horn. "You, turn him over. Let's gaze for a while upon his *angelic countenance.*"

She said the last words with a sneer and urged her horse forwards towards my corpus. The huntsman dismounted. He grabbed clumsily at the body and turned it over none too gently onto its back.

I looked down at the familiar form. Its eyes were closed and its mouth hung vacantly open. There was a large and livid bruise upon its temples, and its left leg was stretched out at an odd angle, like it had been broken. It was covered with cuts and scratches. The short sword was still stuck, uselessly, in its belt.

"Is it dead?"

"No, mistress, see, the chest moves. It seems stunned, but it still breaths."

"Aah... so the angel is still alive..."

She looked down at the body, musingly.

"You know, I have never tasted angel flesh. They say that it must be eaten whilst the spirit remains within the corporeal form. Once that has left, of course, the corpse is simply human. And that is far too common a taste to be considered a delicacy.

"Before we kill him, I must try this flesh and drink this blood." As she spoke, she saw the remaining huntsman move towards the body, hunger and desire gleaming in their eyes.

"And what do you think you are doing, churl? You may eat when he is dead. The flesh of a living angel is not for the likes of you."

At this, she dismounted, and still carrying her whip, walked towards the body, hitting out at the dog-things as they milled around her and, clearing a space, she bent over my poor corpus and took the sword from its belt. She gave it a single, contemptuous glance and hurled it into the bushes on the edge of the clearing. Returning her attention to the main event, she bent forwards, using the steel point at the end of her whip to push aside my jacket and then rip open my shirt.

The demon stared down at me contemplatively. "The heart, I think... Yes, the still beating heart of a living angel. That will be a taste to savour." As she spoke, she ran the nail of the forefinger of her left hand across my now exposed chest, circling the area around my heart, drawing blood and going deeper and deeper with each revolution.

Drawn to the smell of the blood, the dog-things gathered round her, some of them beginning to whimper and yelp in frustration. They pushed in to her, coming closer and closer until she lashed out at them with the whip, which she still held in her right hand. And now the blood-lust was upon her and nothing could distract her from her prey. She was completely engrossed in my body. Sitting astride me now, she lifted her finger to her mouth and sucked the blood greedily, running her finger round the edge of her teeth and smearing the crimson on her pallid lips. Then she lowered her other head to my chest and began licking and lapping at the wounds she had made.

I gazed around me, looking deep into the forest.

It was nearly time.

It had begun.

As I watched, the huntsman with the single horn collapsed silently on to the forest floor, a golden arrow piercing his chest; before the others had chance to raise a warning, two more arrows had found their homes.

I looked into the trees, and there was Sara, almost completely concealed and sitting securely upon the spreading branches of an ancient oak tree, her crossbow loaded, and a triumphant smile upon her face.

I raised a questioning eyebrow and she held up her hand.

Five fingers.

All the huntsmen were dead. She had played her part to perfection.

Now it was my turn.

With what I couldn't help but notice was a remarkably smooth landing, I came to rest in the clearing. Sensing my presence, the demon raised her eyes from the corpus and stared straight into mine.

Fury followed surprise and then mingled with terror in her eyes.

"Enepsigos, daughter of darkness, you are foul in my sight."

The full force of my anger burned livid within me, and the power of my rage hit her like a lightning bolt. She shuddered at the force, knocked backwards into a crumpled heap by the side of my body.

As she fell, I caught sight of the wound on my poor mangled body, open and raw. I could see my heart, exposed now to the open air, still valiantly pumping my life's blood, but growing weaker with each second.

I had taken my eyes off the demon, and she had rallied. She stood facing me now, teeth and talons bared, livid crimson droplets of my blood still fresh upon her lips.

"And you taste good, Angel." She smiled at me. "Perhaps I will just finish what I started."

Swiftly, she bent down towards my body, her fingers bunched together and aimed at my heart.

But I had regained my composure. Sure, I liked my corpus, but it meant absolutely nothing compared to my desire to see justice done and to send this bitch-queen to the deepest, darkest pit of Hell for all eternity.

"You are foul in my sight," I repeated.

I knew the words, I knew the ritual.

I grew taller, stronger, towering now above the tallest trees. My power was eternal and immense. I could touch the stars and command the Heavens.

"You are foul in my sight." My voice was like thunder.

I stretched out my hand and the demon was raised from the ground, pulled upwards towards me, kicking and screaming as she felt my power and was unable to resist it.

"No... You... Will... not. You ...cannot." She screamed and spat at me; a mix of saliva and my heart's blood hit me on the cheek. I ignored it.

"I am Enepsigos. I am the huntress. I am the queen of the damned. You will not do this."

I felt the force of her will roll out towards me like a tsunami. But what harm can a tsunami do to the eternal power of the universe? It washed over me, its waves retreated. And she went limp.

"You are foul in my sight."

I had done it.

Like King Solomon before me, I summoned a triple chain to bind her, but unlike Solomon's; my chain would be truly unbreakable. His had broken when the prophecy Enepsigos had made had come to pass and the temple of Solomon had crumbled into dust. My chain was forged from adamantine and tempered in the deepest fires of the Inferno. It would not break.

I bound her, hand and foot and as I secured the final link within the chain, she turned to face me.

"Beware, Angel, I can see what you cannot see.
You cannot see what is staring right at you.
You always forgive but will not be forgiven.
You will not destroy what is going to destroy you.
And when you are destroyed, my chains will break and I will devour you."

Whatever.

Demons always say stuff like that.

I thrust her from me and saw her fall, the chains dragging her down through the soil beneath, down to the deepest dungeons in the prison of Tartarus, deep below the surface, where she would now remain for all eternity.

The earth closed up over her head and as it did so, I started to feel the power of divine justice begin to ebb away from me.

I was standing in the clearing and there appeared to be no sign of the dog-things or the horses. I looked down at my sad and sorry, bruised and battered corpus. Sara was kneeling beside it, her hands held just above the surface of my body. She had a look of complete concentration on her face and I decided to say nothing to disturb her.

As I watched, the wounds began to heal, my breathing deepened and colour gradually returned to my skin. I really had gone quite green about the gills.

Then, one eyelid flickered, and then the other. The eyes opened, and I saw Johan's compassionate gaze staring at me from my own so-familiar face.

"It's all okay, Zach. All systems are go in here, believe me. I told you I'd look after it."

I said nothing.

Me-Johan sat up. "We did take a bit of a mangling, but we had to make the wounded rabbit believable."

I nodded.

"I'm going to vacate the property, if that's alright with you?"

I watched as Johan emerged from my corpus and gave himself a bit of a shakedown.

As he did so, Sara got to her feet, brushing her hands together, before wiping them down the sides of her trousers.

"All done, your leg might tingle a bit when you first walk on it, but the bones are absolutely solid. You'll have a scar on your chest though. Not much I could do about that."

She looked at me.

"Another centimetre and this corpus would have had it. She nearly had your heart in her hands you know. Bitch. What did you do with her?"

"Triple-binding in eternal chains and flung in to Tartarus."

"Good one." Sara gave my foot a gentle nudge with her boot. "Come on, you had better get back in the saddle. We need to get home and let Lisl know everything's okay."

I felt a strange reluctance to re-enter my corpus. Not so much because I knew I had come so close to losing it, more because the image of Enepsigos sitting astride me trying to eat the heart out of my body was taking a long time to go away. I was worried it might have polluted me in some way and I was putting off the moment when I would find out if it all felt the same.

"Yes, come on, Zach," urged Johan, "we must be getting on." His face fell as he remembered what was going to happen that morning. "I only have a few more hours to spend with Heinrich."

Thinking about Johan's troubles put my slight qualms about my corpus into perspective, and once I was safely inside, I was relieved to discover that it was all fine and dandy – in fact the slight twinge in my left knee that I'd had since my days in Bosnia seemed to have vanished completely.

Sara had already disposed of the Minotaur and the guy with antlers. We carried the bodies of the other three huntsmen to the river and hurled them into the Lethe. They would never be found there.

Johan said that the horses had scarpered as soon as I had arrived in the clearing in my full-on celestial manifestation and they'd sussed that no-one was watching out for them.

I was a bit worried about this, because a horse roaming freely with a saddle, bridle, reins and no rider was unlikely to go unnoticed even in the boundary lands. But it turned out that this was no problem; Sara said she'd rounded them all up as they entered the forest and had taken their gear and dumped it in the river before setting them free again.

Johan said that the dog-things had hung around for a bit longer. We could see where they'd had a go at the bodies of the huntsmen, which was a bit disgusting, but in the end, they too had all run off into the forest. I wasn't too worried about them; there are hundreds of creatures like that roaming wild in the boundary lands; a few more wasn't going to raise any eyebrows.

There was now almost no trace of the events that had taken place in the clearing; we had retrieved the short sword from the place in the undergrowth where Enepsigos had thrown it and apart from a few broken branches and the odd spot of blood, Johan and Sara said it looked exactly as it had when they had found it and set up the whole 'wounded rabbit' routine.

We had taken a big risk, and we had pulled it off. The hunt was destroyed and we had dispatched one of Eligor's most powerful demons to the depths of Hell.

Sara and Johan had played a blinder, and secretly, I felt I hadn't been too shabby either; as we walked back towards Johan's cottage I felt more positive than I would have believed possible.

In the east, the sky was brightening. Night was over and the first battle had been won.

~ *Chapter Nineteen* ~

Johan had gone on ahead of us as he was keen to spend as much time as he could with his soon to be departing son. Sara and I walked a tad more slowly, enjoying a gentle stroll through the still moon-lit forest.

When we got back to the cottage, all was silent. Johan had gone upstairs to be with Lisl and the children, so Sara and I headed into the kitchen, where we thought we could talk without disturbing the family above us, and decided to try and get in touch with Manny.

He answered on the third ring. The line was not good; there was always a lot of interference when you called across dimensions and I had to stand right by the kitchen window to get any kind of signal at all, but we could just about hear each other.

I gave him a quick update, telling him about our reunion with Johan and Lisl and our two encounters with Enepsigos and the Wild Hunt. He sent his best wishes to his old associate but although he was pleased to hear that we had managed to consign the Hell-Queen to the pits of Tartarus, I could tell that he really wasn't happy that we had been tracked down within hours of crossing the boundary.

"The only way they could have got onto you so quickly is if they had inside intelligence. Eligor would've been expecting you to go in via the Avernus Gate, but from what you say, they were onto you almost as soon as you crossed the boundary from the Elysian Fields. Who else knew your plans?" he demanded.

"No-one," I replied. "Unless you count Raphael." I told Manny that we had called into the HTC on our travels, and that we had briefly met up with Sara's old mentor, but it seemed absurd to even consider the Archangel capable of giving away our plans.

"Hmm… well, I don't like it." Manny was clearly unsettled. "The reason we sent in such a small force was to keep you under their radar. If we'd have suspected they were going to sniff you out the minute you crossed the border, we might as well have dispatched a battalion of the Potestas and had done with it. This was supposed to be a stealth mission; enter, secure the target and leave - but within six hours of being there, you've destroyed the Wild Hunt and totalled one of Eligor's most trusted generals; not exactly activities which will go unnoticed."

"But we cleared up the scene… no-one would know what went on there," I protested.

"Yes, I'm sure you did, but I am also pretty sure that Eligor will be expecting regular status updates from Enepsigos, and when he doesn't get one, he will know immediately that something is wrong."

I had the phone on loud speaker and at these words I stole a quick look towards Sara. I could see from the expression on her face that the elation we had both experienced as a result of the successful execution of 'Operation Wounded Rabbit' was beginning to ebb away - and fast.

"You need to get out of there." Manny was insistent. "And you need to find a way of doing it that leaves no tracks.

"The one advantage you have is that at the moment, no-one knows for sure exactly where you are. Eligor is bound to send out search parties and you need to make damn certain that they can't follow your trail."

Recognising Manny's concerns, I outlined to him our plans for the next stage of our journey; to stick close to the banks of the Lethe, heading towards the Lake of Fire, where we could use the vast quantities of spiritual energies unleashed there as a cloak to hide our emanations until we reached Malebolge[43]. From there, we would be able to use the cover of the ditches to head straight towards the Medusa Gate and Eligor's stronghold.

This seemed to calm Manny down a bit; he accepted that the plan would probably give us our best chance of avoiding further detection. It was clear that his main preoccupation was how we could get away from Johan's without

---

[43] "Malebolge is the eighth circle of Hell and has a reputation for being one of the most violently horrific areas of special interest within the Inferno. Fraudsters, hypocrites, extortionists, seducers, thieves and blackmailers feature prominently in the area's roll call, each undergoing specific and unpleasant punishment within the sunken ditches that make up the majority of the area's topography. Well worth a visit if you have a strong stomach and enjoy seeing good old fashioned retribution being carried out in its most classic setting." *Lonely Planet Guide to the Inferno*, 1997

leaving a trail. He wanted there to be no trace of us in the area at all – so it would be all the more difficult for the trackers he was certain Eligor would send after us when he got no news from Enepsigos, to find us and run us to ground.

As we had been talking, I had started to think of a way we could do this, and if I could get it to work it would also shave hours off our travelling time. But I needed some time to think it through and it would all depend on Johan and Lisl's co-operation.

I roughly sketched out my idea to Manny, who agreed, fairly reluctantly, to let me try it. He was about to end the call, when I remembered something.

"Hang on, Manny; did you manage to get hold of the Katibeen? Any news on what actually happened at Kathryn's flat?"

For a second, the line was quiet.

"Yes," he said at last. "I contacted the Katibeen and I managed to speak to one of the angels who recorded her last moments on earth.

"Kathryn was an innocent. She knew nothing of the evil in Alex's past; he hadn't told her anything about his family or the danger he and Sophia were in. I am sure he was just trying to protect her – or possibly he thought she wouldn't have believed him if he had told her the whole story.

"Her heart and mind were full of simple, human dreams and desires: weddings, babies, you know the story. According to the Katibeen, her actions and intentions were straightforward and pretty much on the straight and narrow."

"But what happened?" I insisted "Who killed her? The Katibeen would have been there when she died. Didn't they see whoever did that to her?"

Manny was silent again. When he began to speak again, his voice was low; his words slow paced and deliberate.

"It took a long time for her to die. It was a painful and unpleasant death and one that she certainly did not deserve. You know that the Katibeen don't appear until the very last moments before life is extinguished. They make the final record of a human's actions and intentions, at the very last second, before the soul passes over into the spiritual realm.

"At this point, Kathryn was alone. The Hell-Beast had clearly been in the room with her; her blood was still dripping onto the bathroom floor and from the mess, it looked like something had been lapping at it. There were bloody footprints on the floor, but the creature was no longer there. The Katibeen are not permitted to move away from the dying person, they have to stay with the body until the actual point of death, so they weren't able to tell me anything about what might have been going on anywhere else in the flat, but they assured me it was quiet, which was a good thing, as it meant they could just make out Kathryn's last words.

"She was barely conscious, but they were pretty sure that she knew what she was saying." He paused. "Zach, her last words were confused... maybe... they don't even make a sentence - but the Katibeen were absolutely sure that the last thing Kathryn said before her life's blood finally ebbed away was: 'Alex, must tell Alex... Jaoel... he's not...'"

"Not what?" I interrupted. "Manny, what did she mean?"

I thought back to the flat, to finding Kathryn's still warm body – and to the attack that had sent me sprawling on the bathroom floor.

"I told you before, I was pretty sure Jaoel was in the flat when I got there, I think he was the one who brained me – and would have sent me on a one way ticket to Limbo-land if Sara hadn't arrived when she did."

As I spoke, I looked up at Sara. She gave me a quick smile when I mentioned how she had helped me and moved in closer towards the table, where I'd placed the mobile on loudspeaker so we could both hear what Manny was saying.

"Do you think this means that Kathryn saw something?" She spoke softly, leaning forwards, closer in to the phone. "Could Jaoel have revealed himself to her in his true form? Was he the one who helped Belphegor perform the sacrificial rites?"

As I listened to Sara's half-formed conjectures, about a thousand thoughts were racing through my brain; we had had our suspicions before, but this seemed to be something approaching tangible evidence. I swallowed, and voiced the question that all three of us were probably thinking:

"Manny, do you think Jaoel is the traitor? Is he the one who helped Eligor kidnap Alex and Sophia? Is he responsible for Kathryn's murder?"

"I don't know, Zach." Manny sounded uncertain. "There are still a whole bunch of things that don't add up... but whatever the situation, Jaoel has got a lot of questions to answer – and the longer it takes for him to come forward and speak to us, the fishier it gets. All I can tell you for sure is that we're searching for him.

"I don't know if you saw them, but K has deployed a battalion of the Potestas under the command of the Angel Nathanael to find and eradicate the rogue angels. I think that they left the celestial plane just after you arrived. One of their specific tasks is to locate Jaoel – and to bring him into the Agency for questioning."

"Yes," I answered. "We saw them. They passed us on the road; all very present and correct and gung-ho, weapons at the ready and loins fully girded. More than a match for Jaoel I would have thought."

Much as I disliked Nat and his rather brutal mode of operations, part of me felt that Jaoel deserved every damn thing that was coming to him.

I dragged my mind back to the main point of the conversation to ask one more question about poor Kathryn. "Did she say anything else?" I asked.

"No," Manny replied. "It was the end for her. She passed over and the Katibeen guided her onwards. They told me that she was a good soul. Nothing special, but innocent and basically well-intentioned; just another victim of the Maniscalos and their infernal desire for power."

He sighed and then stopped speaking. After a few seconds pause I asked, "Is that it? No more information?"

"No," Manny replied. "Nothing else. You had better get going. Call me when you can… and get your sorry ass back here as soon as possible. That goes for you too, Sara."

And the line went dead.

I looked over at Sara, who had clearly decided to say very little the whole time Manny had been on the phone. She was not alated and without her wings she seemed smaller and more vulnerable. She had wrapped her arms tightly across her upper body and was not looking at me; her chin was tucked tightly into her collar bone, and as I stared at her, I saw a single tear roll down her cheek.

Fiercely, she wiped it away and raising her eyes to mine, I saw both anger and determination in her gaze. I moved towards her; I'm not quite sure why, but as I did so, she stiffened and edged away from me.

"No, Zach, don't try to touch me. I am so wound up I would probably electrify you." She began pacing, backwards and forwards, walking from one side of the tiny room to the other, muttering to herself.

"There was no need for that girl to die like that; no need for all that mess and pain." She rounded on me. "They could have put her out of her misery quickly, you know, and the ritual would still have been just as effective."

She had stopped pacing and stood right in front of me, staring straight into my eyes.

"Raphael taught me all about summoning rituals. It's not the life-blood itself

~ 132 ~

which opens the portal, but the inflicting of the mortal wound. You can do it just as well with a beheading or a shot to the heart. But not for those bastards; they wanted a lingering death… a death they could… savour." She almost the spat the last word at me.

"Well, yes," I replied, somewhat lamely, more than a little confused by what she had said. Why had Raphael been tutoring her on demonic rituals? Surely they weren't part of the Healer's standard curriculum?

"They aren't actually the nicest of people to deal with. It's all part and parcel of being a demon – alongside the general evil and debauchery, you usually find a predilection for inflicting pain and an obsession with bloodshed. Goes with the territory you might say."

Sara gave me a brief smile at this.

"But how come the tutorial on summoning?" She had piqued my curiosity with her throw-away comment, and I wanted to find out a little bit more about what the old Archangel had actually been teaching her. "What's that got to do with being a healer?"

Sara looked a tad confused "What… oh no, it was just a conversation we had one day. No big deal." As she spoke, she picked up our kitbags, strapped hers on her back, and threw the other in my general direction. It landed at my feet.

"I'll tell you all about it another day, but like Manny said, shouldn't we be getting a move on? And don't you need to make sure that Johan and Lisl will actually buy into your suggestion? It's an awful lot to ask of them."

She was right. What I had planned would be asking a lot of my old friends. But I really couldn't think of a better way out.

I opened my kitbag and pulled out a water bottle and a couple of protein bars, and as I tossed one across to her, I looked at the clock on the mantelpiece. It was already 08.00.

"Johan will be downstairs any minute. I think he said the chariot was coming at nine."

I took a long, deep swig from the bottle and passed it to her. "You'd better drink this. The last thing we need is to get dehydrated." She raised the bottle to her lips and drank deep; emptying it in a single draft.

It flashed through my mind that we now only had one bottle left, and there was no chance of getting any fresh supplies.

There was a sound above our heads. Feet on the floorboards, then footsteps on the stairs. Seconds later, the door opened and the whole family came into the room. Johan and Lisl were both dressed in black; he in a suit that had seen better days and which hung limply on his tall, rather gaunt frame, whilst Lisl wore a simple, sleeveless linen dress, with a vast lacy shawl draped over her shoulders.

In contrast, Heinrich and Lottie were both resplendent in white. They reminded me of John and Yoko; Lottie even had a big floppy hat held tightly in her left hand. She ran straight to the window and climbed up on a stool, clearly on the look-out for the chariot.

"Good morning," said Johan. "I hope you don't mind, but we need to get ready. The chariot will be here soon, and we can't afford to be late. This is too important for Heinrich."

He looked at his son, no longer with anger, but with love and acceptance. Lisl reached over to her husband and took his hand. Her other rested gently on Heinrich's shoulder. She smiled at us, and said,

"It's a great shame that we had to meet again in such unfortunate circumstances... but we're all so glad that everything went well last night." She gazed up at her husband, and gently gave his hand a squeeze. Then turning to look at us, she continued,

"I think it did Johan good to get back in the game again. It made him remember all the times he had with the Agency. To think about the excitement... the challenge; realising that he did a good job; that he made a real difference.

"I think it made him see that he has to allow Heinrich to have the same chances."

Johan lifted his wife's hand to his lips and kissed it. "Whatever happens, we have each other, Lisl. We have Lottie. We are still a family. So many others are not so fortunate."

He turned to Heinrich and reaching out his other hand, gently stroked the side of his son's face.

"I am so proud of you," he said. "Any man would be proud to call you his son. Whatever happens today, and whatever life you are bound for, your new family will be truly blessed."

After a moment in which no-one spoke, Johan moved towards us and Lisl and Heinrich joined Lottie at the window.

"Perhaps you should go now before the chariot arrives. It's probably not a good idea for them to see you."

"Aah," said Sara, "that's something we wanted to talk to you about. We've had... an idea, you see..."

Johan looked questioningly first at me, then at Sara. He glanced quickly towards his family. They were all clustered together, looking out of the window. Heinrich had picked Lottie up so she could see better; she had put on her hat and was chattering incessantly. All of them seemed to be sublimely indifferent to what the three of us were doing.

Gesturing towards the table at the other end of the room, Johan moved slowly towards it, saying rather resignedly, "Now why does that not surprise me?"

He sighed, and then gave me a rather world-weary grin.

"So, come on then, you two. Perhaps you'd better tell me a little bit more about it."

~ *Chapter Twenty* ~

Having been earthbound for quite a while, I knew very little about '*This is your next life*', the programme that Heinrich was going to appear on, and even less about Celestial Information and Entertainment Limited (otherwise known as CIEL), the broadcasting company who made and distributed the programme, and an organisation which had in recent years become a major player in non-terrestrial broadcasting.

When I'd last lived in the Heavens, in my little flat in Ma'on, we'd only had two channels, both provided by the rather worthy Celestial Broadcasting Corporation (CBC). Programmes had been mostly educational or inspirational (with, in my opinion, rather too much exposure for the celestial choirs and their incessant praising). The pompous presenters were almost exclusively selected from the most senior ranks of the seraphs. And everything had been black and white.

Now it appeared that there were more channels than you could shake a stick at, everything was in glorious technicolour and they were even beginning to pilot 4d viewing, a full-on sensory immersion, in which the viewer could experience not only sights and sounds, but smells, touch and taste as well.

There was also a new breed of presenter; gone were the sombre seraphs with their RP speech and public-service principles, now cheeky, irreverent cherubs like Arat and Dal, the comperes of '*This is your next life*', were by no means an exception. From what Sara said, they were even beginning to allow ghosts, spirits and other non-angelic celestial beings to get in on the act; she told me that sister act Mary and Martha had recently been brought out of retirement by the CBC and were now presenting a hugely successful cookery programme '*The great celestial bake off*', which was apparently now beginning to rival CIEL's offering '*Let them eat cake*', presented by Marie Antoinette and Mrs. Beeton.

CIEL, an outfit set up by the Archangel Ramiel[44] in partnership with the powerful antipodean spirit Murgnin[45], had taken the lead in driving this shift in celestial broadcasting away from education towards entertainment. Whilst some regarded the organisation as an unholy collaboration between the Heavenly Host and some of the more powerful boundary landers, there can be no doubt that its aggressive combination of sport, reality TV, populist drama and 24/7 news, has been a hit.

Sara also told me that in recent years, the relationship between CIEL and the inner circle of the Heavenly Host had been actively managed by K in order to support the work of the Efficiency and Reform group. Their growing worries about the shift in the balance of power on earth, coupled with continued pressures on celestial resources had led, so Sara informed me, to a deliberate policy of support and de-regulation for CIEL, who in return had been providing entertainment aimed at keeping the celestial masses quiet, entertained and a bit dumbed down.

Programmes such as *'This is your next life'* and *'I'm a celestial, get me out of here'*, were, Sara said, highly successful in promoting the drive for increased reincarnation, reducing the pressures on celestial resources, by glamorising life on earth.

'This is your next life', the programme which Heinrich would be appearing on later that day, was filmed live, in studios right next to the Lake of Fire, the place where recently deceased human souls made their way for judgement.

Sara had told me more about the programme as we walked back from our encounter with Enepsigos and the Hunt.

Apparently, it always started with an interview with one of the previous contestants, filmed just hours after their passing; they were shown a quick re-cap of their life and achievements and asked to comment on how they felt their most recent life had worked out.

Incidentally, that's why the studio was built right next to the Lake of Fire.

---

[44] "The Archangel Ramiel is the bearer of divine visions and has responsibility for ensuring these are seen and understood by all new souls entering the celestial realms. One of the first creative directors of the Celestial Broadcasting Corporation, his involvement in the development of CIEL was seen by some as a surprising departure, but has been fully supported by his colleagues within the highest echelons of the Heavenly Host. He is on record as stating, 'We must move with the times. Give the people what they want, and they'll come to see it'." *The Angels' Year Book,* 1907
"[45]Murgnin, a powerful spiritual being descended from the Australian Rainbow Serpent, has his roots in the Aboriginal dreamtime, where he developed a reputation for trickery and fast talking. He is a hugely energetic and influential presence in the boundary lands and has recently married for the fourth time at the ripe old age of 7,000,085." *A Guide to the Three Realms, 2016*

Sara said that the programme's researchers had a direct line to the Katibeen, who filled them in on the death-dramas as they were happening, and were always on the look-out for the big stories.

The judgement of the soul was then filmed and they were sent on their way to their celestial destination. It was, so Sara said, immensely good for ratings if they made it through to the Elysian Fields or the Isles of the Blessed – and even better if they were condemned to Tartarus or one of the other Infernal prisons for a period of punishment or remorse.

"What if they've been really bad?" I asked. "What if their souls are judged to be beyond redemption? Do they film them actually being devoured? Surely even Murgnin and his crew must draw the line somewhere?"

"That's an interesting question," Sara had replied, "CIEL have been lobbying the Host to allow televised devourings for some time now, on limited access, adults-only subscription channels. They want to set up a special dream nexus to broadcast them terrestrially as well, as a type of nightmare-deterrent for potential sinners, but there's strong opposition round the top table, led mainly by Gabriel and Michael, and K doesn't think that will be happening anytime soon."

"Well thank Heavens for that," I said, somewhat ironically. "How does your mate Raphael feel about it? Surely he can't think something so barbaric should be peddled around for entertainment?"

"Raph's actually quite relaxed on the subject. He thinks the threat of a bit of fire and brimstone doesn't actually do anyone any harm. In fact, he thinks the more liberal Archangels aren't doing the Host any favours." She warmed to her subject. "If people really thought about the consequences of their actions and realised that eternal damnation meant just that, Raph thinks we might genuinely be able to put the fear of God into people once more."

"I thought you wanted to temper justice with mercy? Remember Isra? You weren't too keen on the un-tempered wrath of God back in St. Basil's were you?"

"Yes, but that was for Isra, surely you see that the rules for angels are different? Humans are lower beings. They should follow the guidance the Heavenly Host has provided and must be prepared to take the consequences if they disobey."

I was a little shocked by this. The Sara I had grown up with had been a bit of a free thinker, more aligned to the liberal end of the spectrum. Now she was parroting the views of the hardliners.

"Easier said than done, I'm afraid; do you know exactly how many '*Books of Guidance*' there are out there for humanity to follow, each and every one of them proclaiming itself to be the 'truth', the unambiguous word of God? I mean, half of them are set up in direct contradiction to the others. They can't even agree on something as simple as dietary taboos, so to expect humanity to agree on the more complex principles is basically a hiding to nothing."

I sighed. The decision, taken early on amongst the Heavenly Host, to grant humanity free will and to encourage the human spirit to develop its own levels of awareness and self-actualisation had been both contentious and bloody. Revelation of The Word had taken place at a number of points throughout human history, but rather than resulting in a single world view or a shared religious theosophy, the terrestrial's innate tendency towards bursts of creativity and innovation, constrained and boundaried by the ongoing tribalism inherent in most of mankind, had led instead to the development of the ragged tapestry of belief systems which currently exists across planet earth.

And this in turn, had helped to spur on some of the planet's most bloody wars and conflicts and was responsible for inspiring innumerable acts of intolerance and atrocity. The hardliners within the Host now believed that humanity was incapable of resolving its differences, incapable of ever developing a society in which tolerance and acceptance of others became the norm. Instead, they argued that the time had come for a worldwide celestial revelation of the 'Truth' to be followed with a regime of absolute obedience, not just on earth but across all spheres.

However, the more liberal wing presented a different case, arguing that much of what was most beautiful and valuable within the human spirit was generated by freedom of thought and expression. In their view, humanity should be supported to move towards a more advanced level of spiritual tolerance and acceptance of others, by being able to choose freely, rather than by being forced to obey.

I thought about arguing the point with Sara, but to be honest, it was all rather too much for me. Definitely above my pay-grade and something I didn't usually think about from one century to the next. I knew where I stood back on earth, and to be honest, I wasn't that interested in politics. Most importantly, the last thing I had needed at this point was an argument with Sara.

I could tell from the way her shoulders were set that she wasn't happy with the way the conversation was going, so I turned half towards her and smiled, raising my hands in a placating gesture and suggested we leave the political niceties for another day.

"Tell me a bit more about the show?" I asked her.

She harrumphed a bit; I could tell she hadn't liked me disagreeing with her, but I think she recognised the olive branch I was sending, and she eventually carried on with our previous conversation.

She told me that after the newly deceased previous contestant has been judged and sent on his or her way, the two presenters, Arat and Dal, introduce the six souls who are going to play the game. They are usually shown relaxing with their friends and family, and Arat (or Dal) would fool around a bit with them, asking them to talk about their past life on earth and their hopes and aspirations for the next one.

Sara said they usually have a fairly standard mix of contestants: young and old, black and white, different belief systems etc. etc. but that they all tend to be fairly good looking. "Ugly contestants don't go down so well," she explained. "But there's usually loads of sympathy for someone who had a disability in a past life. There was one chap, lost the use of his limbs in the trenches and died in agony in a field hospital in France in 1916. He won the top prize when he was on - came back as David Beckham."

"So what do they have to do?" I asked. "What do they actually have to do to win?" Sara explained that the contestants have to go through a series of challenges, some of which, like the 'Talent' round, are judged by the audience in the studio and at home. Other tasks include things like physical endurance or general knowledge. The overall winner gets to be reincarnated in to that week's 'Star Life'.

She explained that the next four contestants on the weekly points table get one of a more random set of reincarnation destinies, none of which will be exceptionally fabulous, but equally, none of which will be existentially awful. The person who gets the least points has to spin the wheel governed by the 'fickle finger of fate' and will end up with the booby prize – a life characterised in some way by disaster or disadvantage.

Finally, the show ends with Arat and Dal leading the winner out to say tearful goodbyes to his or her family. Quite often, everyone joins in a universal weep-fest, and even the cheeky cherubs themselves are not immune. (Sara even said that the shows where Arat wipes away a tear and manfully pats Dal's shoulder in a gesture of shared sympathy usually get higher ratings than the ones where they both appear to be unmoved.)

The winner is then led centre stage, where Arat (or Dal) pours out a large glass of Lethe water, hands it to the winner, and encourages them to drink, accompanied by great back-slapping and cheeky grins to the TV audience. After the cup has been drained, down to the very last drop, obliviating every memory and removing all sense of personhood, personality or past life, the winner is escorted out, past their now unrecognised family and friends (who are usually still weeping and emotional), through the 're-birth portal' where their soul is absorbed and sent on its way to its new life.

'This is your next life' had just finished its 150th series, and was described, or so Sara said, as one of the jewels in CIEL's crown. Personally, from what I had heard about it so far, it didn't really sound like my cup of tea, but be that as it may, I was currently sending out great waves of thanks for its existence.

If our plan worked, not only would we get away from Johan's with no-one being any the wiser, but we would be able to make our way into the ditches of Malebolge within hours.

And our plan? Oh, I forgot I hadn't told you.

We were going to commandeer the chariot that CIEL was sending to transport Heinrich and family to the studio.

And if everything went according to plan, it was going to take us right up to the gates of the Lake of Fire itself.

~ *Chapter Twenty One* ~

The plan was simple. Dangerous - definitely; foolhardy - possibly. But simple.

Johan had already told us that the CIEL chariot would be arriving at around nine in the morning. Two charioteers and a small film crew. They would spend around an hour filming Heinrich at home, in the bosom of his loving family, in order to create a short montage of shots and soundbites to use at the beginning of the programme. Once this was in the bag, the family and crew would set off for the studios, a journey which should take no more than two hours.

Whilst the filming was going on inside, all Sara and I needed to do was to get the real charioteers out of the way, sweet-talk them into taking off their clothes and inveigle them into allowing us assume their identities. We would then transport Heinrich, Johan, Lisl, Lottie and the unsuspecting film crew straight to the studios, park up the chariot and make good our escape. As I said; simple.

As we outlined the plan we talked quietly and at speed so Lisl wouldn't hear us or begin to worry about what was going on at the other end of the room.

Johan said nothing as we sketched out our ideas. We sat, huddled together at the table, and as we talked, Johan's left hand tapped lightly onto the wooden surface; whether in irritation or impatience I wasn't sure.

When we'd finished, he remained quiet; his face closed, giving away nothing about what he was thinking. But I knew him well and I thought we were on the way to convincing him. Johan was an expert tactician and one of the best field operatives I had ever worked with. He understood that the stakes were high, but he also knew exactly what it would take to pull off what we were proposing.

He looked up, shifting his astute but still rather troubled gaze towards Sara, possibly thinking about the work she had already carried out that night. Five of the Wild Hunt had died at her hands. She was no lightweight, but he was clearly considering if she had what it would take to deliver. I knew that he would never support a plan which, if it went wrong, could very easily put his family at risk. There was no way he would help us unless he was absolutely convinced that we could do it.

She felt his gaze upon her and, without seeming to be aware of what she was doing, she moved closer to me, so that her shoulder brushed lightly against my arm. Instantly, I could feel her warmth, that connection which seemed to flow so strongly between us, but beneath it, I could sense something else, an unease, and something more, something which seemed to me to be the first vestiges of fear. Was it Johan's silence that was making her nervous? We both knew that without his help the plan wouldn't stand a chance. Or was she starting to realise, finally, exactly what it was that we were taking on? Within the next few hours, if all went to plan, we would be well away from the boundary lands and deep within the hellish territories of the Inferno itself. I couldn't blame her if she was starting to get a little nervy; hey, if I spent too long thinking about what we were doing and where we were headed, I'd be bricking it myself.

But before I had chance to dwell on this any further, Johan shifted his gaze away from Sara and winked.

"You're one hell of a risk-taking bastard, Zach. You always were... But we always made it out in one piece didn't we?"

I decided not to remind him about that time in Northumberland.

"Who's going to actually fly the chariot? I seem to remember you lost your licence a while back."

"I am," said Sara, before I could get a word in edgeways.

"I'm K's personal charioteer, and I can fly anything CIEL see fit to send over." As she spoke, I sensed the confidence returning to her, the small waves of fear receding. She stood up and reached into her kitbag. "Here's my licence, if you have any doubts about it." She tossed something over to Johan, who caught it, examined it and returned it to her with a nod.

"Okay. You can fly. I trust you to handle that chariot and to get us to the studios safely. But it's going to be getting you into the driving seat that's going to be a challenge."

We agreed. Without a doubt, this was going to be the hardest part of the plan, and it depended entirely on Sara's ability to sweet talk and beguile the unsuspecting charioteers into taking just one small sip of Lethe water; enough to bring on short term memory loss, but not enough to do any permanent harm.

Johan listened as we told him what we intended.

"Alright… you've convinced me." He looked at the clock on the mantelpiece. "They should be here in about fifteen minutes – that gives you enough time to get what you need from the river; so you'd better get going."

"What about Lisl and the children?" I glanced quickly towards the window. Heinrich was no longer carrying his sister. She was standing on a chair and leaning out of the open window, looking up in to the sky, searching amongst the clouds for the first sight of the chariot.

Looking beyond her, I noticed that a number of people had gathered just outside the garden fence; most of them were also scanning the skies.

Heinrich's TV appearance was clearly hot news in the neighbourhood; more people were turning up all the time and by now, there were at least a hundred figures standing by the fence. I noticed that there was very little noise, they were standing silently, perhaps out of respect for Johan and his family, and the loss they would suffer as a result of their son's big adventure.

Lisl and her son were now close together, her head resting on his shoulder, her arm around his waist. They were not talking. I got the feeling that all the words had been said and that all Lisl wanted before the media circus began was to be as close as she could to the son who would have left her forever by the end of the day.

Johan shook his head. "No, I don't want to involve them. It's far less risky that way. If you're careful, they won't even notice the switch. Lisl is only interested in Heinrich, and Lottie just wants to be on TV. As far as they're concerned, I doubt they will even give the charioteers a second glance."

I nodded. "Right, Sara, you get yourself ready, they'll be here any minute now. I'll head down to the river and sort out the water."

Johan got up, preparing to join his family on the other side of the room. "We owe you," I said, reaching out my hand towards him, but stopping short of clapping his shoulder. I couldn't actually touch him, and whatever the intention, putting your hand through someone's shoulder was more than a tad creepy.

"Whatever happens, I'll make sure Manny knows exactly how much you've done for us."

Johan shrugged. "It's what we do… you know that. I signed up for it years ago…."

I knew him of old – he'd never wanted to get sentimental over business, and today was clearly no exception.

"And we're running out of time; you'd better get on with it – pronto. Just don't get caught."

He walked away from us and as Sara took out a mirror and began putting on lipstick, Johan moved towards his wife and son, embracing both of them, and joining them in their silent vigil at the window.

I left the house by the back door, ran down to the river and filled a small flask, being careful to wipe the sides clean and to get none of the waters of oblivion on my skin. Although it was most effective when drunk, the waters could also affect you if they touched any part of your body, and I needed to ensure I was firing on all cylinders; we couldn't afford even one tiny slip in concentration if the plan was to succeed.

I slipped into the cottage through the back, and not a second too soon. As the door shut, behind me I heard the first blast of the celestial fanfare which always accompanied your traditional Angelic Chariot, and thirty seconds later, it had landed, in all its pomp and glory, upon Lisl and Johan's back lawn. I ran upstairs and concealed myself behind the curtains on the front landing. I could see out, but I didn't think that anyone could spot me as long as I didn't move too much. There was no sign of Sara. I assumed that she was at her post, but I had no way of checking. I hoped that the fear and uncertainty I had felt in her earlier had now been replaced with the meticulous planning and absolute sangfroid which I hated to admit I had come to rely on. She was the lynch-pin of this operation, and if she messed up, I had actually no idea about how we were going to get out of there without drawing Eligor's attention on to both us and Johan's family.

Putting such thoughts behind me, I took a good look at the vehicle which had landed on the lawn.

Much as I hated to admit it, the CIEL chariot[46] was really quite impressive –

---

[46] "Here we have an Ezekiel Five that looks like it's been involved in some kind of unfortunate smelting incident. It hasn't though. CIEL assures us it's quite on purpose. It's called the Celestial Glory Edition, and the manufacturers say it is one of a kind. The body kit is carbon fibre and the orphanim's wheel trims are burnished platinum, with diamond finishing. All exterior decoration has been refinished in pure silver. The Glory's 6.6-litre V12 orphanic engine power hasn't gone unaltered. Power is up from 623bhp to 730bhp, cutting the 0-62mph time by a fifth of a second to 4.4 seconds. CIEL's done away with the 155mph limiter, too, for a 186mph top-end. Tasteful upgrade or gaudy monstrosity? Whichever it is, it is bound to get you talking." CBC *Top Chariot*, 2016

in a vulgarly baroque sort of way. The ornate, jewel-embossed rectangular body was decorated in CIEL's corporate colours of sky-blue and silver, and an angel, fully alated and equipped with a ceremonial trumpet, stood at each corner. Along each side of the chariot were the eight heavenly wheels, known as 'orphanims', which provide both the vehicle's power and its stability, making the four winged, silver horses actually pretty redundant. I decided that they were probably only there to make an impression; and I grudgingly had to admit that they succeeded.

The two ghostly charioteers were dressed in skintight, all-in-one blue and gold body suits and were now dismounting from the box. Johan had been rather disgruntled when he informed us that CIEL tended to use spectres for their more manual, less glamourous jobs.

They were tall and well-muscled and were both fairly slender. As they were wearing winged helmets which covered their hair and obscured their faces, it was hard from this distance to make out if they were male or female.

One went straight round to the horses, who seemed to be a bit spooked; stamping their feet and snorting rather inelegantly. There was quite a bit of foam flecked around their mouths and their eyes were rolling. Perhaps they had been startled by something as they were landing, or maybe they were picking up the lingering scent of the Wild Hunt? Whatever it was, they weren't happy and charioteer number one seemed to have his – or her – hands full getting them to calm down.

Whilst this was going on, charioteer number two had opened the door at the side of the vehicle and was helping a couple of rather nervous looking angels to dismount. Both carried small silver cases, which I guessed must contain the gear they needed to film the interviews, and both looked a little green about the gills. The angels at the corners of the chariot stayed where they were, but lowered their trumpets and stood sternly to attention. I noticed that each had a silver sword at their waist, and each angel had placed a hand on their sword-hilt, as if in readiness for an attack. I guessed that they were Hayot Angels, whose only function was to guard the chariot and to provide the requisite celestial fanfares whilst in flight.

By this time, Heinrich and Lottie had rushed out into the garden, with Lisl and Johan following rather more circumspectly in their wake. The small crowd outside the garden moved closer in to the fence, eager to hear what was going on.

The first of the angels was also carrying a clipboard. He took a quick look at it and moved forwards more purposefully towards Heinrich, holding out his hand in greeting: "Hello... you must be Heinrich, so pleased to meet you; we've heard so much about you." They shook hands and he looked quickly about him. He seemed worried about something, and his colleague was definitely unsettled. She kept gazing upwards, as if scanning for something in the skies. "And this must be Lottie... what an utterly adorable hat you're wearing..." He moved forward, closer towards the house, where Lisl and Johan were standing, arms around each other, leaning in against the door frame. "And you must be - Lisl?" He leant forward and air-kissed the space around her left and right cheeks. "And," he checked his notes, "Johan."

Johan nodded, without moving forwards. Perhaps he was worried that he too would have to get involved in the air-kissing.

The angel didn't seem affronted by Johan's lack of response; there was clearly something else on his mind. "What little beauties your children are... you must be so proud. And I love those outfits... But let's not stand here gabbing, there's so much to do, and we have no time to waste."

The female angel moved forwards. "Can we get inside...? Like, now, please?"

If they were surprised by the rather peremptory nature of the request, Lisl and Johan didn't show it. Instead they nodded, and moved aside, indicating with an outstretched arm that the angels were welcome to walk in to their house.

The guy with the clipboard went on in, followed immediately by Lisl, Lottie and Heinrich, but the female turned back towards the chariot, casting what was undoubtedly a worried glance upwards and then back down towards the horses and the two charioteers.

She had a high-pitched, rather arrogant voice. "We'll be as quick as we can, and we can always finish off at the studio if we need to. It's a bloody nuisance, but we need some shots of the cosy cottage for the montage. Mummy and Daddy's tearful farewell will look great framed against the humble fireplace – but once it's in the can, I want out of here."

The second charioteer nodded and moved towards the vehicle, clearly beginning to check that everything would be okay for take-off. The guy standing by the horses was clearly not so happy.

"I don't think that's a good idea. Whatever that thing was up there, it's frightened the horses, and we have no idea if it's still around. I think we should contact Head Office and ask for instructions. We could always just leave the horses here you know. We don't actually need them. You know that the chariot flies perfectly well without them."

He moved to stand further away from the horses, closer in towards the shelter of the cottage roof, his feet slightly apart and his arms folded mutinously across his chest.

"I've no time for this." She moved swiftly towards him. "You know we ran over budget last week because you lost the original footage and we had to shoot everything again."

She was now standing right in front of him, and she was clearly not a happy bunny. She had the forefinger of her left hand outstretched and I think the only thing that was stopping her from prodding it hard against his chest was that it would have passed straight through his ghostly frame.

"I am just about fed up with your attitude, your incompetence and your refusal to do what you are told. You're just a bloody ghost. Who do you think you are, trying to tell me, an angel of the second sphere, what to do and how to do it?

"We will not call head office.

"We will not be late on the job.

"We will not arrive without the horses.

"And we will not do anything that will make Murgnin think we are anything other than consummate professionals." By this time, she was shouting. "Do I make myself clear?"

The poor guy was by now completely intimidated; he just nodded and uncrossed his arms.

"Right. Now, get some water for the horses and have everything ready for take-off. I want to be out of here in twenty." Without waiting for a response, she turned on her heel and went into the house.

Now I was in a bit of a quandary. If I was to follow the plan to the letter, I needed to get straight out into the garden with the Lethe water, find Sara and administer the diluted draft of oblivion to the charioteers. We only had twenty minutes to make the switch, and with every second, the pressure was mounting. But I needed to know what had happened out there. Exactly what had spooked the horses so much? What had they seen – and where was it now?

I took a swift look out of the window and saw Sara boldly open the gate and saunter across the lawn towards the first charioteer, who had just filled a bucket of water from the tap in the garden and was lugging it rather awkwardly towards the horses.

~ 148 ~

She looked amazing. Her hair was not scraped back into the severe bun I had become accustomed to; instead it fell almost to her waist in rippling waves of copper. She was still wearing her combats, but she had unbuttoned her shirt by at least three buttons, revealing a cleavage which could only be described as impressive. She had reached the first charioteer and was now standing in front of him, her head slightly to one side, one hand on her hip, the other outstretched towards him. The second charioteer was nowhere to be seen. I assumed he or she was on the far side of the chariot, checking the tyre pressures or tuning up one of the trumpets, or some such mechanical task that would be needed to ensure a safe and speedy departure.

The story we'd planned for Sara was simple; she was an angel on vacation, spending some time in the boundary lands and she just *loved* chariots. He would be flattered; she would be a little silly... She would coax him away from the chariot to the edge of the forest, where I would be waiting. We would overpower him, slip a few drops of the waters of oblivion down his hopefully not too greatly protesting throat, and Bob, as it were, would've been our uncle.

Once we had one charioteer, it would have been a piece of piss to grab the other. We had reckoned on ten minutes flat to do the switch-round. But that was then.

At any other time, I had no doubt that she could have pulled him in hook, line and lusty, libidinous spectral sinker, but the game plan had changed. He was under orders to get the chariot ready for a twenty minute turnaround and on top of that, there was something threatening in the skies above him which seemed to have turned a bog-standard journey into a dangerous mission.

That thought decided me. I still had a few minutes to play with; I needed to find out exactly what had happened to the chariot on the journey over here. I thought that it would be bound to take them a while to get all their equipment ready, and that they would probably be telling the tale whilst they were setting up. This, I thought, would give me chance to do a little eavesdropping and still get to Sara in time. I calculated that as long as I got outside before they started their interviews, I would be fine.

Decision made, I turned my back on Sara and the chariot and moved silently away from the window towards the top of the stairs. I leant as far forward as I dared, straining my ears to pick up what I could of the conversation that I could just about hear through the open sitting room door.

~ *Chapter Twenty Two* ~

"No, nothing for me, thank you." It was the male angel. "Already had three espressos this morning... anymore and I'll be as high as a kite... and we don't want that now, do we? Not after all the excitement we've had this morning." I heard a nervous giggle. Lisl was obviously doing the standard hospitality spiel and the angels were following the usual underworld-refusal etiquette.

He gave another little laugh, which sounded to me to be reaching the early verges of hysteria. "Now, Heinrich, I just need to put a dab of powder on here... and a little touch of colour here... There. Penny darling, are you ready to roll? We don't want to hang about now do we?"

I heard a few murmurs and the sound of what sounded like a chair being dragged across the floor.

"Right." It was the female. Penny. I cast about in my memory, trying to place her. Then it came to me. I was pretty sure she was the Angel Peniel, a fairly small-fry seraph, who I had come across once or twice, back in the dim and distant. I seemed to remember that she had tried and failed to get in to the Potestas, and had been extremely put out not to have been accepted. Recalling the way she had spoken to the charioteer, she clearly still had a chip on her shoulder about something.

"Heinrich, you sit there." She spoke clearly, annunciating every syllable, like someone who had had every vocal idiosyncrasy erased through years of elocution training, and her tone was still fairly peremptory. She didn't sound like the sort of person who was very good at putting others at their ease.

I thought of Sara and the way she had reassured Isra back in St. Basil's, the way she had helped me manage my anger and emotion. Whatever the quality was: empathy, understanding, intuition maybe; she had it in spades – and Penny didn't seem to have any at all.

There was some more muffled conversation. I couldn't make out what anyone was saying, then, when Penny spoke again her voice was getting sharper, more high-pitched. "Johan, Lisl, can you sit across from him? Yes, that's right.

"Finally!" She gave a loud and rather theatrical sigh.

"Now, Lottie, how about you sit on your big brother's knee? And can we lose the hat? Yes, I know it's lovely, but it takes up too much of the shot."

I heard a rather mutinous wail from downstairs. Lottie was clearly not impressed.

"Oh for goodness sake; we can take a shot with the hat when we get to the studios. Can't we just get on with it now? I just need a few words here in the happy homestead and then we can be on our way."

It sounded like Penny was losing it.

"I want to get out of here before that Chimera comes back for another look-see, and I think you guys probably don't want to mix with him either, even if you are already dead."

"What?" I heard a roar from downstairs. Then the sound of furniture being pushed back roughly. "What do you mean – Chimera?" Johan's anger exploded. I heard another wail and then sobbing. Lottie had started to cry.

"Now please, just keep calm. Penny was just saying that... of course there isn't a Chimera."

It was the other angel. He sounded scared, and seemed anxious to diffuse what was on its way to becoming a very heated situation.

"It's just something we say in television..." He was floundering. "Something to... gee people up... get the juices flowing.... You know, get a little urgency into the proceedings. As Murgnin says... 'time is money' – and we haven't got all day you know?"

"Seems like a bit of a stupid thing to say," muttered Johan. "You don't want to mess with Chimeras whatever the reason... I'm really not sure I want to go through with this."

At this there was another wail; this time from Heinrich. "Oh no, Dad... you promised... come on. We can't pull out now... this is just another stupid excuse 'cos you don't want me to do it. Of course there isn't a Chimera. She was just saying it."

"Yes... sorry... sorry, my fault entirely." Penny's voice was calm again. "Stupid thing to say... of course there isn't a Chimera.

"Now, are we okay to carry on?"

There was a pause. I heard a chair scrape again and some more muffled conversation. After a few seconds, it sounded as if things were now back on track.

I heard Penny speak. She had now adopted a gentle and interested tone, which was clearly her television voice, "So, Lisl, how do you feel about Heinrich's ambition to be reborn as the first person to walk on Mars?"

I didn't wait for the answer. I reckoned we had less than fifteen minutes before they would wrap up downstairs. And I was also pretty sure that Sara was not going to be best pleased with me. I was seriously off schedule. Without further ado, I went into the back bedroom and jumped out of the window.

Even without alation, angels are pretty good at that sort of thing, so I landed rather niftily in the cabbage patch, brushed myself down and moved cautiously round the corner of the house towards the front lawn and the chariot.

I was expecting to find Sara cosying up with charioteer number one and had decided that it wouldn't be a good idea to cramp her style; I thought I'd go slowly and try to keep out of sight if I possibly could.

When I got round the corner however, I saw that Sara was, indeed, up-close and personal with the Lycra-clad spectre – but so were about twenty others. There were another five or six figures milling around at the front of the chariot, stroking the horses and I could just see, out of the corner of my eye, another fifteen or so clambering in and out of the chariot itself. This was to the absolute frustration of charioteer number two, who was completely beside herself, almost weeping with frustration as she tried to make them get out and go back to where they had been standing, on the other side of the garden fence.

It was clear in an instant what had happened. The gawpers at the gate had obviously been emboldened by Sara's example and had taken the opportunity to have a really good look at CIEL's state of the art chariot. I couldn't blame them; it was a pretty impressive piece of kit – but this was neither the time nor the place for sightseers.

At that moment, I caught Sara's eye. She raised her eyebrows, and gave a slight shrug of her shoulders. Then she nodded towards the door of the cottage and shook her head giving me the signal that she thought that time was too short and we should abort the plan.

But giving up is just not in my DNA. I reckoned we had less than ten minutes until Penny had her sound bites in the can – but that would be enough, providing we worked quickly.

Making a rapid scan of the scene around me, I reckoned that I only needed to work on the garden and the area immediately beyond the fence. There was no-one to be seen anywhere else – I just needed to make sure that I only stopped time in a very limited area – and I had to be absolutely certain that time within the four walls of the cottage continued to run on as normal. Chronoprohibery is something angels can do – but it is not something that can be done to them. I had to make sure that Penny and her sidekick didn't get even the tiniest sniff of what was actually happening - and if Johan and co. suddenly went all catatonic, I reckoned that even that self-obsessed little madam would guess that something was not as it should be.

Once I was certain that I had my co-ordinates, I constructed my time corridor and in an instant everyone except me, Sara and the Hayot Angels was caught in suspended animation.

I wasn't worried about the Hayots – on a cognitive level they were really only a few steps up from the horses. They continued to gaze placidly about them, totally oblivious to the freeze frame going on around them. Sara, however, was another matter.

As I rushed over towards her, I could see that she was not happy.

"What the fuck...? What are you playing at, Zach? We can't do this... we have no time to spare. They will be out of that door any minute now."

"Shut up," I said. "We've plenty of time if you stop panicking. Just get your guy and come with me."

I grabbed the second charioteer and carried her at a run round the corner. Without looking to see if Sara was following me, I took the small flask of Lethe water from my kitbag and carefully measured five drops of water into her slackly open mouth. I tilted her head backwards to make sure she had swallowed it and as I did so, Sara staggered round the side of the house with charioteer number one slung over her shoulder. Swiftly, I administered a slightly larger dose to him and gestured to Sara to put him on the ground.

"Right, we need to move quickly. Put your clothes into your kitbag and get into the Lycra."

I had already started stripping. Sara hadn't moved. I rounded on her.

"This is no time for false modestly. Stop being so bloody precious and get your kit off.

"Do it!"

As I shouted, she seemed to snap out of her reverie and began quickly unbuttoning her shirt. Within thirty seconds she was standing next to me, wearing not much more than her modesty.

Being a gentleman, I averted my eyes, but not without noticing that she had done some great work on her corpus... and that she had a small tattoo, I wasn't quite sure what it was, a flower, or maybe a butterfly, just at the base of her spine.

By this time, I was already half into the all-in one body suit. I had decided to put my own boots back on and just hoped that if I was standing up-front in the chariot, Penny wouldn't even notice. I grabbed Sara's and stuffed them into my kitbag – tossing her the rather dinky silver ankle boots we had unceremoniously pulled from the uncomplaining form of charioteer number two.

As Sara carried out the final adjustments to her costume, I moved the two semi-naked charioteers into a sitting position by the back wall and, taking out a couple of pairs of wrist restraints, manacled them to the fence, just to make sure that they wouldn't come wandering out into the front garden as we were about to take off. As they were both spectral beings, I knew that the physical restraints wouldn't hold them in check for too long, but I counted on the confusion caused by the Lethe water to keep them shackled for the short-term.

I grabbed both our kitbags and quickly checked my watch – we had about forty-five seconds before time came back on track again.

"Right, let's get back out there – and first priority is to clear the garden of those bloody sight-seers. We've also possibly got another problem." As we ran back to the chariot, I told her what Penny had said about the Chimera. At first, she said nothing. She kept her head up, looking away from me, and her shoulders were set in a tense and angry line.

She clearly wasn't happy with me. Maybe because I had shouted at her; maybe because I had seen more of her than she had wanted me to see. I didn't know exactly, but as far as I was concerned, she would just have to get over it.

When you are out in the field, you have to respond to situations as they happen. There's no time for false modesty or drawing-room etiquette. And if she didn't like it, well, she was just going to have to toughen up, because as far as I was concerned, this was only just the beginning. There was going to be an awful lot more mess, violence and unpleasantness to contend with before we got out of the Inferno and back to normality.

Finally, she spoke. "Well, I suppose that could make sense. Something had clearly spooked them on their way here. The horses were not at all happy, in fact, I think we may have problems getting them back up there."

"Can you handle it?" I knew she was an experienced charioteer, but I had no idea if that had included a crash-course on horse-whispering.

She didn't look at me.

"Just watch me," she said, and with that she turned away and began walking straight over to the horses, which had just emerged from the time-trance and were now stamping their feet and blowing through their nostrils. To be honest, they did seem to be a little edgy, but whether that was because of a close encounter with a Chimera, or just a reasonable reaction to being poked and prodded by all the sightseers, I really couldn't tell.

I gave one glance towards Sara's purposeful back; the muscles on her legs now firmly hugged in blue and silver Lycra, and decided to leave her to it.

First thing to do was to find a place for the kitbags; I dumped both of them up front in the box of the chariot, where hopefully no-one would spot them and then took a quick recce of the situation. There were still far too many people milling about on the lawn and I had just begun shepherding them back through the garden gate as the cottage door opened and Penny, closely followed by Heinrich, Lottie and Lisl, came out.

Ignoring the now rapidly retreating crowd, Penny strode straight towards the chariot, glancing quickly upwards as she did so. She reached Sara, who was still calming the horses and they began to talk in low voices. I couldn't hear what they were saying, but whatever it was seemed to satisfy her.

The others followed more slowly – Heinrich waving a little shyly to some of his friends on the other side of the fence, who were now calling out to him and holding up placards saying things like 'Good luck Heinrich' and 'Mars Here We Come'. When they got to the chariot, Penny opened the door and they all got in, Heinrich and Lottie standing up at the front of the passenger area with Penny, whilst Lisl found herself a more comfortable seat at the back.

The other angel and Johan came out of the cottage, and made their way over to the chariot. As he got close to me, Johan seemed to stumble and as I reached down to help him up, he whispered hurriedly, "Did you hear them back there? The Chimera?"

I nodded, saying nothing.

"Can you deal with it?" He was back on his feet now. I moved towards him, giving the appearance of brushing down the sleeve of his jacket. He looked straight at me, and I winked.

"Is everything alright now, sir?" I said to him, in my most courteous, cabin-crew type voice (one that admittedly, I don't use very often).

"Everything is now ready for your journey, and we hope that your ride today with CIEL will be a pleasant one."

I winked again, and this time, after a second he winked back.

Hopefully he was now feeling reassured – which I must admit, would have given him a rather higher confidence level than I was feeling at the moment. We were about to commandeer a vehicle neither of us had flown before, owned by one of the most powerful corporations in the celestial realms; possibly heading right into the path of a hostile Chimera. To say I was nervous would have been something of an understatement.

As I struggled to get my nerves back on track, Johan and the other angel climbed in, both taking seats at the back alongside Lisl. I made sure the chariot door was secure and went round to the front of the vehicle. Getting up into the box, I found Sara expertly carrying out the final checks on a fiendishly complex-looking control console.

She was still pissed off with me. I thought I had better make some sort of apology, and also try to reassure her that everything was now quite nicely back on track.

"Look, I'm sorry. I know it was risky, but we did it didn't we? We're here safe and sound… and that lot," I gestured back towards the angels, Lisl and the children, "haven't spotted anything out of the ordinary."

No reaction.

I was blustering. "I know you can fly this thing… and I'm actually not bad with chariots, despite what Johan said about me losing my licence, so all we really have to worry about now is getting away cleanly at the other end…"

This time, she looked at me, with both contempt and disbelief in her expression. Without saying a word, she raised her eyes skywards. There were very few clouds, the sun was shining and the sky was the palest, early-morning blue. But far away, towards the horizon, I spotted a dark and strangely menacing shape, which seemed to be flying slowly back and forth, as if scanning for something…

"Oh and… er… the Chimera… Yes, we may need to worry about that."

Finally, she spoke. "No, we don't actually."

She sounded both professional and more than a little dismissive. She nodded towards Penny, who was standing a little way away from the children, and was also rather surreptitiously scanning the sky. "I told her that we have a special cloaking device on this model and that we can fly the whole way to the studios under cover."

I looked at her, a little nonplussed. "And do we?"

She gave a little shrug. "All I need to do is bring down the darkness."

~ 156 ~

Without waiting for a reply, and totally ignoring Penny, who had just spotted the shape on the horizon and was now tapping urgently on the glass panel which separated the box from the rest of the chariot, Sara moved towards the console and began to call down upon us the darkness of the twelfth hour of the night.

Within seconds, the garden was filled with a darkling mist; we could no longer see the faces of the people standing on the other side of the fence and the cottage had vanished into the gathering gloom. She turned towards Penny, gave her a thumbs-up, and received a rather quavering half-smile in return.

She then turned to me, with a look of challenge in her eyes. I'd always liked her eyes. Even back in the day when we were working together on Jacob's Ladder and she had that crush on Samael, I'd been a sucker for them. Brown, with little flecks of gold. Eyes to drown in.

I couldn't help it. I melted.

"Sara, you are a bloody miracle..." I moved towards her, but however much I wanted to, I didn't dare touch her; Penny and the other angel might have been watching and it would have looked most unusual for the charioteers to be embracing.

As the blackness engulfed us, she turned to face me and finally, she smiled. Now we were safely cloaked within the cloud, she put the orphanims into gear, the Hayots raised their trumpets to their lips to sound the fanfare for take-off and Sara grabbed the reins of the four silver horses, which were now calm and completely commandable. She had everything under control.

There was nothing for me to do – and as if she read my mind, she turned to me saying, "You might as well put some music on, we've got at least two hours in this damn thing, and we're not exactly going to be able to pass the time looking at the view."

I gave her a quick grin and rifled through the CDs in the glove box. Bypassing the classic rock and jazz-funk fusion which had clearly been the favourite in-flight listening of the chariot's previous crew, I found what I was looking for and slipped the CD into the console.

There was only one track that would do. As we rose into the Heavens, the horses' shining wings valiantly cleaving their way through the clouds and the Hayot Angels playing their muted triumphal fanfares, the chariot was filled with the sound of Space Rock; *Hawkwind* and *Silver Machine*.

~ 157 ~

~ *Chapter Twenty Three* ~

It didn't last long. Sara humoured me for about five minutes, but then her sarcastic comments combined with the insistent knocking on the glass panel made it pretty clear that this was not exactly a popular choice, so I switched over to a collection of pleasant and inoffensive jazz classics, mainly featuring Ella Fitzgerald on vocals. Now that is what I call the voice of an angel.

Sara's "cloaking device" worked perfectly and we managed the whole journey without incident or interference. As we closed in for landing, she lifted the cloud cover and we flew to earth in what can only be described as biblical splendour; orphanims blazing, sunlight catching on the silver of the horses' wings, casting fragments of light like a halo around the chariot, and the Hayots playing the show's theme tune on their golden trumpets like a celestial Herb Alpert and his Tijuana brass.

We made a text-book landing on our allotted spot at the back of the studios, exactly on schedule. I wanted to congratulate her, but everything I could think of to say sounded patronising, so I just gave her a thumbs-up and carried on with the safety checks on the control panel. She didn't seem particularly pleased by this and after sending a rather withering glance in my direction, Sara leapt out of the box and went to open the chariot door for the passengers. I saw that Penny was smiling as she led the way into the building. She had got exactly what she wanted, and was once more the cool, calm professional. Her colleague followed her, looking a little the worse for wear from the flight through the darkness. I noticed that this time he was carrying both of the silver bags and his previously rather jaunty air was conspicuous by its absence.

I climbed out of the box more slowly, making my way to the front of the vehicle to check on the horses. I was clearly not out of Sara's bad books and I was still worried about my boots; the last thing I needed at this stage was for someone to rumble me. Because of this, I had no chance to say anything to Johan as he and his family disembarked and, following the angels, made their way towards the studio entrance. As he reached the doorway, Johan paused to let the rest of them go in before him. At last, he stood alone on the tarmac. He turned towards me and, squinting slightly in the sun, raised his arm in a gesture of farewell. I did likewise.

Then he opened the door and went in.

I stood unmoving for a minute, my thoughts focused on Johan and what the week ahead would bring for him and his family. We would never have come so far without him. He had helped us at a time when his personal life was in turmoil. He was a good guy – I'd always known it. And now I owed him. Big time.

My reverie was shattered when something heavy landed at my feet. Sara had thrown my kitbag at me.

"Come on, we need to get the horses stabled; then we can get changed and make our way out of here."

I picked up my bag and went to help her sort out the horses; we took two each and led them to the stables, where we handed them over to a couple of waiting grooms and made our way towards the rear of the studio building. I'd spotted a couple of outhouses which we could use to get back into our normal gear.

We tossed the Lycra body suits into a rubbish bin and took a quick look around us. There was a lot of activity around the studio building itself. People had already begun to queue outside the front gates; I guessed that these were probably the audience getting ready for their weekly fix of 'This is your next life'. At the rear of the building, technicians were milling around frantically doing whatever it is they do with wires and cable. Another chariot had landed and a third was just about visible on the horizon. As we watched it, we quickly saw that all was not as it should've been.

It was travelling at speed but seemed to be flying erratically. As we gazed on in disbelief, we saw the dark form of a monstrous creature moving swiftly towards the chariot. There was no doubting what it was, even from this distance it was possible to make out the Chimera's mutated and distorted form; the head of a lion, a vast and muscular dragon's body and wings and the long, threatening tail of an enormous snake. It flew closer and closer, and as it dived towards the chariot box, its powerful, scaly wings grazed the flank of one of the flying horses. The horse screamed, and the beast sent out a jet of fire which engulfed the terrified animal, causing the chariot to lurch alarmingly in the air.

The horse, mane and tail ablaze, reared up and lashed out at the Chimera, catching it with its silver hooves, and knocking it to one side. As it fell, the beast sent out another jet of flame, missing the horses, but singeing the undercarriage of the chariot, which was still rocking in the air and was becoming increasingly unstable.

The beast righted itself and began to fly upwards, away from the chariot, higher and higher as if positioning itself to dive for one final, catastrophic attack. But as it did so, the four Hayot Angels who guarded each corner of the chariot spread their wings and launched themselves upwards, their swords held aloft and their faces set grimly for battle. Three of the Hayots flew towards the Chimera; the fourth banked slightly and then flew swiftly towards the still screaming silver horse.

Hovering beside it, the angel gazed upwards and raised his arms to the Heavens. Both Sara and I knew what he was doing; the Hayot was calling down into himself the celestial powers of healing and regeneration. Within seconds, the angel was glowing with heavenly radiance; he held out his hand towards the terrified animal and then blew gently, his breath visible and glistening like a spider's web on an autumn morning. The web surrounded the horse, putting out the flames and calming him, and as the blaze subsided and the screaming stopped, the horse bowed its head towards the angel, who reached out his hand again, gently stroking the pure white muzzle, before launching himself upwards towards the Chimera.

The matter was dealt with swiftly. We saw the Chimera fall from the skies, its wings in tatters, and deep gashes along its neck and flanks. The Hayots may not have been too bright, but they were programmed to protect and defend, and no-one could say that they took their responsibilities lightly. Their business finished, the angels sheathed their swords and resumed their positions. The chariot set off again, heading straight for its allotted landing space at the studios. It had all taken less than half an hour, but had caused a major rumpus on the ground.

A film crew had recorded most of the action from the roof of the CIEL building and there was a massive amount of activity around the landing site as reporters vied with nurses and lawyers to get to the chariot first. I reckoned that this would be the lead item on CIEL News for at least the next four hours, and it would provide even more publicity for '*This is your next life*'.

From what Sara had told me, this would go down extremely well with K and his Efficiency and Reform buddies, and it might even get Eligor off our back for a while, as it would be completely clear from the footage that the chariot that had been attacked by the Chimera had contained an innocent cargo of game show contestants – not a Justice Angel to be seen amongst them.

"Come on," I said to Sara, "this is the perfect opportunity. Let's make a break for it now; looks like everyone is too busy dealing with the drama to notice if we slip out the back gates."

She nodded, we both strapped on our kitbags and walked, unchallenged and in broad daylight, straight towards the gates of the studio compound. The scene we had just witnessed seemed to have put our petty squabbles into perspective; in any case, it reminded me that we had some serious shit to deal with and that quarrelling wouldn't help. I remembered what Raphael had said to us as we were leaving the HTC and decided that it would be a good time to clear the air. I cleared my throat. "You were great you know? Up there…"

She looked at me, not quite decided if she was ready to be friends again.

I carried on. "And I'm sorry for being an idiot back at Johan's."

That seemed to do the trick. The corners of her mouth just twitched into the beginnings of a grin. "And I'm sorry for getting so uptight. If you hadn't hung back in the cottage we'd have had no idea about the Chimera, and who knows what would have happened if we'd met it in mid-air. There's no guarantee that the Hayots on our chariot would have been a bunch of Samurais like those guys back there."

I grinned back at her. "Quits?"

"Quits."

~ *Chapter Twenty Four* ~

As we passed through the gates, we entered a bleak and desolate landscape. The sky, which had been blue and almost cloudless when we stood within the boundaries of the studio compound, was now a dull and rather sickly grey. Red clouds streaked with foul-smelling, sulphurous vapour almost completely covered the dull face of the large and oppressively darkened sun, which seemed to squat in the sky, very close to the horizon.

Despite the fact that the sun was out and it was still not yet noon, there was very little light and the shadows cast by the sandstone outcrops which dominated the landscape were abnormally long and sinister.

The studio had been built on a vast natural plain which stretched from the walls of the Tartarus prison to the west and continued right up to the eastern edges of the Lake of Fire, bordered and crisscrossed by the rivers Archeron, Lethe and Styx. Whilst there was still some neutral territory in the area, for example, inside the boundaries of the CIEL compound and within the halls of the palace of judgement itself, now we were out in the open we could no longer count on the comparative safety we had found within the boundary lands. We were heading towards the heart of the Inferno and most of the people we would meet from now on were unlikely to be exactly friendly towards angels.

We decided the best thing to do would be to find some cover, give our bodies a bit of refreshment and then check out our co-ordinates. We would have to be very cautious about how we moved forward from now on and we needed to know exactly where we were. We could see a river in the middle distance and I was pretty certain that it wasn't the Lethe; we were rather too far north. Given that, I guessed that it must be the Styx, which also flowed out of the Lake of Fire and which made its way north-west, along the borders of the Inferno.

~ 162 ~

Sara spotted a small, ramshackle hut about half a mile away down the road and we agreed to head towards it. We saw no-one and there was no other sign of habitation. As we walked, I kept looking upwards, my eyes vigilantly casting across the skies in case another enemy was lurking. This caused me to miss my footing twice and, as Sara reminded me as she helped me up after my second tumble, it was a pretty pointless exercise anyway, as there was fat chance of seeing anything up there with all the cloud cover.

As we reached the entrance to the hut, I felt a vibration against my shoulder. I reached into my kitbag – it was Manny. Not wanting to take the call until I knew it would be safe to talk, I pressed the reject button and followed Sara inside.

It took a while for our eyes to adjust. If it had been gloomy outdoors, it was pretty much stygian once we got inside (which is, I suppose, what you might have expected). There was hardly any noise; just a sort of wheezing and rumbling that seemed to come from the very back of the building, but once inside, the smell was so strong and so disgusting it almost seemed to scream at you.

I heard Sara gag and felt her push past me. I didn't try to stop her, in fact, I couldn't blame her. I'd come across this particular fragrance once before, maybe three thousand years ago, and I'd never found anything that would trump it in terms of sheer fetid revoltingness. But if I was right, we could be on to an absolute winner.

Quietly, I retraced my steps. Sara was standing with her back towards the cottage, taking great breaths of air. I rammed my phone into my back pocket and began a quick search in my kitbag for something we could tie round our faces to provide at least some protection from the stench. I didn't find any handkerchiefs, but as I fumbled about in the depths of the side pocket, I found the phial of eucalyptus oil that the pharmacist back at St. Basil's had given me.

I dabbed some on my upper lip, just below my nostrils and offered the phial to Sara, who raised an eyebrow and gestured questioningly towards the doorway.

"Don't tell me you expect me to go back in there. I have never smelled anything so disgusting in my life." She looked at me questioningly. "What the hell is in there anyway? It's beyond gross. That whole shack needs demolishing if you ask me. And a little dab of essential oil is not going to make any difference."

"What is in there, Sara, is probably the answer to our prayers." She looked at me with a glance that contained a subtle cocktail of scepticism and disbelief, topped off with a glace cherry of resignation.

"Come over here and keep quiet. We're lucky that we don't seem to have disturbed them when we went inside the first time."

We walked across to the other side of the track, where a couple of blighted and unproductive olive trees provided cover of a sort.

"There's only one thing I know that smells like that and that is the Graeae – or rather, to be more precise, the Graeae's dinner."

"You mean the Grey Sisters? The ones with just one eye and one tooth between them?"

I nodded, speaking quickly and trying to keep the excitement out of my voice. "Yes, that's them. They can only eat food that has rotted to putrefaction, the more maggoty the better." Sara wrinkled her nose in disgust.

I continued. "They have almost no sense of smell themselves, so the stink doesn't bother them. In fact, I think they only know their food is ready for them when the stench has become so overpowering that they are finally able to smell it."

"Well, that's all well and good," said Sara, still looking with complete distaste at the almost derelict building across the way from us, "but I don't understand what the presence of the Grey Sisters and their stinking supper has to do with the price of fish."

"They may only have one eye and one tooth between them, but they know everything that's going on down here - and if anyone can tell us exactly where Eligor is keeping Alex and Sophia, they can."

"Yes, and we're just going to walk in and ask them are we?" Sara folded her arms and looked mutinous. "I really can't see the Grey Sisters wanting to play ball with a couple of angels. And from what I hear, they keep some very dodgy company. Aren't they related to the Gorgons? I don't know about you, but I don't fancy being turned to stone anytime soon."

"Well, yes. There is that. But most people down here keep pretty dodgy company, what with it being the Inferno and all. We really aren't that likely to bump into Judy Garland or Princess Diana you know. And beggars can't be choosers. If we can get them to talk, it will save hours of wasted time."

She looked at me for a second, and then closed her eyes, as if seeking to distance herself. She said nothing for a minute or two, and I didn't press her. There are times when you just have to let people work things out for themselves.

"Okay." She looked straight at me and uncrossed her arms. "What's the plan? And you'd better give me some of that damned eucalyptus."

Quickly, I sketched out my idea. She looked sceptical, but finally she nodded in agreement and, having first made sure that we had rubbed on as much of the eucalyptus oil as we could stand, we crept quietly back across the road and into the silent, stinking shack.

The rumbling, wheezing noise had stopped. There was now no sound at all and we could see nothing in the fetid blackness. We moved slowly, cautiously placing one foot in front of the other, terrified that we would knock into something or fall over. We stayed close-up along the side of the left hand wall, gradually edging ourselves towards the back of the building, from where we had heard the sound of the sleeping sisters. Despite the eucalyptus, the smell was revolting. I was thankful that I'd given my corpus very little in the way of food over the last forty-eight hours; if I'd been in here with a full stomach, I think I would have hurled by now.

Something stirred a few feet away from me; I heard a cough, grating and phlegm-ridden, and then the sound of spitting. Rustling noises, like rats scrabbling in a rubbish bin, and then someone spoke. The voice from the crone's toothless mouth was old, but not weak or quavering.

"Ith there thomeone there...? Eyno, can you thee anyone? I'm thure I heard thomething moving..."

Her voice was deep and ageless; her lack of teeth giving her speech a strange lisping impediment, which I later found was shared by all the sisters. She sounded like a cockneyfied and rather sinister Violet-Elizabeth Bott. There came more rustling, more coughing; then the sound of a more definite movement, someone getting to their feet.

"Shut it, Deino, we can't hear nuffin wiv you makin' that bleedin' racket. Path me the toof. If there ith thomeone there, I want to be able to bite the little bleeder."

Behind me, I felt Sara shrink back against the wall. She didn't like it in here, and I can't say I blamed her. The rustling sounded again, then the noise of something metallic being knocked over or kicked, then another disgusting, hawking cough. I moved quickly, all my senses attuned to the noises in front of me. Praying I had got it right, I put out my hand and felt a small, sharp and surprisingly heavy object drop into my outstretched palm.

Yes! I mentally punched the air. I'd got it.

As you probably know, Eyno, Deino and their lovely sister Pephredo, share a single tooth and a single eye between them. I tucked the tooth into my pocket and waited.

"I thaid give me the bleedin' toof. What're you playin' at, Pepi?"

The sister I took to be Eyno must be standing right next to me. Immediately, I moved backwards, slightly to my right, towards the person who had unwittingly handed me the tooth. As I did so, I gave Sara's foot a quick nudge. We had to do this bit together.

I reached out into the darkness, grabbed tight hold of the ancient crone standing beside me, and gagged her with my hand. At exactly the same moment, I heard a dark, guttural voice say,

"No, Eyno, it'th my turn wiv the toof, you 'ad it all dai yesterdai. You give me the eye. If there's any bathtards in here, I'll find 'em."

Eyno made a protesting noise, but the voice rang out again. This time it was more threatening.

"I sed giv me the toof. Do it."

The crone I was holding onto was squirming in my arms, trying to kick my shins, and doing her best to bite my fingers with her toothless jaws. She was a revoltingly malodourous bundle and I was pretty relieved a few seconds later when a completely different voice rang out.

"Zach, I've got it."

It was Sara. Immediately, I let go of my captive and pushed her away from me towards the back wall.

Pulling my phone from my pocket, I turned on the torch app and moved back towards Sara, who was holding the eyeball between her thumb and forefinger, her arm stretched out slightly behind her, as if she wanted to touch the revolting object as little as possible and to place it as far from her own field of vision as she could.

I shone the light on the three ancient sisters, who were now standing together in an angry huddle in the corner of the hut. Next to them was an overturned cauldron. That must have been the thing we heard being knocked over as the sisters had got to their feet in the darkness. Its decomposing contents were now leaking onto the floorboard and I could just make out what looked like a canine femur, its mouldy and maggot-ridden flesh still partly clinging to the bone.

Behind me, I heard Sara begin to gag again; I swiftly pointed the beam towards the sisters and away from their dinner.

I checked my watch. It was nearly one o'clock.

"Good afternoon, ladies; so nice to see you again." The sisters said nothing. One of them, I think it was Deino, turned towards us and spat.

"Charming. So lovely to be welcomed into your... gracious... home. It is, of course, such a shame you can't see us, but hey, that's the way the cookie crumbles."

"I know that voithe." It was Eyno.

She stepped away from her sisters, her sightless eyes raised towards me, a look of furious recognition on her face. "You're an eyngel. You in'erfered wiv our bithneth before. Watcha want thith time, you bathtard?"

"Aah, so you do remember me, I'm flattered; it was quite a while ago you know. Now, all I need from you is a little information and then we'll be on our way and you can get on with your particularly appetising dinner."

"Fuck off, eyngel." It was Pephredo, the one I had captured whilst Sara was acquiring the eye. She'd grabbed a knife from the floor and was now making her way towards us, unsteady, but determined.

"Now we can't have that, can we?" Sara moved out from behind me and with whip-crack speed, kicked the knife out of the sightless crone's grasp sending her reeling backwards into the wall of the hut.

She stood in front of me, shoulders back and slightly breathless, one hand closed in a fist around the sister's single eyeball.

"You may have met Zach before, but you've never met me, and believe me, you do not want to piss me off. Any more stupidity and I will break every bone in your stinking bodies and as for your eyeball; I will grind it beneath my boots.

"Now, you'll listen, and you'll tell us what we need to know, and then we will be on our way. Do you understand?"

The three sisters grumbled and muttered and then Eyno stepped forwards. "Athk utth your quethtionth, then go."

Pephredo was still on the floor; her sisters went to sit beside her, their three ancient, malevolent faces turned towards us in the torch-light.

Sara moved back to the side wall; I went to stand next to her and we began questioning the Grey Sisters. They were evasive at first, but after I threatened to grind their tooth to powder alongside the eyeball, they began to co-operate.

It appeared that Deino had actually seen Sophia and Alex yesterday. It had been her turn with the eyeball and she had been taking picked-over bones from the cauldron to Cerberus, the three-headed Hell-Hound who guards the Avernus Gate.

"Heth such a good doggie, and he doeth love hith bone marrer." Deino gave a surprisingly sentimental smile.

"Lovely. But what about Alex and Sophia?" I was determined to get the questioning back on track. It emerged that the brother and sister hadn't looked hurt, but were clearly distressed and afraid and both of them were handcuffed and blindfolded. We asked how Eligor had managed to bring two living souls into the Inferno and Eyno told us that they were both wearing Orphic talismans, which provided a basic level of protection and should allow re-entry into the land of the living. At least this provided us with an answer to our worries about how we would be able to keep them safe once we'd rescued them. The talismans should hold good for the journey back – and we still had that bloody stupid stick Sara had insisted on bringing along for the ride. I glanced across at her, and sure enough its gilded tip was just poking out of the top of her kitbag.

"So where did he take them? Where are they now?" Sara was getting more urgent in her questioning.

After quite a bit of maundering around and a number of highly evasive answers, we found out that Sophia and Alex were being held in Eligor's stronghold, just as Johan had suspected.

Eyno gave a nasty cackle, "And they're not alone. Eligor found thome very pretty playmateth for them. Thome very pretty playmateth indeed."

All three of the sisters were laughing now, almost hysterical, their voices cracked and distorted; breath coming in short bursts from their ancient lungs.

I turned to Sara. "Come on, we won't get any more from this lot. We know where we have to go now, and I say we get going."

She nodded. "And what about this?" she glanced at the object she still held in her hand.

"Oh, I think we keep these for a little bit longer." I took the eyeball from her and stuck it with the tooth into one of the side pockets of my kitbag. "As a guarantee that this lot stay silent."

I looked back at them. "You get word to Eligor that we've been here, and your precious treasures will be gone for ever. You stay silent and I'll leave them with the ferryman."

Gesturing with the phone, I sent a pathway of light towards the door of the hovel and Sara quickly moved along it. I walked more slowly, going backwards towards the entrance and never taking my eyes off the Grey Sisters who were now looking towards me with hatred. As I reached the doorway, Pephredo got to her feet, her sightless eyes deep holes within her ancient face and her scaly hand raised towards me.

"But he knowth you're here, eyngel. He knowth exactly what you're up to. And he knowth that thomeone will betray you. Thereth a traitor to the Heaventh in the Inferno. And when they bring you down, your boneth will be ours."

~ *Chapter Twenty Five* ~

I staggered a little as I emerged from the hovel. The light, which had seemed so dull before we went in there, now seemed startlingly bright in comparison and I missed my footing on the threshold; my mind focused on the crone's words rather than on where I was going.

Sara had returned to the clump of trees and taken the map from her kitbag. I pulled out the water bottle and took a swig, wiping my mouth with my hand as I did so. I wanted to wash away the foul taste of the Grey Sisters and to get rid of the remnants of the eucalyptus oil, which was starting to irritate my skin. I handed the water to Sara; after she'd finished, the bottle was about half empty. There were four cans of Red Bull left and we would need to save two of these for Sophia and Alex. If we didn't get a move on, our bodies would soon start to become dehydrated, and then we really would be in trouble.

"Look," Sara pointed to the map, "I think we're about here. That means it is probably only about 10 miles to the ditches of Malebolge. Do you still think that's our best chance?"

I ignored her, my mind still on the words that Pephredo had thrown at me. "Did you hear what she said to me as we were leaving, did you hear what that old bitch had to say?"

Sara shook her head. "No, I didn't hear anything; I got out of there as quick as I could. What is it?"

"She told me that Eligor is on to us. She told me that there is a traitor to the Heavens right here, in the Inferno."

Sara stared at me, her face suddenly blanching; her eyes were open wide with shock. But before she could say anything, I felt my phone vibrate in my pocket. It was Manny, and this time, I was going to talk to him. Putting my hand out to silence Sara, I pressed the button to accept the call.

~ 170 ~

"Zach, where are you... and what's going on in there?" It felt good to hear his voice. Manny had got me through more operations than I cared to remember and he'd never let me down. I quickly got him up to speed with everything that had happened since we had left Johan's.

"Were you involved in that incident with the Chimera? The footage is going viral. That's not exactly a way to stay inconspicuous." Manny's voice had a bit of an edge to it and I had to calm him down, telling him about everything Johan had done to help us and giving Sara a rave review as a charioteer.

I quickly told him about our encounter with the Graeae. "So we're pretty certain that Alex and Sophia are still being held in Eligor's place. We reckon it is only about 10 miles from here to the ditches of Malebolge; all being well we should be through them in a couple of hours. My main worry is..." but here Manny stopped me before I could tell him what the Grey Sisters had said about the traitor.

"Your main worry should be that Jaoel is in there with you."

"What? Jaoel... in here. How do you know?"

"One of the Potestas went to question the doorkeepers at the Avernus Gate. Turns out Jaoel took the ferry across the Styx at around midnight on Sunday. He paid his way, and they let him through. We don't know where he is now, but I reckon he knows exactly what you have been sent in there to do. And he will want to do anything he can to prevent you from succeeding."

Sara who now looked less pale, but was clearly surprised to hear the news about Jaoel, moved towards the phone. "Manny, what's going to happen with Nat and the Potestas? I thought they had been sent out to track down Jaoel. Has K told them to stand down?"

"No. There has been no decision to stand down the Potestas." Manny was speaking low and fast, like he didn't have much time, and was worried about being overheard. "That's one of the reasons I'm calling you. K has called a meeting of the full council. He doesn't just want Nat's platoon to be engaged. He wants reinforcements. And he wants to send them straight into the Inferno."

"But that means war." I was horrified. It was one thing to fight injustice, to right wrongs and to mete out divine punishment; it was quite another to march into the Inferno and stir up a Hell's nest of demons who would be only too happy to take the fight back to earth. The consequences of a war would be catastrophic for humanity and it would make our chances of getting Alex and Sophia out of there alive almost non-existent.

"How long have we got?"

"K is with the council now. Gabriel and Michael are trying to dissuade him, but they don't seem to have much support. If the decision goes his way, I reckon the order to mobilise will be given immediately and the forces will be on their way by midnight." Manny sighed. I knew how uncomfortable he would be feeling. What he was doing was sailing very close to disobedience, and we all knew the consequences of that.

"What about Raph...? Where does he stand on this?" Sara spoke quickly; there was an edge of uncertainty in her tone. She and her old teacher had been pretty close, and I think she was hoping that he wasn't part of the faction urging the Heavenly Host to go on the offensive.

"The Archangel Raphael is not at the meeting. K consulted with the others and they agreed to continue without him." Manny paused. We let this sink in. Raphael was one of the inner-circle; it was almost unthinkable that they would take a decision like this without involving him.

"Zach, Sara, listen to me; the only way to stop this is to capture Jaoel before Nat can get his forces together. You need to bring him back to the Agency, along with Alex and Sophia, and let the council decide on his punishment. Maybe that will be enough to stop everything imploding. Do you understand me?"

"I *understand* you, Manny, but that doesn't mean we can actually do this thing." I was still reeling from the shock that we might be about to be plunged into a cosmic war-zone. Our task had always been a tough one but now we had to factor in the added responsibility for the capture of a rebel angel on top of the rescue of the two human hostages, who were only being held by one of the most powerful of the Dukes of Hell in a stronghold protected by at least sixty legions – and we had about nine hours to play with.

He didn't reply. Then we heard noises in the background; a door slamming, raised voices, Manny spoke, low, fast and urgent into the phone. "Zach, Sara, I've got to go. The council's breaking up, Gabriel and Michael have just stormed out, I don't know what's been decided, but I can guess. And it doesn't look good. You know what you've to do. And there's going to be hell to pay if you don't get back here with Jaoel by midnight."

The phone went dead.

"Did you hear that?" I thrust the phone in Sara's face and she had to pull backwards to avoid it. I always become less well co-ordinated when I lose my temper.

~ 172 ~

"Nine hours. Nine hours. He wants us to capture Jaoel, rescue Alex and Sophia, outwit the forces of evil and present ourselves back at Canonbury Tower, all present and correct. In nine bloody hours."

I was more than a little angry with Manny for hanging up on us; I felt stressed and put upon and my little outburst must have come over as particularly melodramatic because Sara instantly assumed a ridiculous pose.

"Flash, I love you..." She was wringing her hands and looking up at me, quoting from an old movie, in a truly atrocious American accent.

It was so absurdly unexpected, that after I had taken in what she was actually saying, I became a little hysterical.

"But we've only got fourteen hours to save the earth," I replied in equally cod and unconvincing tones. Sara laughed; she leant into me, her shoulders brushing against my chest, her hand gently coming to rest in mine. I felt the shock of her touch careering through me, a warm ripple of celestial energy that made me gasp as I looked down at her. And this time there was no-one watching. This time, I kissed her.

Her lips were soft and slightly parted; I could just feel the firmness of her teeth as I kissed her harder, pulling her closer to me. The faint odour of eucalyptus still clung to her, but beneath it was another smell: warm, and spicy; intoxicating. This was what human bodies did, what human bodies wanted.

But we were angels. As swiftly as the kiss began, it ended. We pushed apart from each other. Sara wiped her lips with her right hand. I turned away from her, not knowing what to say.

"Well, that was... interesting." Sara looked at me speculatively. She licked her lips. I didn't want to meet her eyes, so I looked away and said nothing. We were silent for a moment, and then Sara spoke again.

"We'd better get a move on." Clearly Sara was not quite as much at a loss for words as I was. She looked upwards and I followed her gaze. "I reckon we chance it," she said. "I think we should fly to the ditches. It's probably our best hope of making it - and it's definitely the fastest. What do you think?"

The skies were still heavy, a dense dull grey and despite it only being just early afternoon, the darkly over-blown sun's rays were weak and gave little heat. But much of the sulphurous cloud cover had lifted and I could see nothing up there that seemed likely to threaten us.

Normally, I wouldn't have gone along with it. An angel in flight is vulnerable from both above and below. There's nowhere to hide up there; you become a target the minute you spread your wings, and a pretty big one at that.

But my emotions were all over the place; Manny's revelations, Jaoel, the increased threat to Sophia and Alex. And Sara; most of all Sara. The touch, taste and smell of her had triggered something in me and not just because of the physical responses of my corporeal body. It went deeper. And I did not know what to do with it.

I didn't do this. I never had.

And because I wasn't thinking straight, I decided to risk it.

"Okay. Let's go for it." I gave a quick glance in her direction. "Are you ready?" She secured her kitbag to her belt. Then she nodded.

We moved apart from each other and stretched out our arms. Within seconds we were fully alated and as one we reached upwards into the grey and threatening yonder. With an almighty surge of power, we forced ourselves onwards, thrusting towards the skies. Our wings beating in unison, we rode the currents until we were far above the ground and on our way towards the evil ditches of Malebolge.

Last time we'd flown together, when she had raced me to the gates of the Elysian Fields, I'd gloried in the power and majesty of being an angel in its element. This time I was unable to lose myself in the sensual thrill of flying. There was no pleasure to be found in soaring above this blasted and desolate landscape, where our shadows cast traitorous shapes upon the ground and the cirrus clouds provided no hope of shelter or concealment. And my mind could not let go; I couldn't just become absorbed in the simple physicality of flight and speed, air and currents. My mind was full of Sara.

Sara, pushing me hard up against the wall of my flat before we set out to St. Basil's, showing me she wasn't the timorous little desk-bunny I had assumed she had become. I thought about the way her touch had become attuned to mine, the way she'd calmed me down when I was on the verge of hurling Isra to oblivion and how she had given me her strength when I had needed it. She'd used her own feathers to bring me round after I had been attacked in Kathryn's flat, an almost unheard of intimacy between Angelic-kind.

And then, the other thoughts; the questions and the doubts. Once again I wondered why she hadn't told me that Nat and the Potestas had been mobilised. I thought about her secrecy, her anger when she thought I was going to look inside her kitbag; her curious reaction when we found out about how Kathryn died. It hadn't been the death that shocked her, but the fact it had taken so long, had been so inefficient.

I remembered her rudeness to Johan and Lisl when they let slip that the defection of the Fallen Angels was common knowledge in the boundary lands. But Johan had trusted her. And she had proved her worth so many times.

My thoughts were racing, image followed image and I couldn't sort out what it was that I was feeling. She flew beside me, silent and glorious, her copper wings riding the air with grace and magnificence, her eyes constantly sweeping the skies for danger.

We had calculated that Malebolge was about 10 miles away from the Graeaes' hovel and we were flying at speed. In less than fifteen minutes we'd made it; we began to circle slowly, looking for somewhere suitable to land. We flew above the vast cavern, looking down on the trenches which ran in concentric circles, each connected to the other by a series of rickety bridges. Some were built deep within the ditches, rising on stilts above the treacherous depths; others were cobbled together from planks of wood and roped across the divides, swaying perilously each time a rush of steam forced its way upwards, carrying with it the sobs and screams of souls in torment.

There was a sort of shanty town at the edge of the cavern. Huts and hovels made of scavenged wood and old tarpaulins, rusted-up containers, abandoned skips and broken down trucks that would never move again had become ramshackle dwellings, creating a home of sorts to those who chose – or were forced - to live in this benighted place.

We circled, flying high above the ditches so our shadows remained small and, we hoped, would not create suspicion if they were seen. There were figures moving across the bridges. Some it seemed, had once been human, their bodies now distorted, twisted and racked by the torments they had suffered, punishment meted out in accordance with their sins.

Along one ditch there stretched a chain of prisoners, shackled together, their clothes mere rags; their bodies were little more than skin and bone, bleeding flesh and open, weeping sores. Behind them, urging them on, we saw their demon jailers, whipping and scourging their prisoners, forcing them forwards in a constant deathly shuffle. This was the first of the ditches of Malebolge, where panderers and seducers served their sentences.

Flying on, we saw below us a deep, steep-sided gorge, with a dark, sluggish river winding through it. There was an uprush of wind and sulphurous steam accompanied by an even more disgusting smell. Fetid and foul, the stench of human excrement wafted up towards us, and looking down, we could just make out the shapes of those condemned to walk through the river of slow-flowing shit: flatterers, liars, shit-stirrers and deceivers. This was the second ditch - and the punishment meted out here most certainly and revoltingly fitted the crime.

We were now on the look-out for somewhere to land safely. As we passed over the third and fourth ditches, Sara pointed to one of the larger buildings on the edge of the next ravine; a two storey shack with a wooden porch and swinging saloon doors like the ones in the old Western movies. It stood right at the edge of the straggling shanty-town and had a sort of back yard, fenced in with rusted corrugated sheeting.

It seemed as good a place as any. Scanning the skies again, all seemed clear. There was nothing above us, and although we could see figures moving to the front of the building, there didn't seem to be any sign of life or movement in the back yard. Folding back our wings, we both began to dive downwards, the air rushing past us as we descended. Sara reached the ground first, a nice landing, crisp and clean.

I wasn't so lucky. I'd aimed a tad low and as I flew into the compound, I clipped the tips of my wings on the jagged top of the rusty fencing, losing a couple of primaries and causing me to falter as I landed. Winded, I staggered to my feet and then I sensed, rather than saw, a shape coming at me from the shadows at the side of the building. Before I could do anything, my arm was twisted roughly up behind me, damaging my pinions even further. I felt the touch of a blade at my throat and then a voice I thought I recognised murmured, "You really should take more care, angel. That was sloppy. Very sloppy indeed."

~ *Chapter Twenty Six* ~

I was pinned up against the corrugated fence and could see nothing of what was going on behind me. The knife blade was cold against my skin and if he pushed my arm much harder, I thought it was going to break. I heard Sara scream, there was a thud, and then the sound of two bodies colliding. The pressure on my arm lifted and I was free to move.

I massaged my elbow, which felt quite sore from being forced into such an unnatural position and flexed my wings. There didn't seem to be too much damage, but I decided to err on the side of caution and de-materialised them. They made me way too conspicuous and anyway, they would heal better in the celestial dimension.

Turning round, I expected to see my attacker on the ground, locked in mortal combat with Sara. What confronted me was a very different picture. Sara had also got rid of her wings and she and the stranger were locked in the sort of embrace that told me she knew whoever it was very well indeed. He was tall, probably not much shy of seven feet, and he bent over her protectively, holding her to him in a great bear-hug of an embrace, one of his huge hands round her waist, the other resting on her shoulder.

My immediate instinct was to get away. Whatever this was, I didn't like it, but before I could say or do anything, they pulled apart, and with a thrill of disbelief, I saw that the other guy was Raphael; the Archangel, master of healing and leading light of the Celestial Council.

Sara disentangled herself and ran towards me, and at the same time, Raphael gave me a slightly shamefaced smile and extended his hand towards me.

"Forgive me, Zach." His voice was mellow and unexpectedly calm given all the excitement. "I was perhaps a little... over enthusiastic... in trying to teach you a lesson."

Sara had reached my side and put out her hand to touch me. I shrugged her away. I just didn't understand what game these two were playing, and I was in no mood for a bit of the warm and fuzzy.

"You don't understand." Sara spoke urgently. "Raph's here to help us. It's really good news."

"Well he's got a funny way of showing it. He could have broken my arm back there." I rubbed my elbow again, rather melodramatically this time.

"Zach, I'm sorry." Raphael took another step towards me and he was no longer smiling. "I was just trying to make you think a little. You flew straight into this yard without checking it out properly. I could have been anyone, anyone at all hiding under the eaves, and you'd done nothing to ensure your safety."

I let his words sink in.

I looked around me; Sara was standing a couple of feet away, looking like an abandoned puppy. Raphael remained silent, staring straight at me. His eyes didn't flicker as I held his stare.

And I had to admit it; he was right. As I checked it out I could see that the yard was full of sheltered places, nooks and crannies where anything could've been hiding. The passage at the side of the building was big enough to conceal three or four fairly sizeable demons; I grudgingly admitted to myself that I was lucky that the only thing that had been hiding there was actually somebody who, apparently, was on my side.

I gave him a nod and looked away. "Point taken," I said.

Then, not wanting to seem like a spoilt child who's just had his comeuppance, I walked towards him and held out my hand. "Good to see you again."

Raphael smiled. His eyes did that sort of Morgan Freeman crinkly thing as he took my hand and grasped it in his. I steadied myself for the shock, but when his celestial energy reached me, rather than knocking me backwards, it just settled inside me, warm and reassuring like a cup of sweet tea and actually went a long way towards removing the last traces of my hurt pride.

"But what are you doing here?" This is what I couldn't understand. Raphael was supposed to have been in Islington, at the council with the other Archangels. What was he doing deep inside the Inferno – and how had he found us?

"I take it you know what's been going on?" Raphael looked quickly first at Sara, then at me.

~ 178 ~

"If you mean about Jaoel and this crack-brained scheme of K's to send in the militia, then yes, we've already spoken to Manny."

Raphael took a few moments to get us completely up to speed. The news about Jaoel had sent fairly seismic shockwaves throughout the Heavenly Host. Most of the other Archangels had headed straight over to the Agency when K had summoned them. Raphael, however, had had other ideas. He told us that he'd made it clear that he was completely opposed to the idea of sending Nat and his militia into the Inferno in pursuit; and he put his foot down big-time when K began talking about mobilising reinforcements.

"But I could see that he wasn't really listening." Raphael shook his head slowly, his hand rubbing his chin in a way that made me think that he was feeling either nervous or guilty about something.

"This isn't easy to say. I've known K for years; there's no doubt that he is a great leader. He cuts through the crap, gets things done... but he doesn't always think things through. And he's not always exactly... objective."

Raphael looked straight at me. "Did you know that K was the angel who drove Adam and Eve from the Garden?"

I shook my head. I didn't know very much about the early days; before humans inhabited the earth. From what I can remember, life had been really boring back then. Just the lauding and the magnifying and the constant bloody singing. Things didn't start to get interesting until the third realm was colonised, and of course, that all started with Adam and Eve.

"It was awful really. That poor girl, she had no idea what she was getting into. And he – Adam that is – was completely useless. He just went to pieces when they were given their marching orders and she had to pretty much carry him out of the Garden. I remember seeing them both as K pushed them through the gates, still practically naked, cold and trembling. They were covered in mud, their feet were bleeding from walking so far, and they were reeling from the shock of what had happened as they had just started to comprehend what they had lost."

"Sure, K was only doing what he had been told to do. He barred the gates and he took out his flaming sword and he made damn sure that they would never again have access to Paradise. When he had finished, that poor girl was beside herself."

"I don't have a quarrel with him doing his job, but... you know, Zach... when I looked into his eyes as he did it, I could see that he was relishing every single moment."

I understood what he meant. Some angels seemed to get rather too much of a kick out of the more unsavoury aspects of our celestial responsibilities. Nat was one example; I was pretty sure that Jaoel with his masterly ability to create nightmares and inflict hallucinations via the dream nexus also fell into this category – and now it seemed that K was another.

But I was worried by what Raphael was saying. It sounded like he was pretty close to actually entering into a direct conflict with K, and that could really be seen as nothing but out and out rebellion. If he was telling the truth, then I could understand why he felt a bit queasy about some of the stuff K had done in the past, but quite honestly, by now he should've recognised that that was just the way it was.

You can't judge angels by the sort of soft and fluffy ethical standards developed by humans. We are created to be instruments of divine justice, to follow the rules and mete out vengeance and punishment in accordance with the Law.

I've been around for a long time and I know for a fact that it isn't always easy; on a couple of occasions I've had to do things that I've found hard to stomach, but I've had to accept that is just part of the deal. I agree that it's probably a lot easier for angels like Nat, who actually seem to quite enjoy summoning up the old fire and brimstone and watching them do their worst, than for more sensitive souls like Manny and me. In fact, that's why Manny decided to retire from operations about seven hundred years ago, after the massacres of Bezier and Carcassonne. But just because he no longer had the stomach for field work, I'd never heard Manny come close to questioning authority in the way Raphael seemed to be doing.

But then I remembered how he had sounded just a short while ago on the phone. He was worried that K was going too far, that the decision to send in reinforcements was not actually an enactment of celestial justice but an unprovoked act of aggression. This got me thinking. I didn't really know Raphael, but I did know Manny, and I had complete and utter faith in him.

Deciding to withhold judgement for the moment, I looked up. Sara seemed to be completely absorbed in what Raphael was saying. I wondered how she was feeling. She knew both of them; Raphael had been her teacher and mentor for over three hundred years and she'd worked in K's private office since the collapse of the Holy Roman Empire. If I was feeling conflicted, Lord knows what was going on inside her head.

"But why are you here, Raph?" asked Sara. "Why didn't you go with K to the council? Manny said that Michael and Gabriel don't agree either. Why didn't you try harder to get K to change his mind?"

"Because it would have been stupid, pointless, and ultimately, counterproductive." His voice had an edge to it that I hadn't heard before. I was surprised at how menacing he sounded. This was no longer the gentle guy I had met at the Healing centre. This was a warrior.

"Yes, Michael and Gabriel are well intentioned, but when the chips are down, they'll probably just stand by and let it all happen. The rest of the council are running scared about the defections and there's been a seriously influential faction pushing for a much harder line for some time now. The way I see it, if the reinforcements invade, then all hell will be let loose. What started as a relatively minor incident will escalate and those angels on the council who are arguing for a second coming, this time backed up with a regime demanding absolute obedience from humanity, will have manoeuvred themselves into a position where everyone else is running scared. As soon as that happens Mankind will have lost their free will; the third realm will be populated by what will be little more than a race of slaves, forced to obey celestial instruction with no opportunity for challenge or debate and destined for eternal torment if they put one foot out of line."

"So no big deal then?" I said.

Sara snorted and Raphael shot me a look which could have withered fruit on the vine.

"Look, this must be stopped. Jaoel must be found, and Sophia and Alex must be taken to testify." Raphael sounded like he was getting to the end of his tether.

"When K started summoning the council to meet him at the Agency, I decided that you two were our best hope of sorting out this mess. Sara had told me you were heading in via the Malebolge ditches, so I high-tailed it over here to wait for you. Archangels have free passage throughout the three realms anyway and I got here unhindered and, to the best of my knowledge, unobserved. I have a feeling that the fun and games with the Chimera over at the CIEL compound might have had something to do with that." Sara and I exchanged glances.

"I'd been here about half an hour when I saw you on the horizon. The rest you know."

"Well, I for one am really pleased to see you." Sara gave Raphael's hand a swift squeeze and sent me a quick questioning glance.

~ 181 ~

"Yeah. Me too." I gave them both a quick smile and bent down to pick up our kitbags. "But we need to get moving. From what Manny said, we're on a rather tight deadline."

I tossed Sara her bag and as I did so, something shiny fell out of it and clattered to the floor at Raphael's feet. Sara rushed to pick it up, but he got there first.

"Is this what I think it is?" Raphael raised an inquisitorial eyebrow at Sara, who nodded, warily.

"I never gave you permission to remove this." His tone was icy.

"No… Sorry… I didn't think you'd mind." For the first time, Sara had lost her cool. I'd never seen her looking so shamefaced.

"This is a celestial artefact, Angel Sarandiel." I was starting to feel quite sorry for her.

"The Golden Bough has hung in its place of honour since Aenaes returned from the underworld. It is a priceless treasure." He was holding it reverently, not letting Sara anywhere near it.

"A unique fragment of the Ancient World, a link between cultures and belief systems that has remained untouched for millennia… And you just decided to pick it up and bring it along for the ride?

"Do you know what you are, Angel Sarandiel?" He towered above her now, terrifying in his righteous indignation.

Sara said nothing.

"What you are, Angel Sarandiel is a bloody genius."

~ *Chapter Twenty Seven* ~

I started, not sure if I had heard right and Sara hiccupped in surprise and relief as Raphael picked her up and swung her round, the Golden Bough clasped tightly under his arm.

The hugging didn't last long; Raphael dropped a slightly dazed Sara to the ground, then picked up his own kitbag and turned towards the side gate saying, "Right, let's be off. I reckon the fifth ditch is our best bet – and that's over there to the right."

"Hang on," I said. "Confused much. I still don't get it. Can someone please explain why that bloody piece of wood is so important?"

"I already told you." Sara sounded more than a tad impatient. "Back at your flat. The Golden Bough is a talisman which provides safe protection through the underworld."

"Yes, I get that, but that's to allow humans – the living – to enter and leave unscathed. We can do that anyway."

"It's slightly more than that," Raphael said. "The Golden Bough is a powerful artefact, its powers of protection generated by the sacrificial death of a human being. It was a gift to Persephone many, many years ago, when there was rather less delineation between the Heavens and the Inferno; when Aenaes placed it on the gates to the Elysian Fields, there was still relatively free movement between the realms. But for at least two thousand years, the Fallen have been unable to cross that particular boundary and there has been a strong campaign to return the Bough to the palaces of the Inferno. Eligor is one of the most vociferous campaigners; indeed, he's promised free passage and a significant pay-back to any being that will bring it to him."

"Whoa. Just wait a second." I had just taken in what Raphael had said about the Bough. "What was that about human sacrifice? We just grabbed the thing from the gateway after we left you at the HTC; so if it needs a sacrificial death to activate it, then I'm afraid it will be running on empty."

"I assume that you utilised Kathryn's death to empower the talisman?" Raphael looked at Sara, who nodded.

"Yes, when I got to her apartment, there were still sufficient vestiges of the life force remaining for me to harness it."

I stared at her, not quite grasping what she was saying. "But you didn't do any rituals at Kathryn's apartment. You just brought me round with your burning feathers and we pretty much high-tailed it out of there straight away."

"You were still unconscious, Zach." Sara sounded like she was explaining something incredibly simple to a rather dense five year old. "I didn't have much time, so I did the ritual first before waking you up. I was worried that if I'd had to wait for you to regain consciousness, it would have been too late."

Raphael nodded approvingly. "Good... That was quick thinking, Sara, just what I'd expect from you."

Sara's whole body shifted into smirk mode at the compliment.

"Any more questions, Zach?" He too had the air of a patient schoolmaster addressing a well-meaning dunce. I was not liking this at all.

I shook my head.

"Right, that's enough talking. We need to get on with this." Raphael and Sara moved off swiftly towards the steps leading down to the fifth of the evil ditches. I followed at a rather slower pace.

I was puzzled; Sara had mentioned the Golden Bough for the first time back at my place when we were getting changed and grabbing essentials, but she'd said nothing about death rituals and sacrifice. So she'd managed to use poor Kathryn's death to charge up the talisman, but it hadn't been the opportunity that poor girl's sad demise had presented that had made her think of the Bough; she had already said that she wanted to bring it along several hours beforehand. What if we hadn't just chanced to stumble on a convenient corpse on our journey? What would Sara have done then?

As these thoughts ran through my head I looked at the two figures striding on ahead of me. They were walking in step with each other, their arms swinging at their sides in a matched and purposeful rhythm, Sara's head slightly leaning in towards Raphael. There was no doubt that they were extremely comfortable with each other, and that they trusted each other completely.

~ 184 ~

I felt uneasy, remembering what Sara had told me about how she and Raphael had worked on summoning rituals as part of her training; it had rung a few warning bells at the time, but I had just decided to let it ride. I would have given almost anything to have been able to talk this through with Manny, but that wasn't going to happen. There was no time to make a phone call and even if there had been it would have been fairly difficult to have a private conversation.

I decided the best thing to do would be to keep my thoughts to myself and as I followed the others down the steep granite stairway that led into the depths of Malebolge I gave myself a bit of a talking to. How could I feel so suspicious of one of the most trusted and benevolent of the Archangels? And why was I questioning the integrity of a companion I had known for millennia, for whom I was beginning to feel a whole host of unexpected and unfamiliar emotions?

If I was being truly honest with myself, I recognised that I was probably more than a little pissed off that I was so clearly last in the pecking order in the new scheme of things - and I also had to admit to myself that I was not happy that Sara seemed to prefer Raphael's company to my own.

Somewhat chastened, I completed my descent and found the other two waiting for me. They had both put on long, hooded robes; Raphael handed one to me as I joined them.

"Put this on. It'll absorb the last traces of your celestial radiance. If they're scanning for us, they won't pick up anything so long as we've got these on. What you might call a 'cloaking device'." He grinned as Sara groaned at the awfulness of the pun and the atmosphere between us lightened. I did as he asked me, pulling the robes on over my head, covering my kitbag and pulling the hood down low over my forehead.

I looked around me. We were standing in a sort of entrance lobby, with rough stone passages leading off it in several directions. There was very little natural light and a strong smell of burning tar. Above us, I could still see the sky, which was now dark and overcast, with clouds moving fast across the slender face of the crescent moon. The wind was rising and although we were sheltered down here in the ditches, we could hear it rattling through the ramshackle buildings on the edges of the cavern. Then, above the growing tumult of the gathering storm, I was certain that I could hear the sound of voices and the shrill and urgent call of a hunting horn.

As I looked upwards, I saw a huge winged creature soar across the front of the moon, flying slowly, wings outstretched, casting about to left, then right, its tail acting as a rudder as it swept back and forth on what could only be a surveillance mission. I gestured to the others and as we looked on we saw another come in to view. Behind it came another, and then another, until we could see five Chimeras, flying in loose formation, scanning the ground and the skies ahead of them. We shrank instinctively back against the walls of the tunnel, pulling our cloaks more tightly around us.

As we watched, we realised that the Chimeras were simply the avant-garde of a demonic army, for now, following behind them we saw a mighty chariot, pulled through the air by eight black horses who breathed fire as they galloped forwards across the skies. The charioteer stood tall and menacing, illuminated by bursts of firelight. He was enormous, bare-chested and horned. His skin looked dark, dull and metallic and from his shoulders sprouted huge vulture-like wings. He cracked his whip, which ripped viciously across the backs of the horses and raised his horn to his lips; the air was rent with the unmistakable sound of a call to battle, combined with the terrified screams of his bleeding horses.

"Eligor," breathed Raphael. "In his true form, as I haven't seen him for five thousand years."

"And look." Sara pointed upwards, a slight quiver in her voice. In the wake of their master, we saw the approaching army. Eligor commanded sixty legions of the Fallen, and there they were, spread out across the skies above us. A nightmare parade of demons and Fallen Angels, some flying together in well organised squadrons, tight in formation, purposeful and silent, others astride monstrous creatures, winged lions and tigers, great beasts with yellow eyes that shone, harsh and malevolent as they cantered forwards through the air, their riders whooping and cheering with battle fever. There were chariots, some large like Eligor's, containing rows of wingless archers, each armed with crossbow and arrows and ready for the fight, others small and light, with single wolf-headed charioteers who added to the noise and hurly-burly by throwing back their heads and baying with blood-lust as Eligor sounded his battle cry.

On and on they came until they filled the skies; there were so many of them that they blotted out the moon and our only light came from the occasional burst of fire from the flying horses as they coursed by above us. We remained silent and motionless in the dark tunnel, not wanting to do anything which could bring us to the attention of Eligor's forces.

I was aware that my body had gone into panic mode. My heart-beat was up and I could feel the rush of adrenalin; my breath was coming in short bursts and it was becoming increasingly difficult to breathe. I forced myself to get back in command of my poor corpus and as I looked at Sara, I could see that she was as tense as I was and that she was having an even more difficult time keeping in control. From beneath her hood, I could see drops of sweat beginning to sheen on her forehead; she was starting to tremble.

My Sara.

I couldn't help it; I finally admitted to myself that whatever happened, what I felt for Sara was unlike anything I had ever felt before and when we got out of the Inferno, I was going to have to do something about it. I moved my hand towards her and found her fingers waiting for mine. Under the shelter of our cloaks, we grasped each other's hands; she was burning up, her skin dry with a raging heat. I focussed my mind and called into myself the certainty of divine justice and the joys of celestial peace. After just a few seconds, the power began to flow through me and into Sara. Her grasp on my hand tightened and as we held each other, I felt her slowly relax. Soon, her skin regained its normal temperature, she gave my fingers one last squeeze and as she did so, the skies above us cleared, the last of the stragglers had passed us by and we had remained undetected.

I moved slowly away from the wall, keeping one eye on the sky, just to make sure nothing else was looking down on us. I took quick stock of my bearings; we needed to be heading due north, and it looked like the second passage to the left was going in roughly the right direction. Soundlessly, I gestured to Sara and Raphael to stay where they were whilst I went to check out the lie of the land.

They both still seemed to be in a state of shock, but whilst Sara gave the very faintest nod to show she had understood me, Raphael did nothing. He was still staring, transfixed, at the now empty skies. I went over to him and, lifting his hood, placed my hand against his forehead. It was stone cold. His eyes were open, but they registered nothing as I waggled my finger rather foolishly in front of them. I realised that his corpus had gone into complete catatonic melt-down[47].

---

[47] "**Catatonia Corpus** is a state of neurogenic motor immobility and behavioural abnormality manifested by stupor. It is associated with high levels of psychiatric and or physical stress, fear or anxiety. The condition manifests itself through complete close down of the physical functions of the corpus and can result in the angel being unable to release itself from its physical manifestation until the stupor has abated. Early signs of Catatonia Corpus include shortness of breath, high temperatures and a palsied shaking of the limbs and upper body. There are a variety of treatments available; the administration of food containing high sugar content can be a successful first-line treatment strategy. Electro-convulsive therapy is also sometimes used, but this requires admission to St. Basil's Hospital for angelic care and rehabilitation. A sharp smack around the face has also been known to produce positive results." *The Anatomy of Angels*, 1895

I'd seen this before with inexperienced operatives out in the field. I dug in my kitbag and found a can of Red Bull; forcing his mouth open and tipping back his head, I managed to get quite a lot of it down his throat. There seemed to be no immediate reaction so, grabbing the back of his head firmly, I gave him a good slap round the jaw, just as he opened his eyes.

"What the…?" Raphael spluttered sticky droplets of Red Bull all over me and put his hand to his face, where a mark showing the imprint of my hand was rapidly emerging.

"Catatonia Corpus," said Sara, who now seemed to be pretty much recovered. "You had completely gone. Zach brought you back with this." She waved the empty can of Red Bull at him.

"Hmmm… well in that case, did you need to hit me quite so hard?" Raphael didn't seem very happy with my emergency first aid, and I must admit that I had taken out some of my frustrations when I hit him. It had been, by any standards, a bit of a belter.

"You didn't seem to be responding and I needed to get you back." I looked a little shamefaced. "Sorry if I went a bit too far."

Raphael looked at me, and our eyes locked. I think he could see right through me. He gave his chin another rub; a bruise was now beginning to form on his jaw-line.

"Well, let's say we're quits. I think that makes up for me holding a knife to your throat." He smiled his elder-statesman smile and once again, I couldn't help but warm towards him. "Thanks, Zach, you thought quickly and you did what was right. No ill feelings?"

"No ill feelings."

"How about you, Sara, did Zach have to beat you up as well? Or did you manage to keep your composure whilst all that," he glanced upwards, "was going on?"

"No, I was fine. Zach helped me before it got too bad." She threw me a quick glance. "But I don't think I would have managed without him."

I shrugged. "It's nothing, I've seen it before, it happened to one of the Katibeen out in Syria. You just learn to watch for it, and do what you have to do if it happens." I was feeling uncomfortable. I don't like being thanked. I do my job. It's no big deal.

"If you two are okay now, I suggest we get under cover. We weren't spotted that time, but who knows what else might be up there." They both agreed and we moved in single file towards the second passage on the left.

We walked for a while in silence; then Sara spoke.

"Are you sure that was Eligor?"

"Oh yes, without a doubt that was Eligor and his sixty legions." Raphael's voice was still a little shaky. "I haven't seen anything like that since the First Rebellion. It brought back some very unpleasant memories."

"Where do you think they were going?" I asked.

"They seemed to be flying towards the North East, which probably means they're heading for Erebus[48]," Sara replied.

"That would make sense if they are planning to defend the area beyond the Avernus Gate," I agreed.

"And even more sense if they are planning to invade."

Sara and I both turned to Raphael in horror. We had never considered an invasion. Our main concern had been about preventing celestial forces from committing an unprovoked act of aggression. But what Raphael was suggesting would be a hundred times worse.

"Surely not? The balance of power is still too much in our favour for them to attempt that. The Fallen can't launch a major attack on either the celestial realms or the earth whilst we hold the Heavens." I was taken aback. Raphael could not be serious.

"If there's a major split within the Heavenly Host because of K's actions, it will be difficult for us to claim that we are in control. If we are divided, we are weakened. And if we're weakened, then we open the doors to the Fallen."

Sara and I said nothing, letting the implications of what Raphael had said sink in. Sara rallied first.

"Well, then we need to be getting a move on. And the good thing is that Eligor's place will probably be less strongly guarded now. If he's taken his forces to Erebus, then hopefully he'll only have left a skeleton force back in Dis, and that will make it easier for us to get hold of Alex and Sophia."

What she said made sense.

We all adjusted our cloaks and Sara took out her crossbow. She had just started to assemble it when Raphael stopped her.

---

48 "Although the straggling city of Erebus straddles the Inferno between the Styx and the river Archeron, it is lacking in the charms to be found in other, nearby riverside towns and cities. Situated on a flat plain, it's devoid of the mountains and dramatic landscape that characterise the areas around the Lake of Fire and has none of the quirky appeal of downtown Dis. As the first stopping off point for souls newly departed from the mortal coil, it is chaotic and constantly busy, but it really has very little to offer the discerning traveller in the underworld." *A Guide to the Three Realms* - 1945

"No, let's keep our weapons close, but keep them hidden, we don't want to look like we're aggressors. Do you have a dagger?"

She nodded, taking it out of her kitbag and securing it at her waist. Once we had all checked our weapons we had a drink, finishing the last of the water. Then we moved off down the tunnel and into the unknown.

~ *Chapter Twenty Eight* ~

Like all of the evil ditches, the fifth ditch of Malebolge is reserved for the punishment of a particular type of sinner. Someone, for example, who used their knowledge of off-shore accounting to avoid paying reasonable taxation, or perhaps a politician who took bribes in order to smooth the way for certain pieces of legislation. Maybe even a business-leader who knowingly suppressed information regarding product safety or environmental performance in order to turn a quick profit. A very particular and choice bunch of scum-bags that are likely to find themselves heading hell for leather towards ditch number five once their souls have been examined and found wanting.

It is the unpleasant destination for peculators, grafters, extortionists, blackmailers, corrupt politicians and unscrupulous businessmen. Their punishment is to be thrown into a river of boiling tar, which represents the sticky fingers and dark secrets of their corrupt dealings, and where they must remain until it is judged that they have atoned. If they try to get out before their time is called, then they become prey to the Malebranche, a particularly nasty group of demons, armed with grappling hooks and barbed spears, whose sole function is to either push their sorry arses back into the river, or to tear them to pieces.

In the main, we weren't too worried about the goings on in the fifth ditch. What went on there was fairly self-contained and provided we could avoid an encounter with the Malebranche, we should be able to steer a fairly quick and easy course through the tunnels and reach the Medusa Gate in about an hour.

At first all went well. We moved quickly and quietly, speaking seldom - not just because we didn't want to disturb anyone, but, to be honest, none of us were feeling in the mood for desultory chit-chat. Our path took us along the edge of the river, which was deep and slow moving, and emitted a noxious miasma of burning tar. At some points, there were pools, black and murky, often full of piteous individuals forced to remain submerged within the boiling liquid, their skin cracked and peeling, their eyes red with the constant tears that provided the only cooling to their tortured bodies.

Patrolling the length and breadth of the river was the Malebranche, a strange group of twelve winged demons, who were fated to dwell forever within the ravine. Some were extremely tall and at least one was no bigger than a human toddler, but they were all red skinned and scaly, with long, razor sharp claws. They carried their grappling hooks and spears strapped to their backs and flew up and down the river, constantly on the lookout for anyone trying to climb the banks in order to gain a few moments ease from the relentless torment.

As they flew, their grappling hooks knocked against their wings, making a sound not unlike a garden wind-chime, alerting us to their presence and allowing us to draw back into the shadows along the edges of the river bank to escape detection.

Then, as we turned a bend in the river, we saw a very old man haul himself painfully out of the boiling blackness, to lie panting on the bank. His skin was a scarlet mass of livid burns and when he looked up, we were unable to make out much of his face, which was covered in great blisters, shiny and suppurating. Sara turned away in distaste, but Raphael was about to move towards him, his healer's instinct aroused by the sight of so piteous a creature. As he did so, we heard the incongruously melodic chimes of demon-wings knocking against wood and I pulled Raphael back into the shadows just in time.

Two of the Malebranche alighted on the river bank, just a few feet from where we were hiding. One was about 6 feet tall and immensely fat, with curly hair and a cavalier goatee, which gave him a surprisingly eccentric and misleadingly benevolent appearance. His colleague was considerably shorter, probably about 4 foot 6, and stockily built. When he turned towards us, we were shocked to see that he had the face of a bulldog, his jowls drooping over his lower jaw and his pointed bottom teeth protruding upwards.

The man on the bank cowered in front of them, holding his hands above his head. He began to speak, and at first, we could not understand a word he was saying:

"제발 자비를 보여 구걸. 내가 당신을 애 원, 제발 자비를 보여 구걸. 내 가 당신을 애 원!"

Strange sounds repeated over and over, but within seconds, our Angelic decoders[49] had kicked in. He was speaking Korean, and he was begging the demons to have mercy.

"That's a good one," said the taller of the two demons, getting out his grappling hook and beginning to matter-of-factly push the old man back into the boiling tar. "What do you think, Cagnazzo? Should we show him... mercy?"

The dog-faced demon laughed, a sound which was a combination of a high-pitched giggle and a bark. "Well, I reckon we show him as much mercy as he showed all the people he sent to the death camps."

He bent down towards the figure, which was now struggling unsuccessfully against the grappling hook that was slowly pushing him back, feet first, into the river. Reaching out his hand, the demon used his claws to rip a long, thin piece of flesh from the upper arm of the man who was now screaming in renewed agony as the tar engulfed his feet, legs and buttocks.

"Want a bit, Barbariccia?" He dangled the seared flesh in front of the nose of his companion, who looked at it for a second before regretfully shaking his head.

The dog-faced demon pushed the flesh into his mouth, jaws working, drool slavering from his overhanging jowls. "It's very nice... nice and crispy. Done to a turn you might say."

"Oh for goodness sake, you know I'm supposed to be on a diet." The taller demon looked crossly at his companion. "But I just can't resist Korean take-out." He bent down towards the river, where the head of the old man could still be seen just above the surface. Reaching out with his grappling hook, the demon pulled him upwards and cut a neat slice of flesh from his belly.

"We've let you off lightly this time, Kim, my old mucker. We could have flayed you from top to toe like last time if we'd been in the mood. Don't forget, you've got another thousand years of this before there's even a chance of parole – and the way you're going, there's not a hope in hell of getting remission for good behaviour."

He dropped the old man back into the river, where he sank, screaming, into

---

[49] "An angel's mother tongue is the music of the spheres, a language without words, containing within it all that is universally true and beautiful. However, angels have the ability to speak and understand all humanly constructed languages (and several others beside) via the celestial decoder situated within the right hemisphere of the angelic brain. In order to prevent Babel-like confusion, the decoder sets itself to the language it is currently encountering and needs to use, and may take several seconds to adjust if a new language is introduced." *The Anatomy of Angels,* 1875

the depths, the naked wounds on his body cauterised immediately by the boiling tar.

"Do you want some, Cagnazzo? No... oh well, all the more for me then."

They spread their wings and launched themselves into the air; as they disappeared round the bend we heard the dog-faced demon remark, "Well, that was a nice snack, but it's a shame we forgot to bring any kimchi."

We got shakily to our feet.

Sara moved a little way downwind from us and was sick.

Rummaging in my kitbag, I pulled out one of the last of the cans of Red Bull, opened it and passed it to her. She took a deep swig, washed out her mouth and spat onto the path. It was baking in the tunnels, and I could feel that my body was really thirsty, so I took a few sips before passing it on to Raphael, who would probably have finished it off if Sara hadn't pulled his arm down and taken the final drops for herself.

"Sorry," he said, "I'm out of practice with physical materialisation. I just hadn't realised how thirsty my body was until I took the first sip. Have we got any more?"

I shook my head. "No, only two cans left and we have to keep those for Alex and Sophia." I offered round what was left of the mint cake, but none of us felt hungry. I think that watching the two Malebranche had rather put us off snacking for the time being.

We carried on for another mile or so, occasionally hearing the chimes of the flying demons as they patrolled the river and its tributaries, but not encountering anything untoward. We had nearly come to the end of the tunnel and could now just make out the dark skies ahead of us, illuminated by a smattering of stars and the crescent moon whose light, though faint and rather sickly, was a welcome relief after the subterranean gloom. To our right, the river carried onwards, flowing through a sluice gate into unseen caverns and eventually, so Raphael told us, making its way to the Lake of Fire itself.

Ahead of us, the path began to climb upwards, at first gently, but within 500 yards the slope had become so steep that we were forced to clamber on our hands and knees, grabbing onto the rocky outcrops or finding hand-holds in small crevices as we urged ourselves onwards and upwards. As we neared the top of the ravine, we could see the climb was going to become more difficult as there was a sharp overhang which stretched out over the ravine by about five feet. To negotiate it, we would have to find hand-holds strong enough to bear our weight as we pulled ourselves precariously out towards the lip of the ravine and over the edge. Below us flowed the river of molten tar. And above us, anyone or anything could be waiting; we were completely unable to see over the edge on to the plain and the lands beyond the evil ditches.

We came to a halt, all three of us craning our necks and bending backwards as we tried to work out if there was an easier way to do this.

"Why don't we just take off our cloaks and fly up there?" said Sara. "We're nearly there; surely it won't matter if they spot us now?"

I thought she had a point, but Raphael shook his head vigorously. "No, we can't see what's waiting for us, and we definitely don't want to trigger their interest when we are so close to reaching Eligor's stronghold." He turned to me. "What do you think, Zach?"

I looked again at the overhang. It had a very uneven surface, great lumps of rock stuck out like bad teeth through the chalky soil. There also seemed to be tree roots mixed in with the rocks and vines of some sort trailed over towards the far left of the cliff edge. I thought I just might make it if they turned out to be strong enough to bear my weight.

"I'm going to give it a go." And without waiting for a response, I turned away from them and found my first hand-hold. It was solid. I transferred my weight to the second rock; I was now leaning forwards by about 45 degrees and the pressure from my kitbag was dragging me downwards. My next move would mean kicking away from the path and dangling out over the ravine; I reached for the third rock and it remained steady.

Swinging out, I grabbed a sturdy tree root which curved like a small hammock, its two ends embedded in the earth above me, allowing me to hold onto it with both hands. The edge was now about two feet away from me, and I decided to risk it. Using the root like a trapeze, I began to swing, backwards and forwards, until I felt I had gained enough momentum to release myself. I let go and twisting in the air, grabbed onto the vine roots trailing loose over the edge of the ravine. They seemed sturdy enough and I clambered upwards, relief flooding through me as, head and shoulders now firmly above the ravine, I scrambled for a stronger hand-hold in the thin grass. Then, sickeningly, I felt the vines give; I began to slide backwards, inch by terrifying inch.

Letting go with one hand, I reached into my robe, grabbed the dagger from my belt and thrust it deep within the thin and crumbling soil, hoping it would hold. Three times I got no purchase, but on the fourth attempt, as the vines snapped and I jerked sickeningly towards the edge, it remained steady. I rested for a moment. I could feel my heart banging against my ribs, and my hands had become so sweaty I thought the dagger might slip from my grasp. Concentrating all my resources, I began to pull myself upwards, one painful jolt at a time, and was finally able to swing my legs over the edge.

I came to rest in a panting and exhausted heap on the rough and spiky grass.

"Zach, are you okay?" It was Sara. "Is it safe up there?"

"Yes... I'm fine..." I sat up and looked around me; the landscape was bleak. A few feet away was an ancient oak, its trunk almost completely covered with ivy, great skeins of which grew out along its exposed tree roots, which I could now see had been the source of the vines that I had used to pull myself over the cliff edge.

Apart from that, there was little to be seen in the way of natural cover; a couple of scabby thorn bushes and a few large boulders to my right; to my left, a wide expanse of dry and dusty down-land, stretching out for about a mile towards the horizon. In the weak light of the crescent moon, I could just make out the outline of city walls, and beyond them, I saw little specks of lights; this, I assumed, was the City of Dis.

I went back to the edge of the cliff. The overhang was so extreme that I couldn't see the others, so I stretched out full length and peered over into the ravine. They were standing, huddled together, leaning back into the cliff wall.

"It's okay – there's no-one up here. Sara, you go next. You can use the same hand-holds I did and then swing yourself out to me from the tree root. I'll hang over the edge and catch you. Then both of us can help Raphael."

She spoke hurriedly to Raphael, who said something in reply, but I couldn't quite catch what they were saying. The wind was getting stronger; blowing across the plains and over me, down into the ditches, causing little eddies and waves to form in the molten river below.

"Okay." She looked up at me and nodded. Her eyes seemed huge in her pale face, her copper hair pulled tightly back, but still emitting a faint and ethereal glow in the pale moonlight. Her mouth was set in a thin, determined line. I could tell that she was scared - and I could tell just how hard she was trying to hide her fear from me.

"Hold on a second." I scrabbled to my feet and cut away a couple of chunks of turf to create some sort of toehold. Then I roughly plaited together six or seven of the longest and thickets strands of ivy and tied these around my waist. Preparations complete, I returned to the edge of the cliff.

"Now, Sara. Go for it. I'll catch you."

She found the first and second hand-hold without difficulty, and then swung her right arm out to grab for the third. It was a seamless and almost elegant movement; she looked up at me and grinned.

"Good girl."

"Don't be so bloody patronising." She was biting her bottom lip in concentration, and, as the wind got higher, drowning out all sounds from the river below, she moved with apparent ease to the under-hanging tree root.

"Okay. Now, take your time, just swing out and aim for my hands." I stretched out as far as I could over the cliff edge.

"You'll catch me?"

"I'll catch you. I promise."

Sara nodded and shut her eyes, building her concentration for what she had to do next. She swung backwards, forwards, backwards again, and then, on the highest point of her trajectory, opened her eyes and launched herself into the air. I reached out, urging myself towards her, stretching as far as I dared over the mouth of the ravine. My fingers touched hers, I felt the now familiar warmth of her and I reached towards it, desperate to hold on. But my hands were still slippery and as my fingers came together, they closed onto empty air.

~ *Chapter Twenty Nine* ~

Sara began to scream as she fell, her cloak flapping uselessly around her, towards the rocks and the molten river below. I scrabbled back up on to the cliff edge, struggling clumsily to extract myself from the ivy which seemed to be pulling tight against my waist.

As soon as I was free, I threw off my cloak and alated instantly, leaping high into the air and shooting downwards into the ravine with a dive that was at least twice as fast as a peregrine falcon's.

As I levelled off about two feet above the surface of the river, I cast about me, looking for something which might indicate where she had landed, working on the faintest of hopes that her fall might have taken her to the river bank, rather than into the vast, slow moving expanse of burning tar which flowed inexorably beneath me.

It was hopeless... there were no ripples, just the slow belching sound of the molten bubbles, coming to the surface and bursting, emitting little gusts of steam. The sides of the ravine had narrowed and I was below the worst excesses of the wind. I could hear the chimes of the Malebranche getting closer. Then I realised that they were above me, and turning aloft, I saw a host of demons, soaring upwards towards the edge of the ravine. One of the demons seemed misshapen and was flying in a rather laboured fashion; as I got closer, I saw that he was holding something in his arms. It was Sara.

I flew upwards, landing some way away from the cliff edge, just behind the ancient oak. Raphael was standing not far from the ravine, fully alated and in his celestial form.

I looked down and saw his corpus, sitting slightly lopsided, tucked away behind the oak tree and partially covered by his discarded cloak. Any desire to remain inconspicuous had seemingly been cast off along with his cloak; he stood, mighty and awe-inspiring in his celestial radiance, sword outstretched in a gesture, which even the dullest and most incompetent of the Fallen would have been able to understand.

In the sky above us, the Malebranche remained airborne, hovering in ranks behind the one carrying Sara.

"Now then, here's a suggestion." The demon sounded surprisingly pleasant and rather jaunty, like a voice-over for car insurance. "Why don't you put that thing away…" he gestured with his long and almost prehensile tail towards Raphael's outstretched sword, "then I can put down this little pretty, and we can have a good old chinwag."

I wasn't quite sure how to play this. I didn't think the Malebranche had seen me – they all seemed utterly fixated on Raphael and the sword. I could have remained where I was, but skulking in the background has never been part of my modus operandi, so I sloughed off my corpus and dumped it in a sitting position next to Raphael's, draping the cloak over both of them.

As I felt the flow of celestial energy course through me, I was surprised that I didn't get a significant sense of spiritual danger. I could clearly feel the almost constant pricking of my thumbs - which you would expect in the depths of the evil ditches, but I was not sensing any particular threat from the Malebranche. I moved out from behind the oak, until I was standing next to Raphael, wing-tip to wing-tip.

"Ooh. Now what have we here? This is a surprise... is it BOGOF day and no-one told us?" A few of the demons behind him actually tittered. "I'd heard we could expect two angels passing through our humble ditches, but three… it's like those bloody London busses; we've not had visitors for nigh on nine hundred years and now three turn up all at once."

The flying demon did seem genuinely surprised to see me, but not unduly worried. I clearly didn't represent the same level of threat as an Archangel with a magic sword.

"Come on, Raphael," I said. "Put that thing away for now. Let's get Sara back on to solid ground and we can take things from there."

Seeing the sense in my suggestion, he returned his sword to its scabbard. The demon with the long tail flew towards us, landing about five feet to Raphael's left – just out of reach of the sword, but, I calculated, still in close enough for him to aim a rather nasty swipe in our direction with his barbed and vicious looking tail.

The demon then deposited Sara quite gently on the ground and I thought I

~ 199 ~

saw her fingers brush his cheek as she turned away from him and run towards us. Could she even work her magic on the demons of the evil ditches?

But all thoughts were pushed from my mind as she reached me and, seeming to not even notice that Raphael was present, flung herself into my arms and kissed me. Even though she was corporeal, as her lips met mine, I could feel the full power of her angelic energy mixing itself with mine. As we clung together, I thought my head was going to explode with the intensity of sensation; stars seemed to be forming, growing and then erupting inside me. I could feel currents of pleasure coursing through me in a way I'd never thought possible. I opened my eyes and found she was staring at me, the crescent moon reflected in her eyes and a look that seemed to combine both triumph and excitement on her face.

"Sara."

I said her name, and as I did so, I became aware that I could feel nothing but air around and beneath me. I looked down, and realised that we had levitated and were now about 50 feet above Raphael and the demon with the long tail. This was a phenomenon I had heard about from other angels, but had never experienced myself. Not wishing to suffer the ignominy of tumbling to the ground in front of a bunch of ditch-dwelling demons, I instantly took control of my wings and we descended gently and in a relatively dignified fashion.

Raphael was looking at us; I was unable to quite make out the expression on his face, but Sara just went up to him saying, "Oh, Raph, don't get mad. It's all going to be okay. This is Malacoda, he's the leader of the demons in this ditch, and he's not too bad really."

"Thank you, dear lady." The demon called Malacoda gave a little bow. "What you angels sometimes forget is that, on occasion, we are actually on the same side."

I saw Raphael give a little snort of disbelief.

"No, no, don't get sniffy, you listen to me." Malacoda had seated himself on a nearby boulder and was gesturing at Raphael with both his outstretched finger and the very point of his extraordinary tail. "We demons of Malebolge have a duty to perform under section 3A, paras 1 to 7 of the Retribution, Restitution and Rehabilitation Act. We have the extremely difficult and onerous task of ensuring that the punishments defined and demanded by divine and eternal law are carried out exactly as stated in the regulations." It sounded like he had swallowed the rule book.

"And that," he said, looking me full in the face, "ain't really too different to what you do, Angel Zachriel, when you mete out justice and retribution in the earthly sphere."

He had a point. But how did he know who I was? I knew I was good, and I'd been around the block quite a few times by now, but I wasn't quite that egotistical or foolish enough to think I had the sort of reputation which would proceed me into the Inferno.

I saw Raphael relax slightly. He could see the logic in Malacoda's argument, but I wasn't sure if he had picked up on my concerns.

"Yes, we are all subject to the demands of divine law. You have your part to play, I give you that."

"And you've got the Golden Bough." Malacoda looked at us knowingly. "We were told to watch out for you, and to give you clear passage through the ditches, because a certain… personage… is extremely keen to get his scaly little mitts on whatever you've got in your kitbags."

Raphael glanced at Sara, who cast her eyes downwards. "I didn't say anything. He already knew. He asked me if I had it when he grabbed me as I was falling. I told him I wasn't going to say anything until he brought me back to you."

"Who told you about us? And what exactly did they say?" I asked brusquely, my hands reaching towards my kitbag. If those old hags, the Graeae had betrayed us, then this would be a perfect place to get rid of their impedimenta. I couldn't see their eye and tooth lasting long if I threw them into the boiling river of tar which was flowing so conveniently beneath us.

"Oh… you are a jumpy one and no mistake." He looked at me as if I was a parish spinster, surprised in the vestry by a rather large spider. "We heard all about two angels entering through the boundary lands yesterday afternoon. The Lady Enepsigos reported to my Lord Eligor that her Wild Hunt was on your trail, and there has been a general alert ever since."

He looked at us a little pityingly. "You see someone on your side's not really all they seem. Not quite the article as it were. We've been getting information for quite a while now, and we knew something like this would happen when Eligor brought those two live-uns back here for a bit of fun and games."

"You mean Alex and Sophia?" I asked quickly.

"That's them. The very ones. She was a lovely little thing. Long brown hair, nice figure… Lovely… Not quite so pretty now though."

"You've seen them?"

"Where are they?"

Sara and I had spoken together.

"Oh yes, Eligor asked us to give them The Tour." Malacoda smiled as though this was a great honour, and he was only too pleased to share his reminiscences. "They've been round all the ditches, sampled a little bit of everything, so to speak. Ditch seven[50] was a bit of a problem for her. Terrified of snakes she was." He looked up at us, shaking his head as if recounting the idiosyncrasies or peccadilloes of a naughty but well-loved child.

"And of course ditch nine[51] really did it for young Alex. Not too keen on the disembowelling you see. She didn't really notice them by then, what with the snake bites and all. Particularly bad around here..." He gestured loosely, indicating his head and neck. "Me, I can take it or leave it. A bit messy, but, you know it's in the rule book."

"And we're here to make sure everyone follows the rules." He stood up and moved towards us, his jovial manner had completely disappeared.

"Now, we won't harm you, because Eligor told us not to. And we do what we're told. Don't we, boys and girls?" He turned back to the other demons, which were still hovering at the edge of the cliff top. There was a great clamouring of wings and banging of grappling sticks as they, presumably, indicated their agreement.

"But we don't want to see you again. If you come back here, we can't be held responsible. The rules say 'safe passage, one way only'. There's no return ticket. Even for Archangels. Do you understand, Mr. Smart Arse, All Superior Archangel Raphael? We weren't expecting you, and to be honest, we really never want to see you again."

Raphael didn't bother to dignify this with an answer, but I wasn't prepared to just leave it at that.

---

[50] "**The seventh ditch of Malebolge:** This ditch is where the souls of thieves must meet their punishment. It is filled with serpents, snakes, vile reptiles and even, on occasion, small and unpleasant dragons that torture the thieves endlessly. The bites of some of the snakes cause the thieves to spontaneously combust, only to regenerate their bodies for further torment in a few moments. A very interesting excursion for those attracted to Herpetology, but protective clothing is an absolute must!" *A Guide to the Three Realms, 1972*

[51] "**The ninth ditch of Malebolge**: Reserved for those who in life, promoted scandals, schism, and discord particularly those who caused schism within the church or within politics or bullied others via trolling and revenge porn. They are forced to walk the length and breadth of the ditch, bearing horrible, disfiguring wounds inflicted on them by a great demon with a sword. The nature of the wound mirrors the sins of the particular soul; while some only have gashes, or fingers and toes cut off, others are decapitated, cut in half, or are completely disemboweled." *"Ibid"*

"But why were you expecting us, me and Sara? Who told you who I was?" I had worked out now that I'd called Raphael by name in front of them, so it was no surprise that they knew who he was, but Malacoda had addressed me formally, by my full name. And I was determined to find out how he knew it.

"Like I said, there's someone on your side who isn't quite what they make out to be. From what I heard, they contacted Eligor before you even left the earthly plane and told him to expect you. To expect two angels, the Angel Sarandiel," he gave a mocking little bow towards Sara, "and the Justice Angel Zachriel."

"Jaoel," I said the name just under my breath. "It can only be Jaoel."

"And where is the traitor now?" demanded Raphael. "We know they have entered the Inferno."

"Now that's a bit of a tricksy question right enough..." Malacoda's rather more flippant manner had returned. "We think that they're heading towards Erebus, like every other bugger but us. We aren't allowed to leave the ditches, you see, so we can't be part of the gathering... but everyone else is headed there, just waiting for the word."

"What word?" I asked quickly. "Is it war?"

"Ooh... now that would be telling..." He winked at me, unpleasantly.

"We never asked for trouble you know... and if that high and mighty, arrogant bastard Lord Kemuel thinks that he can just walk in here with a band of the Potestas, without a by-your-leave, he's got another thing coming and I'll tell you that for nothing." Malacoda was walking away from us now.

"There's rules you know... and rules have to be followed." He spread his wings and launched himself into the air. "I think you know your way from here... Dis is over there." He pointed towards the lights I had spotted earlier. "You can see Eligor's stronghold to the left of the city walls, just through the Medusa Gate. Last I heard those two live-uns were being kept in the dungeons." He turned right and pointed towards the horizon. "And Erebus is over there.

"Give my regards to the girly. Little sweetheart she was. Such a shame about her hair. Lovely head of hair she had. Really lovely..."

He gave a little giggle, and then waving the others to follow, he dived back into the darkness of the evil ditches.

Raphael turned to Sara. "Not too bad really? That was one of the most unpleasantly pestilential presences it has ever been my misfortune to encounter."

"Oh come on. He didn't harm us, and he's given us some rather useful information, don't you think?" Sara had adopted her sweet-talking voice. I'd heard it before when she was trying to persuade Johan to let us commandeer the CIEL chariot.

"I thought he was a slimy and disgusting little bastard. He gave me the creeps." I wasn't going to let her get away with this one completely. "But it was clear from the get-go that he'd no intention of actually harming us. After all, he did save Sara from a deep-fried encounter with a river of tar, which I for one am going to count resoundingly in his favour." I looked at Sara and she blew me a kiss. Like a sap, I felt myself melting.

"Basically, I think Sara's right. The only problem is we now have a really difficult decision to make."

They both turned to look at me.

"We've got less than five hours left to play with... So do we head towards Eligor's stronghold, which by the sounds of it is practically unguarded, and rescue Alex and Sophia, or do we head towards Erebus and hope to head Jaoel off at the pass?"

~ *Chapter Thirty* ~

"Or alternatively, should we split up?" Raphael's question caught me off guard for a second.

"It seems to me that Zach's got a pretty good chance of getting Alex and Sophia out all by himself. He's done this sort of work before, and to be honest, we might just slow him down at this stage." He had a point. Although we had seen Eligor's heavy mob setting off on their journey to Erebus, it was unlikely that he would have left the place completely unguarded; it would be easier to get in under the radar if we didn't turn up mob handed.

"And, not being funny or wanting to pull rank, but I think that I've got a better chance of pulling off the negotiations if we have to do a deal with Eligor." Raphael looked across at us, nodding in Sara's direction. "And you've worked with K long enough to know the ropes as far as diplomacy is concerned, so I think we should go to Erebus together."

Again, you couldn't fault his logic. Eligor would be flattered that one of the most senior of the Heavenly Host, an Archangel no less - had come down into the Inferno; there was no doubt about it, Raphael was one of the big boys, and he had a much better chance of pulling off any deals than I did. I was beginning to nod in agreement; Sara, on the other hand, did not look quite so convinced.

"But the whole point of me doing this was so I could help rescue the humans. If I don't get some opportunity to practice my healing techniques on non-celestial beings, I can't complete my diploma." She sounded like a spoilt school girl whose evening goggle-boxing had been disrupted. I couldn't believe what I was hearing.

"Sara, get a grip for fuck's sake. This expedition has gone much, much further than the original brief. You must see that?" I was on the verge of getting

~ 205 ~

angry. "We're less than five hours away from the potential break out of an intra-dimensional war, and you're worried about your bloody Brownie badges?"

"Well, it is a little more serious than that, Zach. Sara has been studying for nearly three hundred years for this. I can see that my idea might make her just a little... disappointed..."

Raphael was trying to conciliate, but I got the feeling that he too was rather surprised by Sara's reaction. It made me think of the way she had flown off the handle at Johan when he let on to us that the recent spate of angelic defections were common knowledge in the boundary lands, rather than the state secret she had taken them to be.

"Come on, Sara, it makes sense if you go with Raphael. And if we get lucky, you'll be able to work with Alex and Sophia once we get them out of here, so your trip won't be wasted if we all pull our fingers out and get on with it."

My words might have been a bit harsh, but as I spoke, I gently stroked her left arm, from elbow to wrist and back again. She moved closer to me, her material body gently buffering against me, little thrills of warm, loving radiance rippling between us. I didn't want to leave her... and then I thought that maybe she had said what she did because she felt the same, and just didn't want to admit it in front of Raphael.

She sighed and looked up at me, her eyes wide and questioning. We didn't need words. I nodded and looked towards Raphael, who had spotted the surreptitious stroking and was being ultra-tactful. He'd moved a little way apart from us so as to give us some space.

"Okay. Sorry. Let's go with your plan, Raph. I was being an idiot." Sara moved away from me and pulled the map from her kitbag. "Let's just get our bearings – but don't you guys think you'd better get back into your corpuses? I doubt we'll be coming back this way, so if you want to keep them, this is your last chance."

She was right, so we both went back to the oak and retrieved our stinking, filthy bodies. It was quite unpleasant getting back into mine; like getting into dirty underwear after a shower, or having to put on yesterday's clothes after a night on the tiles when you didn't quite make it back to your own bed. It hadn't had a proper wash in a couple of days now and could really do with a shave. Some of the clothing was particularly rank and as I experimentally ran my tongue round my teeth, they felt almost furry; I could practically see the bacteria gathering on them. As I wriggled myself back into every finger and toe, I could also feel the weight of sheer physical exhaustion it was experiencing. It had been awake for over thirty-six hours now; it was soon going to be running on empty. I promised myself that once I got out of here, I would book the poor old thing into St. Basil's for a proper service.

Raphael's nose was wrinkled in an expression of disgust which didn't sit well on his normally benign features; I guessed he was not enjoying the experience either.

"Oh stop being so precious, you two." Sara was laughing at our obvious – and completely ridiculous – discomfiture; we were on a field operation in Hell after all, not a gentle saunter through St. James' park: dirt, blood, sweat and tears went with the territory.

Sara's gentle mockery broke through what was left of the atmosphere. Raphael gave his jacket and trousers a final and rather ineffectual brushing down with a clump of goose-grass and moved towards the boulder where she had laid out the map. Whilst they weren't looking, I rifled through my kitbag for something to use as a mouth wash. I took a quick swig from one of the phials of germanium we had brought with us in case either Alex or Sophia was affected with celestial radiance sickness. It didn't taste that brilliant, but at least it made my mouth feel a bit more hygienic – and I hoped it would've killed off any lingering traces of bad breath.

I made my way over to the others; they seemed to have reached some sort of conclusion, Raphael was now rummaging for something in his kitbag and Sara was expertly folding up the map.

"I think we're clear on where we're going – we need to keep tight to the far edge of the ditches and then head along the side of the River Phlegathon. It looks as if we are slightly going back on ourselves, but that can't be helped." Sara stowed the map back in one of the side pockets.

"You won't need a map I don't think, Zach, we're practically up close and personal with the outskirts of Dis as it is." Sara was right. I clambered up on to the boulder and looked around me. The road to Dis stretched out and away to our left; the nearest buildings were less than a mile away through the Medusa Gate, a large structure which straddled the road and cast a long shadow over what I thought was the entrance to Eligor's stronghold itself. I felt a light touch at my waist and saw Sara holding out her hand; I grabbed it and pulled her up on to the boulder, and we folded into each other, my arm around her shoulder, hers around my waist.

~ 207 ~

"Right; are we ready?" Raphael was matter of fact and commanding – and his interjection was extremely unwelcome. "Zach, Sara, stop gazing into the distance like a pair of moonstruck tourists; we need to get moving if we're to have any chance of getting this done."

Always one to resent being told what to do by those who based their authority simply on hierarchy rather than experience, I felt an instant flicker of doubt. I'd had no chance to contact Manny and I felt exposed and uncertain. If I had learned anything from those misspent hours watching b-movies in the basement of the Canonbury Tower between assignments, it was Never Split Up. It always leads to disaster.

How come Raphael was now the one calling the shots? It had all happened so fast; a few hours ago, Sara and I were working as one to outwit the Graeae; we had been a partnership; we'd clicked, and we'd been good together. Now we were separating; I was heading off to face I knew-not-what in the stronghold of one of the most powerful of the Dukes of Hell whilst Sara was walking towards enemy-lines on what now seemed to me to be the flimsiest chance that Raphael could sweet-talk Eligor into handing over a rogue angel.

I felt Sara's arm tighten round me and I knew she must be feeling the same. This was our mission. Why should Raphael have it all his own way? Fired up, I disentangled myself and jumped to the ground.

"Now look, Raphael, I'm not so sure this is the best plan, after all." I moved swiftly towards him and he turned, somewhat startled by the challenge in my voice. As he looked at me, I saw a flash of what might have been fear cross his face, but it was too fleeting for me to be certain. He pulled his shoulders back and raised himself to his full height.

"What has changed your mind, Angel Zachriel? Tell me what worries you – but hurry, we really do not have much time." His face had regained its usual benign aspect but he was speaking to me formally now, a subtle way of reminding me of both our respective ranks and my duty. He was an Archangel, and I was honour-bound to obey him.

When I had taken up my commission as a Justice Angel all those years ago, I had pledged to act in obedience, to 'seek out and punish that which is evil'. I had always upheld that oath because I believed in it. I was proud of what I was, and the work I had to do. And when push came to shove, I was now faced with a direct command – how could I let a small flicker of personal doubt tip me over the edge into defiance?

"It's nothing, Raphael. You're right, I can do this alone. And Sara will be an

~ 208 ~

asset to you at the negotiation tables." I looked over towards her, but she had her head down and was putting things in order in her kitbag. When she'd finished, she slung it over her shoulders and went to stand next to Raphael.

"So, I'll head towards Eligor's stronghold and if I'm successful, I'll take Alex and Sophia straight up to the Avernus Gate. Do you want me to wait for you at the ferry?"

Raphael thought for a moment. "If you get there with time to spare, then wait for us, but if we haven't arrived by eleven, get Charon to take you over; your first priority has to be getting Alex and Sophia to safety. Contact Manny as soon as you get on the ferry – and don't forget to send it back for us once you reach the other side."

Raphael reached into his kitbag and pulled something out. It was the Golden Bough. "And take this. It will help keep Alex and Sophia safe." He was about to hand it to me, when Sara reached towards it and tried to pull it from Raphael's hand.

"No. We need it." Her voice was harsh and urgent. "He's got germanium and asphodel and Lord knows what else that the pharmacist at St. Basil's gave him." She pulled again, but Raphael's grip was stronger.

"Please, Raph, it's the only thing which will give us safe passage to Eligor." She was pleading now as she slowly dropped her hand from the Bough and took a step backwards, lifting her great eyes to his face. "I don't think I can do this without it."

Raphael said nothing, he just stepped forwards and handed me the Bough. I took it uncertainly, looking first at Sara, who seemed to be pleading for me to hand it back to her, and then at Raphael, who just curtly nodded to my bag and then turned away.

"Now, Sara, don't forget that you are with me. What could hurt you if you stand beside an Archangel?" She gulped a little and then gave him a small smile. He nodded approvingly at her and looked back towards me. "Make your farewells. We leave now."

I moved across to where Sara was standing, but she turned away from me. "Don't, Zach," she said. "I can't bear it. Just go. I'll see you at the ferry." And with that, she set off towards the farthest edge of the gorge, her shoulders back and determined and the faint light of the moon gleaming on her burnished hair. I needn't have bothered with the mouth wash after all.

"God speed, Angel Zachriel." Raphael gave me the traditional farewell before he too turned away and began the journey towards Erebus.

~ 209 ~

"God speed to you, Archangel, and God speed to you to, my Sara." I said the words in my head, for there was now no-one left to hear them. Without further ado, I turned my back on the rapidly retreating figures and set my course towards the Medusa Gate and Eligor's stronghold.

~ *Chapter Thirty One* ~

The road was deserted and although it was steep and unpleasantly hard underfoot, I made good progress and was within spitting distance of the Medusa Gate in less than fifteen minutes. I kept glancing upwards, but the skies seemed clear, although it was becoming increasingly overcast and I couldn't tell if there was anything flying above the cloud cover. I'd put my cloak back on just in case, but it was beginning to seem like an unnecessary precaution. It was bulky and didn't fit particularly well around the shoulders and was definitely not making the walking any easier. I had just about made my mind up to discard it when I heard something coming up the hill behind me. Immediately, I abandoned the road and took cover in the trees.

It was the sound of an engine, but a very quiet and smooth running engine, so quiet in fact that I only just had enough time to conceal myself before a vehicle came in to view.

It was spectacular. A Rolls Royce Silver Ghost, circa 1910 if I was not mistaken, and one of the most beautiful cars ever made. Its long, elegant body was a delicate shade of blue, set off to perfection by polished maple panelling and silver headlamps and wheels. As it sailed past me with a serenity and grace which seemed strangely out of place in this stark and infernal landscape, the driver turned slightly to the left to chuck a cigarette out onto the roadside. As he did so, I saw his face, illuminated in the spotlight that shone down from the top of the Medusa Gate. He was handsome, in a haughty and rather dissolute way, his face all right-angled perfection, with a strong, almost aquiline nose and a full and beautifully proportioned mouth.

I recognised him instantly and fell back amongst the tree roots in shock. I hadn't seen him for thousands of years, but there could be absolutely no doubt about the identity of the driver.

It was Samael[52], ex-member of the Heavenly Host, the first commander-in-chief of the Justice Angels, Fallen Archangel – and the wanker responsible for breaking Sara's heart, back when we were working security duty together on Jacob's Ladder.

As I watched in silence from the bushes, the car drove on, through the Medusa Gate and then turned left, taking what I knew to be the road that led to Eligor's stronghold.

When the coast was clear, I returned to the road, pulling grass off my cloak as I went. My mind was racing; there were about a thousand thoughts chasing around in my head. What was Samael doing here? Why wasn't he in Erebus with the other Lords of The Fallen, preparing to defend their territories against the Potestas? And why was he making for Eligor's stronghold?

I wondered if this could just be a coincidence; I knew that many of the more ostentatious of the Fallen had luxury pleasure palaces in Dis; perhaps he just wanted to get the Roller shut away safely before heading back into the theatre of war. I knew I wouldn't have wanted to leave such a magnificent machine just lying around for looters and vandals if she'd been my baby.

And then I thought of Sara. The hours when we were supposed to be monitoring the traffic flow on Jacob's Ladder, and instead I had done nothing but listen to her frenzied outpourings about Samael, giving her tea and sympathy, and on one memorable occasion, a whole Melchizedek of champagne in an attempt to lift her spirits. (It hadn't worked, she'd got very drunk, fallen off the Ladder and I had had to carry her home, unconscious.)

The story was really a bit of a cliché; he had spoken to her once, made some comment about her hair, given her a smile. And that had been it. As far as Sara was concerned, her heart belonged to Sammy.

At least, it had then. It was different now. I thought about the way we had stood together less than an hour ago, looking out towards Dis, her body pressed against mine, the warmth of her hand on the skin of my back. She was my Sara

---

52 "The Archangel Samael was once ruler of the fifth Heaven and held dominion over death. Known as 'The Venom of God', he was commander-in-chief of the Justice Angels and for several millennia was the executioner for high-profile death sentences directly decreed by divine law. A notorious seducer (he has married at least three demon wives) he is a destroyer and enemy of humanity. He has been held responsible for instigating the Fall of Man and is thought to be the father of Cain, who brought bloodshed and murder into the human world. Despite this undisputed roll-call of evil-doings, there is still some uncertainty as to the true nature of Samael and some authorities insist that, although he is without doubt one of the Fallen, he still remains under the command of divine law." *Know your enemy – The Angels' Guide to the Legions of the Fallen*, 1987

now, and if that bastard came anywhere near her, Fallen Archangel or no, I would harness the full might of divine justice to knock him off his arrogant, straight nosed perch.

Feeling all fired up and full of righteous indignation, I marched through the Medusa Gate and went left, seeing no-one as I did so. I took the first turning and within two minutes I'd reached my destination – bordered by two, tall, wrought iron gates, painted gold and scarlet. Eligor's coat of arms, a rather horrible image of two scarlet wolves (rampant) disembowelling a lamb (couchant), was displayed prominently on both gates. If I had been in any doubt as to who owned this property, a small brass plate was attached to the side wall, noting that this was the 'Property of the Lord Eligor' and that 'Trespassers will be Persecuted'.

The gates were closed and beyond them I could see a courtyard in which a floodlit fountain was playing. To the left and right I could just make out lawns and well-kept but rather unimaginative ornamental gardens. About 10 yards from the great golden basin of the fountain was the entrance to the house. It was a Southfork monstrosity of a hacienda, which was approached via a covered and red-carpeted walkway, its ceiling supported by eight Doric columns. The walkway led from the ornate and unbelievably vulgar gold and scarlet marble steps to a half-opened doorway, through which I could just see a black and white tiled floor. To the left of the steps, parked rather haphazardly as if the driver had been in a bit of a hurry, was the Silver Ghost.

Samael was nowhere to be seen, but a small demon with a forked tail and three metallic looking horns had just turned on the engine and was probably about to manoeuvre the car to a rather less obtrusive spot in its allotted garage.

This was not what I'd expected. Maybe I'd read too many gothic novels, or perhaps I was suffering from a surfeit of LOTR and Game of Thrones, but I had been looking for the mighty stronghold of one of the Dukes of Hell - and rather than finding the traditional dark, forbidding moated fortress, with ravens nesting in the battlements and the obligatory dank and dingy dungeon, I had stumbled across the sort of place that looked like it was trying its hardest to keep up with the Kardashians.

Still, I was not going to let my disappointment get the better of me. I knew better than to assume that just because the place looked tacky and unthreatening, didn't mean that it really was just tacky and unthreatening. I was going to treat the silent and apparently almost deserted hacienda with the same level of caution I would've used if it had been Sauron's fortress at the foot of Mount Doom or the sinister bastions of the Dread Fort.

I had just decided to follow the outskirts of walls round to the rear of the building to see if there was anywhere I could easily scale them, when I caught sight of something moving in the hallway. I decided to take off my cloak; weighing up ease of movement against anonymity. On this occasion, ease of movement won hands down.

As I was stuffing it back in my kitbag, the door of the building was flung open and a woman made her way out on to the walkway. She was tall and incredibly slender, with short, dark, spiky hair. She strode the length of the walkway, coming to a halt on the edge of the marble steps. She raised her right arm and turned her wrist slightly, as if checking her watch. Then, raising her left hand to her brow to shield her eyes from the blaze of the floodlights, she peered towards the road.

"Hello, you... by the gate... I'm talking to you." The voice was low and pleasant although undeniably commanding; she had a slight lilt which I thought sounded European, but I couldn't quite work out if it was French or Spanish.

Trying to keep calm, I didn't move or say anything. She began to descend the stairway, making her way past the fountain towards the tall, wrought iron gates.

"I can see you, you know. It is the Angel Zachriel isn't it? You might as well come out..."

I remained frozen.

"We are expecting you... In fact you are actually just a little late." Her voice was closer now; I heard the gates open. There was nowhere I could go, nothing I could do...

"Well, finally we meet." She was standing beside me, her small, well-manicured hand outstretched and a smile on her face, which would have been charming if it hadn't revealed that all her teeth were filed to the sharpest of sharp points.

"I'm Lilith. It's a pleasure to meet you at last. May I call you Zach?" She looked me up and down, taking in my tattered clothes, dirty face and what could no longer even think of passing itself off as designer stubble. "But where is your charming companion? The little Angel Sarandiel? I was looking forward to meeting her also. My husband has told me so much about her."

And then it all clicked in to place.

Way back in the day, Lilith had been Adam's first wife, made, as he was, from dust, and equal to him in every particular. The story goes that all was definitely not rosy in Paradise – and she had soon got fed up with the missionary position night after night. She started pressing Adam to be more inventive, which did his sense of manly pride no good at all. And she insisted on being on top some of the time as well; there were no beds in the garden, and to be honest, I didn't blame her for not always wanting to be forced to writhe around in the dirt with the bugs and who knows what as yet unnamed flora sticking into her.

He, on the other hand, was quite happy with the way things were and didn't want an uppity wife challenging him to think about her satisfaction as much as his. To cut a long story short, after a number of rows and altercations, Lilith upped sticks and left Eden, settling for a while somewhere on the shores of the Red Sea. There she met Samael, who if he hadn't already joined the ranks of the Fallen, was tipped over the edge by his obsession with the sex-mad seductress.

Lilith and Samael married and at first all seemed hunky-dory, but when she heard that Adam had a new wife, this time created from his rib, allowing him to retain his dominance, she was jealous. She persuaded Samael to take her back to the garden, where between them they tempted and tricked the innocent Eve into breaking her vows. Some people say that Lilith is happy to swing both ways, and that she had an affair with Eve before Adam had actually consummated the relationship, but I don't know if that's just malicious gossip. As I said before, I'm a bit hazy about pre-history, but what I do know is that unlike poor old Adam and Eve, who ate of the fruit of knowledge, were banished and became mortal, Lilith left the Garden of her own accord and retained her immortality.

I'd heard that she and Samael had had a bit of a volatile marriage over the years – he'd been linked with at least two other Hell-Queens and his bed post must have been whittled to nothing with his countless conquests amongst humanity. Lilith had always given as good as she got, and her reputation as a succubus, temptress and seducer was legendary.

Poor Sara hadn't stood a chance when she became infatuated with Samael; back then she was still in pig-tails and had as much poise and self-possession as a spaniel. Samael liked them sophisticated, worldly and experienced - and looking at Lilith as she stood smiling up at me, her almond shaped eyes sparkling and a wicked smile on her delicately tinted pale pink lips, I felt an enormous debt of gratitude to Raphael for taking Sara to Erebus with him.

It would have knocked her for six if she'd had to meet Samael again – and I don't think that what I now knew to be Sara's carefully constructed carapace of elegance and sophistication could have withstood a full-frontal attack from the lovely, but terrifying Lilith.

Her hand was still outstretched. I looked at my grimy dirt-soiled palm and gave it a quick rub on the seat of my pants before holding it out towards her. She allowed herself to touch just the tip of my fingers and then turned back towards the house, calling out to me over her shoulder, "Well, come on in… as I said, you're actually a bit late. We were expecting you an hour ago."

Silently, I walked behind her across the courtyard and up the marble steps, which I found slippery and unsettling to walk on; Lilith however, in her 6 inch stilettos, seemed to negotiate them without any difficulty.

Although I hoped that I appeared calm, my mind was working overtime. What was she talking about? She said she'd been expecting me and she didn't seem to be behaving in a way which suggested she felt threatened or unsettled by a Justice Angel turning up on her doorstep. I decided to say nothing for the time being, let her think I knew as much as she did, and not betray for an instant that I was feeling more and more out of my depth with every single step that we took.

As we walked through the hallway, the doors closed silently behind us; I turned to see two enormous jackal-headed footmen, dressed in the Eligor livery of gold and scarlet, take up their positions in front of the closed doors. I mentally crossed this off as a possible escape route and continued to walk with Lilith across the hall and into a large and ornate salon, decorated ostentatiously in the baroque style and containing furniture which looked either too flimsy or too uncomfortable to sit on.

"Ghastly isn't it, darling?" Lilith looked at me with amusement. "Eligor is a sweetie, but his taste is somewhat… underdeveloped. Let's head over to the guest suites, they're rather more simpatico."

We had now walked out into a covered atrium, heading towards a more elegant looking area at the back of the development.

"Don't you think they're simply gorgeous…? I had Frank Lloyd Wright do them for me. He wasn't keen at first, in fact it cost an arm and a leg before he finally agreed…" She smiled over her shoulder at me, once again revealing those disconcerting rows of pointed white teeth. "Still, I've been told that he's getting about wonderfully in his wheelchair and I made sure that it was his left arm that darling Sammy gave to the Hell-Beast, so that's alright isn't it?"

The room was indeed lovely, large and well-appointed, with a relatively low ceiling and long windows, each embellished with beautiful yet simple stained glass in shades of ambers and greens. The floors were wooden and covered with woven Kashmiri carpets; there were no pictures on the wall, but each table held a large spherical terracotta pot containing arrangements of natural flowers. At the end of the room the wall was made of exposed golden-hued brickwork, and it was here that I spotted the only really incongruous item. Slap bang in the centre of the wall was a large fireplace, sunk back deep into the wall, with seats all around it, like the hearths in old Elizabethan manor houses. Across the fireplace was a spit, and on the spit was what looked to be the body of a small child. As I watched, a figure rose from the depths of the fireplace and gave the handle of the spit a vigorous turn. He had his back to me, but I was pretty sure it was Samael; I'd recognise that arrogant arsehole's posture from any angle.

The spit span round rapidly, sizzling in the flames and sputtering meat juices and fat into the hearth, where they were greeted with enthusiasm by the creatures that lay there. As I looked down with mounting horror, I recognised that these were more of the dog-things that had accompanied Enepsigos and the Wild Hunt.

"Oh there you are, Sammy darling… but must you play with your food like that? I have asked you before to be careful; you know it makes such a mess of the oak flooring." Lilith walked over to the fireplace and ran a proprietary finger down the man's spine.

"And we have guests. Darling Zach has finally arrived, but *sans la petite ange*… such a shame for you my precious… I know you were simply dying to see her again."

The man gave a grunt and leant forward into the fire where, by the sounds of it, he was having a bit of trouble pulling something away from the spit. He finally managed it and when he turned towards us he was holding the crisp and golden remains of a child's arm. He waved it in our direction rather vaguely.

"Ah, Zach… Welcome… Welcome. Not been here that long myself, in fact I thought I might have met you on the road… would have given you a lift in the old Roller if I'd seen you." I'd forgotten how much his clipped and precise old-Etonian tones got on my wick. In actual fact, he hadn't been to public school any more than I had. We were old souls before mankind had first discovered the 3Rs, and the fact that he had chosen to assume those plummy, pampered and privileged tones was just one more thing I realised I hated about him.

"Shame you haven't got Sara with you… I was quite looking forward to a

~ 217 ~

bit of a reunion." He gave me a conspiratorial wink. "Still, you're here now. Fancy a munch? They call this 'long pig' you know; or perhaps it should be 'long piglet' in this case." He let out a short bray of a laugh and took a huge bite from the upper arm, waving it again in my direction.

I knew that I needed to keep calm. Whatever was happening here, Lilith and Samael were not going to get a rise out of me. They seemed to think I knew exactly what was going on, and I was damned (possibly quite literally) if I was going to disabuse them. I had tangled with demons before, and the one thing you couldn't do was show them any weakness.

Lilith had made her way to a small cupboard on the far right of the fireplace and was mixing drinks. She came towards me, carrying two tall glasses of something that looked incredibly cool and refreshing. There were little drops of water forming on the side of the glasses and I could see a small flotilla of ice cubes nestling desirably beneath slices of lemon and lime.

"So rude of me, darling, please, you must be so thirsty…"

She handed me the glass, a slight smile on her lips and a questioning look in her eyes. Without thinking, I took it from her and had almost raised it to my lips before I remembered where I was. My poor corpus was so dehydrated by now that my physical reactions had almost overridden my thought processes. I felt like throwing whatever she'd given me back in her face, but managed to control myself sufficiently to put it down on one of the nearby walnut tables. I didn't use a coaster and I took a small but very real pleasure in hoping that it would leave a ring mark.

"Naughty, naughty, Lilith… Now you didn't really think I'd fall for that one did you?" I pretended to laugh off what I took to be her first move, something which, if it had been successful, could have held me within the Inferno for all eternity.

She pouted charmingly, raised her own glass, toasted me and drank. "Oh well, one can but try…"

She seated herself on the long, cream-coloured sofa which ran almost the entire length of the room and patted a place which was rather too close to her leather clad thighs for me to sit with any hope of comfort. She took another sip from her glass and looked up at me expectantly. "Now, let's get down to business."

I side-stepped the sofa and pulled out one of the chairs from the dining table, reversing it, so I could lean my folded arms on the chair back. Out of the corner of my eye, I saw Samael wander over to the cupboard, grab what looked like a can of lager and head out into the garden, taking another enormous bite out of his revolting spit-roast as he did so.

"We were expecting you about an hour ago as I said. And we really didn't think you would be alone. You're clearly a little more resourceful than we'd given you credit for and, interesting as it would be, I don't have time to find out what you've done with your little sidekick."

I decided it was time to come clean. Whatever was going on, I didn't sense anything particularly threatening and she was right, time was passing and I thought we might as well just cut through the crap and get on with it.

"I'm not sure what you were expecting, lady, but I'm here for one thing and one thing only." It was time to get formal. Reaching into my jacket, I pulled out my ID and flashed it across at her.

"I believe that the owner of this property, the demon Eligor, otherwise known as Duke Eligos, is holding two humans captive against their will and in contravention of divine law. I am an agent of the Celestial Justice Forces and I have come to recover said humans, return them to their natural and appropriate environment and will use all reasonable force in the pursuance of my duties. I therefore demand, under the conditions laid out in…"

I had really got into my swing, but before I could get any further, she waved aside my ID with a contemptuous flick of her hand and got to her feet. "Yes, yes, you can stop all that regulatory mumbo-jumbo. You've come for the live ones. Take them. We don't need them anymore."

This threw me: "What… where are they? What do you mean you don't need them anymore?"

She laughed coldly, and now there was no longer even the slightest pretence at cordiality. "They have served their purpose. And now you can serve yours."

She leant over and took something from a small lacquered bowl; it was a single key, small and insignificant. Throwing it to me, she turned and began walking towards the garden door. Her top was low cut, displaying most of her back, which was tanned and well-muscled; she had what looked like a tattoo of a moth or butterfly at the base of her spine.

"They are in the basement; take them and go. Please excuse me if I don't remain to see you out; time is passing and Samael and I now need to discharge our duty and join the others in Erebus."

As she reached the doorway, she looked back at me, teeth bared and a look of complete loathing on her face. "I know what you did to Enepsigos. And I know what she said to you before you cast her into Tartarus. Believe me, angel,

~ 219 ~

when the time comes for your destruction, I will join her in devouring you…
and it will be a pleasure."

She was gone.

Slightly stunned, I looked around me. The place seemed deserted except for
the dog-things which were still hanging around the fireplace, so absorbed in the
smell of the pitiful and unsavoury remains that were still slowly rotating on the
spit that they didn't turn a hair as I walked past them.

So Sophia and Alex were here, and it sounded like they were still alive. I
couldn't be sure what Lilith had meant when she said that they had served their
purpose, but I had my suspicions and if I was right, it was even more important
for me to get them out of the Inferno. I also knew that I needed to get in touch
with Manny as soon as possible.

I had no idea where the basement might be, but the key Lilith had thrown at
me was new and much more in keeping with the Frank Lloyd Wright part of
the property so I decided to head back into the covered atrium to see if there
were any signs of it.

Directly opposite me was the entrance to 'Southfork'; the wall to my right
was entirely made of glass and housed a swimming pool and bar. By a process
of elimination, I walked over to the left hand side of the atrium, which was a
weathered old brick wall covered in wisteria. It had a few narrow windows
spaced every twenty feet or so, about two thirds of the way up the wall. Right
at the end and almost entirely covered by the wisteria was a door. I tried the
key in the lock. It turned easily, the door opened inwards and I found myself
staring down a steep concrete staircase into what looked like the ground floor
of a run-down and deserted multi-storey car park.

I could hear nothing and the smell of petrol and stale urine simply
reinforced my first impressions. Remembering to put the key in my pocket, I
gingerly stepped over the threshold. The staircase had handrails which had
once been painted a rather bilious yellow, but the paint had chipped away,
leaving them rusty and in some parts, worn so thin that they looked as if they
would perish if you actually tried to hold on to them.

The walls of the stairwell were brutalist concrete and predictably covered
with the apparently universal graffiti any car park user can rely on. Enormous
penises flowered above me and garish tags, smiley faces and a set of telephone
numbers which would have been incredibly useful had I been seeking good
head, street drugs or bondage and domination, were set out at regular intervals
as I descended.

I walked down three sets of stairs, eventually reaching the ground floor, which was dark and shadowy, lit only by the faint and flickering light from an EXIT sign screwed on to the wall above a heavy and old fashioned fire door. Next to the door was a battered parking payment machine. It had been kicked in some time ago and now its only purpose was to act as a message board for those who used it to display business cards advertising a range of insalubrious and frankly unbelievable personal services - and the perhaps even more unhappy individuals who desired them.

The smell was truly atrocious down here. Reaching into my bag, I took out the eucalyptus oil I had used when paying a visit to the Graeae. Rubbing it under my nose, my eyes gradually acclimatising to the darkness, I looked about me and saw that there was another door, round to the back of the stair well. It was marked 'PRIVATE STAFF ONLY'.

I tested it; it wasn't locked and I saw no reason to knock. Making sure my dagger was secure in my waistband, I kicked open the door and went inside.

The light was dazzling. I was momentarily blinded and fumbled in my bag for my UDs. Cramming them on, I was then able to take in white padded walls and neon track-lighting; about fifty high-powered halogen spotlights shone into every corner and cranny of the room.

There were two narrow hospital beds against the far wall; as I approached, I saw that they were screwed into place and there was a disturbing array of hooks and chains fastened into the ceiling above them.

Lying on the beds, their bodies imprisoned in straitjackets, their faces held in some sort of ghastly metal masks which forced their eyes to remain wide open, staring incessantly into the dazzling lights, were two silent and motionless figures.

I was certain that I had finally found Alex and Sophia. But what I didn't know was if it was now already too late.

~ *Chapter Thirty Two* ~

The figures on the beds hadn't responded at all when I'd kicked the door open and from where I was standing, I really couldn't be sure that they were even breathing.

Swiftly, I pushed the door shut behind me and secured it with the safety lock. I'd decided it would be better if I was locked in with Alex and Sophia rather than leaving the room open and accessible to all and sundry. I had no idea if the coast really was clear out there and I didn't want any interruptions. It seemed sensible to shut down the majority of the track lights. The switches were by the door; I flicked a handful of them and within seconds the unbearable dazzling whiteness was gone. I left only a few spots to illuminate the centre of the room, which would give me more than enough light for what I needed to do.

Once I had sorted out the most obvious source of their discomfort, I went over to the beds to see what sort of state they were in. As I got closer, I was able to see a slight pulse in Alex's temple and could just make out an almost negligible movement in Sophie's throat.

I felt a great surge of relief; despite the odds stacked against them, they were alive. I seemed to be all fingers and thumbs as I undid the straps around first Sophie's mask and then Alex's, loosening the sharp pincers which had forced their eyes to remain open and instantly reducing the pressure on their temporal lobes.

As soon as her mask was removed, Sophie simply closed her eyes and slipped into an even deeper state of unconsciousness. Alex, on the other hand, looked at me in terror as if he was expecting my presence to herald some new and yet more arcane form of torture. I began to speak slowly, to try to find a way to reassure him as I fumbled to undo the straps of the straitjacket which imprisoned him.

"Alex, it's alright, it's okay…" I tried my best to sound kind and reassuring, even though I knew that I must look quite terrifying, what with my unkempt hair, filthy face and dishevelled clothing.

He was staring at me as if I was some kind of yahoo, a creature of nightmares, rather than an angel who had literally gone through Hell to try to find him and return him to safety.

I tried again. "Please don't be frightened Alex. I really am a friend. I'm here to help you." As I spoke, I managed to work free his final bindings, then I stood back to allow him the dignity of releasing himself.

"Alex, I know who you are, I know that Jaoel deserted you, I know what you've been through. I'm here to help you."

Once Alex felt his bonds relaxing, he almost immediately pushed himself upwards and back, until he was half sitting, half cowering against the wall. Still he said nothing.

His lips were cracked and bitten and there was a vivid and unpleasantly suppurating scar running across the left side of his face. The eyes that were now gazing uncomprehendingly into mine were bloodshot and watering, the result of being forced to stare constantly into the halogen lights. I remembered the germanium and went to fetch it, bringing with me my kitbag, which still contained the food and drink we had saved for them.

I passed Alex the phial of germanium and pointed to the eye-dropper. "This will help. It's germanium, used to treat the effects of excessive radiance. I got it at St. Basil's, in Chelsea."

At the mention of a familiar location, Alex raised his head. "Ch… Chelsea…? You come from Chelsea?"

"No, Alex, I'm an angel, like Jaoel, like Sophia's Guardian, Ely. I've been sent here to help you…; to bring you home."

I pointed to the bottle. "Try it… it will help."

"Can't take stuff from the Inferno… Sophia told me… we mustn't…"

I understood immediately. Sophia knew her stuff, she'd been reading Dante's *Inferno* the day she met Alex in Old Street. She'd warned him not to eat or drink anything that was given to them.

"It's alright. I brought this in with me, from a hospital, to help you; to help both of you. You must trust me…"

And for some reason, he decided that he would. Maybe he thought that he had nothing to lose, or maybe I'd somehow managed to convince him, but he unscrewed the stopper and put two droplets of germanium into each eye. He blinked and within seconds, I could see the inflammation abating and his eyes beginning to return to normal.

"Have you got anything to drink?"

I reached into my bag and brought out one of the last remaining cans, plus what was left of the mint cake. Telling him to take it easy and not eat or drink anything too quickly, I moved across to the other bed and began loosening the ties on Sophia's straitjacket.

She still had not moved. Her eyes remained closed; her breathing slow and shallow. She had livid welts across the side of her face and neck, as if she had been sprayed with something toxic and I could see what looked like bruising and a puncture wound just behind her left ear. Her beautiful long hair had been cut off and shaved almost to her scalp. There was no doubt that she was in a bad way.

"How did you find us?" I turned to see Alex sitting up, the straitjacket was now on the floor and he had emerged dressed in jeans and a checked shirt, both of which looked very much the worse for wear. Round his neck was a thin leather thong from which hung a small bronze disc; he must still be under the protection of the Orphic talisman, which should allow him to move safely through the Inferno. To be honest, he looked like shit, but at least he seemed to have decided to trust me.

I told him as much as I could about what had happened since I had been raised, unceremoniously, from my pit, by Manny's phone call on Sunday morning. It had been less than two days ago, but believe me, it felt like a lifetime.

"But what we don't understand is what happened to you and Sophia, how did Eligor manage to get hold of you, and how did he bring you here?"

When Alex finally told me what had happened, it was all so simple I couldn't believe that we hadn't managed to work it out.

What had happened was this. At around seven o'clock on Saturday night, Alex, Kathryn and Sophia were having a drink in the kitchen of Kathryn's flat off Old Street when Sophia's mobile rang. It was the person they knew as Duke Eligos – the guy whose party they had been to the previous night, and who seemed to have the hots for Sophia. Duke asked her over for a drink and suggested Alex come too. He didn't mention Kathryn, whose nose was then put decidedly out of joint by not being invited.

Alex, being both a good guy and aware that he stood more chance of a leg-over if his sister didn't need baby-sitting, decided that he didn't want to spend the evening with Eligos either. Sophia, who seemed to be rather on edge about something, was really keen to go out and as it was a cold, wet evening, Alex said he would drop Sophia over there, stay for one drink and come back within the hour.

They drove round to Eligos' flat in Old Nichol Street, but there was no-one home. Sophia was more than a little pissed off at being stood up, so they went to the offy, grabbed a couple of bottles of wine to make up for it and went back to Kathryn's. The minute they opened the door of the building they were seized by the being Alex now knew to be Eligor and transported into the Inferno.

I had to hand it to them; it was so neat it was text book. Alex and Sophia had left Kathryn alone for less than an hour, but this was more than enough time for Eligor to summon Belphegor and his vile Hell-Beast and for him to carry out the ritual sacrifice which opened the portal into the Inferno.

"The only thing that's kept me going is knowing that I managed to keep Kathryn out of it." I looked up at Alex, who was now pacing unevenly back and forwards along the cell wall, trying to flex and stretch the muscles which had been cramped up in a straitjacket for at least the last six hours.

"I hadn't told her anything about my family; about the whole witness protection thing... she'd have thought I was off my rocker anyway if I'd tried to make her understand about Guardian Angels.

"Eligor grabbed us as soon as we entered the building, Kathryn would have been upstairs in her flat the whole time. She wouldn't have had a clue about what was really going on; in fact, if I know her, she was probably getting really pissed off that we were so late coming back." He gave me a small, slightly rueful smile, which instantly lit up his bruised and battered features.

"She's not going to believe a word of this... well... why would she? It's not exactly an everyday story of country folk..." He looked up at me, and I could finally see the beginnings of trust in his startlingly dark blue eyes.

"You must have had experience of stuff like this before... you're an angel aren't you...? So what do you think I should say to her?"

He didn't know she was dead. And I had to tell him.

It was one of the most difficult things I had ever had to do. I felt as if I had just forced my way into his life to offer him a way out of all the shit that was happening around him, only to push him under, just as he was beginning to get his head back above the surface.

After I had told him about Kathryn, he sank down on the bed, his head in his hands. He began to rock, slowly, backwards and forwards; then suddenly, he threw himself hard against the wall, so his head smashed against it. He threw himself backwards again and again, each time slamming his fist on his knees, each time saying the word 'no', at first almost under his breath and then more and more loudly.

I went over to him and touched his shoulders, thinking about Sara and the way she had been able to channel her healing touch to help for Isra. As I concentrated, I felt my hands begin to tingle; they seemed to become weightless, as if they would float away from me if they could. They were now very pale and surrounded by a slight luminescence. I let them rest on his shoulders and as I did so, I felt him shudder and then finally, relax. He stopped hitting his head against the wall and became silent. His breath was coming in deep gasps and then he began to cry. Through all this, I held him.

And at last, the crying stopped.

"Alex, I know this is incredibly hard for you, but we need to get out of here." I hoped that the strength I had just transferred to him would be enough. Lord only knew what he had been through, but time was running out for us, and I needed to move quickly.

"I have to take you back now. We can't hang around here any longer. When you get home, there will be people to help you, but for now, we need to get through this. It's just a few more hours. Do you think you can hold on for me?"

"Too right I can." Alex had pulled himself to his feet; his strength had come back to him and the anger which was driving him was almost tangible. "I am not going to let those fuckers win this. Do you know what they said to us when they put us in here? They told us that they didn't want to kill us... but that by the time they had finished with us, we would wish that we were dead.

"They made us watch things... do things..." He looked down at the floor, his shoulders quivering with remembered disgust and terror. "But I don't want to talk about them now... They wanted to drive us insane... and I'm worried that they might just have succeeded with Sophia."

He turned to look at his sister, who still had not opened her eyes or moved in any way since I had entered the room.

"I don't know about Sophia, maybe she's just buried herself so deep within her consciousness that she just isn't ready to come out."

I'd seen things like this before, in Syria and Bosnia, Afghanistan and Iraq; and going further back, in the pogroms and concentration camps, the crusades and the inquisitions. The human mind is actually a very resilient thing, and sometimes, when it has seen too much, or been forced to live through stuff it just can't cope with, it sort of shuts down, almost like going into hibernation, until it is ready to begin to heal.

I hoped this is what was happening to Sophia, but whatever the situation, the one thing I was certain of was that we couldn't just leave her here.

I swiftly unwrapped the rest of the straitjacket and pulled it off her, exposing what she was wearing underneath. Like her brother she was still wearing the small ancient amulet on a leather thong around her neck. I remembered that she had been expecting to go on a date when she'd been kidnapped, so her clothes were particularly unsuitable for a foray into the Inferno. She was wearing a classic LBD, originally designed to be clingy and low-cut but now hanging in tatters across her back and stomach. Her tights were ripped into a mass of ladders and there were great livid bruises on her lower legs and thighs. She had no shoes – which didn't actually matter that much, as I had decided that I was going to have to carry her.

I took another quick look at her poor tatters and dragged the cloak out of my kitbag, hastily pulling it over her head. Whilst it had been too small for me, it completely swamped Sophia. But at least it would give her some protection from the elements, and perhaps its innately positive qualities would be of some help to her in her silent and unreachable torment.

"Right, is there anything here you need to bring with you?" It was time to get this show on the road. Alex shook his head. I strapped on my kitbag and then turned to lift Sophia gently onto my shoulder. She weighed very little, and didn't even stir as I picked her up; a fireman's lift may not look very decorous, but it was by far the best way to carry someone if you needed to be able to climb stairs and keep at least one of your hands free.

"Okay, I've got Sophia, but will you be alright walking on your own?" I'd noticed when he had been pacing the room that he was limping. If the bruises and lacerations on Sophia's legs had been anything to go by, I wouldn't have been surprised if Alex hadn't got some rather nasty injuries as well.

But I had to hand it to the guy – he was a stoic.

"No problem... I'll be fine."

I checked my watch. It was twenty to nine.

I was now travelling with a brave, but extremely weak human and carrying another who I didn't think would regain consciousness anytime soon. The ferry was about sixty miles away, and we needed to get there in less than two hours.

I unlocked the cell door and stepped out into the dingy, urine-smelling vestibule, Alex walking just a couple of steps behind me.

Instantly, I could sense something wasn't right. There was another presence close by to us, and it was something not human. We heard a noise in the stairwell above us, the outer door banged and there were sounds like footsteps pounding the concrete. Something was in here with us, and it was heading towards us at a run.

I turned sideways, thinking possibly to retreat back into the padded cell where Alex and Sophia had been imprisoned, but the door was now shut fast, and Alex was leaning against it, panting as a result of his exertions.

I shifted Sophia slightly on to my right shoulder to make sure I was holding her as securely as I could and reached in my belt for my dagger, positioning myself at a right angle with the stair rail, in order to provide what shelter I could for Alex and to ensure that Sophia was as far away as possible from direct attack. As I did so, the intruder careered round the last corner of the stairwell. Looking up, I found that I was gazing directly into the face of an angel, alated and in full celestial manifestation, sword at the ready and the light of battle in his eyes.

"Oh my God… It's Jaoel," breathed Alex, before he collapsed on the floor behind me.

~ *Chapter Thirty Three* ~

For a second, I just stood there, gobsmacked. I wasn't quite sure what I'd thought might have been hurtling down the stairs towards me, but it certainly hadn't been Jaoel.

I'd never met him before, but I'd heard a lot about him over the years. He had been very matey with a couple of the big boys – in fact there had been a time when he and the Archangel Michael had been pretty much joined at the hip. He'd been the angel tasked with the education and conversion of Abraham and a century or so later had been given the responsibility for taking the first Patriarch on a quick tour of the three realms, which had included a whistle-stop tour of the Lake of Fire and the judgement of souls.

He'd resurfaced a few times across the years, although never in quite so high-profile a role and had developed a bit of a reputation for being the go-to-guy if you were wanting a bit of spiritual persuasion via the manipulation of the dream nexus. I knew that he specialised in Hell-fire and damnation and I was pretty sure that he'd used this to good effect when working with Sophia's Guardian, Ely, trying to persuade her to seek out her long lost brother.

Assigned the role of Guardian to Alex, Jaoel had been given the almost unheard of dispensation to remain in semi-permanent material form so that he could protect him more effectively when they fled both Sicily and the bloody vengeance of the Maniscalos. He had appeared to be absolutely loyal to his duty and as far as I knew, had seemed squeaky clean until the events of the past weekend had set warning bells ringing and he had become the Universe's Most Wanted.

All this flashed through my mind as I stared up into the cool blue eyes and fumbled in my waist-band for my dagger. Neither of us moved. He said nothing, but his eyes left mine for a moment and took in the crumpled body of

Alex on the floor behind me and the still unconscious form of Sophia who I was holding rather precariously over my right shoulder.

Suddenly, he leapt forwards, and in a single movement dropped his sword and, grabbing Sophia from my arms, gave me an almighty shove, which knocked me back against the wall. Losing my balance completely and trying to avoid landing on Alex, I fell awkwardly, hitting my head on the rusty corner of the broken-down payment machine.

Jaoel retreated to the base of the stairs, where he now sat with Sophia clasped in his arms. I pulled myself to my feet, rubbing the side of my head which was now throbbing painfully. I could feel a slight trickle of blood and I hoped I wasn't going to get blood poisoning. I'd been rather lax about tetanus injections for the poor old corpus in recent years.

I bent over to check on Alex, whose eyes were now beginning to flicker open, I helped him sit up, back resting against the wall, head between his knees.

"Hello, Alex." The voice was low and uncertain. "I'm… so… sorry… so very… sorry." Unlike Alex, he still had the slightest trace of an Italian accent.

"Jaoel… why did you leave us?" Alex raised his head to look at the other angel, whose wings were now folded submissively against his back and who had not for one second loosened his grip on Sophia. He shook his head, but didn't reply.

"You bastard…" Alex sounded more hurt than angry. "I trusted you. I'd always trusted you. You were supposed to protect us… To protect Sophia… but you ran out on us."

"It wasn't like that…" Jaoel's voice was shaky, his words tentative and penitent. "I was angry, confused… I'd only just told you that I could no longer be your Guardian… I didn't understand what I was feeling… But believe me; I would never have left if I'd thought this was going to happen. We'd just performed the Talisman ritual – the Abracadabra… I thought she was safe." Jaoel lowered his head; he didn't seem able to look at Alex. He hugged Sophia closer to him, one hand stroking her poor wounded head.

"Now, let's get this straight," I said. "You told Alex that you could no longer be his Guardian, performed the regular evening ritual and then just buggered off, leaving these two," I nodded at Alex and Sophia, "and that poor girl Kathryn, with a complete stranger who'd just walked in off the street and a temporary protector who anyone worth their salt could see was more than a little flaky?" I'd got into my stride now and walked over to Jaoel, louring over

~ 230 ~

him as he sat on the bottom of the hard and unforgiving concrete stairs. "Is that how it was?"

"Who are you?" Jaoel looked up at me. "What's all this got to do with you anyway?"

"Who am I? Who am I, matey? I'm the one who got called in to sort out this mess, after you and that half-wit Isra mucked up. That's who I am. These guys disappeared on your watch and Manny pulled me in to try to find them."

"He rescued us, Jay." Alex spoke quietly. "He found us just now, and he says that he can get us out of here." He looked up at me. "But I don't know if Sophia's going to make it."

I checked my watch again. Time was tight, but I needed to understand what was going on before we went anywhere. Where had Jaoel appeared from? And why was he here? He didn't seem to be offering any threat to Alex and Sophia, but I had to get to the bottom of why the nexus had been terminated before I could make any decisions about what to do next.

Whilst I had been thinking, Jaoel had been concentrating all his attention on Sophia, speaking quietly to her and gently stroking her bruised and damaged face. Alex had got to his feet and he was now sitting on the steps next to Jaoel, holding Sophia's hands in his and warming them.

"Sophia, Sophia, my darling, wake up," Jaoel was whispering to her and I listened in astonishment, but comprehension was just beginning to dawn.

Just then, Sophia moved a little in Jaoel's arms. I saw her shoulders shudder and her breathing deepen. She opened her eyes and looked up at him.

"Jay, oh, Jay… is it really you? Oh my God…" Her voice was weak, so faint I could hardly make out her words. She had no chance to say anything else as he pulled her towards him and kissed her. I could see tears in his eyes and I understood it all.

Jaoel had fallen in love with Sophia.

He had lived for ten years in a human body, guarding her brother and building the strongest of mental connections with Sophia as she grew up. He had been removed from the company of other angels, had had no chance to live even for one hour as a celestial being and he had needed something, someone, as a focus for his energies.

Angels who spend much of their time earth-bonded need to dematerialise regularly in order to refresh their spiritual flow, to cleanse and to regain their celestial balance. Jaoel had not been able to do that, so he had done the next best thing. He had fallen in love.

I rummaged in my bag and pulled out the last remaining can and as Jaoel helped the dehydrated Sophia drink it, Alex told me the rest of the story.

When Sophia had finally arrived in London, he and Jaoel spent pretty much all their time with her, and it was clear that his Guardian's feelings for his little sister were growing stronger by the day. Eventually, Jaoel confided in him. It all came to a head after that dreadful party in Old Nichol Street, where the person they knew as Duke Eligos had tried to get Sophia drunk and – apparently – into her knickers. Jaoel decided at that point that enough was enough; he told Alex that he was going to take the drastic steps of renouncing both his guardianship and his angelic status in order to marry Sophia. This must have been what his last text to Isra had meant when he'd said *'big day tomorrow – you only live once'*.

Alex urged him to sleep on it, but the following day, Jaoel told Alex that his mind was made up. He terminated the nexus, leaving Alex guardian-less and when Alex and Kathryn went out, he told Sophia what he had done. Rather than falling into his arms, however, she was furious. She couldn't believe he'd terminated the nexus and left Alex without protection (and to be honest, he could have contacted the Agency for a temp, so she definitely had a point there) and what's more, she was not prepared to see him sacrifice his angelic status just for her sake.

To cut a long story short, they'd had a blazing row and when Alex and Kathryn returned, Jaoel made himself scarce, going out onto the balcony and not wanting to talk to anyone. Alex said that he saw him talking to someone on the phone at around half past five. He came back in to the flat and then went off somewhere. That was the last any of them saw of him. Remembering Isra's story, I reckoned this must have been when Eligor arrived pretending to be Ely. Jaoel must have been operating on auto-pilot when he helped cast the Talisman – no wonder he didn't bother checking the photograph.

I'd heard enough. Jaoel might have been a bit of a love-struck idiot, but he wasn't a traitor. If I could get all of them back before midnight, I thought I had a pretty good chance of averting the crisis, but it was now nearly twenty to ten. I went over to Jaoel.

"My name is Zachriel, but call me Zach," I inclined my head in a slight bow of greeting; like I've said before, angels are quite wary of touching each other, "and I think we need to be getting a move on. There's one hell of a situation going on out there, but I don't have time to brief you on it now."

"Call me Jay." He gave me a half-smile, then said, "I've just come from Erebus; it's crazy there, armed troops on the streets, the legions massing in the public squares... whatever's going on, it's not funny."

"Right." There was no time to brief him properly, his words only served to confirm the need for action. "We'd better get a move on. Jay, can you carry Sophia?" He nodded.

"Which way are we going?"

"What alternatives do you think we have?" I asked him. He pointed to the door.

"That takes you to Erebus. It's how I got in. I'd gone there looking for Eligor; I'd heard he had Sophia, and I was hoping to run him to ground. I got there a few hours ago and did a bit of digging, calling in a few favours, you know?" I nodded.

"Anyway, I found out that there was a connection between Eligor's place in Dis and the back streets of Erebus. Some sort of wormhole he maintained to allow him to move quickly between the two cities. I exerted a little... pressure... and it didn't take too much for me to find out where it was. Strange how your average demon gets a little worried when you mention Tartarus..." He grinned. I was beginning to like this guy.

"So, I came in here, dashed up the steps and had a quick recce round Chateau Tacky looking for any trace of Sophia or Alex. Of course, I found nothing, so I was making my way back downstairs empty handed when I heard the door opening and you guys coming out into the hall. You know the rest."

"Okay, well, I don't think Erebus is our best bet. The Avernus Gate is quicker, and if we're lucky, I think I know a way to get us to the ferry in less than an hour."

"You're not thinking of flying? There are Chimera up there you know, and I'm not risking Sophia again."

"No, not flying. Come on, let's get going." I picked up my kitbag and began climbing the stairs, Alex following me, slowly but with determination. Jay had picked up his sword and sheathed it; he needed both arms for carrying Sophia, who was nestling in to him, her head resting on his shoulders.

I pushed open the door and looked round me. The coast was clear and I knew exactly where I was going. I led the way across the atrium, back into the hacienda, through the room full of baroque monstrosities and out into the hallway. I picked up a set of keys from a lacquered bowl on a table by the door and led the way out, down the marble steps and around the side of the house, where I was pretty certain I would find the place where Samael's minion had parked the Silver Ghost.

It was at that moment that we heard it; an unearthly howl, followed by another and another. And then we saw them, charging towards us across the grounds. Samael's dog-things, fangs bared, hackles up, hungry for flesh and baying for slaughter.

~ Chapter Thirty Four ~

I looked around me. Alex was too weak to move quickly and Jay had his hands full. There was only one thing for it. I handed the car keys to Alex, telling him to make for the garage at the side of the house and told Jay to go with him. He was about to protest, but the dogs were almost on us.

I didn't want to do this. I wasn't even sure that I could go through with it… but I couldn't see any other way out.

I pulled my knife from my belt and hacked at my left arm. It took four blows, but I did it. I had cut my arm off below the elbow and with my right hand I hurled the bloody flesh and bone towards the main gate, hoping the dogs would be distracted. The ploy worked; at least six of the brutes rushed at it, snapping and fighting in their frenzy to reach the raw meat.

This was it. I had to do it. I ripped off my kitbag and threw it towards the garage and stabbed myself hard in the legs, chest and stomach. As I fell to the ground, my poor corpus struggling for its final breaths, the dog-things were upon me, driven wild by the scent of blood and the chance to sample living meat.

The pain was intense. I felt each bite, each rip and tear as my flesh was pulled away from me, as my sinews ripped and my bones splintered in the jaws of the Hell-Hounds. My mind was exploding. I couldn't do it; I couldn't find the calm I needed to escape my physicality.

And then, as I neared the end, as my strength ebbed and even my desire to carry on seemed to have abandoned me, I thought of Sara, her face, her touch, the softness of her lips. As I felt my ribs cracking and my heart's blood draining from me, I finally found the strength to force my mind to transcend, to move my spirit to the celestial plane and achieve full angelic manifestation.

The force sent me upwards, fully alated and I hovered for a second, looking at what was left of the corpus I had loved so well and which had seen me through so much. But this was no time for regrets. I needed to move before the dog-things finished their feasting and began looking for other flesh to devour. I swiftly came back down to earth and had just grabbed my kitbag from where it had fallen when the garage doors opened and the Silver Ghost appeared with Jay at the wheel.

"Get in... and you'd better ditch the wings. There's not that much room in here."

Wordlessly I obeyed.

Jay steered the Roller round the side of the fountain, away from the remains of my corpus. He probably didn't want Sophia to see what had happened.

"You alright, mate?"

I nodded. I think he sensed that I didn't want to talk about it. Putting the car into gear, he drove smoothly towards the gates. As we approached, they opened automatically and we drove out onto the silent and deserted roadway, on our way to the ferry and the Avernus gateway; on our way out of the Inferno.

I did not look back.

For what seemed like ages, no-one spoke. I had made Jay pull the car over once we were clear of the Dis city limits and treated Sophia's face with germanium. It seemed to calm the worst of the swelling and I gave both Sophia and Alex a spoonful of asphodel for good measure. They were both dozing on the back seat and I was not in the mood for idle chit-chat. Jay handled the car well, the road between Dis and the ferry was a good one, and we were eating up the miles. We must have been driving for about fifteen minutes when Jay finally broke the silence.

"How're you feeling? That was a bit grim back there. I've not seen anything like that since Jezebel got her comeuppance."

I shrugged. "Easy come, easy go I suppose."

"Had you had it long?" He was talking about my corpus.

"About twenty years. To be honest, it was starting to wear out, needed attention, didn't run as well as it used to. But I was used to it." He nodded.

"Yeah, I know what you mean; you get a new one, wear it in, get it so it feels just right, you know exactly how it works... and then – dog meat." He smiled at me, ruefully.

"Dog meat." He was right, this was just the way it was, and I had to get over it. I decided to give him a quick update on everything that had happened since this whole crazy thing had started and had just got to the bit about Kathryn's murder when he interrupted.

"I know, I saw her, just before she died. And I think I might have heard you arriving. Someone came into the flat whilst I was in there, but given the circumstances, I didn't stop to see who it was."

I thought about the unknown person who'd knocked me unconscious just after I found Kathryn and I remembered what Sara had said about another presence in the flat. I asked him to go on.

"I'd stormed out straight after Isra left on Saturday night. I'd had enough of the lot of them, had enough of humans and being in a human body, I headed to the river, dumped my corpus round the back of Blackfriars station and materialised in my true form for the first time in ten years. I spent hours flying above the Thames, down to the coast, out over Europe; just feeling the power of being an angel."

"Gradually, I calmed down. I'd flown for miles, I think it was when I looked down and saw that I was flying above the Sicilian coastline that I really came to my senses. Seeing below me the land we had been forced to flee from, remembering all Alex and Sophia had been through, I felt terrible. Ashamed of myself, and terrified about what might be happening back in London. I knew that I'd left them in a position of great vulnerability."

"So you came back?"

"I came back. But it was too late. I arrived at the flat at around half three on Sunday afternoon. I found Kathryn. She was still just alive, just barely, but there was nothing I could do."

I thought about what the Katibeen had said about Kathryn's last moments, something about Jaoel. "Were you back in your corpus?"

"No, I'd had enough of it. It had begun to feel like a prison to me if I'm honest. I was fully materialised, and I'm glad of it. When Kathryn saw me, I swear that she smiled; she must have thought I was an angel come to guide her to Paradise. I held her hand as she passed over, and when the Katibeen arrived to record her, I went in to the kitchen. Out of respect. You know?"

I nodded. "Yeah, I've done that, back in Syria. It's best to get out of the way, let them do their job."

"Anyway, I stayed there for quite a while, just trying to get my head round what had happened. There was this book there, hideous thing, covered in human skin, out on the counter in the kitchen. I'd just realised what it was when I heard the front door open. I turned off the kitchen light and pulled the door shut." I remembered heading into the flat, thinking the kitchen was deserted, finding Kathryn.

~ 237 ~

Jay continued. "Whoever it was went down the hallway and into the front room. Then I heard them going into the bathroom. I thought that finding Kathryn's body would keep them busy for long enough for me to get out of there; I was just about to head out when the door opened again. I didn't wait to see who it was, just opened the kitchen window and legged it."

Jay hadn't actually seen anyone, so I was still no clearer about who had actually coshed me. I asked him what he'd done next and he told me that as anyone with half a brain could see that Kathryn's death had been a ritual sacrifice, he was pretty sure that it had been used by Belphegor to open a portal, allowing Eligor, Sophia and Alex into the Inferno. He decided the only thing to do was to follow them and to try somehow to rescue them. So he flew back to Italy, landed on the shores of Lake Avernus, and made his way in to the Inferno.

When I told him that he'd been spotted crossing the river and that K and the Heavenly Host had taken him for a traitor, he seemed to think it was funny, but the smile was wiped off his face pretty sharpish when I went on to explain that they'd decided to use this as an excuse to plan an invasion.

"That's why I need to get you all back there before it kicks-off. Manny's pretty sure they'll be ready by midnight, so if I haven't managed to get the three of you in front of K and the rest of them, all shipshape and Bristol fashion, then who knows what will happen."

"And Eligor's geared up for it?" Jay was sombre now. "That explains what was happening in Erebus. They're ready for it. And from what I can see, they aren't just preparing defences. The forces gathering were being psyched up to attack."

I told him that that was what Manny and I had been afraid of, and that Raphael had also predicted that Eligor and his forces were planning to go on the offensive.

Jay looked a tad startled when I mentioned the Archangel, and I realised I'd been so busy talking about Kathryn that I hadn't filled him in on what had happened to me and Sara whilst we'd been in the Inferno. I was just telling him about Johan and 'Operation Wounded Rabbit' when a tremendous noise broke out in the back of the car.

Alex had woken up and had wound down the window; he was now frantically banging on the side of the car and screaming, "Stop. Stop the bloody car. It's Kathryn."

We were pretty close to the ferry now, driving along the side of what I was sure must be the River Archeron. Going in the opposite direction to us was a long stream of walkers, progressing slowly, in a long but straggling line. I knew what they were. These were the shades of the recently dead, who'd just crossed on the ferry and were making their way towards the Lake of Fire and the judgement of souls.

"Stop, for pity's sake." Alex was getting frantic. "If you don't stop, I'm getting out anyway. It was Kathryn, didn't you hear me?"

"Hold tight, Alex. Don't do anything stupid." The last thing I needed was for him to hurl himself into the dust at this point. We were so close to the ferry that I could see the harbour lights about half a mile further on down the road.

Jay looked at me and I nodded; without slowing down, he pulled a handbrake turn and we headed back along the line. Within thirty seconds, Alex was banging on the panels again. Jay brought the car to a shuddering halt and Alex flung open the door.

"Kathryn... Kathryn." He tried to run towards the line of walkers moving slowly away from him, but his injured legs wouldn't hold him and he sprawled in the dirt still screaming and calling Kathryn's name. It seemed as if no-one in the line of unhurried marchers could even hear him; they took no notice of his increasingly desperate calls as they continued to walk, one slow, steady step after another in silent and unfaltering procession.

He pulled himself to his feet; by this time Sophia had awakened and she too had got out of the car. It took her a while to reach him as it was clearly an effort for her to put one foot in front of the other. They stood together, supporting each other and looking helplessly after the line of shades which was now disappearing into the distance round a tight bend in the road.

"Are you sure it was Kathryn?" Her voice sounded harsh, as if it was an effort to talk; she was still dehydrated and I had nothing left to offer her.

"Yes, yes, I know it was her. I'd recognise her anywhere... We can't lose her now." Alex turned towards me and Jay; we'd both got out of the car and were leaning up against the side panels. "You've got to help me, Jay. God knows, you owe me."

"Alex, she's passed over." I tried to reason with him, to explain what was happening and why Kathryn hadn't responded when he'd called to her. "She's on her way to be judged and then to start her new life here. She won't see you, she won't hear you; you're still a mortal and now she's a member of the spirit world."

"But she'd see Jay. She could speak to Jay, or to you." Alex was insistent.

~ 239 ~

"You're spirits too and you could reach her. I need to talk to her, don't you understand...? I need to tell her I love her. You can't just leave it like this..." And Alex started to move after the line, staggering towards them, his sister holding him round the waist, his arms round her shoulder until both of them were brought sprawling to the ground again.

"He's right, Zach." Jay tossed me the keys. "You stay here with these two, and turn the car around. I won't be long," and with that he alated and thrust himself up into the air, flying low, just above the line of spectral walkers. Before he reached the bend in the road, he swooped down and lifted a slender woman with long blonde hair out of the line of travellers. No-one seemed to notice or object; the person who had been walking behind Kathryn just shuffled a little closer to the person in front so the line wasn't broken.

I did as Jay asked and turned the car back towards the ferry, and almost before I'd done so, Jay was back, carrying a rather pissed off and bedraggled Kathryn.

"What the bloody hell do you think you're doing?" She was hitting him ineffectually, and when he finally deposited her somewhat roughly on the ground, she moved away from him and crossed her arms belligerently. She had a very English voice, the sort you hear reading the news or asking about the provenance of the Dover sole at the fish counter in Waitrose, and she clearly wasn't afraid to express herself. "I don't know what you're doing here, Jay, and I have no idea what sort of benighted mutant you are, but I've had about enough of this. I've been sacrificed, left for dead, and abandoned by my boyfriend. I've been cut open, sewn up and cut open again. I've had to queue for over twenty-four hours to get on to that disgusting ferry and when I finally got on it, there was nowhere to sit, I couldn't get a cup of tea and it stank to high Heaven. I haven't been able to change out of this utterly revolting gown they decided to put me in when they took my body away to do the postmortem and now that I am finally getting close to somewhere where I'm told there might be one tiny, weeny jot of civilisation, you come and drag me away, right back to where I started in this godforsaken place."

She was right, the postmortem gown wasn't very flattering, but in a way she was lucky. Some of the spectres were marching along butt naked, and to be honest, that was even less of a pretty sight.

"And Lord knows why they needed to do one." Kathryn was in her stride now; there was clearly no stopping her. "Even a first year med-student could see that I'd been ritually slaughtered, disembowelled and exsanguinated. I

~ 240 ~

mean, cause of death could hardly have been more obvious, but that's the way it seems to be, protocols and process rather than old fashioned common sense. And now you've pulled me out of the line and I've lost my place, so I have no idea how long I'm going to have to hang about in this Hell-hole until I can get something sorted. Bloody, bloody nightmare." And then she started to cry.

She hadn't noticed me, so I thought I'd introduce myself and try to get her to calm down as her hysterics really weren't helping. Alex was standing next to her, calling her name and trying to touch her shoulder, but she clearly couldn't hear him, and she kept making little flicking motions like she was swatting away a fly.

I opened the side door of the Roller, and as I did so, my kitbag fell to the ground and I saw the Golden Bough sticking out of its side pocket. I knew that Sara had wanted to bring it along because apparently it helped mortals gain safe passage through the spirit realms. I'd never really understood what all the fuss was about, but finally I thought I could see why it might come in handy. Logically, or so I assumed, to give them safe passage, the spirits must be able to see and hear the mortals. So I thought that maybe if I handed Alex the Bough, then Kathryn might be able to see him.

I pulled it out of the bag and tried to give it to Alex, who just ignored me. Not surprisingly really; why would anyone want to take hold of an old gilded stick when he was trying to comfort his sobbing spectral girlfriend? Finally, I stuffed it into the pocket of his jeans and immediately, the scales fell from her eyes.

It all got a little messy. First she hugged him; then she hit him. Then she kissed him, and when it seemed as if we had achieved at least some sort of harmony, I bundled them both into the back of the car next to Sophia and we set off again. I told Sophia to hold on to one end of the Bough as well and as soon as she did so, Kathryn could see her too, and there was instantly more emotional reunion stuff - but no hitting or kissing this time.

Whilst Jay carried on driving, Alex, Sophia and I got Kathryn up to speed about what had happened. She didn't want to talk about what had been done to her at the hands of Belphegor and his Hell-Beast, and to be honest, I didn't blame her. It was going to take a long time and a lot of therapy before she would be able to deal with that one, and I made a note to recommend the HTC to her once she had gone through her judgement and passed on into the realms beyond.

She did say that she remembered seeing Jay just before she died, and that her last memory of her mortal life was thinking that she needed to tell Alex that his friend had the face of an angel; Jay grinned at me when we heard that one.

We were now getting very close to the ferry. I looked at my watch. Ten thirty. We were going to make it.

I told Jay to find somewhere to ditch the Roller. The road to the harbour mouth was too narrow to drive down, so we pulled in by the side of the river and left the car just waiting there; we even left the keys in the ignition. I hoped someone who deserved it a little more than Samael did would find it.

I led the way, Jay and Sophia wandering on behind me; he'd ditched the wings and was carrying her piggy-back, which seemed to be causing an utterly unnecessary level of giggling. Alex and Kathryn brought up the rear, walking slowly, hand-in hand, their heads close together as they talked.

She had a bit of a temper, but she was alright really; I could see that she was just right for someone like Alex, who I'd come to realise was quite gentle and more than a little self-effacing. I reckon that he probably needed his arse kicking every now and then to make him get on with stuff, and I could see that Kathryn had been just the woman to do it.

I hadn't let myself really think about what I was going to do when we got to the ferry. Kathryn was a spectre and her place was down here – in the boundary lands of the hereafter. But I could tell that Alex wouldn't wear it; as far as he was concerned, they had a future and he wasn't going to let a little thing like the fact that she was dead and he wasn't, get in the way.

I cast my mind about, trying to think of other times, other cases, where something like this had happened. It was almost unheard of for someone to be allowed to return to the mortal world. But there were precedents and I was trying to remember exactly what had happened when Orpheus tried to get his girlfriend Eurydice released from Hades, when I heard a scream.

There was another, and then a sound that I was certain was that of a whip slicing through the air. I looked around me – behind me stretched the plains and the winding road back to Dis and the ditches of Malebolge. To the east I could see the mountains of Erebus and the molten glow of the Lake of Fire on the horizon; ahead of me, over the hilltop was the river, and it was from there that I could hear the screaming.

And I knew that voice; it was the one voice I longed for, the voice I'd thought of when I needed the strength to pull myself from my ripped and bloodied corpus back in the grounds of Eligor's stronghold. Forgetting the others, I ran towards it, over the crest of the hill and down towards the

~ 242 ~

Archeron, which stretched out into the rippling darkness, the small house lights of the boundary lands on the other side just visible.

There, by the side of the jetty, were two figures.

One was a female, chained and bound her face livid and bleeding from a recent cut. The second was an angel, fully alated and imperious, towering above her and about to bring down his whip.

I could not believe what I was seeing; the first figure was Sara... and the angel... the angel was Raphael.

~ *Chapter Thirty Five* ~

As I ran, I alated and, opening my wings, soared into the air, racing towards the sound of Sara's terrified screams. Within seconds I was beside her, landing on the river bank in the space between her and the towering archangel and bending to take her in my arms.

"Do not touch her." Raphael's voice was cold and implacable and as he spoke the whip cracked again and I felt it snaking round my waist, pulling me away from her.

"What do you think you're doing?" I pulled at the cord round my waist. "Get this fucking thing off me... What are you doing to Sara... you evil shit?" And then I was sure I knew the truth... and I could hardly believe it.

"It was you all along, wasn't it... you're the traitor... I know now it wasn't Jaoel...? But you; an Archangel...?" I wrenched myself free and fell forwards on to the bank, reaching out for Sara and pulling her close to me. She was breathing hard and whimpering, little gasps and fragments of words that I could hardly make out as I rocked her in my arms.

Reaching down, I pulled at the chains that bound her using my powers as a Justice Angel to release her, and they fell apart as I touched them. Sara's arms now freed, she wrapped them round me and at her touch the conduit between us opened; I was feeling the depth of her terror, experiencing the dread which was running through her as if it was my own. Her emotions, her thoughts, her deepest fears were open and exposed to me, like mine had been to her when she had calmed and restored my spirits. And now it was my turn.

"Oh, my darling, my love, my Sara." I whispered words, said things that I had never thought I'd say, holding her to me until I felt the fear abating. I wiped the tears and specks of blood from her face with the hem of my robe and set her down beside me, her hand in mine and then I turned to Raphael.

The Archangel had moved away from us to the edge of the ridge, and was speaking in a low voice to Jaoel who was standing a little bit apart from Alex, Kathryn and Sophia. When he saw that I had freed his captive, Raphael gestured to the others to stand back and he alone moved down the hill towards me. As he approached us, arms outstretched, palms facing upwards in a centuries old gesture of conciliation, he looked magnificent and despite the undoubted power which radiated from him and the things I'd seen him do, he seemed to be both benign and sorrowful as he came near.

"Don't trust him, Zach… don't believe anything he tells you," Sara whispered urgently, holding my hand even tighter and pressing herself into my side.

"Zach." He began speaking in a low and surprisingly gentle voice, but then he shook his head, saying, "No, for what I need to do, I must address you formally. There is no other way and you of all angels, will understand the duty that will place upon you."

Raphael was now standing about six feet away from us. He extended his wings and lifted his arms to the sky, and then, in a voice of depth and authority, raised as if calling upon the very Heavens to witness his words, he spoke. "I, the Archangel Raphael, first in rank and power and servant of the divine laws call upon you, the Angel Zachriel, to release the Angel Sarandiel and return her to my custody. In the name of the powers and the authorities, the principalities and the dominions, the virtues and the strongholds, I command you."

I stood, rigid, uncertain. If I disobeyed, I would be breaking every vow I'd ever made. If I did what he asked, I was giving up the only creature I'd ever truly loved at the behest of a being that despite his words, I was almost certain was a traitor, a Fallen Angel.

"Zach, don't do it… Give me the Golden Bough and I can stop this." Sara spoke low, her voice still not much more than a whisper. She took something from her pocket and handed it to me. "Look, it's the ritual, from the book, the book in Kathryn's kitchen." Her hands were pawing at my kitbag and unfastening the straps. "He's the traitor… Don't you see? And we can get rid of him. We can stop it… give me the Golden Bough and we can send him where he can never bother us again…" I looked at the paper she'd handed to me, involuntarily; my flesh crawled as I unfolded it.

By this time she'd upended the bag and was shaking out the contents onto the river bank. "We can send him to Limbo and we'll be free of him… free to do what we want to do… don't you see?"

~ 245 ~

What was she saying…? I couldn't understand her, couldn't quite make sense of what I thought I'd heard her say. I could say nothing, think nothing, I seemed to have no will, no power to think straight, my mind was foggy.

And then it cleared. Sara had moved away from me and was kneeling on the bank, desperately searching through my kitbag, frantically rifling through the pile of stuff she'd created. Her jacket had ridden up and there, just at the base of her spine, I saw it again.

That small tattoo.

Just like Lilith's.

"It isn't there, Sara. What you're looking for; it isn't there. I gave it to someone who needed it. Who needed it to do exactly what you told me it could do, back then, back when I thought I knew you." I edged away from her, moving towards Raphael, slowly, like a mourner. She stretched out her arms towards me, but I flinched away from her.

"It's you, isn't it? It was you all along. Not Jay, not Raphael. But you."

Without taking my eyes away from her, I approached the Archangel and knelt before him. "By the powers and the authorities, the principalities and the dominions, the virtues and the strongholds, I, the Angel Zachriel do submit to you and honour you. I give unto you the Angel Sarandiel."

At these words, Raphael lifted his arms once again and the chains which had fallen at Sara's feet when I had released her rose in the air and wrapped themselves around her. She struggled as they enclosed her and then she spat at me; its bitter wetness hit my cheek as I knelt there trying to comprehend exactly what she had done – and why she'd done it. I was still holding the paper she'd passed to me, the ritual from the Necronomicon. Slowly, I tore it to shreds and let the wind take the pieces as I threw them from me.

I just stayed there, not moving, unable to fully process what had happened, not really sure what was going to happen next. Sometime later; it might have been hours, or maybe only seconds, I felt a slight shock as a hand touched my shoulder and looking round I saw Jay. I grasped it and he pulled me to my feet.

"You okay?" He looked me over, not quite sure what to say, how to play this… "That can't have been easy."

I didn't respond. I still couldn't get my head around what had just happened.

"Thank you, Zach." Raphael had now moved towards me and was opening his arms like he was going to hug me, but I didn't think I could handle that and when I side-stepped he didn't seem offended.

"How did you know it was her? I thought you trusted her, I thought she was your Star Pupil...?" Only Raphael could give me the answers I was looking for. I needed to know what he'd known and for how long. And if I felt bitter about what had happened, about being played for an idiot, could you blame me?

"I only had my first real suspicions in Malebolge; she seemed too pally with that demon, and he knew far more than she'd had chance to tell him when he rescued her from the burning river." Raphael spoke quietly, with a grim determination. "To be honest, I was uneasy about your mission from the start, I'd heard on the grapevine that you were a bit of a loose cannon, and I hadn't been happy about Sara being partnered with you in the first place." He gave me a wry grin at this point. "And then, when you almost didn't get admittance to the Heavens because your purity ratings were so low, I became really jumpy."

I spluttered a bit at this. Although it was bad form to talk about it, my spiritual purity ratings were A-one, and Manny had even confirmed that to K before we set off.

"I know that now," Raphael said, "but when I saw the readings, I was worried. That's why I got so heavy about stuff back at the HTC. And to be honest, that's why I decided to join you rather than stay with the council. But now we know what was actually happening, it all makes sense."

"Does it?" I still didn't know what was going on.

"She's a parasite, mate. Locked on to you and took your ratings to supplement her own." Jay spoke matter-of-factly, as if such a thing was commonplace.

"Pretty much right I'm afraid," confirmed Raphael. "You must have noticed that she's different from other angels. She worked with me for three hundred years and I've never met anyone with the same level of ability. Her touch channels powers; powers of healing, of calm and restoration. But it works both ways, she can give and she can take."

I thought back... and he was right. When we'd gone through the sensor at the Pearly Gates, she'd been holding my hand. At the time, I thought she'd done it because I was nervous. Now I knew that it was just to hook onto my ratings.

"Didn't you notice how your mood would shift when she touched you? That was the thing that finally convinced me." Raphael was still looking deeply unhappy. I recognised that in many ways, this had been much harder for him than it had been for me. He'd worked with Sara for centuries, come to trust, respect and even, perhaps, love her. I'd only really known her for a few hours. And she'd betrayed both of us.

"Remember when she got so angry about my suggestion that we split up? You thought it was a good idea until she put her hands on you, and then she almost drove you to rebellion. That's when I knew for sure. That's when I was certain that I had to get her away from you."

I thought of the look of fear that had flickered across his face before we went our separate ways, and now I understood it.

"So did you go to Erebus? I still don't quite see how you came to be here."

Raphael explained that as soon as I was safely on my way to Eligor's stronghold, he had confronted Sara and put her in chains. He'd decided that the best thing to do would be to bring her back to the council via the quickest route possible, the Avernus Gate. He wasn't so worried about finding Jaoel now he had the real traitor in custody and he just hoped that I would follow on behind with Alex and Sophia.

What he hadn't taken into consideration was that Jaoel was also looking for Sophia – or that we would find the Roller and make such good progress to the ferry. It seems that Sara hadn't sought to deny anything. In fact she'd taunted Raphael on the journey, telling him that she had been using her special powers of time-adjustment to get in contact with Eligor from the outset.

Although your bog-standard chronoprohibery doesn't work on other angels, Sara was a Mistress of the Hours and had abilities that don't come as standard. She'd used her skills to create small moments of frozen time to get messages through without anyone else being aware of it. She'd even sort of hinted at it when we were driving towards St. Basil's, telling me that if she was doing such a thing, I would have to arraign her, because she would have fallen. And I'd thought she'd just been being dramatic.

This was why Raphael had been using the whip – her powers only worked if she was calm and in control, and keeping her enraged meant that she was unable to let anyone know that she'd been rumbled.

But what I couldn't understand was why she'd done it. What had happened to tempt her, to draw her into the darkness, to make her risk her immortal soul and the punishment of an eternity in Tartarus? I looked across at her, her slender frame bound in chains, the breeze from the river lifting the edges of her jacket, and once again, I saw the tattoo.

I went a little closer; it wasn't a flower or a butterfly, but a moth. A Death's Head, beautifully drawn and inked in delicate greens and blues. I recognised it instantly. It was the mark of Samael, the Angel of Death. When we'd been greenhorns, back on Jacob's Ladder, she'd had a t-shirt with the same picture.

She'd worn it out, wearing it every day, washing it every night. At first she'd worshipped him from afar; just a teenage crush I'd thought, but then one day she met him. He'd spoken to her, told her he liked her hair. And that had been that.

Like a fool, I'd thought she'd got over it but I now knew she hadn't. He'd marked her, like he'd marked Lilith. And she was his, doing his bidding, biding her time over the millennia, until now, when the balance of power had become so fragile and K was under pressure to make a stand.

She had connived her way into this, gaining the trust of the Archangels, waiting for a chance to set up the dominos so that the only outcome could be war. And we'd played into her hands. I was starting to feel anger. Righteous indignation, combined with a personal desire for vengeance was beginning to simmer as I thought of the way she had played me.

"So what do we do now? We need to get these guys on the ferry; do you think it's still a good idea to take her with us?" Jay's question broke into my reverie. It raised a whole shed-load of issues and Jay was right, we really did need to get moving.

Raphael considered: "I think this is the time and the place for justice. It would serve no purpose to bring her back with us now. We have Jaoel, and we have Alex and Sophia. To take her with us is unnecessary. Do you agree with me, Zach?"

I looked at him and nodded. But this wasn't going to be pretty. "Jay, get the others out of the way. Make your way towards the ferry, we'll meet you there. This isn't going to take long."

Jay looked as if he was about to protest, but at a sign from Raphael, he went over to Sophia, hoicked her up onto his back and headed off towards the jetty, Alex and Kathryn following close behind.

"Can you do this?" Raphael's tone was gentle.

"Can you?" He looked away.

I stared as the figure on the river bank, bound in chains and yet still so delicate, so beautiful.

This was Sara. My Sara, who I'd known for all my life and had oh-so recently re-discovered. Sara, who had given me what I never thought I would experience, who had warmed me and inspired me and touched my heart with her courage and her beauty.

This was Sara, who had betrayed me and who had betrayed the Heavens.

I am a Justice Angel; I am a vehicle of the divine will and the divine law. I would not think about what she'd done to me, for I am but one being, and my personal concerns are as nothing. I let my mind go blank and called the powers of the universe to fill me, to make me a vessel of their will.

I felt the power surge within me and I grew mighty. I towered towards the skies, my wings outstretched, my head back as I became as one with the supremacy. Stretching out my arms, I called her to me.

"Sarandiel, daughter of darkness, you are foul in my sight."

She was raised up, her body limp now, her long, copper hair streaming out below her as I drew her upwards.

"You are foul in my sight."

She began to writhe as if the chains that bound her burned her living flesh. She screamed in agony, her body racked with pain, her skin starting to crack and peel as if there was a fire burning from within her. And then she looked at me. Her eyes stared at mine and there was no anger. She said my name.

"You are foul... you are foul... You are..."

I couldn't say it, for she was Sara, she was not foul, she was my love. My love, with the copper hair and burnished wings... I was diminishing... The power was ebbing and I was fading. I turned to look at Raphael, who could only gaze at me a look of fear and pity in his eyes.

And then I heard a crack, as if the very earth was rent asunder and from the depths of Hell I heard a voice screeching in triumph.

"You cannot see what is staring right at you.

You always forgive but will not be forgiven.

You will not destroy what is going to destroy you.

And when you are destroyed, my chains will break and I will devour you."

To my horror, I heard once more the curse of Enepsigos; her chains were breaking and soon she would be free.

I looked again at Sara and slowly, very slowly, her lips parted and she smiled a smile of triumph. And in that smile, I found myself. The seconds ticked... the bonds were breaking...

"Daughter of darkness, you are foul in my sight."

Her smile faded. I felt the power return a hundred-fold and surge within me. I had no doubts, I was implacable. I knew what I must do and so I pulled her up, high, high above the abyss which had opened up beneath us.

"You are foul in my sight."

I heard the chains clank fast around Enepsigos, deep down in the depths of Tartarus, and knew that I had bound her for eternity.

"You are foul in my sight."

And then I threw her, sending her falling, falling, falling. Down and down through the timeless depths she spun, her hair cascading round her 'til her final scream became a single fading echo.

When she had gone, the abyss closed up and I felt weakened and unsteady as the power drained away from me.

"That was well done," Raphael spoke simply.

There was nothing more to be said and so we turned and walked towards the jetty.

~ *Chapter Thirty Six* ~

When we got there, we found ourselves in the middle of a bit of an altercation. As I'd feared, the ferryman wouldn't countenance taking Kathryn, and Alex was refusing point-blank to leave her behind. Sophia was sitting on an old lobster-pot by the side of the dock looking bored and Jay was trying to pour oil on troubled waters in what was clearly a futile attempt to find a solution to the problem.

"I'm sorry, but it's in the regs. We can't take dead-uns back over, and to be honest, you live-uns should never of got 'ere in the first place." The ferryman was dressed in a battered old Guernsey and oilskins. He had the sort of face which said that he'd pretty much been-there-done-that; and what he hadn't seen, wasn't worth seeing.

"But what about Eurydice? You bent the rules for her." I thought I'd see if an argument from precedent might butter his parsnips, but he was having none of it.

"Special case, a dispensation from upstairs. You got one of them?"

When we shook our heads, he turned away from us and went back to preparing the boat for departure. "We sail in fifteen minutes. Make your mind up about what's happennin', 'cos I ain't waiting on yer."

"Alex, you must go." Kathryn sounded quite determined. "If you don't go back and testify then all this was for nothing."

"I won't leave you. The only reason you're here is because of me." Alex sounded quite desperate now. "And anyway, I can't face being back there without you. If you make me go back, I'll just kill myself anyway."

Jay looked from one to the other in utter frustration, and then he banged his hand to his head. "I've got it... We haven't got much time, but I've got it. Raphael, can you remember how to do the separation ritual? I did it years ago when I took Abraham on his astral tour of the three realms, but I'm not sure I remember all the words."

Raphael nodded. "Yes, I can do that, and it only takes a few seconds. You'd better explain your plan to Alex though, as in this case, there'll be no going back. Once his soul is separated from his body, he won't ever be able to restore it."

The plan was simple but brilliant, and I had a part to play in it too. Basically, Raphael and Jay were going to split Alex's soul from his body, leaving his spirit here in the underworld under the protection of the Golden Bough, whilst I was going to inhabit his corpus and take it with me back to the third realm.

I hadn't really given much thought as to what I was going to do for a corporeal body once we'd returned. In the past, I'd have just fashioned one, like angels normally do when they need a more permanent physical presence. To be honest, I was still feeling the loss of the old corpus and if I'd thought about a new one at all, I'd just assumed that I'd get one as similar as possible to replace it.

Taking Alex's would be a different kettle of fish altogether. For a start, the last few days had put it through the mill, and it looked to be in an even worse condition than mine had. Even more reason to pay a visit to St. Basil's once we got back. Another slightly daunting prospect would be that this corpus would not be a blank slate. It would retain Alex's memories, thoughts, impressions and preferences and although I would be able to modify them over time, it was likely to take a while for me to get used to it. This would have its advantages though, as I would be able to accompany Sophia to the court hearings and give the evidence that was needed to bring down the Maniscalos.

All in all, it seemed like a good plan and in less than five minutes Alex was standing all faint-outlined and spectral on the quayside next to Kathryn. Sophia, with the Golden Bough clasped tight in her hand so she could see him, was giving him a tearful farewell.

I scriggled my way into Alex's corpus. It was a bit of a tight fit, but I'd get used to it. Picking up my kitbag, I decided I would take some time on the ferry to give it a bit of a tidy – after Sara had chucked everything out onto the river bank I'd just bundled everything back inside and it was in a shocking state.

At last, we were ready to set off; it was half eleven. As soon as we were halfway across the river I could contact Manny.

Sophia said her last goodbyes to her brother and she and Jay made their way on board. Raphael followed; I stayed just long enough to thank Alex once again for the use of his corpus and to make sure he had Johan and Lisl's address. After they'd been through the judgement rigmarole at the Lake of Fire, I thought it would be nice for them to have someone they could stay with for a bit, until they'd decided what they wanted to do next.

I was just about to get on board when something vast and hairy forced itself in between me and the gangplank. It nudged one of its heads into my stomach and laid the other two at my feet. It was the ferryman's dog and if there was ever a soppier creature in the three realms than this one then I'd yet to meet it. I fumbled about in my pockets and the mess that was my kitbag to see if there were any scraps of cereal bar, but I found something so much better. Scratching him under his chins I tossed three dried-out pig's ears up the gangplank and prepared to follow him on to the ferry.

The network was pretty poor, but I managed to get a signal before we were quite halfway across the river. I gave the phone to Raphael first; it was vital that we spoke to K as soon as possible, and I knew there wouldn't be a hope of him talking to anyone as lowly as a mere Justice Angel.

He wasn't on the phone long; handing it back to me after exchanging only a few words. I grabbed it from him, hoping to speak to Manny, but whoever had been speaking had hung up.

"Are we in time? Is it going to be okay?" I asked urgently.

"I don't know," answered Raphael. "It seems they were able to mobilise more quickly than we gave them credit for. K told me that Nat and the Potestas are due at the Avernus Gate at any moment."

"We have to stop them." Jay spoke urgently. "If they push through the gate it will be seen as an invasion. Even Eligor wouldn't dare to attack the Celestial realms without provocation, but the minute the Potestas march through that gate, he has the excuse he's been looking for, and all out war's going to break out."

The ferry had almost reached land now; ahead of us I could see the mouth of the tunnel, cut through the living rock of the mountains, which would take us out through the Avernus Gate and back to the third realm. When we docked, the harbour was quiet and seemed deserted and although there were still lights glowing from some of the little houses dotted here and there on the shores of the Archeron, no-one was about.

As we ran down the gangplank, I hurled some old coins at the ferryman as payment for his troubles. I also remembered to hand back a rather squidgy parcel containing one eye and one tooth.

"We need to get moving," shouted Raphael, as we ran headlong along the jetty. I wasn't sure if it was my imagination, but I was certain that I could hear the sound of engines rumbling ominously down the tunnel ahead of us. "Can you fly and carry Sophia?"

Without pausing to answer, Jay alated and leapt into the air, Sophia held in his arms. Raphael followed, with me lagging some way behind them. Flying was no problem for him; he hadn't even bothered to resume his physical corpus, but it took me a little while to get my new body to behave itself and I didn't think I'd be pulling loop the loops for quite a while yet.

We were in time. Or to be more precise, they were in time.

Flying slowly, hampered by an unfamiliar corpus and an increasingly painful set of strained muscles, when I finally emerged from the tunnel I could see that it was all pretty much done and dusted. I spotted Manny and made an appallingly shoddy landing, forgetting that he knew nothing about my new look.

He gave me a double take, clearly recognising the face as that of Alex Maniscalos, but not understanding how the kidnapped human could suddenly have grown wings. I briefed him quickly, brushing over what had actually happened to my old corpus and he gave me an update on the political situation.

It turned out that once K had been convinced that we'd not only caught and punished the Fallen Angel, but that we'd also successfully rescued the human hostages, he called off the potential incursion at once. Far better to be seen as a leader who worked towards peaceful solutions than to be remembered as the person who had brought about the first war across the three realms in over a thousand millennia. I thought it unlikely that he would let slip the little fact that the Fallen Angel who'd betrayed us had actually been one of his inner-circle...

I looked across and saw a CIEL camera crew swing into action and could just catch his imperious, rather self-satisfied tones beginning to speechify.

"Fellow angels – and all inhabitants of the celestial realms... I am so proud to be standing here in front of you today – back in control... and not just in control of our wonderful Potestas, but in control of the three realms. To the Guardians, and the Justice Angels, I want to say thank you. You've been a great team...

"And to those who say we are in trouble, getting weaker, betrayed from within, I say: Keep The Faith... We will find those who betray us. We will find those who undermine us... And they will pay..."

At that point, I switched off. I'd heard it all before. From the ranks behind me, I could hear grumblings as Nat and his army of trigger-happy Potestas began grudgingly making their preparations to head back to base without a single shot having been fired.

Back in Erebus, the legions would be waiting for the signal, and today, because of Raphael, because of Jaoel, and perhaps, just a little bit, because of me, it would not come. Perhaps we would need to go to war one day, but I for one was happy that that day had not arrived yet.

I saw Sophia and Jay making their way unhurriedly towards me. They'd managed to find a bottle of water and she was draining it dry.

"I'm going to take Sophia back to Rome with me. She's already re-connected the nexus with Ely, her Guardian so we'll seek sanctuary there. Once she's testified, I'm going to renounce my Angelic status and we'll get married."

"We'll need you to join us, Alex... I mean Zach... We both need to testify, and your story is even more powerful than mine." Sophia's voice was no longer harsh and croaky, but a tear was forming as she spoke to me. I could see that she was missing the brother she'd only just got to know again before he'd been taken from her.

"Sophia, Alex isn't completely gone. As long as I'm here, in this body, a little bit of him is still with us." She looked at me uncertainly.

"I've got all his memories." I cast about inside my mind to find something to convince her. "I know all about Paulo you know." Her eyes widened and then she blushed.

"You promised you'd never tell... You promised..."

"And I never will." I winked at her and gave Jay a little knowing smirk... It wouldn't hurt to keep him on his toes, I thought. And after all, isn't that what brothers-in-law were for?

"You take care now." Manny was nodding approvingly at Sophia and the soon-to-be-humanised Angel. "We'll meet in Rome in a week or so, and then all this business can get sorted." They nodded and wandered quietly away along the lakeside, with no real destination but each other.

"And as for you..." He checked his watch. "It's after midnight, but I think they've got a lock-in down at Charlie's… do you feel up to putting the new body through its paces?"

I looked at him and shrugged, which he clearly took for agreement. Being one of the Agency's head honchos has its perks and within a couple of seconds, he'd opened a multi-dimensional window onto the familiar streets of Islington and wordlessly, I followed him into the damp despondency of the November night.

I knew that tomorrow I'd have some explaining to do, a report to write and, because of Raphael's involvement, I'd have no choice but to tell it as it happened, treachery, betrayal, eternal damnation and all.

But for now, I didn't want to think about where I'd been and what I'd done; as I walked into the darkness, all I could think of was her smile.

END

Lightning Source UK Ltd.
Milton Keynes UK
UKOW04f2218270917
309986UK00001B/5/P